SASS
& Serendipity

Also by Pamela Masters

THE MUSHROOM YEARS
A Story of Survival

SASS & Serendipity

To Carol with love
Pamela Masters
Apple Hill 2005

Pamela Masters

Henderson House PUBLISHING

Copyright © 2005 Pamela Masters. All rights reserved. No part of this book may be reproduced, stored in a retrieval system, or transmitted in any form or by any means (electronic, mechanical, photocopying, recording, or otherwise) without prior written permission of the publisher, except in the case of brief quotations in a critical review.

DISCLAIMER

This is a truthful work of nonfiction based on the author's life experiences. However, some of the names and identities of persons, locations, businesses, places, and events have been changed.

3001 Camino Heights Drive, Camino, California 95709, USA
www.hendersonhouse.com

Publisher's Cataloging-in-Publication

Masters, Pamela.
   Sass and serendipity / Pamela Masters.
   p. cm.
   ISBN 0-9664489-4-4

   1. Masters, Pamela. 2. Illustrators--United States--Biography. 3. Technical illustration. 4. Outer space--Exploration--Miscellanea. 5. California--Biography. I. Title.

NC975.5.M346A2 2005   741.6'092
          QBI05-800201

Printed and Bound in the United States of America
Cover: Howard Goldstein Design & Illustration
Book Design: Pete Masterson, Æonix Publishing Group

*To Rebel and Gillian
and to their men,
Bob, Nick, Dale and Dakota,
and to the memory of Jay,
my special love.*

Acknowledgements

My thanks to Bob Greenwood and Bill Rowan for their guidance and encouragement, and to Sandra Williams, an exceptional editor and dear friend. Without them, this book would never have come to be. And many thanks also to all the priceless people who slipped in and out of my life, becoming unforgettable memories. You will never know what your friendship meant to me …

Thank you all!

Author's Note

I was born in 1927 in Honan Province, China, and raised in a little British treaty port on the Gulf of Chihli, a few miles south of where the Great Wall runs into the sea. The summers there were glorious, with lots of happy visitors to liven my days, but the icebound winters were lonely and dull, and dragged on forever. My quiet, serene sister Ursula, didn't seem bothered by the boredom, but it drove me nuts. To lighten the days, I dreamed up all types of mischief, and soon got used to my British father calling me a "cheeky brat."

I guess, in the States, Mother's homeland, cheek today would be synonymous with sass, and everyone knows the meaning of that. But serendipity sometimes needs to be clarified. I think my favorite definition is from *The New Oxford American Dictionary*: "the occurrence and development of events by chance in a happy or beneficial way."

What better word to describe my life so far?

Chapter 1

San Francisco, September 14, 1946

Something magical happens when you approach the Golden Gate from the Pacific at sundown. The bridge is no longer a gigantic span of red steel with majestic suspension spires, but an exquisite golden tiara.

That September evening, while our troopship, the *General Meiggs,* cut through fishing vessels and pleasure boats as it neared San Francisco Bay, the magic of the moment brought back memories of the last time I'd visited the States ... before the war.

The year was 1939. I was twelve, fresh from a Franciscan convent in North China, and in for one hellacious "reverse" culture shock! Having been born and raised in China, Chinese quite often seemed to be my first language. I'll never forget Mother hailing a taxi when we got off the ship, and the cabdriver turning and asking, "Where to, ma'am?" He was American—*not* Chinese! That shock followed me through hotels, restaurants, and department stores, and I continually caught myself speaking in Chinese when I thanked the salespeople and waiters for their service. I don't know who was more surprised—them or me.

Dad had cut that lovely visit short when war broke out in Europe that year and he saw the United States getting deeply involved in the Allied cause. "It's going to be a hell of a lot safer in this part of the world," he'd written in late November, and, before Mother could fully digest that letter, he wired us return tickets to the Orient on the *SS President Taft*.

We returned home to North China on my thirteenth birthday, February 1, 1940, and for almost two years it looked as though Dad's prediction about us being safe had been right. That is, until the attack on Pearl Harbor.

It was then that Japan turned her wrath from the embattled Chinese people to the Allied nationals in the Orient—first holding us under house arrest, then following up with internment in a Japanese prison camp in Shandong Province.

I have to admit, the teen years I spent in the prison camp weren't all bad, even though we had appalling living conditions and scant food rations. I learned a lot I could never have learned anywhere else ... the most important of which was to enjoy each day as it came, to look forward, never back, and to live each moment without regret. And unknown to me at that time, I became invincible.

It was the silent gift of survival, which for the rest of my life made me never doubt that whatever I dreamed would come true; whatever I wanted to do I would succeed in. It was like being tattooed with the words "What would you do with your life if you knew you couldn't fail?"

Of course, every once in a while reality set in, and I'd have to stop and take stock. But it was never the big issues that foiled me; it was always the inconsequential little milestones that would topple along the way, making me step over them as they faded into the mists of yesterday.

I have to admit, no such thoughts were in my mind that sparkling September day as Mother, my sister Ursula, and I arrived in San Francisco. I'd already forgotten yesterday completely in the excitement of coming back to the States. And as the old troopship sailed under the Golden Gate, I saw more than a view of that lovely sprawling metropolis, its windows ablaze with the setting sun: I saw the future, and it looked fantastic.

I kept thinking of Bill, my fiancé, who would be meeting me at the pier. We'd met in North China after the war, in the teeming, metropolitan city of Tientsin where I was working for the First Marine Division as a court reporter. It was a gut-wrenching job for a nineteen-year-old, even one who had seen the depth of man's inhumanity to man. At the end of many a general court-martial I would see young marines—younger than I, and who'd fought their way up through the Pacific—get twenty years at hard labor because some boot-lieut assigned to their defense didn't care, or didn't have the ability to handle their cases. Bill and his marine buddies helped me get over those rough times, and, although he had only left for the States in July, I already missed him.

A while later, as I leaned over the railing watching tugs nudge the troop transport into her berth, I noticed crowds of relatives and friends waving frantically on the pier, and heard their screams of recognition and joy. But I didn't see Bill anywhere. *Oh, well, he's probably there, lost in the crowd, or something...*

Then I thought of Margo, my older sister, a marine war bride who'd been shipped to the States right from our prison camp in August of '45, along with thousands of battle-weary marines. She'd arrived in San Francisco not knowing if her POW husband was alive or dead, and not knowing a soul she could turn to if he wasn't there to meet her. She, who'd been married on December 4, 1941, and had already lived through four years of hell and separation, finally succumbed to pure panic *until there he was!* He had been jammed in by swarms of joyous greeters, but being resourceful—and in uniform—he cut around the jubilant marine band, got into the front row, and made like a happy piccolo player!

Mother came toward me through the crush on the deck, and I saw tears in her eyes. "What's up, Mumsy?" I asked anxiously, as I'd seldom seen her cry.

"I don't see Donald anywhere." Donald was her brother, an engineer at Lockheed in Burbank.

Oh, well, I thought resignedly, *that's two for two.*

"Oh, damn, what are we going to do now?" she asked. "I was so sure he'd be here and have taken care of everything, I didn't even call ashore for hotel accommodations."

"You need a hotel?" It was Paolo Caggiano, an Italian businessman from Shanghai, and an ex-inmate from our old prison camp. "I booked reservations at five hotels, as the first time I came here I got bumped by an earlier arrival. Now I always take care of myself first, and the hotels can lump it when I don't show up."

He was on his third trans-Pacific trip. First class, of course. He happily told us he was profiteering on war surplus and planned to recoup all the losses he sustained while in camp. At the rate he was going, I had no doubt he'd succeed royally. When things got really hectic on the lower decks, my sister Ursula and I had gone up to visit him, and invariably he'd order us a sandwich or a drink, and regale us with intriguing stories of both the old and the new Shanghai.

"Here," he said to Mother, handing her a slip of paper. "I think you and the girls would prefer the Manx. It's a small, quiet hotel. Not as pricey as some of the others, but it gives excellent service and is central to everything in San Francisco."

"Oh, thank you so much," Mother said, adding thoughtfully, "I wonder if there'll be any problem as there are three of us, and I'm sure you only made reservations for one."

"Tell 'em to put an extra bed in the room if it's needed. You have a reservation now, don't let them give you a rough time."

Mother thanked him again for his kindness, and he wished us luck and happy landings, then wandered off to say more goodbyes.

Margie Thomas came up to us about then and, putting a kindly arm around my shoulder, said, "Where the hell is he?"

"Who?" I asked, startled, wondering if she was expecting to be met by someone.

"Bill, damn him. Why isn't he here to meet you?"

I found myself going to his defense immediately. "Margie, it's a heck of a long drive from Pasadena to San Francisco. I don't even know if he's got a car yet."

"Don't make excuses for him. It's inexcusable."

I'd forgotten that Margie and her husband Gerry knew Bill, and that they had often joined us at the country club in Tientsin, swapping tall stories and enjoying the luxury of its ambience after our years of deprivation. She was the mother of Lisa, my closest friend in the prison camp, and she was coming to the States to join the American side of her husband's family.

Margie had lightened up our days on the old troopship. And our nights, too. I wish I'd kept a diary of that incredible trip, but only the highlights stand out now.

I knew how hard Mother had worked to get us passage to the States, but I had no idea she hadn't been able to get us a stateroom. I believe she was as shocked as we were when we were all herded aboard the ship in Shanghai and escorted to our quarters below decks. The women and children were led to the forward holds, the men taken aft, to meet their families only on deck and at mealtimes during the day. It must have been rugged for families to be separated like that. Luckily for us three, we were assigned the same hold, but not the same "bunk-stack," as I called the tall tiers of canvas cots.

For a person with mild claustrophobia, that was a nightmare of no mean proportions for me. I was on the second bunk up, with a hefty woman below me who always slept on her side with her huge hips pressing against the canvas of my cot. And above me, I fared no better. That woman was so heavy, the canvas sagged down and almost touched me. I had only two positions I could sleep in: either on my back or my stomach. I chose the latter, as it was less frightening and I didn't have to see the huge mass pressing down on me. I'd have done anything to have gotten the top bunk, but the woman who had it wasn't about to swap.

Another problem went way beyond the crushed sleeping accommodations. There were hundreds of Jewish refugees on board who were being given free passage to the States on humanitarian grounds, and they had just celebrated Rosh Hashanah. During the ten days of penance that followed, they couldn't eat food from the galley, so they prepared and ate all their meals in our hold. I swear they lived on fish, pickles, and garlic, each food vying to outstink the other. It was nauseating, and there was no way to get the pungent odor out of the hold.

The fact that the Jewish men came down and ate in our quarters during the day didn't bother us that much. We realized it was a religious observance, and most of us tried to be tolerant. But it was a different situation at night when we finally came down into the stuffy, smelly hold, peeled off our sweaty clothes, and started climbing into our bunks. Their visits then became insufferable.

My earliest encounter was on the first night, when I was trying to wriggle on my stomach into my bunk and felt a coarse brush rub against my leg. Turning in total shock, I looked into the bearded face and beady eyes of a rabbi! I let out a yelp that could be heard all through the hold, but, not surprisingly, no one paid attention, as the men in their long robes and yarmulkes were going systematically down the aisles kissing their wives and children good night!

This went on for several nights. And slowly our tolerance turned to outrage. Here we were, a group of women of all ages, shapes, and sizes, most of us in our next-to-nothings under sweltering conditions, having to put up with men whom we didn't even know invading our privacy.

Finally, a group of us got together on deck and let off steam. No one seemed to have a solution that didn't entail our reporting the situation to the captain. We didn't want to do that. We hadn't ratted in the prison camp, and we weren't going to do it now.

"I've got a solution," Margie said, but for all our probing, she wouldn't tell us what it was. She just said cryptically, "Don't worry, after tonight we won't have to put up with them any more."

That evening, when I saw her go down into the hold earlier than usual, I followed quietly. I watched silently from the shadows as she pulled her suitcase out from under her bunk-stack and, rummaging through it, lifted out a filmy nightgown and negligee. She was tall and extremely attractive, and when she pulled off her clothes and slipped into the gossamer gown and sheer robe, she looked stunning. She primped her hair, touched up her makeup, and sallied aft.

A little while later the rest of the women and children came stomping down, babies crying, children yelling, and our nightly bedtime ritual started all over again. There was a difference this time though: we had no male visitors.

Margie came in about half an hour later with a look of triumph on her face. Her filmy attire caught everyone's eye, and the group that had plotted with her on deck earlier in the day gathered around asking what had happened.

"Oh, I sashayed down into the men's hold, smiling sweetly and asking each one in turn if they knew where my husband's bunk was. I took my time, and needless to say, except for the fully dressed rabbis I got an eyeful of next-to-naked men of every conceivable shape and size scuttling for cover.

"Of course, Gerry knew I was coming. He waited until the hold was in a total uproar, then he shouted to the men and told them that I would be coming down to kiss him good night every night until the Jewish gentlemen stopped their embarrassing trek to the women's sleeping quarters!

"As promised, I don't think we'll have to worry about them anymore."

There was no doubt I needed Margie on that trip, just as I'd needed Lisa, her daughter, in the prison camp. Lisa had opted to leave camp for Australia with her maternal grandmother, rather than return to Tientsin with her mother and stepfather. I found myself hoping she's made the right decision.

When the gangplank was lowered in San Francisco, the first to go ashore were the Jewish refugees and their families. It was great to see them being greeted by their friends and kinfolk in the States, and I said so.

Paolo had come back and caught my remark. He raised

an eyebrow and said, "*Refugees?* They are Shanghai businessmen who know a good deal when they see one."

"How can you say that!" I said angrily, recalling pictures of the Holocaust and the hell most Jews had lived through.

"How can I say it? Hey, I've been doing business with them for years—even way before the war." He patted me on the back, and added, "Keep your kind heart. The world needs more of them." Then he was gone.

⁓

The Manx lived up to the recommendation Paolo had given it. The room was pleasant, the beds comfortable, and the service great. The following morning, the desk clerk arranged for us to be taken to the station, where Mother was able to get us three tickets to Glendale with little fuss. Coming over to Ursula and me, she said, "It's the milk train, not the express; probably that's why I was able to get the tickets so easily. It'll take a couple of hours longer, but on the plus side, we'll probably see a lot more of California."

That was an understatement.

That had to be the slowest train trip I'd ever taken in my life, even slower than the freezing trip to the prison camp. As the conductor came down through the car checking tickets, a wobbly drunk bumped into him and said, "Shkooshe me, when do I get off the train?"

"Where are you going?" the conductor asked.

"U-m-m … duh … Glendale," the drunk said in a slurred voice that rose in happy surprise when he finally remembered his destination.

"I'm afraid you have a long trip ahead," the conductor said placatingly, adding in a louder voice so we all could hear, "Please people, we make a lot of stops on this train. No one, I repeat, *no one* is to get off at any stops until we reach Glendale.

I will come and tell each of you who has tickets to Modesto, Fresno, and Bakersfield so you can get ready to disembark."

Sure enough, about twenty minutes later we pulled into a whistle stop and the drunk staggered off the train. I pointed him out to Mother, but she just shrugged and said, "Don't worry, God takes care of drunks."

"He does?" I asked, as the train gave several jerks. "Well, we're pulling out, and that dumb idiot is still on the platform, waving like crazy!" As he tried to chase the train, Ursula and I couldn't stop laughing, wondering what he was going to do next and how he was going to get to Glendale.

We shouldn't have worried.

When we finally stopped at Fresno hours later to let a family off, the drunk climbed back on board. I looked at Ursula, and she at me, and we both started to laugh again.

I leant out into the aisle and touched him as he went by. "How'd you get to Fresno in time to catch the train?" I asked.

"In time?" he asked. "Why, I hitchhiked. I've been sitting in the station for over an hour waiting for you!" I could tell his little excursion had definitely sobered him up.

I'd forgotten how lovely the California countryside could be. It was a perfect time of the year to see all the truck gardens, vineyards, orchards, cattle ranches, and dairy farms. There was a cool coastal breeze blowing, and all the cows had their rumps to the wind. I'd learned about that when we'd spent that year in the States in '39. An old-timer had told me then that you never needed a weather vane in cattle country.

I tried to get lost in the scenery around us, afraid to contemplate what it would be like to get to Glendale and find I'd been stood up again. I found my emotions ranging from anticipation to panic and back. I remembered telling some over-serious GIs I'd met in China after the war that the only reason they had a crush on me was because they were homesick and hadn't been with an American girl in ages. I told them to wait till they hit the States and the girls all came running after them. Now I was wondering if that was what had happened to Bill. That his not meeting us was more than not having wheels: it was having too many adoring looks from love-starved females. *Out of fifty-some-thousand marines in the Orient, why did I have to pick a no-show?* I thought glumly.

When we finally pulled into Glendale station, it was already dark. There weren't many people on the platform, so it wasn't hard to spot Donald and darling little humpbacked Grandma.

Never one to show emotion, Donald came over with a crooked smile and gave us each a perfunctory hug. Not a word about not seeing us for going on seven years. No mention of us having survived a Japanese prison camp. No understanding that the abrupt use of the atomic bomb at the end of World War II was to prevent the Japanese war ministry from carrying out their directive "to annihilate all prisoners and civilian internees and to not leave any trace." Just Donald's "How was the trip?" as though we'd come up from Phoenix or somewhere.

I couldn't believe Bill was nowhere to be seen. I clipped myself under the chin, and said silently, *To hell with you, I've survived worse than this!*

While Ursula and I were hugging diminutive Grandma, who was standing silently with tears running down her precious, age-crinkled cheeks, Donald looked around for our luggage.

"There isn't much, Don," Mother said. "We came over in the hold of a troopship with what we each could carry. There's

21

the stack over there, we should be able to get it all into the trunk of your car."

"If not, I've brought some rope, and we can tie it on top," Donald said. It all seemed so mundane, almost awkward, and I didn't know whether to laugh or cry.

Just then Bill came rushing up out of nowhere, swept me off my feet, and yelling a brief "Hi!" over his shoulder to the others, gave me a resounding kiss, and hissed in my ear, "Come and see my new car!" His excitement was contagious.

It was a late model, prewar Dodge coupe, and immaculate.

"Isn't it a beaut? Guess what I've named it? Remember Cumma–shaw, the old Jeep in Tientsin? Well, it's Cummashaw II."

"Cummashaw, yo-mei-yo!" was a cry for alms from the street urchins in Tientsin. Every time we had to stop for the milling crowds in the streets and byways, they'd swarm all over the Jeep, begging for *"Cummashaw!"* and sometimes they would prefix their plea with a touch of Marine Corps humor: "No mama! No papa! No flight pay!" I looked into Bill's smiling blue eyes and started to laugh ... from those happy memories, but mostly from relief.

Okay, Margie, I said silently, it's just as I thought, he didn't have any wheels, that's why he wasn't in San Francisco!

Chapter 2

We'd just moved in temporarily with Don and his wife Marian when Margo called, asking Mother to come to New Orleans as her first baby was due and she wanted Mumsy with her. Mother, afraid Bill and I were getting too serious to be left totally unsupervised, suggested that I go with her. Needless to say, her suggestion went over like a freight load of mung beans, but being Mother, she prevailed, and I went.

It was mid-September, and Algiers Naval Base, in the Mississippi Delta south of New Orleans, had to be the soggiest piece of real estate in the United States. It rained without letup for all of the two weeks we were there, and the slimy mud made it almost impossible to leave the little base housing unit where Margo and Jack lived.

The trip to New Orleans was pretty frantic, and when we finally arrived, a couple of plane hops, several bus transfers, and a ferry trip later, Margo had already gone through her ordeal and was back home on the soggy little island with a precious, bawling baby boy. The delivery had been really rough, and I was glad we were there to help her get through those first painful days. I can't ever remember seeing Margo so weak and listless, and the darn weather did nothing to cheer her up. Of course, the only one in the house above it all, and enjoying his new life to the fullest, was noisy young Jack Bishop, Jr. When his proud dad came home in the evenings, I remember him humming the *Marine Hymn* softly to his new son. Seems it was the only "lullaby" he knew!

When Margo got to feeling better, we'd sit around reminiscing. It was then that she told me of a headline story in the Sunday supplement of a major New Orleans paper that featured Becky Durande, a marine war bride who'd been in our prison camp, and whom the other brides had nicknamed "What's-the-Use." Becky came to camp with an absolutely adorable little baby boy, and an attitude of apathetic despair that brought fury and frustration to the other war brides. Like Margo, Iris Sydow, and Thyra Retske, Becky had married just before the marines were to ship out from their China station on December 11, 1941. When Japan declared war on December 8, all the North China marines, including Becky's husband, Johnny Durande, were taken prisoner and put in military camps.

The war brides met fifteen months later in Weihsien Prison Camp, a civilian camp, and they couldn't help thinking how lucky Becky was. At least she had a beautiful son to remind her of her husband's love. But she didn't see it that way. I recall Margo asking her one day, right after we got to camp, if Johnny knew he had a son.

"N-a-a ..." she said, her voice sounding like the bleat of an unhappy lamb.

"Did he know you were pregnant before he was taken prisoner?" Margo asked kindly.

"N-a-a."

"Oh, Becky, you've got to write him and tell him! That's the kind of wonderful news a guy needs when he's a POW."

"What's the use?" she asked, the bleat turning into a whine.

"What do you mean—*what's the use?*" Margo asked, dumbfounded. She'd been writing Jack every month, not that she was expecting that he would receive all her letters, but if even one got through she knew what a boost it would be to his morale.

"What's the use of writing," Becky whined. "He'll never get it."

"You don't *know* that!" Margo said, exasperated.

Thyra took her and shook her hard. "Write a damn letter!" she exploded. "Or a card. Anything. Mr. Egger from the Red Cross is here to take our letters to Tsingtao to mail them for us. You've got time. Write him ... *now!*"

Becky started to whimper, "What's the use? What's the use?"

Through the years I'd ask Margo if Becky had ever written Johnny. The answer was always no. Margo learned later from Jack that Johnny didn't make it. All the other guys were getting cards and letters; not many, but enough to let them know their gals still loved them. Johnny never got a word. Before long he became ill. Very ill. Nothing that a man with a will to live couldn't have come through with flying colors. But Johnny didn't have that will. He was certain Becky had left him and didn't care. He knew nothing about his adorable son. So he gave up.

Now here was this headline story about a brave war bride and her darling five-year-old son being welcomed into the arms of Johnny's loving family. And Becky, reveling in every moment of it, was playing the bereaved widow to the hilt.

∽

When we got back to California, the first thing Mother did was hunt for an apartment for us, because her earlier joy at seeing Donald had been tempered by a big disappointment.

It happened when we left the Glendale station and Mother realized we were not heading for Grandma's little home on Satsuma Avenue in North Hollywood. It was a pretty little house on a half-acre of land, and Grandma had had an extra room built on when we visited her in '39. Mother had been dreaming about the place, and about staying with Grandma. She knew her mother was getting old and fragile, and she had planned to take care of her in her declining years, while we girls got part-time jobs and completed our higher education. She hadn't realized how much she was depending on this arrangement. It would have helped us so much, as Dad had lost all his investments in China, and the only nest egg left was his retirement fund in England.

That evening, after we'd stowed our luggage in the trunk of the car, Mother commented on the route we were taking, and Donald said in his blunt, offhand way, "Oh, I sold Mother's place back in '43. You can't believe what houses were going for during the war, and I thought it would be good to take advantage of the market."

"So Mother's living with you now, then?" she asked.

"Oh, no. Marian and she don't get along. I found Mother a nice little one-bedroom place across from Buena Vista Studios in Burbank, and I go over and see her once a week, and take her grocery shopping. In fact, we're heading there now. We'll drop Mother off, then head on home."

I looked to see how Grandma was taking all this, and noticed she'd fallen asleep with a sweet smile on her precious face.

If homes had been at a premium during the war, rentals were even harder to find when it ended. By dint of persistence, Mother finally found us a large, downstairs studio apartment on Woodhaven Drive in the Hollywood Hills. It had obviously been a cellar or rumpus room in its day, but the owners of the home above had converted it into an apartment of sorts to take advantage of the high postwar rents. It had a partitioned-off sleeping area, but only a communal bathroom reached by climbing a steep flight of stairs to the main house. There was also a wall phone at the head of the stairs which we were allowed to use in an emergency.

On the plus side, it was clean and nicely furnished—though rather dark, as all the walls were paneled in pine, and the lovely large windows the owners had had installed looked out on a tree-studded hillside that blocked any sunlight from coming in. It had a minimal kitchen consisting of a tiny refrigerator-range combination, with an equally tiny sink beside it. But after all we'd been through, it was home—and it was heaven!

And the nicest part of all was that it was on the Beachwood Drive bus line, which took us down to Hollywood and Vine, the hub of our little universe, where we could catch streetcars and buses in all directions to get to our jobs in the daytime, and Ursula to her drama classes at night.

And so my new life took shape. I spent my days at work, my nights at home, and my weekends with Bill.

∽

Looking back on the jobs I had, I couldn't help thinking that the short, brush-up secretarial course Ursula and I had taken at a well-known business school in downtown Los Angeles while we were still living with Don and Marian was a total waste of time. It had been a terrible ordeal. Eight hours a day of pounding typewriters, taking dictation, transcribing letters, and being told that we'd never amount to a hill of beans. I think the worst disservice the school did was to make all the students terrified of any new employer they might get. They painted them all as ogres, with no patience, heart, or ethics.

Ursula and I would come home evenings totally exhausted, getting off the streetcar at Lankershim in North Hollywood and trekking the long blocks up to Victory Boulevard where Donald lived, wondering all the while if the business world could be as rotten as the sadistic school personnel painted it to be.

Of course, it wasn't.

Ursula's first, and only, job was with the prestigious Beverly Hills Bank, whose clients were all movie moguls and stars. I remember drooling at her stories of them: how down-to-earth some were, and how others would be so stuck-up she'd wish they'd take a pratfall just so she could laugh at them.

Unlike Ursula's, my first job lasted just under two weeks. It was with a "subliminal" advertising agency on Melrose Avenue. If I had not been given a description along with the address, I'd never have found the place. There was no way of knowing it was a business address, except for the street number on a massive oak door. The offices were plush and, like the outside, completely unrevealing. My job turned out to be assisting Janet Price, the president's personal secretary. She was a charmer who always called him "The Boss," and she did a great job of showing me the ropes. One of the things I learned from her was that I was *never* to talk about the agency or what I did with anyone.

I'd never heard of subliminal advertising and asked her what it was. It turned out that the firm worked with all the radio actors and writers—at that time television had not yet come of age—and whenever some performer would say, for instance, "I'll have a scotch on the rocks," the agency would have the writer change it to "bourbon on the rocks" and collect a nice fee from a group of bourbon distillers. The same went for household appliances, toiletries, soft drinks … the list was endless. They must've been doing all right, as they had a warehouse in the back full of gratuities to hand out to obliging actors and script writers.

I'd only been there a week when I was promoted to handling the reception desk outside The Boss's office. Janet told me to always get a client's name so I could announce them when I showed them into his office. I enjoyed it, and found most of the writers and radio personalities intriguing, unaffected people. That is, until one fateful Thursday morning.

That morning the heavy oak door opened, and a funny little short, round man came in. I didn't know him from Adam, but I stood up, smiled, and said politely, "Good morning. May I have your name, please?"

To my horror, he responded with screams, squeals, and shrieks till I thought he would self-destruct. Before I could gather my wits, he pushed me out of the way, slammed through the president's office door, and shouted, "What the hell is that Bostonian bitch doing out there? Who the hell does she think she is, asking me for my name? Get rid of her now, or I'm *gone!*"

I felt my face turning every shade of red and wished I could turn into a bug on the wall and crawl away. Janet came rushing out of her office about then and beckoned for me to follow her.

"Who the heck is he?" I whispered. "And how dare he speak of me like that?"

"He's a famous animator."

"A famous *what?*" I asked.

"He's the voice of a whole slew of cartoon characters on radio, and our top account. I should have warned you about him."

"Yes, you should," I said curtly.

"It's not your fault," Janet said kindly. "It's your British accent. We all like it in the office—in fact, that's why The Boss put you on the reception desk. We never thought anyone would take offence at it, but I'm afraid we were wrong. Why don't you stay in my office and I'll go handle the front desk."

It took a while for things to calm down, and after Janet had gushed over the loud-mouthed creep and shown him out the door, she came into her office and said, "The Boss would like to see you."

I went into the holy-of-holies and was greeted, not unkindly, with, "I don't think I have to say anything. You heard it all. That gentleman is my best account and I can't afford to lose him. When I finally got him to cool down, he made a generous offer and said that if you took elocution lessons I could hire you back."

"He did, did he?" My humiliation started to turn to anger. "Well, tell him from me, I think *he* needs elocution lessons. Thank you, but I'm leaving—goodbye." I was damned if I was going to give anyone the chance to fire me.

"I'm sorry it had to end like this."

"So am I," I said, and meant it.

"Won't you wait till Janet has the bookkeeper write out your check?" He looked so concerned, I thought he'd cry.

"No thanks, please mail it to me." Collecting my purse from the desk drawer, I raced across the lobby and out of the building. I made it just in time! Tears started to flow, my nose started to run, and my brave new world took a nosedive.

My second job fared better. It was with Massey-Greenfield Homes, with offices on Cahuenga Boulevard. They had a lumber mill in the San Fernando Valley that built prefab home kits which were shipped to eleven western states and Hawaii. I thought the concept was great, and, with the housing crunch the way it was, it had nowhere to go but up. When Leon Moscowitz, my boss, found out that I was also an artist, he asked if I would sketch the home elevations along with performing my secretarial and office duties. I couldn't believe I was being paid to do a job that was so much fun. I especially enjoyed running off the renderings on the mimeograph machine and inserting them in the press kits we made up for the franchise sales promotions.

The crew in the head office was fun, too. There was Shirley Neal, an ex-army master sergeant who had driven across the States to California in an open 1927 Model-T because she couldn't take another New England winter, and "Smiley" Travis, who was charming and as happy as his name. And among the sales crew, there was Leon's top franchise man, Joe DuBois. I remember when he first handed me his card and I said, "It's nice to meet you, Mr. Dubois," giving it the correct French pronunciation. He looked at me queerly for a minute, then said, "Look, missy, that's *Doo-Boys*—don't give me no uppity French name."

I stood corrected.

Inadvertently, it was Joe who brought my happy house of cards tumbling down. He'd been gone for almost a week, and I learned he was trying to line up a new franchisee in Nevada. It was Friday afternoon when he burst into the office with, "I've *done* it!" I was manually feeding paper into the mimeograph machine, and spun around to congratulate him. It only took that split second. I fed the last sheet of paper into the rollers along with my right index finger, and promptly lost the tip. The nail and bone were still intact, but the whole fleshy pad was sucked off into the machine.

I remember little else of that afternoon, as the pain was excruciating. I do recall Shirley and Joe rushing me to the

Hollywood Receiving Hospital and having the doctors bawl them out for not getting my fingerpad out of the rollers so they could sew it back on. It was weeks healing after that, and years before the nerve endings under the nail finally numbed out. Typing was almost impossible for the longest time, because if that finger landed awkwardly on a key I'd just about go out through the roof.

Leon, always considerate, said he'd pay all my medical bills but asked that I please not file for disability as he didn't have any insurance. It was while I was on limited duty at the office, sitting around getting bored at doing nothing, that I started going through files and cleaning up old projects. It didn't take long for me to find out that dear old Leon had been spending the franchise money on himself. He'd told me earlier about his beautiful new home in Bel Air, and more recently of the forty-foot yacht he'd just bought, but I always assumed he was a man of means. When I found out what was really going on, I brashly went into his office and told him, whether he liked it or not, what he was doing was embezzling, and I didn't want to be a part of it. He told me it was all legit; he could do what he liked with the money as long as he supplied the kits to the franchisees. As I knew nothing about how, and if, the kits were being shipped, I couldn't argue.

It all came to a head a few weeks after Easter, when the Cardozas of Hawaii came over to the mainland to find out why none of the kits they'd paid for were being shipped. After Leon had blustered his way out of a tight corner, telling them that lumber was still hard to get, Mrs. Cardoza came over to me, gave me a beautiful bottle of the perfume that her family made in the Islands, and asked quietly what was going on. I was in a quandary. I liked them. They were hardworking people who didn't deserve to be taken to the cleaners. I couldn't lie to her. I ended up suggesting that if she didn't feel comfortable, maybe she should check into Leon's business practices.

When she and her husband left, I turned in my resignation, went home, and quietly took stock of my life.

I knew I could always get another job, that wasn't my problem. My real problem was that during the months I'd been with Massey-Greenfield, my personal life had received a slug in the gut.

Chapter 3

Looking back, I found there was a certain magic in the air when I returned from New Orleans the previous October. I could feel that our time apart had been good for both of us. I was bubbling over with plans for our future, and although Bill wasn't quite that elated, I was happy to see that while I'd been gone, he'd applied at both the University of Southern California and the University of California at Los Angeles. The reason he was more subdued was that he'd been turned down by both universities, and I was glad I was back, because he wasn't taking it very well.

As a native son, he was furious at being bumped by veterans from out of state who were going to college under the brand-new GI Bill of Rights. It was a rotten break, but he didn't give up, and, after finding he couldn't get in at UCLA, he tried all the other California campuses, but to no avail. Ultimately, desperate, he applied to Arizona and was accepted by the University of Arizona at Flagstaff. As a native Californian, I could feel his disappointment, but he needed to finish his studies and get his degree, and he only had a couple of semesters to go, so it was "Arizona, here I come!"

I couldn't help measuring the time he'd spend in Flagstaff by the years I spent in the prison camp, and I thought, *Hell, six months is nothing!*

"When do you start?" I asked.

"Not until January," was his despondent reply. After a long silence he added, "Guess I'd better find a part-time job to fill in the days, or I'll go bonkers."

It was a lovely, cool Saturday in October, and we were sitting on the patio of his folks' home in Altadena. Looking at Bill, I found it impossible to match his glum mood, as the week before I had started my new job with the subliminal advertising agency, and my world was glowing in several luscious shades of pink.

While we sat in quiet contemplation, I watched his dad, a Panama hat hiding his thinning hair, puttering under a late-blooming jacaranda, its cloud of lavender blossoms challenging the intense blue of the sky, and I recalled how nervous I'd been the first time Bill had brought me to meet his parents. It turned out I shouldn't have worried. They were gracious and charming, and his dad did all he could to make me feel at home. For some reason, he reminded me of Fibber McGee, of the *Fibber McGee and Molly* radio show I'd listened to during those long wet nights in the soggy South. I loved radio for that reason. I could picture the different characters anyway I pleased, and I pictured Fibber looking like Bill's dad, Ed.

His mother, Elaine, was definitely not a sharp-tongued Molly. She was more the charming social type, who knew how to make everyone feel at home in her home. Strangely, I felt there was some insincerity in her graciousness toward me, but maybe that was because Bill was her only son, and I could sense her sizing me up at every turn.

I found his folks were very well-off, in an unpretentious way. Their home was small but delightful, with a panoramic view of Los Angeles that on a clear sparkling day went all the way to Catalina Island.

Before long I found out how they handled their home

without servants. The household work was divided up in a seamless sort of way, with Ed taking care of the lovely front and back gardens, which, for some reason, they insisted on calling "yards." For someone who'd always been under the impression that a yard was where one hid things like clotheslines, trash bins, and unwanted odds and ends, I had quite a time referring to their gardens as yards. Be that as it may, Ed had a wonderful green thumb, and both the front and back yards were absolutely delightful.

Elaine, on the other hand, ran her immaculate home with the deft touch of one born to it, especially in the kitchen, where she was a superb cook. The only place she drew a line was when it came to doing the dishes. As it was before dishwashers were a household item, she always called Bill in to do them. I couldn't help wondering how she'd made out while Bill was in the service, and figured Ed must've done the chore for her then.

I also found out she was loved and spoiled completely by the two men in her life. As she didn't drive, they were her glorified chauffeurs and provided all the polite little amenities that went with professional chauffeuring. She had built helplessness into an art form, and all she had to do was raise an eyebrow, or look up sweetly with a query on her face, and they'd jump to do her bidding.

As far as Bill was concerned, I was glad he was going to look for a part-time job, as there's just so much scrubbing and polishing one can do to a car before it gets to you. I have to admit he did a great job on Cummashaw, though, waxing and buffing its old paint job till I could see my reflection in it. The same went for all the chrome-ware and hubcaps. There's no doubt that if cars could get along on spit and polish alone, Cummashaw would last forever. I remember asking him once what its engine looked like, and he opened up the hood and showed me. It was obvious by the disinterested way he did it that he really didn't care about the car's guts, only its appearance, and he as good as admitted he didn't know a darn thing about what made it run.

I noticed the sun shining off Cummashaw's hood, and I thought back to another time, and another Cummashaw in China. That old Jeep's hood had been so battered and bruised no sun would ever shine off it, but it had more spirit than any vehicle I'd ever known. And as the memory grabbed hold, I recalled a trip we'd made in it to Peking.

Bill and Cope, Ursula's latest boyfriend, wanted to see that fabulous city, and we told them they'd better take us along as tour guides ... or else!

I have to say, it didn't take much persuading on our part.

To justify the trip, the first thing Cope did was get some official papers to deliver to Marine Headquarters in Peking. And as we'd lived our whole lives dodging skirmishes, irate warlords, and Japanese invaders, Mother and Dad didn't blink twice when Ursula and I asked if we could go along with them.

The day we took off was cold and blustery. The road to Peking was around a hundred miles long, not very wide, and built in concrete sections that made the old Jeep bounce every time we hit the seams. It was not very kind on our butts.

About halfway there, Bill and Cope said we gals had better learn how to use the M-1 and side arms they'd brought along for protection ... just in case. We stopped at a desert-like area; actually it was the beginning of the Gobi. It soon became obvious that I was a rotten shot and couldn't hit any of the big old shrubs I aimed at, but Ursula turned into Annie Oakley! The break lasted about twenty minutes, then we all piled back into the Jeep and took off for the great walled city of Peking.

Most of the cities in China, from the smallest hamlet to the biggest city, have walls around them. The townships straddle the main road, with massive wooden gates at either end that can be closed in the event of an attack by marauding bandits, making them self-sustaining forts.

We'd been driving quite a while when a big walled city loomed up ahead of us. I got all excited and shouted, "Hey, that's Peking!"

A fork in the road veered off to the left about a quarter mile before the city gates. Bill was driving, and he asked which road to take. I said smartly, "The right, of course. *That's* Peking!"

In those days I knew *everything!*

So we took the right fork and drove through the huge, imposing gates, expecting a Marine Corps Jeep to get a joyous welcome. But it didn't happen. In fact, the atmosphere was downright hostile.

"This can't be Peking," Cope said, as we sped along. "They don't like us one bit!"

When the crowds got even angrier, he said, "Let's turn around and get outta here *now!*"

But smart-aleck me said, "Keep going, we'll just drive out the gates at the other end and be on our way."

By this time, Bill was stomping on the gas, with chickens, pigs, and ducks flying in all directions. When we got to the far end of the road, to our horror there were *no gates*. Where they were supposed to be, there was a big graveyard!

Bill spun around a cluster of grave markers on two wheels, and we tore back through the city with the Chinese yelling, hurling rocks, and cussing us all the way. Cope told us to keep down, as they might be armed with more than rocks, but Bill had turned us into such a fast-moving, erratic target, I don't believe there was any way they could've hit us with live ammo.

One thing we learned, it definitely was *not* Peking!

I was quite subdued when we finally drove through the massive gates of the old historic city and headed for the marine headquarters to deliver our so-called official papers. Then Bill and Cope took us to the British legation, where we were going to stay with a family friend at the British embassy, while they found rooms in the Wagon Lits Hotel. The next morning when they joined us for breakfast in the Legation Quarter, Bill noticed a bold headline on the resurrected *Peking-Tientsin Times:* "Fierce Fighting Reported on the Tientsin-Peking Highway." Below it there was a totally fabricated account of a raid that supposedly took place the previous afternoon ... just about the time we were learning how to fire those weapons and the guys were making like gunfighters!

We'd gone up on a Friday after work, and came back Sunday evening after a whirlwind tour of the fabulous city. On the way home, Cope drove. He said if he really hit the gas, the concrete seams wouldn't be as rough on our behinds, so we told him to go for it, Cummashaw roaring along like a happy hound. We were almost to the Tientsin city limits when we noticed a thin, black line across the road. We were going so fast, there was no way we could stop, and all of a sudden we found we were airborne, like a Wile E. Coyote cartoon, landing with a thrump on the far side of a huge, open pit. It was obvious some enterprising Communists had removed a section of concrete, dug a giant tank-trap, and filled it with explosives. Needless to say, we were all badly shaken-up thinking about what could've happened to us if we'd been going any slower.

The following week, the Armed Forces Radio Service moved their headquarters from Peking to Tientsin, and the lead vehicle in the convoy wasn't as lucky as we were; it fell into the trap and was destroyed, along with all the personnel aboard.

Even that sobering memory couldn't stop my nostalgia.

One thing about China: nothing ever remains the same for long.

I had a smile on my face when Bill closed Cummashaw's hood, and he asked what was so funny. And I, thinking of all the important and unimportant things in life, just shrugged and said, "To each his own …"

The remark seemed to trigger something, because he said, "Have you heard it?"

The non sequitur left me out in the cold. "Heard *what?*" I asked, wondering what he was getting at.

"*To Each His Own.* I've decided it's our song."

"Really? It's that good? No, I haven't heard it."

"Tell you what, we'll go dancing tonight and I know you'll hear it at least once. When you do, you'll know why I chose it."

It turned out we didn't have to wait till the evening, as his mother ran out of butter and asked us to go to the store for her. Tooling down Lake Street in Cummashaw, I flicked on the radio. Eddy Howard's voice came over the airways, a little shaky at first as the radio built up volume, then I caught the words and realized he was singing "our song." It was beautiful, and I decided I liked Bill's choice.

∽

Before I knew what had happened, Thanksgiving arrived. The last time we'd celebrated that American holiday was in '39 when we were in the States visiting Grandma. It was a lovely time, with a great feast, and I remember Grandma trying to do everything herself, and knocking herself out with exhaustion along the way. This time, Elaine took over and showed her true colors. The meal seemed to go together effortlessly, while Bill and Ed lapped eggnogs and tried to make themselves useful. In the spirit of the occasion, I asked if I could lay the table.

"Lay what?" Bill asked, and both he and his dad started to laugh uproariously.

"What's so funny?" I asked, confused, and not a little embarrassed.

"Honey, we don't lay tables in the States, we *set* them."

"So?" I asked, still wondering what was so hilarious about my remark.

"Never mind, I'll explain later," Bill said with a grin.

So I "set" the table.

Bill helped me with the beautiful damask tablecloth, then got out the silver flatware, and I started to put the place settings down. Before I got far along, I realized I didn't know what we were having to eat, so I asked Bill, and he went out to the kitchen and talked to his mother. When he came back he said, "We're starting with a crab cocktail. There'll be a fruit salad on the side, along with turkey and all the trimmings, and, of course, pumpkin pie for dessert."

"Thanks," I said and, in typical British manner, set all the pieces down to the left and right of the place plate in the correct order, with the fork for the crab cocktail alongside the knives to the right. Then I placed the dessert spoon and fork at twelve o'clock high, directly above the main plate.

Elaine came out about then, wiping her hands on her apron, and said, "I've taken the bird out of the oven and I'm going to start making the gravy. We should be sitting down to eat in about twenty minutes."

"Smells fantastic," I said, as she looked over the table. Then I saw a look of surprise come over her face, and asked, "Is something wrong?"

"What are these doing up here?" she asked, lifting up one of the dessert spoons.

"They're for the pumpkin pie," I said.

"Well, dear, we don't use spoons for pumpkin pie, we use forks, and we place them to the left of the salad fork." She then proceeded around the table, changing the place settings and picking up the offending spoons.

I know she hadn't meant to sound short and condescending, she had to be tired even if she didn't look it, but for some dumb reason I felt I'd been soundly put in my place.

I took a deep breath and looked across the room through the pretty archway to the sunken living room, trying not to show my hurt. My gaze rested on the beautiful mantel over the provincial fireplace, and I saw the exquisite pieces of carved jade, cloisonné, and inlaid soapstone that Bill and I had picked out in China after our engagement. Not the most practical items to start a new home with, but definitely the most beautiful.

I'll never forget asking Bill what they were doing on his parents' mantel when I saw them on display for the first time. He said his mother was taking care of them for us.

"Where's the beautiful, carved white porcelain vase with the twelve male fairies on it?" I asked.

Bill's face turned flaming red, and he said, "Dad told me when the pieces arrived, he helped Mom unpack them. When she lifted out the white vase and saw the male fairies in all their—I'm sorry, honey, but they really were obscene—poses, she let out a scream and dropped it on the floor and it broke into a million pieces."

"She had no right opening the package in the first place," I said angrily.

"Well, she and Dad thought it had arrived for them and

thought nothing of unpacking it. Don't worry, everything's in safe hands till we get married."

I didn't want to tell him I wasn't worrying about them, I was annoyed that they were being displayed by anyone other than ourselves. We hadn't been able to get an engagement ring in China after the war, so Bill had bought me a lovely, solid jade bracelet to mark the occasion. I felt for those pieces as I felt for the bracelet: they were ours, and no one should have the pleasure of displaying them but us.

There was nothing I could do about it except take it in stride, but it rankled me every time I saw them.

I looked away and saw Elaine going back out to the kitchen. I followed her and asked if there was anything I could do. She was standing over the range, the roasting pan full of turkey drippings simmering gently on the large front surface unit.

"You can watch me make gravy," she said kindly, realizing she had offended me and trying to make up. I did watch, and I learned, and I've made my Thanksgiving gravy just as she did for over fifty years.

∼

The fill-in job Bill found was pretty rugged. He became a relief mail carrier over the Christmas holidays, hiking up and down the hills of Altadena loaded with Christmas mail. He became lean and mean, and insisted he felt he was back in boot camp.

I, of course, had already lost my first job with the advertising agency, and was now with Massey-Greenfield Homes. Everything was an exciting challenge, and even though I knew that after the holidays Bill would be gone for six months and I'd only get to see him over Easter, it didn't dampen my spirits. Everything was coming together beautifully, and the only slight problem I saw looming on the horizon was my having to persuade Bill to let me work after we were married.

I'd had a surprise earlier when I mentioned I wanted to keep on working and Bill said, "No women in our family have ever worked outside the home. And I don't want it to start with you."

How could I tell him housework was not my forte? If I worked, we could afford a housekeeper, the housework would still be done, possibly much better than I could do it, and I would be happier. I knew I had to use every scrap of finesse I could muster to get him to change his mind, but I never doubted I could do it.

When January rolled around, Bill loaded up Cummashaw and headed for Flagstaff, and I went merrily on my way. Without weekends with Bill, I decided I'd do some freelance work to make extra money for my trousseau, and I also went to modeling school and took dressmaking and design. It didn't leave me much time for writing letters to Bill, but I managed a couple a week. Bill, on the other hand, wrote daily. Nothing much, but they were warm reminders of our love for each other and the great future we were looking forward to.

Sometime in February, a couple of days after I'd lost the tip of my finger, Bill came home for a midterm break, and, as luck would have it, Margo and Jack were in town, and also Ursula's fiancé, Cope. She'd met him in the legal office of the First Marine Division in Tientsin when we'd worked there right after the war, and he and Ursula had gotten engaged as soon as she hit the States. I always liked him. He looked like Hollywood's version of a Mafia don, but he had a heart of gold. Jack, of course, I adored. He had the most delightful sense of humor of anyone I knew, and considering the hell he lived through as a POW in the different Japanese prison camps in China and Japan during the war, he'd never lost his droll outlook on life.

Jack was a career marine, and Cope was still in the service, so Bill decided to join them and wear his old marine uniform when we all went to the Coconut Grove for a gala evening of dining and dancing to Freddy Martin and his band.

The war had been over long enough for three tall, good-looking uniformed marines to make a splash anywhere they went, and with us three gals dressed to the nines, we had the maitre d' and waiters falling all over each other to wait on us.

The evening would have been perfect for me if it hadn't been for my darn hand. The pain was still excruciating, and I didn't want to take a painkiller as I wouldn't be able to drink or to toast our future. I wore a slim black skirt, with a loose-sleeved silk brocade jacket over it—the only thing I could wear with my hand bound in a bulky bandage, and my arm in a sling.

Needless to say, I needed lots of help when it came to cutting my filet mignon, and it didn't help matters much out on the dance floor either when my darn right arm in its sling kept getting in the way. I still remember the tab. Including cover, drinks, and a big tip, it ran one hundred twenty dollars! Why I remember it is that Bill hadn't brought enough money, and, as plastic didn't exist in those days, I paid the forty dollars that was our part of the tab.

Come to think of it, Bill still owes me. Wonder what forty dollars at five percent compound interest, adjusted for inflation, would amount to fifty-some years later?

～

I had just gotten through telling Leon Moscowitz that I didn't approve of embezzlement at Massey-Greenfield when Easter rolled around, and Bill came home for the holiday. It was wonderful seeing him again, and the first thing we did was go for a drive up Rubio Canyon. It was one of our favorite spots, and, surprisingly, few other couples had found it. It was a meld of hidden wildlife sounds and rustling leaves, of weathered trees, greening shrubs, ageless rocks and soft white sand, and most of all, it held a lovely feeling of peace and solitude.

The mood was still with me when we noticed the time, backed up and turned around, and started driving home. It was then that the sun shone directly in my eyes, and I reached up to pull the visor down and got stuck by a hat pin.

"Oh-oh, William," I said mischievously, "girls don't take their hats off unless things are getting *pretty* serious."

"What are you talking about?" he said, adjusting his sun visor in turn.

"There's a hat pin in your sun visor. Want to explain how it got there?"

He turned and smiled, saying, "Make anything you want out of it, I'm not talking."

I laughed and forgot the incident.

Early in the week we went dancing at one of our favorite haunts, the Pasadena Civic Auditorium. With no bandage on my hand or sling on my arm, I was looking forward to a great time.

We met many of Bill's friends there, even several ex-marine buddies from China. Don Barnard was among them; he too was attending Arizona State at Flagstaff. Of all the marines I'd met in Tientsin, he was one I wouldn't have missed if I'd never seen him again. He was so arrogant and full of himself, it canceled out any good traits he might have had. I'll never forget the morning my boss, Major Baines, a perfect Southern gentleman, came into the legal office with a grin on his face that eclipsed the sun. He'd just learned his wife in Memphis had given him a son, and he was handing out cigars, proud beyond words. When he handed a cigar to Barnard, the long, lean lieutenant said, "Let me see, you were home last, when? ... *ten, eleven* months ago?"

Baines didn't say a word. He put out his hand as if to shake Barnard's, grabbed his wrist, and flipped him over his shoulder and up against the blistering oil stove in the middle of the room. It all happened so fast I almost dropped my coffee.

"Stand up, and get out while you can! Don't ever come into this office again!" Major Baines didn't raise his voice; he didn't have to. He was at least six inches shorter than Barnard, but his gallant reaction to the off-color remark made him appear over ten feet tall. Barnard got up, his uniform badly scorched, suffering possible body burns, and left the room. There hadn't been a trace of a swagger in his walk.

The band started to play *To Each His Own,* and Bill and I were snuggling on the dance floor when Barnard nudged him and said in a singsong voice, "Sally wouldn't like that."

I wondered what he meant but didn't comment. Obviously, Sally was one of the girls at college who probably had a crush on Bill. Within minutes I'd forgotten all about her, enjoying the evening, the music, and us being together.

A couple of days later, Bill was helping me shop for my trousseau when I noticed he couldn't stop yawning. It certainly wasn't from being up late with me the night before, and anyhow, it wasn't a sleepy kind of yawn. It was a bored, how-the-hell-can-I-get-out-of-this type of yawn. It was unlike him, but I couldn't help thinking that most men hated shopping, especially for girl things, so I suggested we quit and I'd finish up after he'd gone back to Flagstaff.

That night, as I lay in bed, twirling the lovely engagement ring he had given me at Christmas, I kept thinking about the change in Bill. It was as though he'd had a call from someone after our drive out to Rubio and the evening of dancing at the Civic. He was different, but I couldn't put my finger on it. Something was wrong, very wrong, yet I didn't know what. It was frustrating.

When Bill came to take me out that Saturday evening, for some reason my Scotch heritage hounded me without letup. I'd always been *fae*, knew things were going to happen before they did, and during the evening, when I went to the girls' room to freshen up my lipstick, I found I'd unconsciously put the jewelry box to my engagement ring in my purse. I looked at it, mystified.

The evening never really got off the ground. We spent it at the Double-H Club, a noisy little place in Eagle Rock with a pocket-size dance floor, and a bartender who didn't bother to check my age: I was still twenty. I believe that was the only reason we went there. Not that I was a lush, but I enjoyed having a drink, and had done so since I was eighteen.

That evening the sparkle was gone, conversation nonexistent, and the floor so crowded we couldn't even dance to fill in the crushing silence at our table. Although it was still early, I felt there was no need to prolong the ordeal, and, looking at Bill, I suggested we head for home.

"Where to," he said, as he turned the key in the ignition.

"Home home. To Woodhaven," I said.

After long silent miles, we turned up Beachwood Drive, and I looked at the Hollywoodland sign high up in the hills—that was before it had been abbreviated to just plain Hollywood—and I couldn't help wondering, ominously, what was going to happen next.

Just past the halfway mark, Bill made a sharp left off Beachwood, and we wound our way up around the older homes of the matinee idols and simpering stars of the '20s and '30s. The area had been prime real estate in those days, and was still wrapped in that special kind of nostalgia that time never effectively kills.

We pulled out on a spur with a view of Los Angeles below, spreading in all directions like glowing embers.

Bill set the brakes, turned off the ignition, and looked straight ahead.

I said quietly, "What's up?"

"I can't go through with it."

I felt like I'd been hit by a charging bull-elephant and had the life knocked out of me.

"You can't go through with it?" I said slowly, dreading his reply. "Now ... or *ever?*"

"Just for now. It's too soon. I need time to think. To make up my mind ... about lots of things."

"About us?"

"No, there'll always be an us."

I didn't believe him, and I started to cry. Deep sobs, welling up from the innermost depths of my being.

When I finally got control, I became angry with myself. *Lord, why did I have to cry? Why couldn't I take it, and walk away with my head held high?*

"Pam, it's just for now. I need time." I could see he was horribly uncomfortable at my outburst.

I didn't say anything. I still couldn't believe him. I reached into my handbag, got out the jewelry box, slipped the engagement ring off my finger into the box, and handed it to him.

His face reflected total surprise. "You brought the box? You knew something was up?"

"Take me home, please," was all I could say.

As he started up the car he said, "You've got to come to the barbecue tomorrow. I don't want anyone to know we've broken up. At least not now."

I couldn't believe what I was hearing. "You're asking too much, Bill," I said, my stomach churning.

"Please. I told you, it's not over—I just need time."

As we turned back onto Beachwood Drive and headed up toward the apartment, I said a reluctant "Okay," knowing all the while I was being a complete fool. When I slipped out of the car, without a smile or a kiss I said, "See you tomorrow."

Sunday was a nightmare. I'd never been a good actress, and as I looked at Bill's friends, who over the months had become my friends, I realized I'd lose them all if I lost Bill. It was then that I knew I couldn't keep playing the part he wanted me to. I'd have done anything to be blasé and take it in stride, but I wasn't built that way. Around one o'clock, several hours before the steaks were to be tossed on the coals, while the beer was flowing and spirits were high, I said quietly, "Bill, I'm sorry. I can't go through with it. Take me home, please."

"*Now?*"

"Yes, *now*, Bill. Please," I said, hoping I could get away before I lost it and made a spectacle of myself.

As we silently tooled along Los Feliz Boulevard, the numbness slowly wore off and memories started to crowd in. I gulped hard, determined not to let him see me break down in tears again. Bill and I had done so many things together: gone to wild Chinese banquets, shopped in bazaars and thieves' markets, and I'd even taken him on a picnic to a beautiful little park I knew when I was a student in the convent, which had been a near disaster. Unknown to me, while we were in the prison camp, that lovely little park, with its picturesque buildings and tea houses, had changed hands and was now a Communist stronghold, and we escaped by the skin of our teeth.

I glanced at Bill's familiar profile. He was staring stonily ahead, and I was hit with the gut-numbing realization that now I would have no one to bounce my memories off, no one who understood the life I'd led before coming to the States. Funny how I can remember that stream of memories, but not the final goodbye ...

Maybe there never was one.

Chapter 4

On the Tuesday following Easter I found a letter from Bill in the mailbox! I was so elated, I dumped the rest of the mail on the ground and tore it open and read it.

It was his usual fun letter, not long, hardly worth the three cents' postage, but it started me dreaming all over again. I couldn't help thinking the nightmare was over, we'd be a twosome once more, he'd gotten over his darn Easter hang-up ... my heart started to race happily. Then I came to the closing, "Can't wait to get home for spring break!" and my wishful world stopped spinning. I picked up the envelope and looked at the postmark: he'd mailed it the day before he'd left for home, it had just taken its sweet time getting here.

I felt clammy and weak. My letdown was complete.

A few evenings later, Red Bremmer, Bill's best friend, who lived in Culver City and was going to Santa Monica City College, called and asked for a date. He told me Bill had told him the previous Sunday that we'd broken up.

"Do any of his other friends know?" I asked.

"I don't believe so. He made me swear I'd keep it secret."

I wanted to say, *Why? It's going to be pretty obvious if I'm not around anymore.* But I didn't say a word.

I'd known Red almost as long as I'd known Bill, and was really fond of him. We'd met first in Tientsin, when Bill introduced us. Red was in the same outfit as Bill, and we'd often gone out on a threesome together as he had a hard time finding a date. Not that Red wasn't a lot of fun and very attractive, but there were so few girls who could speak English in Tientsin.

I mulled it over for a moment, thinking, *At least he'd be great company and someone I can talk about China with; it might even be a good way to get over Bill.* But then I realized if I took Red up on it, when summer came around I'd be bumping into Bill at every turn, and I knew I couldn't face that.

"I'm sorry, Red, but I can't do it."

"Maybe later? Can I call you?"

"No, Red. I think we'd better make this goodbye. I'm sorry I wasn't up to saying any goodbyes last Sunday. Thanks for the call. Take care of yourself."

After I hung up, I felt horribly alone. No friends, no job, nothing …

First thing the following morning, still feeling completely dashed, I called my employment agency to see if they had any openings for me, pointing out that I couldn't do heavy typing for a while, due to my injured index finger.

"Got just the job for you," my contact said. "Have you ever written insurance?"

"No, but I can learn."

"Good. I think you'll like this place. It's a small agency out in the thirty-four hundred block on Wilshire, and they need someone like you, willing to learn. Want to try?"

"You bet!" Looking back, I think that was the first time I actually believed I was invincible.

I'd never had a problem finding a job, and that one turned out to be great. Talk about characters! I knew where they all got their enthusiasm from: the boss-man, Bob Murphy.

He had more drive than anyone I'd ever met, and it spread throughout the office. His strong right arm was Barry Gilmore, with wicked bedroom eyes, who insisted on calling me "Ming-toy" when he learned I'd come from China. Somehow, the name stuck.

Mary Hutchins was the office manager and a top life insurance underwriter. Betty Randall, the bookkeeper, turned into my closest friend and confidante. Then there was "Lieutenant" Rachel Roberts (née Rebenowitz), with a lovely Brooklyn accent, who prefaced all introductions with her old military rank. Betty always laughed when she heard Rachel introduce herself with "Lieutenant Roberts—Oh, excuse me, I mean Rachel Roberts."

"What's so funny?" I asked Betty, who also had a service record.

"I outranked her, but I'd hate to burst her little balloon."

I learned I was to be handling the marine floater desk. It sounded really important, and I felt certain I'd be insuring boats and meeting all sorts of wealthy yachting types. As it turned out, the "marine" coverage I wrote turned out to be camera insurance for the students at Art Center School and the Fred Archer School of Photography. It was rather a letdown, but I enjoyed writing it and meeting the students, most of whom were ex-GIs. The fact that I usually ended up with a date after capping the sale was a nice little bonus.

The company was growing by leaps and bounds, and before long Bob hired a girl just to take care of the filing. Her name was Millie Whitlock, and she was interesting, to say the least. She was an ex-army nurse, and had really seen the worst of the war. She told me she took the lowly filing job just to keep busy, as she was having a very bad time getting back into civilian life. I commiserated with her for a while, but then got rather annoyed when I found she could foul up a job as simple as filing. It seems she didn't know the alphabet! I kept losing files and having to go through the whole system to find where she'd put them. I mentioned it to Betty one afternoon a couple of weeks later, and she said, "Never give her filing to do in the afternoon. Before lunch she does a great job."

"Do you think she's going out for a liquid lunch?" I asked.

"Uh-uh, she always brown bags it; haven't you noticed? I believe she just sits back in her little office, reading or something."

"Sure doesn't make sense. Maybe she's on medication and has to take it at lunchtime."

"I … don't … think … so!" Betty said emphatically.

"Okay. I'll do what you say, and give her the filing first thing she comes in."

"Good *luck!*"

That didn't work either, as everyone seemed to realize Millie had a problem and loaded her down with filing first thing in the morning. Since I was low man on the totem pole, mine was always held over till the afternoon.

One day after lunch, she left for a dental appointment, and I took the opportunity to snoop around her little office. Sure enough, I found a half-full bottle of vodka, stashed in a brown paper bag, in the back of one of the file drawers. I stood up with a grin on my face and noticed Betty lolling in the doorway.

"What are you doing?" she asked.

"I've found out what Millie's idea of brown bagging is!" I said, holding up the offending bottle of vodka.

"Whoa! Let's see what else she's got hidden!" Betty said, and the two of us continued the search. Sure enough, we found two more bottles cleverly tucked away in very unlikely places.

"What do we do about it?" I asked.

"Go get Mary. I think she's back from lunch."

"Then Millie will lose her job, and she needs it badly."

"She needs therapy worse, Pam. Do her a favor."

When Millie got back from the dentist, her face out of shape and her lips numb, Mary called her into her office. I tried not to listen or pay attention, but my desk was just outside Mary's door, and I could see the three bottles of vodka stacked on the far corner of her desk, and I knew Millie was on her way out. I waited for Mary to say something, but she just looked at Millie, turned her head toward the bottles and gave her a what's-all-this-about look.

To my surprise, when Millie followed her gaze, she exploded. "How dare you go through my office when I'm not here!"

"How dare you bring liquor into the office!" Mary countered, adding, as she reached for an envelope, "Here's your severance pay. Count it. Sign this slip, and leave!"

After Millie'd stormed out of the front door, ranting about injustice and seeing Bob in court, things quieted down, but I still felt lousy.

"Believe me, you did the lady a favor. She should be at the VA hospital being detoxed, or join AA, or something, and you know it," Betty said firmly.

∽

One Friday evening a couple of weeks later, a group of us from the office, plus my date, a really neat photography student named Bill Thrasher, went out to Old Vienna to enjoy the polka music and lap beer. It was a typical Bavarian hofbrau, with Tyrolean costumes, plump barmaids, bellowing accordions, squealing concertinas, and lots of exuberant noise.

I loved to polka, but I'd never found anyone to dance with. It turned out Bill Thrasher danced a mean polka, and I danced and lapped beer all evening. Actually, too much beer.

That's because the polka is so energetic you can't help getting thirsty. At least that was going to be my excuse if Mother got mad at me when I got home.

By the time the "other Bill" had brought me home, I was getting pretty maudlin, and wailing the blues.

He left me with a kiss and a "See you next week," and I stumbled down the outside steps to our apartment.

Ursula was sound asleep when I got in, but Mother was up, and she was furious. "Do you know what time it is?" she hissed, trying not to wake Ursula.

I ignored her query and started to wail about my date being the wrong Bill, and that I'd never, ever get over Bill Stafford.

That's when Mother lost it.

"Here, sit down! Kick off your shoes, make yourself comfortable, and listen—I've got something to read to you."

She went over to the little roll-top writing desk, reached into a drawer tucked away in the back, and brought out a small, blue envelope.

"This is addressed to me, and it's from Mrs. Stafford, Bill's mother." Then she proceeded to read me the letter. Bill was married. In fact, it sounded like he'd just switched brides—as even in my befuddled state I recognized the date as the one we'd picked for our wedding. His mother added she was sorry it hadn't worked out for Bill and me, and that she hoped I was well and had found new interests in life. She concluded by wishing Mother and me all the best.

"How long have you had that letter?" I asked.

"Quite a few weeks."

"Why didn't you tell me?"

"I didn't think you were ready for it."

"When did you think I would be *ready?*" I said, emphasizing the last word very rudely.

"On a night like tonight, when you're being a total fool. *Get over it!*"

I looked at her, and at the pathetic little blue letter in her hand, and said, *"I AM!* I'm *completely* over it! That lousy, spineless, sonofabitch didn't even have the guts to write me himself. Was that the arse I was engaged to? A mama's boy?" Then I started swearing in every language I could think of, rushing around the apartment, grabbing all his smiling framed pictures, some with a moustache, some without, in every uniform the Marine Corps ever dished out. There was even one of him beside Cummashaw I in Tientsin, and again beside Cummashaw II. When I slammed the last picture of him in his dress blues against the refrigerator, the damn glass shattered and a shard slashed my wrist.

"Oh, *s-h-i-t!*" I hissed.

"Don't use that word!" Mother said sternly.

"Look what I've done!" I wailed, holding up my arm with blood spurting out of it.

After putting a tourniquet on my arm and bandaging my wrist snugly, she said, "If it's still bad tomorrow morning, we'll go to the hospital and get some stitches."

Needless to say, it was a mess the following day. I'd had to loosen the tourniquet in the night, and the bandage was soaked. Mother gave it one look and helped me get dressed, and we caught the bus to the Hollywood Receiving Hospital. That was twice in just over six months!

When I signed in and a doctor looked at it, he said, "There's no guy in the world worth it—why don't you girls wise up!"

"Don't … get … me … started!" I said, slowly and deliberately. And all the while he stitched me up and put a clean dressing on, I told him exactly what I thought of men, espe-

cially gutless, chicken-livered mama's boys, and I caught him grinning through my blistering tirade.

When I got up to leave, he patted me on the shoulder and said, "Well, as you sure as heck don't have a broken heart anymore, you can now concentrate on seeing that the wrist heals up. *Capisce?*"

I nodded, thanked him, and said, *"Capisce."*

Several weeks later, as I started to step off the streetcar at Hollywood and Vine, a hefty woman fell against me and I pitched out onto the street, landing awkwardly on my arm. I heard a crack but felt no pain, so I looked down to see what had broken. It was the jade engagement bracelet Bill had given me in China, severed neatly in half. I picked up the two pieces, dropped them into my handbag, and said to myself, *If that isn't a message, I've never heard one.* Then I ran to catch the Beachwood bus.

Chapter 5

It was late July when Dad arrived for a visit; he said he couldn't call it "home leave," as America would never be home to him. I really felt for him. He was still trying to get over the devastating news he'd received in the prison camp after our liberation. It was then, when he'd tried to contact his family in London to let them know we'd all survived, that he learned his family had not. His mother, all his sisters except one, and their husbands and children had been wiped out by a buzz bomb while they were enjoying a brief reunion.

The lovely old homestead on Ashbourne Grove in the Mill Hill district of London had sustained a direct hit, and all that was left was a huge crater in the ground. He was inconsolable. Mother had tried to tell him there was always a home for him in the States, but as much as he enjoyed Americans and what he considered their zany sense of humor, he was a Brit through and through, and insisted he'd feel totally lost in a country as big and diverse as the U.S. He liked "small and cosy," and America could never fall into that category.

Apart from visiting us, he had two other reasons for coming when he did. The first was he needed to buy a car to take back to China, and the second was to get a complete physical. The years in the prison camp had taken a toll on his heart and his health, and he really needed a checkup. There was also a third reason, a happy one. Now that Ursula and Cope were engaged, he wanted to meet Cope's family in upstate New York. So it was that, as soon as he arrived, he and Mother planned a trip to Buffalo, then Detroit, and then on to the Mayo Clinic in Rochester, Minnesota. He picked the Mayo for several reasons, not the least of which was that he'd been to their famous clinic in Peking, and felt it would be like visiting an old friend.

They took the train to Buffalo, where Cope met them, and enjoyed a brief visit with his warm and lively Italian family. Dad had always been a little stuffy around Italians, but had to admit the Cuviellos completely won his heart. There might have been a little envy there too, especially when he was introduced to Cope's two brothers, Mike and Pete. Dad, who'd always wanted sons to carry on the family name, was left with three daughters after Tony, his only son and my little brother, died of dysentery in China while still a toddler.

After the visit, Cope drove Mother and Dad to Detroit to pick up the big, new four-door Mercury sedan Dad had ordered before coming to the States. It had to be a Ford product, as Ford was the only dealership that had reopened in China, and service was still an all-important item when one owned a car in a foreign country. Although Dad didn't drive, he loved cars, the bigger the better. So did Henry, his last Chinese chauffeur, who because of his many wives was named after Henry VIII. When the Japanese commandeered our car, Henry left, and I could only hope Dad would find his old friend again when he returned to Tientsin.

I knew Dad was looking forward, possibly more than Mother, to the drive back to the West Coast after all the physical exams he'd have to go through at the Mayo Clinic. One thing they were both positive about was that he'd get a clean bill of health, and that the trip back would be one happy celebration. And they were right.

The doctors were optimistic about Dad's future. Although he'd had a bad heart for years, they said it was nothing that was not controllable, and that he could lead a long and active life if he avoided stress, cut out rich foods, exercised daily, and kept his temper under control. They gave him some medication to help lower his blood pressure and wished him a safe journey back to China.

It was early September when they returned to Hollywood, and for once Dad, with a vocabulary second to none, was at a loss for words to describe the trip. He was overwhelmed by the size of the country, the endless paved roads, the ever-changing scenery, the splendor of the Rockies, the solitariness of the deserts ...

"So you really enjoyed the trip?" I asked, adding, "No mishaps, no bad incidents?"

"W-e-l-l ..." Dad started, looking a bit uncomfortable.

"Go ahead, tell them, Geordie," Mother said sweetly.

"Tell us what?" I asked apprehensively.

"You tell them, Gee, I'm not up to it," he said, his ebullient tone changing like magic.

"Well, coming home, Daddy forgot who was the chauffeur. He thought I was Henry. That was a big mistake. Remember how he always sat up front with Henry and pulled out the choke, grabbed the hand brake, and tried to change gears while the car was still moving, and generally fouled things up beautifully? Well, he tried that on me several times. It was usually when we were going through some congested traffic in a strange city. I put up with it for a while, but after we'd left the Mayo Clinic, I finally had it up to here," she said dramatically, slashing at her throat with the side of her hand.

"Surprisingly, it wasn't in traffic, but when we were really making good time on an open stretch of road, that Dad started fiddling with the gears and almost flipped the car. I didn't say a word, but when we came to a little whistle stop along the way, I pulled over and told him to get out.

"I guess he thought we were stopping for coffee or something, so he got out. That's when I told him to find his own way home, and put the car in gear and took off!"

"Mother, you didn't!"

"Yes, I did! And I kept going. Luckily, the road took a deep dip before long, and I dropped out of view and pulled over and parked, deciding to let him stew for a while. Quite a long while.

"I returned about an hour later, and he was sitting in the little gas-station-cum-coffee-shop, sipping hot tea, and looking totally contrite and lost.

"I told him the next time he tweaked anything in the car, I'd throw him out and not come back for him."

When she was through, Dad had that naughty-little-boy look on his face, and I couldn't help saying, "Dad, after all the years you and Mumsy have been married you should've known she wouldn't put up with your shenanigans." Then I added, "Actually, you got off easy. With Mother, you never know what she's going to do behind the wheel. You should have been here in '39 when we made a trip down to Tijuana."

"Really? What happened?" He sounded interested again, and I told him the story, hardly believing I could still remember it in such detail.

The year we visited Grandma, we attended North Hollywood Junior High and when summer vacation rolled around we had a ball. Mother bought a car, a lovely '38 Plymouth sedan in a grayish green shade that she named Nike after the winged goddess of victory, and we spent those summer months seeing California. I don't believe there was a spot we didn't visit. We roamed the beaches and the deserts and the mountains, and in August, when our Aunt Ethel from Burns Lake, British Columbia, came down for a visit, we all drove down the coast to San Diego.

We were continually amazed at the unrestricted ease of travel in the States, and after a couple of days in that sun-drenched city, Ursula and I begged Mother to drive on across the Mexican border to Tijuana.

I loved that crazy town with its street vendors and colorful shops. It reminded me a lot of the native cities of China, with their teeming throngs and dusty streets, except here the Mexican merchants and peddlers spoke Spanish and I didn't understand a word. That didn't stop us, though, from loading up on ceramics, baskets, sombreros, and luscious ripe mangoes.

Around five in the afternoon we decided to call it a day, and started heading for home. Somehow, Nike made room for us and all our happy mementoes, and it was a laughing, jabbering group that broke to a stop at the border.

The official was very polite, and the first thing he asked us was where we were born. Given the mood of the moment, Mother thought it was rather funny, so she quipped, "My mother," pointing to Grandma, "is British. I'm a Scot. This lady is a Canadian," and with a wicked twinkle in her eye, she pointed at us and said, "and these two girls are Chinese!"

"That's not funny, lady. Please pull out of line."

Mother got beautifully flustered then and, after acting like a total moron, managed to pull out of line. Needless to say, the hoots, rubbernecking, and pointed comments of the people in the other cars embarrassed me no end.

When we got to the immigration office we were herded into the lock-up area, where the official asked to see our passports. Ethel was the only one who had hers with her. We hadn't planned to leave the States on this trip so had left our passports and visas at Grandma's house in North Hollywood.

Great, I thought, *now what?*

Grandma appeared calmer than most of us, and said to my mother, "Gee, I think you'd better call the British consulate in Los Angeles."

Mother turned to the immigration officer and asked if she could make a phone call. He nodded and gave her the number of the British consulate.

Well, it happened to be five-thirty by then, so there was no answer. And just to round things out nicely, it was Friday, so it seemed we were about to spend the weekend in a Tijuana jail!

"Well, I've really done it this time," Mother said contritely, as she hung up.

"Call again ... and keep calling," Ethel said.

"What's the point? They've all gone home for the weekend."

"Someone *has* to be there, dammit, it's our *consulate!*" I'd never heard Aunt Ethel swear, and I looked at her in surprise.

Mother dialed again, while the unsmiling official fiddled with papers on his cluttered desk. She let it ring, and ring, and ring, and I could see his patience was wearing thin. Finally there was a click, and Mother put her hand over the receiver and hissed, "Someone's answering!" Then she started excitedly to explain our predicament to the consular official on the other end of the line.

Half an hour later, with all parties more confused than

enlightened, we were finally told we could leave, and *please* not to return.

Once more we got to the checkpoint and the officer routinely asked us if we had any fruit in the car.

"Only mangoes," Mother said.

"Hand them over, please."

"Why?" Mother asked.

"You can't take them into California."

"What are *you* going to do with them?" Mother asked suspiciously, eyeing her favorite fruit.

"Throw them away, ma'am," he said politely.

"Oh, no, you're not! We're going back to Mexico to eat them, and don't try to stop us!"

Rage made Mother whip out of line and speed back over the border like the hounds of hell were on her heels.

She pulled over by a big trash bin, handed each of us a mango and a Kleenex, and said, "Eat up, there's more than one way to get mangoes into California!"

When I was through telling the story, Dad was laughing so hard there were tears running down his cheeks.

That evening we decided to celebrate their homecoming with dinner at the Cine Grill, across from Grauman's Chinese Theater. We had drinks while we were waiting for dinner, and listened to a great little orchestra play contemporary songs. When the bandleader asked if there were any requests, Dad raised his hand and asked if they would play *The Last Time I Saw Paris*.

"I'm sorry, I don't know it," the bandleader said.

"Oh, come on, you *must*," Dad said, "it goes like ..." and he stood up and proceeded to sing the delightful song, with the orchestra quickly picking up on it. Of course, I wasn't surprised at Dad's request, as Paris had always been the love of his life.

When he sat down, there were shouts of "Encore!" from the other tables, but he just smiled and waved them off.

If he hadn't been a celebrity for a couple of minutes, I hate to think what would have happened when the dinner arrived a while later and he asked the waiter to take it back to the chef and have him remove half the food from his plate.

Dad, among other things, was a gourmet who loved good food in small portions, and who savored every bite as though it were his last. When he saw our shocked expressions he said, "I'm so sorry, that's another thing that gets to me. Americans always think that if a little is good, more is better. When it comes to food, they're dead wrong. How can anyone enjoy a meal when they can't even find where to begin eating?"

When the waiter gave Ursula and me a querying look, we both grabbed at our plates and said, "Nope, we're fine." Mother smiled and shook her head also when he reached for her plate.

While Mother and Dad had been on their trip, Ursula and I had seen Walt Disney's *Fantasia*. I loved it. I loved the music, the animation, and especially the jazz selection, with its tumbling abstracts and clashing colors. Knowing how Dad loved good classical music, when they got back, we told him he must see the movie.

Several days later, when they returned from the theater, Mother said, "I loved it. Dad didn't. He kept his eyes shut all through the show."

"What do you mean, he kept his eyes shut? How could he *not* like it?"

Dad spoke up. "How dare anyone try to interpret *my* feelings when I listen to music. What they did to the *Waltz of the Flowers* and *The Sorcerer's Apprentice* … Oh, God, it was a travesty!"

"Tell me you liked the music, at least," I said.

"Oh, it wasn't bad, except they edited it to go along with the animation, chopping it up to fit the gyrating hippos and prancing elephants."

Mother gave me a quiet look suggesting I'd better drop it.

⁂

Not long after that, Dad's leave was up and he had to return to China again. The visit had been all too short, but there was so much to do to get the Kailan, the huge coal mining consortium Dad worked for in Tientsin, back on its feet. The years of mismanagement by the Japanese had left the mines in deplorable condition and the coaling ports unusable, and although top management had insisted that Dad take this trip for his health, they'd asked that he keep it down to three months as he was needed back on the job.

We were still in the big studio apartment on Woodhaven Drive, where privacy was almost nonexistent. Often, late at night, I'd hear Mother and Dad whispering, and what I caught was always nostalgic. Dad loved China with a passion. He loved the people just as his father had done. He hated to see them treated like cattle, first by the imperial court, then by the so-called democratic movement that replaced it, more recently by Japan, and now by the Communists. Through all the power struggles that swept through that beautiful country, the people, the backbone of China, were a forgotten cipher. Their numbers were so immense they were looked on not as humans, but as product, to be used and discarded at will.

"Why are you going back, Geordie?"

"I have to, you know that," he said softly.

"You know, as well as I do, that the West's days are numbered in China. What will you do when it all comes tumbling down?"

"I don't know. But for now, I must return." Then on a more plaintive note, "Gee, it's my home, as the States will never be. I know you love this country, but I will always be a stranger here."

"Don't say that. It'll take time, but you will adjust."

"No, old gal, I never will. I'm a Brit, dammit, with no Britain to go home to. They don't want me there. They're too busy licking their war wounds, and I'd be just one more mouth to feed. I think, maybe, if it ever comes down to it and I have to leave China, I might consider Australia. At least we have the same heritage …"

After a long pause, I heard him ask, "Gee, will you come back with me?"

"No, Geordie, I have to make a home here—for the girls, for myself, and, God help me … for *you!*"

As I heard their soft good-nights, the creak of the bedsprings, the rustle of sheets, I knew they were settling down, and that sleep was not far away.

For me it was a different story. Their talk had brought back memories of our lives in China, and of Dad's insistence that we return home from our earlier trip to the States.

While we'd spent that summer of '39 gallivanting up and down the West Coast, enjoying life to the hilt, storm clouds had started to roll over Europe. In early September, Hitler attacked Poland, and Great Britain, honoring her pact with Poland, declared war on Germany. Although the big metropolitan papers carried all the gory details of the German *blitzkrieg*, the students at North Hollywood Junior High were surprisingly disinterested, and I found myself keeping Dad's letters, full of his fears and anxieties, to myself. Surprisingly, there was one letter in mid-October that wasn't full of dire predictions of a possible invasion of Great Britain, and it was priceless.

Dad had always been envious of Mother's popularity and her party-giving that was renowned throughout the small foreign community of North China. But that year Mother wasn't there to don her *Perle Mesta of the Pacific* persona, so Dad decided to throw a party himself, in aid of Britain's war effort. It was to be a Dutch auction. To Brits, that meant the host threw a great shindig, the price of attending being whatever the guests decided to bid on artifacts and furnishings that were put up for auction. The items never left the home though, the fun being in the auction itself and not in acquiring beautiful things, with all the proceeds going to a worthy cause—in this case Britain's war effort.

The day after the party Dad sat down and wrote a letter bursting with pride at the amount he had raised for Great Britain. I remember the height of his success came with the bid from the captain of an American destroyer that was in port. The captain, bless his soul, bid three hundred American dollars for our beautiful player-piano and an inlaid teak cabinet. The piano, which we all played with varying degrees of ability, could be turned into a veritable orchestra with all its built-in accompaniments, and the seven-foot-tall cabinet, lacquered and inlaid with mother-of-pearl, and embellished with gold-leaf scrollwork, had been refinished inside to hold two hundred music rolls in beautiful, individually crafted, felt-lined slots. It had taken our *mujiang,* or carpenter, almost a year to refurbish the inside of the exquisite piece.

Dad couldn't get over the generosity of the American. I remember he wrote, "Darn it, Gee, this isn't even *his* war. It's ours! And yet he felt he had to help." That was a fun letter, and we all commented on Dad's euphoria.

The letter a couple of days later wasn't as ecstatic. In fact, it almost steamed itself open!

I'll try to recall its contents as closely as I can: "Dearest Gee, I'm still seething! Got home to find the piano and music cabinet gone! That American *sonofabitch* sent a couple of his men up to our house while I was at work, and according to Jungya (our houseboy), they had two coolies load them into a mule cart and haul them down to the ship. That evening, when I found them missing and asked Jungya what happened, he pointed to the destroyer steaming out across the bay." Dad ended by suggesting Mother buy me a guitar or some other instrument, as I really enjoyed music and we wouldn't be able to afford another piano for a very long time.

I couldn't get over the irony of the story. It was obvious the American didn't know what a Dutch auction was all about, and he must've thought, in turn, that Dad was the most generous and patriotic man he knew, selling off his prized possessions to come to his country's aid!

Sadly, there is a postscript to this little story: the destroyer, along with the precious piano and music rolls, was one of the first ships sunk by the Japanese after the attack on Pearl Harbor.

∼

The day we saw Dad off at Wilmington brought back such memories. The last time I'd been in that port city had been in January of 1940, when we boarded the *President Taft* to return to China. It had been a beastly day. We'd gotten up at four in the morning, too excited to eat a breakfast, and I remember trembling uncontrollably as we loaded our luggage into Don's car. I knew the trembling wasn't just from the cold; anxiety and loss were mixed up in it somehow.

I kept thinking of the friends I'd made and would be leaving behind, especially Jane Rosenberg and her cousin, Jackie Smith. They were the only ones who took me as I came, British accent and all, and made me feel like I belonged. They were fun and, like myself, hadn't yet arrived at that boy-crazy stage that turned all early teenagers into giggling, overly made-up idiots. North Hollywood Junior High was full of those.

The drive to Wilmington seemed interminable. As we got closer, the fog froze on the windshield, and Donald had a terrible time keeping it clear; when we finally turned onto the docks, we could hardly see the ship for the drizzle and mist.

"Lovely day to be leaving," Don said dryly. "Who knows, you might even get some sunshine once you're out to sea."

"That would be great," I said, giving him a goodbye hug.

"Donald, thanks for everything," Mother said, and I could see tears in her eyes as she silently hugged him and turned abruptly to follow Ursula and me on board.

We'd made it with scant time to spare. The gangplank was raised and the old *President Taft* pulled out almost immediately. As I stood on deck, waving at fictitious friends on the pier, pretending I was getting a gala send-off, I saw Jane and Jackie with their parents, frantically waving flowers and a huge box of chocolates. I couldn't get over it! They'd driven all the way from the San Fernando Valley just to say goodbye, only to arrive too late. I waved back, hoping they knew how much their sweet gesture had meant to me, and yelled, "Goodbye! Goodbye!"

Mother and Ursula joined me then, blowing kisses as we moved out into the channel. Their farewells were symbolic—goodbye to a wonderful memory. Mine had left an ache in my heart.

I knew Dad's departure wasn't going to be any easier.

He was anxious about the car. It had been sent down earlier in the week, and he didn't know how it had been prepared for shipping. As its transportation had necessitated filling out a lot of paperwork for the customs and entry papers for Shanghai at the other end, Dad had hired an accountant who was familiar with overseas transactions, and had left the details up to him.

"Well, you'll have fun exploring the ship and finding where they've put your silent traveling companion," Mother said, smiling.

"That I will," Dad replied. "I hope she's crated and below decks. I'd hate her to be lashed topside, prey to rain and all the elements."

This time it was midday when the ship pulled out. In a way, I wished I was with Dad, going "home," but at the same time I knew home wasn't what it had been all through my growing-up years, and that I was safer here in this great sprawling country than I ever would be in the turmoil that was forever China.

Chapter 6

"Dad was insistent, before he left, that we find ourselves a better place to live," Mother was saying.

"Didn't you tell him it was easier said than done?" I asked.

"Yes, that's why he didn't insist on me looking while he was here. Our time together was too precious and too short."

"It sure was," I agreed, adding, "I didn't tell you, Mumsy, but when we were saying goodbye to Daddy at Wilmington, I got an awful yen to go with him. Then I remembered what you said about staying here and making a home for the family, and I knew you were right."

"I remember that evening," she said, thoughtfully, and I felt myself blush for inadvertently letting on that I'd been eavesdropping. "I thought both you girls were asleep. I think Daddy realized we had to have more space just so we could have more privacy. I remember him saying on our trip that, although the room was large, with us all crowded together, it reminded him of Weihsien." Remembering our adjoining cells and the paper-thin walls, I had to agree.

It was the weekend after he'd left. And it had been a long week. The kind of week, you keep telling yourself, you'll forget within the year, only to find it never happens. I spent most of my waking hours, when I wasn't at work, wondering how far Dad's ship had traveled, whether the sea was calm or rough, what the food was like, and what sort of fellow passengers he had aboard.

"I wonder if Daddy's found the car yet," I said, musingly, "and, if so, what he's named her."

"I've a feeling she'll be the Duchess, like the old Essex in China. Maybe the Duchess II," Mother said with a faraway look. It was easy to see she was dreaming of those wonderful days when the world was ours to enjoy to the hilt. *Would there ever be times like that again?* I shook myself, and said silently, *Never look back ...*

"Incidentally," Mother was saying, "while Daddy was here we set up a joint account at Ursula's bank in Beverly Hills. In fact, I'll have to draw on it from time to time to cover the rent if we find a bigger place."

"Have you been looking?" I asked, feeling guilty that I hadn't offered to help.

"I think rentals are easing up a bit now. I'm on several lists, but it'll take a while."

Ursula wasn't with us that evening; she'd been attending Geller Workshop on Wilshire near Fairfax, and had a small part in a Noel Coward play. I thought it was rather ironic when she told me she couldn't land a bigger part in the play as her accent was *too British!*

That reminded me of an incident, many months earlier, when I'd ridden with her on the Sunset bus. It was a Thursday, and that evening there was to be the dress rehearsal of *A Farewell to Arms* at the workshop, and I'd felt honored when she asked me to go with her.

The bus, surprisingly, wasn't too crowded and we found a couple of seats together, and sat discussing ... I can't remember what. Anyhow, all of a sudden, I felt a prickly sensation down my back, and turned to see the gentleman in the seat behind us leaning forward and listening to every word we were saying. He sat back quickly and lifted his newspaper to cover his face. I turned and looked at Ursula, and said in Chinese, "How rude!"

We spent the rest of the trip speaking Chinese and giggling at his discomfort.

When we got up to transfer to the Fairfax bus, he jumped up and handed us his card. He said we had interesting accents and asked if we would make an appointment for an audition with Georgia Fuller at NBC. He scribbled her name and phone extension on the back of the card, and told us to be sure to go to the Artists Entrance at the side of the building. We nodded, took the card, and stepped off the bus. We weren't about to speak in front of him again—at least, not in English.

I looked at the card. His name was Ken Manson. He was an executive of some kind; in production I believe. Riding a *bus?* It was all very fishy. What executive would ride a bus? All the executive types I'd seen were tooling around in convertibles.

"What do you think?" I asked Ursula.

She'd done the rounds of the agencies. She knew most of the Hollywood types and was not impressed. In fact, when she found that couch-casting was more than a crude cliché, she decided to attend Geller's and see if she couldn't get a break that way.

"Do what you want with it," she said. "I'm not interested."

I'd have completely forgotten the incident if I hadn't picked up a copy of the *Hollywood Reporter* a couple of years later when I was a bachelor gal in Beverly Hills, and read that NBC executive Ken Manson was recuperating from serious surgery, and the columnist wished him a speedy recovery. I couldn't help chuckling when I realized that some executives *do* ride on buses.

I thought, *Oh, well, you win some, you lose some …*

A few days after that, Mother said, looking at the calendar hanging on the refrigerator, "Daddy must be in Shanghai by now. He's home, and I hope everything goes well for him."

"It will, Mumsy, China's truly the only country he loves," I said, wishing it weren't so.

"We're going to have to work on *that*," she said decisively.

She was excited because we were moving into the Hollywood Towers the following month and only had a couple of weeks to go in our cramped quarters. It had taken all her finesse to get the apartment, and she was silently patting herself on the back for landing it. We had passed that ostentatious building on the corner of Franklin and Gower every day when we took the Beachwood bus to Hollywood and Vine, and dreamed of living there. Now our dream had come true.

"The apartment is furnished in French provincial, has a living room, dining room, full kitchen, two bedrooms, one bath, and one maid. Who could ask for more?"

I could tell she was ecstatic.

That was about the same time she got a letter postmarked Honolulu. She let me read it. Dad had found the car under a tarp, lashed on deck, along with three other vehicles. He was not happy about it, especially as he'd paid an exorbitant sum to have her shipped. His letter read, "Enquiries elicited the fact that she will have to shiver on deck, under a tarpaulin, aft, throughout the voyage, together with her three friends." The letter ended with, "Lots of love to you … my dear old sympathetic, understanding lover. Always your own G who adores you."

I handed it back and watched her fold it carefully, touch it to her lips, then get up and put it away in the little drawer in the roll-top desk.

A couple of weeks later, with no further news from Dad, we were busy packing all our clothes and odds and ends prior to the move to our new apartment, and savoring every moment of it. It wasn't until almost eleven that night that we all realized how tired we were, and climbed into our respective beds.

We'd no sooner turned out the light than the phone upstairs rang. I could hear its rings, loud and insistent, and wondered how long it would take the Browns to answer it. Then I heard Mrs. Brown bellow, "It's for you, Mrs. Simmons!"

"Pam, answer it, will you, I can't make those stairs tonight."

"Okay, Mumsy," I said blithely, and ran up the stairs.

The receiver was hanging against the wall, and I picked it up and held it to my ear.

"Donald here. I have a cable from China for you. May I read it?"

"Go ahead," I said happily, knowing it would be Daddy saying he had arrived safely.

Without preamble, Donald read, "We regret to inform you George Simmons died October 12." He added, "It's signed by a W. Pryor, and has KMA after his name."

Dizziness swept over me all of a sudden. I dropped the receiver, and sat heavily on the top stair. I felt my heart being crushed in my chest, and I couldn't breathe. It was as though I were dying too.

Oh, Daddy, Daddy, where are you? I cried silently from the depths of my soul.

I don't know how long I sat there. The squawking voice on the phone telling me to hang up brought me back to the present. I stood up shakily, put the receiver back in its wall cradle, and slowly went down the stairs.

As I came in and shut the door behind me, Mother called out, "Who was it?"

"Donald," I said.

"At this hour? Is something wrong with Mother?" Her first thought was Grandma, whose health was deteriorating rapidly.

"No, Mumsy. It's Dad."

"What about Dad?" There was sudden panic in her voice.

"Don read a cable from China. Daddy died in Tientsin on Octo- ber 12. That's all it said. It was signed by Mr. Pryor."

"Oh, no! *Oh, my God, no!* I wasn't with him. Daddy was terrified of dying. I promised him he'd never die alone … I'd be with him." She kept saying, "Oh, no! Oh, no!"

Why were cables limited to ten words? You can't say anything in ten words. How did he die? Why did he die? The Mayo Clinic had given him a clean bill of health. How could it happen? The questions kept shooting through my mind.

It was a good two weeks later when we heard from Wilfred Pryor, the general manager of the Kailan Mining Administration. The handwritten letter was dated October 14, and the red, white, and blue airmail envelope was postmarked the 16th. It was addressed to Mother in care of Donald's address on Victory Boulevard in North Hollywood, and somehow got rerouted to Margo at the marine base at Parris Island, South Carolina, and forwarded on once more from there. When we finally received it on the 27th, Mother was a bundle of frayed nerves, plagued by unanswered questions. It read in part:

My dear Mrs. Simmons,
I have been thinking of you and your girls in your great sadness … The funeral service was held this afternoon and was beautifully and reverently carried out at the Race Course Road cemetery chapel, and the wreaths were beautiful.

Being unable to communicate with you in time, we decided

on cremation. I felt that, with none of the family in China or likely to return to China, the uncertainty of the future out here, and therefore the worry to you about who was properly tending the grave, it would be better so. I was thinking you might like it—and possibly George would have liked it too—were the ashes to be taken to Chinwangtao and strewn either in the garden of your old home on the bluff, or scattered over the water outside the harbour.

His heart attack was a very severe one and I believe he will have suffered little, if at all—He died on Saturday night—or rather early Sunday morning, and in the able care of Dr. Grice and Mrs. Walmsley.

The office will be writing to you about the car, his will, and his belongings.

My wife is in England and will be returning to me in a couple of weeks time. Were she here she would include her heartfelt sympathy and kindly thoughts with mine.

Yours very sincerely,
Wilfred Prior

It was a gentle letter from a gentle man. He had helped us all in the prison camp, and his concern for everyone was so evident, especially in this letter. Mother was deeply touched by it, and wrote thanking him for his kindness. I know it helped assuage the pain and heartbreak she was suffering.

When Dad's carefully boxed and wrapped attaché case arrived a couple of weeks later, it included his handwritten will, witnessed by two of his Chinese clerks, his prison camp journals, some photographs, personal jewelry, and miscellaneous memorabilia that would have meant nothing to anyone but his immediate family—another kind gesture from his many friends and colleagues.

I found myself thinking back to our "other life." To the days before the prison camp. To all our friends, both foreign and Chinese, who gave so much color to everyday living. It was never dull, always a challenge, and Dad had played such a big part in it. Before I left my little treaty-port home for the convent in Tientsin, Mother had been my teacher, but Dad had been my fount of information. His eidetic memory, his genius for figures, and his boundless vocabulary—heck, I never looked in a dictionary until I went away to school. I always thought it was so unfair that when parents died they couldn't pass on their accumulated talent and mental abilities to their children. I know I would've done anything to have Dad's ever-searching mind.

Ursula's bank advised Mother how to file for probate overseas, and the will was forwarded to Dad's solicitors in London. Within a short while she got a response from them, giving the amount of Dad's retirement fund that he'd religiously deposited to in England, and advising her they would be filing a public notice for several weeks in the London papers, and if there were no liens against it or complications, the funds would be transferred to her Beverly Hills account, less probate costs and the solicitors' standard fees.

It was a great relief to know everything was proceeding well. The transfer of the retirement fund would mean that Mother could live comfortably, albeit frugally, once she had invested the money here. She had been taking a correspondence course in hotel management ever since she'd arrived, as she wanted a job like Ursula and I had, and hosting banquets and managing hotels sounded like the perfect place for her talents.

To her horror, almost a month later she received a letter from some solicitors in London, hired by Harriett, Dad's only surviving sister, denouncing the will as a forgery. The letter stated that Dad had never married, had no children, and that as the sole surviving member of the Simmons family, she should receive Dad's full retirement fund!

When I came home from work that day and took the elevator up to our third floor apartment, I was in a great mood as I'd just been promoted to the auto insurance desk, and had received a nice raise to go with it. Bounding into the living room, I started to blurt out my good news, when I saw Mother's face. "Good God, Mother, what's up?" I said.

She handed me the letter without a word. When I read it I said, "She's nuts, of course! She's shell-shocked from all she went through during the war. We'll be able to prove everything. Don't worry about it. She can't have Dad's money, and she knows it."

"I don't think it will be quite as easy as that. Remember, during all our married life I never went to England, I always came home to the States. And you girls also came to the States. Harriett can honestly say she never saw me or either of you."

"That's rot, and you know it. Heck, Granny and Grandpa sent us presents every Christmas, and on our birthdays; they had slews of pictures of us growing up in China, riding our donkeys, playing in the garden, even snaps of us in our boarding school uniforms taken at the recitals at the end of the school year."

"You forget, those pictures don't exist anymore. They were destroyed along with Dad's family and the home. They're gone, Pam. There really is no record of our existence except in Dad's will, and she's contesting that."

"Mumsy, that's written in Dad's unique handwriting. No one else in the world writes Dad's hand. They can compare it with the pages out of his prison camp journal."

"That's a good point. I'll mention that when I forward all this mess to Dad's solicitors."

Nothing seemed to move fast. Here it was, two years after the war, and everything moved at a snail's pace. It was as though the effort and sacrifice of the war had sapped everything out of everybody, especially English solicitors. Weeks went by before we heard from our attorneys, and they said their hands were tied unless we could find the two Chinese clerks who had witnessed the will. Trying to find two men, who had since left the Kailan's employ, in the teeming millions in Communist China, beat out the old proverb of a needle in a haystack. Even with the Kailan's help, and the hiring of a so-called Chinese PI, the task ran on for months that turned into years. But to no avail.

Mother got quarterly statements from the solicitors on the waning health of Dad's retirement fund. They had been steadily paying themselves out of the account, and it was dwindling at a mind-boggling pace.

Mother's health also was going downhill fast. She developed bleeding ulcers, and was put on medication and a miserable diet. She lost pounds in weight, pounds she couldn't afford to lose, and Ursula and I could do nothing but look on in despair.

"What's the statute of limitations on a probate?" I asked, a couple of years later, when there was still no news from London.

"That's simple," Mother said. "It's when the solicitors run out of money to draw on. And it's getting there fast!"

Almost as though they'd been listening in on our conversation, within days we received a letter from England stating that Harriett's solicitors had informed them that as there was no evidence to the contrary, she would accept the will as bona fide and not contest it further. Obviously her attorneys had advised her there was nothing to go on fighting for.

When the funds ultimately arrived, there were only twenty-eight hundred pounds left in the account. That came out to something like ten thousand dollars. Poor Dad. All he had worked for, and stashed away for their golden years, had been scarfed up by a bunch of greedy solicitors egged on by an equally greedy and demented sister.

When it was finally over, Mother said to me, "One thing, the hell we've been through over this probate would never happen with my side of the family, you can bet on that."

Chapter 7

Through all these trials, life had been ploughing along, leaving fallow fields and furrows to mark its progress.

In February of '48, I celebrated my twenty-first birthday with a gala cocktail party. Mother pulled out all the stops, and Clotilde, our delightful black maid, insisted on helping with the festivities.

I was still working for the insurance agency, and most of the guests were fellow-workers from the firm. Barry Gilmore came without his beautiful, blonde wife, and got maudlin drunk. Not about her, but about Colleen, an Irish girl he'd met in England during the war. He kept rambling on about her, and saying, "Ming-toy, how did you get over your broken heart? I *must* know," his words all slopping over each other, sickeningly slurred.

"It was easy," I said. "I let rage take over. Why?"

"Oh, Colleen, what did I do to you … ?" he wailed, off on another tack.

"I don't know what you did to her, Barry, or what she did to you, but get over it!" I said, remembering Mother's stern admonition to me.

Betty Randall came up then, looked at Barry weeping silently on the couch and, shaking her head, she pulled me away.

"Who's Colleen?" I asked, baffled.

"She and Barry got engaged in England during the war. She was from Ireland, and she came over to marry him. She came with her whole family for the wedding, but on the wedding day Barry changed his mind and married this gorgeous, wealthy, Santa Barbara socialite. Little Colleen was traumatized. Her caring family took her home to Ireland, and Barry's never heard from her since."

"S-o-o-o?" I said with a questioning shrug.

"Well, his marriage is now on the rocks and, just like a man, he's crying over what he tossed away!"

"Poor baby," I said in mock commiseration.

∽

I couldn't believe I'd been in the same job for over nine months. I was bored. Automobile insurance was not as much fun as marine coverage. I never got a date with my clients after writing up a policy, probably because the premiums were ten times that of camera insurance, and they couldn't afford to take me to dinner. Anyhow, most of them were much older than the neat photography students, and not half as much fun. On top of that, Barry was driving me nuts, and it was time for a change. So I gave two weeks' notice and started looking elsewhere.

It turned out I didn't get a day off between jobs. I left Bob Murphy Insurance on Friday and started with US Gypsum on Monday. Again, a job that had no heavy typing, as the nerves in my fingertip had still not healed properly.

My new boss was named Walter Scott, and my job consisted of giving credit clearances for carloads of building materials. I studied the lists of customers and vendors, checked their credit ratings against Dun & Bradstreet on a daily basis, and felt as almighty as God when I approved tens of thousands of dollars' worth of material each day. Walter Scott—whom I dubbed "Sir Walter," and who just loved the title—was gone for days on end, checking the accounts, their inventories, and their stability. Quite often he'd come back from a trip and tell me not to extend any more credit to some firm with a triple-A rating as he had a bad feeling about them. Nine times out of ten, his gut feeling was right.

US Gypsum's offices were on Fifth Street, near Figueroa, in the Architects Building. Nothing like being in the same building with the big boys who were building all the new schools in California!

I liked the company, I loved Sir Walter, and I made one very close friend, Lucille Campo, a tall, statuesque Italian-American with a flare for clothes that put everyone else to shame. Unlike the one with Betty, our friendship moved out of the office and into our everyday lives. We went everywhere together. Lucille lived in a cute little apartment on Rossmore at Melrose. It wasn't far from us, as Vine Street changed to Rossmore when it crossed Melrose.

When spring turned to summer, we started spending our weekends on the beach at Santa Monica. I'd forgotten how the first tan of the season could come on awfully fast if you didn't watch out. I remember it was kind of sneaky the way it happened. We left the beach around mid-afternoon, and I was showing just a faint blush of red on my arms and legs. When we got to Wilshire and Rossmore, Lucy's bus was just pulling up, so she jumped aboard, and I sat and waited for the one that would take me to Hollywood and Vine. As I sat, I got redder and redder. My eyes felt like they were swollen shut, and I was in misery. My big floppy beach hat did nothing to cool me off. I tried putting more lotion on, but it was like adding oil to a hot frying pan, it just seemed to sizzle on me.

I got to thinking I must have just missed my bus, and if that were the case, I'd have almost a full hour to wait. *Oh, hell, what am I going to do?* I thought. I must've gotten dehydrated, because I started to feel nauseated, and panic began to set in. There would be no sense in starting to walk, I'd only get hotter.

"Can I give you a ride?" a man's voice called out as a Jeep pulled up to the curb.

"Thank you, Sir Galahad, if you'd come any later you could have served me with scrambled eggs!"

He laughed outright, then gave me one look and said, "Oh, my God, you're terribly sunburned. Get in, get in, I'll take you home. Where do you live?"

Now, here's a true gentleman, I thought, even with my looking like a boiled squid, he offers to drive me home.

Without hesitation, I climbed into the Jeep and said, "The Hollywood Towers at Gower and Franklin. Know where it is?"

"I know where Gower and Franklin are. I'll get you home in a jiffy. Sorry there isn't a top on the Jeep, but it should only take us a few minutes."

On the drive to the apartment I learned he was an ex-GI who was starting a new record business with his brother. It sounded exciting; I'd never met a young entrepreneur before. When he pulled up under the portico, he asked if he could call me, and maybe we could have a date.

"Do you usually date lobsters?" I asked, trying to smile through my blistered lips.

He ignored my limp try at levity and said, "I'll call you later in the week and see how you're doing. Okay?"

"Okay—and thanks so much."

"I'll need your phone number," he said, smiling.

"Right, you will," and I scribbled it in on a scrap of paper he handed me.

As good as his word, he called the following Wednesday to see how I was doing. Happily, I had completely recovered and, except for some peeling on my shoulders, I was presentable once more, and I told him so.

"Great. What are you doing Saturday? I thought we'd go to dinner and a movie. Would you like to?"

"Why not! Sounds great."

"In fact we'll do it the other way around. We'll see *Die Fledermaus,* it starts at five-thirty, then go on to dinner."

He sounded like a take-charge person, and I rather liked it.

"I'll pick you up just after five. See you Saturday," and he hung up.

"Did I hear you accept a date with Robin What's-his-name?" Mother asked.

"Yep."

"Pam, you don't even know him. He picked you up on the side of the road, for heaven's sake!"

"Mother, you saw what I looked like Saturday afternoon. Anyone who'd pick up a girl who looked like a pickled blowfish has to have a kind heart."

"I don't like it," she said.

"Okay, when he comes Saturday, I'll bring him up to meet you, and if you still feel bad, I'll make some excuse. That work?"

"I guess it'll have to."

When Saturday came around, I was back to normal again, or as normal as I ever am. I was glad I got gussied up a bit, as Robin arrived, not in the open Jeep, but in a spiffy two-door, and he was casually but smartly dressed. I brought him up to the apartment to meet Mother, and I could see she was pleasantly impressed.

Die Fledermaus was a delightful satire, all in German, with subtitles flashing across elaborate backgrounds that made them almost impossible to read, but the music was fabulous and the plot so transparent, it wasn't really necessary for me to follow the dialogue.

When we came out around seven-fifteen it was still quite light, and I found Robin, or Rob, as he preferred to be called, had made reservations at the House of Murphy. When we got there it was just after seven-thirty, and the maitre d' was crossing us off as a no-show. That's when I found Rob had a temper.

"Do I understand you were going to give our table away because we were a minute late!" he exploded.

"I'm sorry, but there's a lineup of people waiting—they don't understand when a table is empty and they can't be seated," the maitre d' said lamely.

"Ever hear of putting a Reserved sign on a table?"

"Okay, we're here now," I said quietly, trying to defuse the situation, and turning to the maitre d' said, "Please seat us."

Rob's mood changed instantly, and smiling widely, he trailed me to our table.

The food and wine were great, and the evening turned out to be really fun. He was an interesting conversationalist, seemed to know a little about every subject under the sun, and the give-and-take was very enjoyable.

The night was dark and moonless when we left the restaurant, and before long I noticed Rob was taking the long way home, turning up and down streets I didn't know, and getting me completely lost. I was slightly surprised at this turn of events, but decided he didn't want the evening to end. Suddenly, his light, bantering conversation turned to crime in Los Angeles, and he started on the Black Dahlia murder that had so stunned Hollywood the previous year. It was still open on the books, with no real suspects in sight, except the possibility of the crime being committed by some serviceman. As we got to Hollywood and Vine, which I immediately recognized, he shot through the intersection, heading west, and I said, "Rob, you should've made a right on Gower or Vine, remember I live up on Franklin."

"We're not going home. I'm not through with the evening, not by a long shot!"

He started then to pour out a lot of grisly details on the crime, details I'd not read about in any of the papers—not that they hadn't been full of gore and guts when the story was still front page news. I noticed he kept giving me strange sidelong glances to see how I was taking it. I didn't like it, but as Hollywood Boulevard was well-lit, I wasn't actually afraid, just a little apprehensive.

Suddenly, without signaling, he made an abrupt right turn on Nichols Canyon, and I found my blood pulsing in my brain. What the hell was he doing? Where was he going? The canyon was dark, and after passing the few homes at the bottom of it, there weren't even any house lights shining. A silent calm came over me and I found my survival instincts taking over. A wisp of conversation I'd heard at US Gypsum came to mind, and I recalled one of the women in the typing pool telling me that she and her husband had just built a rambling ranch house up in Nichols Canyon.

She'd said, "It's like being in the city without being in the city. It's close, yet rural, and Phil is such a country boy, it does my heart good to see how he loves it."

You just did my heart good too, gal, I said to myself.

"Hey, Rob, you know I've got friends up here who've just built a lovely ranch home further up the canyon. They've asked me to visit. Could we go tonight? I know they'll be up, they're both night owls."

He turned and looked at me. I hardly recognized him. Gone was any vestige of his earlier carefree attitude; the look on his face was beyond bad-tempered, it was malevolent.

I shut my eyes for a moment and said a silent prayer.

Suddenly the car was spinning around, almost out of control, and I found we were tearing back down toward the boulevard. There was a stop at the corner, but I was sure he wouldn't bother to make it, so as we approached, I flung open the passenger door and rolled out into the street. He made a skidding right, saw what I'd done, and came to a fishtailing stop.

I'd never moved so fast in my life, banged-up knees and all. I got up and ran down the center of Hollywood Boulevard away from him. A streetcar was coming slowly in my direction, making ready to stop at the next intersection. I dashed alongside it, and when it squealed to a stop and the doors automatically opened, I climbed up and fell into the seat behind the driver.

"What's up, gal? I saw you fall out of that car back there and when I saw you get up and run I knew you were in trouble."

"You stopped for me, didn't you?" I said, noticing the empty car and realizing he normally would've gone on to Highland or some other major intersection without stopping.

"You bet, gal," he said with a fatherly smile, then added, "Are you sure you're all right?"

"I am now," I said, and getting up shakily went to the back of the streetcar to see if Rob was following. There was no sign of him. When we got to Vine, I got off. I knew Gower was closer, but it wasn't as well-lit, and I'd had my fill of dark streets.

～

Thank God for a two-bedroom apartment. Mother didn't

wake up when I crept in. And Ursula, as usual, was dead to the world.

I took a quick, silent shower, gently scrubbed my bruised and battered legs, and noticed quite a few bruises over the rest of me. My right hip hurt like the devil, and I figured it must've taken the brunt of my fall. I quietly slipped under the sheets on the far side of the bed, hoping Ursula wouldn't wake up. I was in no mood to talk about my "date." I could just visualize Mother's "I told you so" look next day, and burrowing down into my pillow, I tried to sleep.

I couldn't. The horror of what I'd gone through wouldn't let me. I even got up once and went to the phone to call the police. Then I changed my mind. Could he be the Black Dahlia murderer? Or was he just one of the hundreds of loonies who confess to crimes for their one moment of glory? I kept seeing his face when he tore back down to the boulevard. It wasn't the face of a loony, it was the face of a maniac. What would have happened to me if I hadn't thought of Vera and Phil? The thought alone brought on a sweat that had me sticking to the sheets.

Finally, I fell into a fitful sleep with nightmares crowding on nightmares. I kept waking, catching myself moaning, and wondering how Ursula could sleep through all my tossing and turning.

Of course, as I shuffled into the dining room Sunday morning looking for a cup of coffee, the first comment Mother made was, "And how was your evening?" She sounded so chirpy, it was obvious she was expecting some happy talk.

Ursula looked up then, and said in her blunt way, "You look like the devil."

As I sat down to the table, my robe fell away from my legs and Mother noticed the bruises and abrasions that had taken on a ghastly hue.

"Were you in an accident last night?" she asked, real concern in her voice.

"You could say that," I said, noncommittally.

"Tell me about it," she said. There was no if, but, or maybe in her tone, so I knew I'd better tell all. I tried to keep my voice even, leaving out the hysteria I still felt, and when I was through she said emphatically, "We're calling the police."

Cool-headed Ursula said, "Let's stop and think. The murder was over a year and a half ago, they had hundreds of confessions from all types of people just trying to horn in on the headlines. Somehow this jerk sounds like one of them. Maybe he gets his kicks out of terrifying his dates. And anyhow, what could you tell them? That you had a date with a guy who picked you up on the street? Come on, how would that sound? They'd probably think you got what you deserved."

"Do *you* think I got what I deserved?"

"Of course not! But that's not the point."

"Ursula's right," Mother said, changing her tune. "We'd just be stirring up a hornet's nest."

Just then the phone rang, and I cringed. Ursula looked at me, nodded, and picked it up. "It's for you," she said. "It's Lucy wanting to know if you feel up to going to Santa Monica today."

I picked up the phone and said, "I think I'll pass, Lou, and let my tan take hold properly before I put another layer on."

"Okay, I won't go either. Why don't you come on over? I had a great date last night, and I'm just dying to tell you about it."

"So did I," I said quietly.

"Great, we'll have an afternoon of girl-talk. See ya!" and she hung up.

"I'm not going to answer the phone today," I said.

"That's okay, Mother or I will, and if that stupid jerk calls I'll tell him you never want to hear from him again."

"Thanks, Urs, but I don't think even he's that stupid," I said.

But he was.

Just as I was leaving for Lucille's he called. Ursula grabbed the phone, gave me the strangest look, and after listening for a couple of moments, emptied both barrels into the mouthpiece, then slammed down the receiver.

Before I could say a word, Mother asked, "That was Rob?"

"It sure was. He wanted to know if Pam wanted to go on a date with him. No apology for last night. Nothing!"

I started to shudder uncontrollably.

"Hey, look at it this way, he isn't the Black Dahlia murderer, he's a thrill-seeker, and he wants to jerk you around some more. He probably got a real kick out of your antics last night."

Surprisingly, Lucille agreed with Ursula when she heard my story. So did Vera at work the following day. "If your sister blasted him, like you said she did, you won't hear from him again. He was just testing the water when he called Sunday."

John Wickham, one of the salesmen, overheard our conversation and said, "Pam, any guy can read a police blotter and get all the gory details on a crime. I'll bet he's one of those creeps who gets his thrills hanging around police stations, nosing into police files, and using the info to make himself sound like a big shot."

By Wednesday, I was sure they were right as he hadn't called again and, when the phone rang, without hesitation I picked it up and said, "Hello?"

It was Rob, and thinking I was Ursula, he asked to speak to me. I knew our accents had him fooled, so I played along with his game and became Ursula.

"You dumb idiot! Can't you get the message? She doesn't ever want to see or talk to you again!"

When I smashed the receiver down on the cradle, a wave of satisfaction swept over me, and I knew that was the last I'd ever hear from him.

Chapter 8

By the time summer waved goodbye, Ursula was in a complete whirl of excitement getting ready for her wedding in October. It was a happy time, the only sad note being that Dad wouldn't be there to give her away. The fact that he had so thoroughly enjoyed meeting all her soon-to-be-in-laws when he went back to Buffalo the previous year made it feel like he'd be there in spirit, and I know it lessened the loss for her.

It was exciting for me, too, as I hadn't been able to attend my sister Margo's hurried wedding in Tientsin on December 4, just before Japan attacked Pearl Harbor, and always felt I'd lost out on one of the happiest days of her life.

We planned to drive back to Washington D.C. for Ursula's wedding, and Mother had the car checked out six ways to center for the trip, including buying all new tires, as she didn't want anything to go wrong along the way. It was a neat little Plymouth sedan, almost identical to the one we had in '39, and I think she bought it for sentimental reasons. I knew she would never buy a Mercury again. Especially a black one. Not that she had anything against the make or the car, but the memories were still too harsh. Several months after Dad's ashes had been scattered in the Gulf of Chihli, Mother got a call from the accountant that the Mercury had been shipped back, and that she owed two thousand dollars on transportation fees.

Mother went ballistic, and said, "Dump the damn thing overboard—I never want to see it again!" I could hear the anguish in her voice.

"Mrs. Simmons, as your accountant, I have to advise you that it's an excellent car and you should keep it."

"You don't seem to understand—it killed my husband, I never want to see it again. Get rid of the damn thing!"

He kept pleading, and she kept telling him what he could do with it in no uncertain terms. Finally, he said, "Then I'm going to buy it off you. I need a car. I like that Mercury. They're still real hard to come by, and it's only just barely been broken in. I'll send you a check, less the transportation costs."

When the check arrived Mother bought herself the little Plymouth, and they seemed to hit it off like old friends.

The Mercury didn't deserve to be blamed for Dad's death. It wasn't the car, it was the Communist takeover of Shanghai in '47, and the ensuing clash on the Bund, that killed Dad.

While Dad was happily watching the unloading of the Mercury, two bumptious Communist officials came up and asked him who owned the car. Dad, in his fluent Chinese, told them he did.

"In the Chinese People's Republic, one car for every five people," the older man said smugly.

Dad smiled, and told them there were five people in his family.

"Where is your family?" the older man asked.

"In the United States," Dad said without hesitation. Then he looked at their faces and realized the mistake he'd made.

"Pu hau! Pu hau!" they shouted in unison, and Dad knew their "No good! No good!" meant nothing but trouble for

him and his precious Mercury that was being carefully lowered to the pier.

The younger official shouted at the crane operator and told him to haul the car back up. Dad shouted in equally strong Chinese for the operator to keep on lowering it. The battle lines were drawn, and the cussing and shouting kept getting louder and louder.

Some of Dad's friends arrived about then. They'd come to drive him to his hotel, expecting to dump his luggage, and then take him out for a night on the town.

It didn't happen.

Dad was losing it. He got so excited he almost slugged the younger of the two officials, and his friends had to hold him back. Finally, after the crane operator had raised and lowered the car for the umpteenth time, the Communists let him lower it all the way down. The relief for Dad was overwhelming, and he thanked them profusely. They looked at him as though he were nuts, and told him he couldn't have the car, it was going to be impounded.

All the things that the good doctors at the Mayo Clinic had told him to watch out for came together like colliding planets, and clutching his chest, Dad let out a long moan and fell to the ground, his face as white as the billowing thunderheads climbing up into the early evening sky.

It was lucky his friends were with him. They rushed him to the hospital where he was placed in intensive care, and after several days, when he was stabilized, he was flown home to Tientsin, and to the able care of Dr. Grice, the Kailan's chief of staff.

∼

At US Gypsum I asked for a month's leave of absence. Sir Walter became so distressed, I felt terrible. "I can't keep the job open for you, Pam, much as I'd like to, as credit checks are so vital to the financial stability of the company. If it were for a few days, I could handle it myself, but my schedule is so tight right now, anything more than a week is out of the question."

It ended up that he pulled a girl out of the stenographic pool and I trained her for my job. It was kind of bittersweet. I hated losing it, but I was so looking forward to the trip East and Ursula's wedding, it seemed a small price to pay.

Of course, there was no way Mother could afford to keep the apartment and also make the trip. We were still going through unbelievable legal shenanigans over Dad's will, and any money Mother had left in the account in the Beverly Hills bank was too precious to squander.

When we pulled out from under the portico for the last time, the car loaded to the hilt with all our precious belongings, there was a catch in my throat. I knew it was rough on Mother too, as she'd grown really fond of the apartment and Clotilde, the maid. Their friendship had been sealed right after my twenty-first birthday when Chloe, as she liked to be called, told Mother that she was going to be a grandmother for the first time, and she was truly excited.

"I'm going to make something for the baby," Mother said. "How about a sweater and bonnet? What color do you think your daughter would like?"

"Oh, red!" Chloe said without hesitation.

It had never struck Mother before that a baby with a dark complexion would look rather ridiculous in baby blue or petal pink. The layette turned out beautifully, and Mother had to admit that red was a really fun color to knit.

Talking about dark complexions reminds me of another event, or near event, that happened just before we took off to go back East.

I say near event, as I didn't learn about it until I received a letter from one of my camp friends saying that Norm Shaw, my favorite dancing partner in Weihsien, had come to Los Angeles, ostensibly to take me on a date and to go dancing. It seems he got all the way to the lobby of the Towers when he chickened out. In his letter to my friend, that was being relayed to me, he said that the American attitude toward people of dark skin was frightening, and he was afraid what would happen if we were seen out together. I thought of Norm, and all we'd gone through in the prison camp, and my old anger at injustice flared up. He was the son of a wealthy British taipan, whose mother was Indian. He was a gentleman, through and through, and a complete charmer.

When the hell is the Western world going to grow up? I thought sadly.

～

The trip back East, where the foliage was aflame with breathtaking autumn colors, was really enjoyable; the car ran smoothly, and the miles spun by. Mother let me do quite a bit of the driving, and I found it to be great fun. I only had two minor incidents, which are probably best forgotten. The first was a dust with the law in Columbus, Mississippi. I got stopped for doing fifteen miles an hour in a thirteen-and-a-half-mile school zone. I was crawling along with my eye on the speedometer, trying to watch the traffic around me at the same time, when I noticed a red light flashing in my rear window.

"Good Lord, what have I done?" I said, under my breath.

"You can't be going too fast, Pam. Maybe he noticed something wrong with the car," Mother said.

I dutifully pulled over, and waited for a very overweight officer to extricate himself from his squad car. When he finally waddled up to the driver's window, I asked him what

I'd done. With a perfectly straight face he said, "Ma'am, you were doing fifteen miles an hour. Didn't you see the thirteen-and-a-half-mile sign?"

"Yes, officer, and I tried to keep to it," I said meekly.

"We protect our children in Columbus, Mississippi, and we don't like speeders. If you weren't in an out-of-state car, I'd write you up. Take this as a warning—thirteen and a half miles an hour does not mean fifteen miles an hour!"

I thanked him for his courtesy and, checking in all directions, carefully pulled away from the curb. When we were out of earshot, and quite a distance from the school, I turned and looked at Mother and Ursula, and we all burst out laughing.

"Consider yourself sternly reprimanded," Ursula said in a gruff voice that contradicted the twinkle in her eye.

The next incident wasn't quite as funny. We were in Georgia. The roads were beautiful and smooth as a billiard table, but so narrow, they left no room to maneuver. It happened as I came down a grade to go under a railroad crossing and met a huge truck heading south. I moved over, ever so slightly, to get out of its way, when my right front wheel ran off the asphalt into slick red mud. I couldn't get any traction, and the car just kept on going till it ran into the dripping bank on the side of the road.

The truck driver stopped well past me in the opposite lane, put out some flares, and came back to offer assistance. I'd gotten out of the car by then, red mud halfway up my legs, and was eyeing the trunk that was beginning to submerge in the slimy mess.

"There's no way I can turn around and try to haul you out," the trucker said, taking off his baseball cap and scratching his butch cut.

"Damn, we've had such a lovely trip till now," I said despondently.

"I see you're from California. That's a long way. Where are you heading?"

"D.C., if we ever make it," I said.

Mother started to get out of the car, and I told her not to. There was no need for all of us to get muddy.

The trucker went back to his vehicle to see if he could raise anyone on the radio. As he climbed up into his cab, he looked across the highway and saw a farmer on a tractor waving at him frantically from the edge of the field that overlooked the undercrossing. I couldn't actually see anything as the railway crossing blocked my view, but after a few minutes the trucker came back and told me a farmer was coming to pull us out with his tractor. We were so relieved, and thanked him profusely. About then I heard the roar of the old tractor engine and turned to the trucker and told him to take off, we'd be fine.

"You're sure?"

"Absolutely. Thanks again."

I leaned in the window and told Mother and Ursula we had lucked out, and should be on our way in half an hour or less.

It didn't take long for the old guy to arrive, and he didn't seem to mind the mud. He had thigh boots on and went straight to work. Within ten minutes we were out of the muck and back on the road, the car looking very much worse for wear. I turned to thank him and he said, with his hand out, "That will be ten bucks, please."

I did a double-take.

"I make more money hauling people out of that spring than I ever could working my fields," he said, smiling. "You'd be surprised how many cars don't make it under that bridge.

On a good day, I make fifty to sixty bucks, free and clear."

"And all the time I thought the Good Lord was watching over us," I said, smiling back.

"Never been called the Good Lord before," he said with a perfectly straight face, climbing back onto his tractor and heading up to his old vantage point.

∞

Of course, we did make it safely to Washington, and the wedding was beautiful. It was held in St. Matthew's Cathedral, and the service was followed by a full nuptial mass. I was Ursula's maid of honor, and a few strings had to be pulled, as I was not Catholic, but somehow it all came together beautifully.

Except for the gardenias!

Too late, I found I was allergic to my exquisite corsage. All through the service, my nose itched, my eyes ran, and I sniffed and wheezed as though I had a full-blown cold. Looking back, I realize all I had to do was unpin the corsage on my shoulder and move it down to my waist, but my mind was so mushy by then I couldn't think straight.

There was also one quick change in the musical selection. Both Ursula and Cope wanted his cousin, who had a glorious voice, to sing *Because,* but the church objected to the line, "*... because God made you mine,*" insisting God did no such thing! They settled on Gounod's *Ave Maria,* and I'm glad they did—it was sung so exquisitely I can still hear those seraphic notes ringing through the cathedral.

One of the first things the Cuviellos did when we arrived at the church was to do away with the tradition of having the bride's family sit on one side of the aisle, and the groom's on the other, as Mother was the only member on the bride's side

After that, formality was thrown to the wind, and the wedding turned into a completely joyous occasion, followed by an equally delightful luncheon at an old livery stable dating back to the early 1800s that was converted into a period restaurant.

When all the festivities were over, Mother and I went back to the Carroll Arms, the quiet, unpretentious hotel that Cope's father had picked out for us. He told us he always stayed there when he was in Washington, and that it was the favorite hotel of visiting senators. I guess the cult of celebrity is strong no matter where you are, Washington being not much different from Hollywood, and I found myself looking around the foyer as I went through, hoping to spot one of my favorite solons. As it was the weekend before the 1948 general election, that turned out to be a fruitless cause.

We left Washington the following morning, and after a couple of days of easy driving, spent election night in Texarkana. I remember going to bed with the papers announcing Dewey had been elected, and waking up in the morning with headlines giving Truman the presidency!

That was my first taste of democracy at work!

Chapter 9

We no sooner got back to Hollywood than Mother waved her magic wand and found us a little house on North Kingsley Drive. It was bare bones, with minimal furnishings, scatter rugs in place of carpeting, a kitchen you could barely turn around in, and only one bedroom. But it met our frugal budget, and we knew it would only be temporary at best, as we both planned to be bringing in good money before long.

While I started back at US Gypsum, Mother completed her correspondence course on hotel management. She figured she might as well be doing what she enjoyed, and being an innkeeper would be as close as she could get to her earlier life and soubriquet as *Perle Mesta of the Pacific*.

My new job at US Gypsum was in agricultural sales. It wasn't as much fun as my old one, but as the girl I'd trained to replace me in the credit department was doing so well, there wasn't any chance I'd get that job back. Anyhow, I decided, it was time for me to learn more about the company, and ag-sales would certainly broaden my horizons.

I learned that agricultural gypsum was used to break up and remediate poor soil conditions; not exciting stuff, but very necessary if you made your living as a farmer. Surprisingly, another product that had nothing to do with agriculture was also handled through the same department. It was nonferrous dental hydrocal, came in two colors, white and ivory, and was designed specifically for use by dental technicians. But the enterprising sales reps found it had a much wider application than that. It was like a very strong ceramic, but being non-ferrous, it didn't have to be fired in a kiln. I forget how long it took for it to set up, but when it did, it could be thrown on the ground and not break or chip.

The reps found young entrepreneurs who wanted to work with it, and I enjoyed seeing all the new ideas they came up with. One such individual had been a GI in the Orient who had come home with several beautiful ivory figurines. He had rubber molds made from them and, using the ivory-tinted hydrocal, was able to reproduce them so it was almost impossible to tell they were not the genuine article. In fact, I brought one home to Mother, and even her practiced eye was fooled by the product, especially as it didn't feel cold like fired ceramic, but was warm to the touch, like true ivory.

That was the only interesting part of the job, as my new boss, Henry Bidwell, like Sir Walter before him, was on the road most of the time, and I ended up being a steno and gofer to all the field reps and technicians. My tender fingertip, which still hadn't healed completely, made the typing part of my work a nightmare. I guess moneywise it was a good job, but I knew I had to find something more challenging and less painful.

That's when I decided to try my hand at freelancing. If I could line up enough fashion design accounts I could quit my "gypsum job," as I called it.

Fired up with enthusiasm, every spare minute I had I trudged up and down the streets of West L.A. and Beverly Hills. I found La Cienega was lined with interior decorating houses, and armed with my portfolio of fabric and wallpaper designs, I hit just about every one of them. Several showed real interest, but I always seemed to arrive when the buyer was gone, and I'd end up leaving my designs with the manager, to be picked up at a later date.

I did land one good account on La Cienega though, but it wasn't in interior decorating. It was a yarn boutique, where the wives of the wealthy came to purchase expensive yarns and receive one-on-one knitting instruction. As money was no object to them, and each one wanted an exclusive design, I enjoyed the work. With a knitting background going back to my childhood, I was able to not only design the dresses, but also to come up with complete knitting instructions when necessary. It really surprised me that I'd finally found a use for algebra! As so many of the dresses called for floral or scenic designs to be knitted into them, I had to find a way to duplicate the design without distortion, and that's where algebraic equations came to my aid.

Another account was with Vyola of Beverly Hills, whose creations were shown in Bullock's French Room and several exclusive salons across the country. She had a patented center seam-line that ran from the throat to the hem, gently following the contour of the body, making every dress she designed fit to perfection. Those in the know always recognized a "Vyola," as this flattering style-line could not be duplicated by any other designer. She was a smart lady to patent it.

I started out as a sketch artist, just sketching the designs Vy came up with, but after a while I tossed in a few of my own. She liked several of them, but said she couldn't afford to pay me a designer's salary.

"Would you consider paying me in dresses?" I asked.

"Definitely! Good idea!"

And that's how I ended up with one of the most envied

wardrobes any girl could wish for. Of course, they were mostly evening numbers: dresses, skirts, silk blouses and wraps. And whenever I slipped into one of them I felt like "Mrs. Astorbilt."

Another of my favorite haunts was Sunset Strip, with its trendy boutiques. I would stroll its length with my trusty portfolio, this time filled with designs of high-style dresses, jewelry, and accessories. Although I always tried to make an appointment with a prospective new account before arriving, I invariably ended up having to leave my sketches with the floor manager, as the owner or buyer was busy with a client, or simply not available. It was disappointing, but I felt I was making inroads, and that I'd eventually achieve success.

One day I saw an ad in the *Los Angeles Times* with the heading "Enjoy the Fabulous Life of a Dance Instructor." It went on to extol the benefits of the profession, and mentioned what a lucrative career it was. I thought it over for a couple of weeks and decided that's what I would do, and then my life would be perfect. I'd do sketching and designing during the day, and teach dancing in the evening. What a healthy and rewarding existence!

When I approached Mother for the fifteen-hundred-dollar loan I'd need to cover my dance instruction, she was less than enthusiastic. "Pam, you have just too darn much on your plate already. You have a full-time job, several freelance accounts that keep you hopping, and now you want to take up dancing?"

"Mumsy, I'm so darn bored with my day job; don't you see, by freelancing and teaching I could break away on my own."

"I don't know. I still think you're trying to take on too much."

It took a while, but I finally got her to agree to the loan, telling her pragmatically that the only way it would not be paid off would be if I died. She told me, just as pragmatically, that I would have to take out a two-thousand-dollar life insurance policy, with her as beneficiary, before she'd consider it.

One call to Mary Hutchins at the old insurance agency settled that, and armed with Mother's check, I went to the Veloz and Yolanda Dance Studio on Wilshire Boulevard and signed up for the dance instruction course.

Somehow, after that my day job became more bearable, as I knew the evenings held either sketching sessions with Vyola or dance lessons at the studio, both of which I enjoyed immeasurably.

I'd only been at Veloz and Yolanda a couple of months when Jay Masters, an evening instructor, and his friend Jerry Goldberg walked out with me at the end of the session and asked if they could buy me a cup of coffee, as they wanted to talk to me. I learned Jay was an engineer at North American during the day, and Jerry had a successful auto parts business.

I was in a great mood, and accepted happily. I didn't think anyone could spoil the evening for me, but I soon found these two sure could. Without any preamble, after our coffees had arrived, Jay said, "There is talk in the teacher's lounge that you'll never be an instructor."

I was aghast, and said, "Why, aren't I good enough?"

"That's got nothing to do with it," Jay said. "It's your clothes. The consensus is, you're filthy rich, otherwise there's no way you could afford the wardrobe you have."

"And it's always been dance studio policy to separate the rich from their money whenever possible," Jerry added cynically.

I burst out laughing. "Ye gods! Would you believe I freelance as a sketch artist and fashion designer, and that I get paid in clothes? I couldn't afford these dresses any other way."

"It doesn't matter what *we* believe. According to Jay, everyone believes you're rich, and your snotty British accent just adds to the picture. The teachers have been told to keep giving you dance lessons, and telling you you're not ready, till you turn old and grey." Jerry didn't make any bones about it.

"I think you're both crazy. I paid for a dance instruction course. I had to borrow money to pay for it. And when I'm through I'm going to become a dance instructor."

"Good luck," Jay said.

"Consider yourself warned," Jerry added.

"Thank you, but I think you're both nuts."

When I got home I told Mother what the two men had told me.

"Well, there's a solution to that. Get Veloz to sign a letter guaranteeing you a job when you've completed the course."

"Oh, Mumsy, how the heck do I do that?" She made it sound so simple. And possibly for her it was. She'd gotten more things done, and more signatures on papers, at her famous parties in China than any bona fide diplomat with the State Department.

"Didn't you tell me you'd been invited to a barbecue at his place this weekend?"

"Yep."

"So … he drinks, doesn't he? When he's feeling no pain, go up sweetly and ask him to write you a letter. Be sure it says that he guarantees you a job with the studio when you complete your course."

I'd been so flattered when Yolanda came in earlier in the week and invited all the dance instructors to a barbecue at their home and made a point of coming over and inviting me. But I was a dithering mess when Sunday came around. I felt like an agent on an impossible mission. All that kept going through my mind was Mother's order to get that letter. I had one thing in my favor—as it was a barbecue, we'd all dressed down for the occasion, and I was wearing a simple cotton dress with a full skirt, and didn't look anything like "Mrs. Astorbilt."

Halfway through the evening, Frank Veloz came up and asked me for a dance. He was superb. I'd never danced with anyone like him. He could make me follow steps I didn't know existed. To say it was a thrill is an understatement. It wasn't long before I realized the floor had cleared and we were the only couple dancing, and when the number was over, the applause was exhilarating.

Okay, gal, now is the moment ... he'll sign anything you ask if you play it right.

"Mr. Veloz," I said, in my sweetest little country-girl voice, "do you think I'll make a good dance instructor for Veloz and Yolanda?"

He patted me on the shoulder, smiled, and said, "The best!"

"Oh, thank you! Would you write me a letter saying that? It would mean so much to me." I couldn't believe I was such a good little actress.

"Of course, of course," he said, obviously quite flattered. "Tell me what you want me to write."

Oh, Lord, this is too easy, I thought, and dictated what Mother had told me, word for word. He wrote it all out in longhand, then signed "Frank Veloz" with a flourish.

I thanked him profusely, folded the note, and put it in my pocket.

When I got home I handed the letter to Mother and said, "I did it! Ya larned me well!"

"That's my girl," she said proudly, reading the letter. "Now file it in a safe place."

~

Once more life returned to normal, or almost so. My days were divided between my job at US Gypsum, freelancing, and dancing. Just a tad busy, but nothing I couldn't handle.

One evening, late, coming home from Vy's, I stepped off the Melrose bus at Kingsley, and while I waited for the bus driver to pull away from the curb, I noticed a man smoking a cigarette leaning against a dark coupe a little further up the street. I got a weird feeling, but didn't worry much as I knew I was only a short block from home.

When the bus moved on, I darted across Melrose and started up Kingsley Drive. Glancing over my shoulder, I noticed the stranger was walking slowly up the other side of the street. *That's not good,* I thought, *he's closer to home than I am,* and I started to walk faster, cutting diagonally across the street, heading for our little place. I looked back again. He was not hurrying, he was walking deliberately, like a predator stalking his prey, and with choking horror I realized he must have seen me walk this way many times before. That's all it took, I started to run like hell, and heard his feet pounding close behind me. I flung open the little garden gate in the picket fence and rushed to the front door, pounding on it like a battering ram. He didn't bother with the gate, he leapt the fence and was just grabbing for me when Mother opened the door and I fell in. She gave him one look, slammed the door, and shot the bolt.

"What happened?" she asked, fear in her eyes.

"He saw me get off the bus and followed me," I said, my voice still shaking.

"We're calling the police!" she said firmly.

"Don't bother, he'll be long gone before they can respond."

"But I saw his face. I could recognize him."

"Even if they caught him, and you picked him out of a line-up, we couldn't prove a thing. Forget it, Mumsy. I'll just tell Vy I can't work evenings any more, only Saturdays."

It was right after that incident that Mother got a call from Las Vegas. The Gunnersons at the Bar-W dude ranch had received her resumé and were intrigued by her background. They had quite a long conversation, and I gathered the more they talked the more they wanted Mumsy, because they asked her if she could start right away. I watched her try to act nonchalant, but I could tell she was bursting inside. When she hung up the phone she couldn't contain herself. "I've done it! I just know that's the job I've been dreaming about."

"Tell me about it!"

"That was Karen Gunnerson, she and her husband, John, own and run the Bar-W. It's a dude ranch just out of Las Vegas. Really high priced, catering to celebrities and movie-types who want somewhere to stay while they get a quickie divorce. She said that most of them come back again and again after the divorce because they enjoy the ranch so much. Said they never have to do any advertising, it's all word of mouth, and very low-key."

"What'll you be doing?" I asked, intrigued.

"According to Karen, I'll be running the show. Seeing everything runs smoothly, planning menus and events, and making sure the guests are totally pampered. The rates are outrageous, but as they include all meals, booze and, I gather, transportation to Vegas for gambling, that's to be expected."

"When are you leaving?"

"Next week. Do you think you can afford this place on your own?"

"Oh, I can afford it, but I won't stay here, not after the horror of last week. While we still have your wheels, can we go apartment hunting? I'd like to find something closer to my freelance accounts, that way I can still work evenings for Vy when she needs me, and not worry about creeps like that one the other night."

"Right. Tomorrow I'll give our landlord notice, and we'll spend the day apartment hunting."

Actually we didn't have to. I picked the second place we looked at on Orange Avenue, a short block from where Wilshire and San Vicente Boulevards intersected. The San Vicente bus would drop me a block from Vy's door, and the Wilshire bus would take me within walking distance of the Architects Building on Fifth Street. On top of that, the studio apartment was just what I needed. It was nicely furnished, with wall-to-wall carpeting and a drop-down Murphy bed. It didn't have any cooking facilities, but it did include the services of an efficient little Filipino houseboy. For me, with my work schedule, that was wonderful, especially when I got back late at night and found the bed made up and back in the wall, and the place spotless. Mother worried that the ninety dollars a month I had to pay would be more than I could handle, but I told her it should be a breeze. If for any reason I did need more money, I'd just line up more accounts. The fact I couldn't cook in the apartment didn't bother me, as I enjoyed eating out, and most evenings, if I wasn't working, sketching, dancing, or attending night classes at UCLA, I had a date.

At that time I was going pretty steady with Colin MacLeod, a Scot, and an aeronautical engineer. After a few hair-raising incidents at stop lights, I found out he was color-blind. I also learned he was in aerial reconnaissance during the war, where color-blindness was a requisite for all reconnaissance spotters. He told me his vision was so acute without color, that he could pick out sniper's nests and gun emplacements that no normal-visioned person could see. I know I should have been impressed, but after we'd just missed being sideswiped at a Beverly Hills intersection, I asked him how he could drive with his handicap.

"Usually, when I approach a stop light," he explained, "I look to see which one of the three lights is glowing. If it's the middle one, I know it's yellow and will be turning to red. If it's the top one, I know it's red and I have to stop. If it's the bottom one, it's green, and I can go through."

"So what just happened?" I asked wryly.

"You happened. You distracted me, and I forgot to run through my little charade."

"Isn't that typical of a man? *You* goof up, and then you blame it on *me!*"

That's what I liked about Colin. We could kid and tease, or we could just sit quietly in some nightclub and watch a three-ring circus playing out before us, and invariably, when one of us broke the silence, we came in on the other's mental wavelength. It was almost spooky. He was just the date I needed to take my mind off those busy, hectic days.

Colin dropped me off at the apartment one evening after an enjoyable date, and asked if I'd like him to see me to my door. I told him it wasn't necessary, and running up the steps, I turned and waved before stepping into the lobby. I was still in rosy euphoria when I got to my door and looked in my evening clutch for the key. It wasn't there. *Oh, hell, I must've forgotten it when I changed handbags ...*

I went back to the manager's office and timidly knocked on the door, hoping she was still up. There was no answer. I knocked again, really loud. Still no response. I stood for a minute thinking, then ran outside and around to my apartment windows. If I was lucky, Ramon might have left one open that I could climb through. I looked up at the first window and, sure enough, there was about a four-inch gap at the bottom. Enough room for me to get leverage and push it up.

I tossed my little evening purse up on the sill and climbed up the wall, using the neatly trimmed juniper beneath the window to give myself an extra boost. Grabbing the edge of the sill I tried to shove the window up. It wouldn't budge. I tried again and again. No luck. *That's probably why Ramon left it open*, I thought. Just as I was wondering where to go from there, a strong male voice said, "Can we help?" and I was bathed in the high-beams of a prowl car.

"Sure can, if you can shove this window up," I said.

"I don't think so," the taller of the two officers replied. "You'd better get down and explain yourself."

"Isn't it obvious? I've locked myself out of my apartment!" I said with a smile.

"Why didn't you get the manager to let you in?"

"I tried. She's not in her office."

"What's your name?"

"Pamela Simmons."

"And your apartment number?"

"One-oh-nine," I said.

I scrambled down and away from the juniper, noticing my nice new stockings were badly snagged, and cussed quietly under my breath.

"Joe, go get her handbag off the sill," the shorter and heavier of the two said, and then they each grabbed an elbow, and steered me up the street to the lobby. I felt like a felon, and hoped no one I knew was watching.

Of course, the first thing one of them did was rap on the

manager's door, while the other went to check the mail slots.

"What did you say your number was?" he called out.

"One-oh-nine," I replied.

"Well, that checks out," I heard him say. Coming back into the lobby, he asked his partner, "Got hold of the manager yet?"

The officer called Joe said, "There's no answer."

Short-and-Sturdy banged on the door and shouted, "Open up! Police!"

I cringed at all the commotion.

Just then a girl's head peeped out of a door further down the hall, and she said, "The manager's upstairs—you want me to get her?"

"Yes, ma'am!"

A few minutes later she came back down with the manager. I was surprised because she wasn't the same woman who had rented the apartment to me. This girl was much younger, a little chubby, and wearing satin evening pajamas.

"You the manager?" Short-and-Sturdy asked.

"Yes. The night manager," she said.

"Do you know it's against the law to leave the manager's office unattended?"

She looked really flustered and afraid.

"Tell you what. You go open one-oh-nine for this gal, and let her in. I won't write you up … this time! But if I ever get a call again, you'll be in deep trouble!" Only he spelled trouble with four letters, beginning with an *s* and ending with a *t*.

The poor kid looked like she was from some small Iowa farming community, with dreams of breaking into the movies, and appeared completely bewildered and out of her depth, and really scared.

I thanked the officers for their help, then turned and

thanked her for letting me in. She bit her lip and started to cry.

~

On more and more evenings after work, I'd jump on the Wilshire bus, and instead of going home, I'd get off at the Veloz and Yolanda Studios and receive several hours of pretty strenuous dance instruction. I loved it. And after I got to know the instructors better, they'd often ask me to join them at a nightclub, and we'd dance some more. That's when I relaxed and practiced the dance steps I'd just learned.

I remember one Friday night a group of us decided to go to the Players Club on the Strip. Bobby Troup was playing, and his repertoire was from *South Pacific*, the new Broadway show that was all the rage. The ambience was both intimate and lively, and I drank it all up in happy gulps. As the men in our group were completely outnumbered by the girls, when several distinguished-looking Hollywood types asked if they could join our party, there were no objections—especially as they insisted on picking up the tab. I ended up with the best-looking man in the group; he had prematurely grey hair, and turned out to be great fun. That he looked like Ezio Pinza only added to his mystique. When the club closed down, they suggested we spend the night at the Bel Air home of Hugh, a buddy of "Ezio," and wind up the festivities with breakfast and a swim. Everyone was game, except straightlaced me. I quickly did some fancy footwork, explaining I had an art assignment early Saturday, and that I'd have to beg off. It wasn't a lie, but I could see "Ezio" was furious. I apologized, and went out to the doorman and asked him to hail me a cab.

While we were waiting for it, "Ezio" came up and asked where I lived. Surprisingly, when I told him my address, he said he knew where it was, that it was right on his way, and he'd drop me off. In fact, his whole mood changed as we drove to the apartment in his racy little open sports car, and he was laughing his head off at my story about the missing door key when we pulled up to the curb.

I told him it wasn't necessary to escort me to my door, but he insisted, saying with a smile that he didn't want a repeat of my last escapade. Then he took my key and opened the door for me. I started to thank him as I entered, but he marched right past me, and before I could even turn around, he'd pulled the Murphy bed down out of the wall.

I tossed my handbag on the coffee table, walked over to the bed and shoved it back up, giving him a glowering look.

He pulled it back down, and glowered back at me with an "I dare you!" sneer on his face.

That made me mad, and I slammed it back up again.

This went on several more times, both of us getting madder by the minute and acting like a couple of stupid, stubborn kids.

Finally, I'd had more than I could take. I slammed the bed back up into the wall and spat out, "The next time you try that, I'll shove the bed back up with you on it, and call the police. *Capisce?*"

It was a lousy ending to what had been a lovely romantic evening ...

Chapter 10

Colin and I were strolling up the Strip. It was one of those lovely clear Los Angeles evenings when the weather's perfect, the stars overhead are competing with the myriad lights of the city, and the streets take on a heady, almost mystical quality.

The boutiques I'd visited in daylight now seemed to have a magical charm, their lighted window displays as brilliant and enticing as the nightclub marquees. We'd passed several of them, remarking on their extravagant displays, when we came to a sassy little boutique I'd had a deep yen to design for, and I flipped out. There, on a beautiful beach, with paper palm trees and a shimmering sea in the background, stood a mannequin in a colorful linen dress, looking cool and enticing. The only thing wrong with the whole scene was that she was wearing one of my creations! I guess I must've looked strange because Colin said, "Lord, Pam, what's the matter?"

"That's *my* dress ... *my* design!"

"Did you know they were going to use it?"

"Heck, no! They never *bought* the design, they have no right to make it up."

"What are you going to do about it?"

"Well, I can't afford to sue, so I guess I'll just have to grin and bear it, and consider it a lesson learned," I said, recalling with alarm all the times I had trustingly left my sketches and designs at different salons.

"I'm so sorry, Pam," Colin said, giving me a consoling hug.

"I didn't think anything could spoil this lovely evening, but that damn boutique sure did," I said, feeling mad at myself for being so stupid and gullible.

We passed a few more attractive windows, but I was so upset I hardly noticed their displays. Then we came to the salon of one of Hollywood's top designers, and I stopped dead in my tracks. There in the window, under a misty moonlit sky, with Italian cypress and a white marble balustrade in the background, stood a tall blonde mannequin, her hair swept up in a French twist, wearing faux diamonds, white opera gloves, and a heavenly creation in subtle blue satin … the exact same number the boutique had stolen from me!

I looked at Colin. He'd recognized it, and was laughing hilariously. It was contagious. I couldn't help myself, and I laughed along with him.

"*Yes gods, this is great!* I've **won**! I couldn't ask for better revenge. What are *either* of them going to say if a client asks how come they both have the same dress in their window? Talk about faces covered in all shades of egg!"

∼

That had to be one of the last evenings I spent with Colin. Not long after that I watched Jay easing his way into my life, and sweet, accommodating Colin being gently eased out. Looking back, I know now that Colin and I would never have fallen deeply in love; we were kindred spirits, and kindred spirits can never really love each other fully. It would be like falling in love with oneself … not that there hasn't been a lot of that through the ages. But it's never fulfilling.

Jay took every advantage of the dance studio impasse to get closer to me, and he and Jerry took turns telling me that I'd never be a dance instructor with Veloz and Yolanda. Of course, I didn't believe them, and said so in no uncertain terms.

"No one can keep me from being an instructor just because I wear expensive clothes. That's crazy!"

And when my course was completed, I went into the manager's office with a broad smile on my face and asked for a job. He told me kindly that there were no openings at that time, but as soon as there was one, I'd be the very first to be called. When I went up and smugly told Jay, with a "*so* there!" in my voice, he said, "Don't hold your breath."

It still really didn't get to me, until Gene Hampton, my favorite instructor, suggested that I sign up for more lessons while I waited for an opening so that I'd keep up on the latest steps and methods.

"Did he say you had to pay for that additional instruction?" Jay asked, when I told him.

"Yes!"

"Well, if they were serious about your being a instructor, there would be no charge. All the teachers get additional training at no cost—it's a studio bonus that goes with the job."

Later in the week, I went out with my "fun" twosome, and Jerry and Jay patiently spelled out the facts of life to me one more time. I could tell they were getting more than a little frustrated with me. Jerry didn't teach at Veloz and Yolanda, but he had been an instructor at Arthur Murray's in Seattle— in fact, that's where he and Jay had become close friends—and he knew the pitch all the studios used to hold onto paying customers.

Jerry turned to Jay and said, "I don't know if you know it, but Vicki's here in L.A."

"Who's Vicki?" I asked.

"My ex," Jay said, uncomfortably.

"Oh," I said, feeling just as uncomfortable.

Jay looked annoyed at Jerry and asked him bluntly why he'd brought Vicki's name up.

"Well, she's in town. She's broke. She needs a job. She's a dance instructor. Why don't we suggest she go to Veloz and Yolanda and see if there's an opening!"

I could tell Jay still had a soft spot for Vicki because he said, "That's not fair, Jerry. We're using her. She'll get all excited and think she's got a job when we know there are no openings."

"We do?" Jerry said, raising an eyebrow. "Well, one way or the other, we'll find out if that's true." Then he added, "We either use Vicki, or Veloz and Yolanda use Pam. What do you say?"

Jay grudgingly told Jerry to go ahead and tell Vicki about the job, and a few days later, to my utter chagrin, I learned she was teaching at the studio!

I felt about two inches tall, hurt, and angry.

∽

It was then I decided I needed to get away for the weekend. Get well away and take a really serious look at where my life was heading. I called Mother and asked her if I could come and visit her in Las Vegas.

"Of course," she said happily. "I was wondering when you'd wake up to the fact that this place is fabulous, and designed for weekend getaways!"

It had to be the most unpretentious dude ranch I'd ever seen, not that I'd seen many dude ranches since hitting the States. Maybe they kept it low-key so that their illustrious guests could have complete privacy. Whatever the reason, if you didn't know it was there, you'd never find it. The entrance, a tall, rustic archway with a small Bar-W burned on the cross-beam, was close to McCarren Field, which, at that time, handled both commercial and general aviation. Except for a few cleared acres around the Gunnersons' home, Mother's home and office, the guest cabins, pool, clubhouse, and chuck wagon—as they called the dining room—the rest of the acreage, which ran all the way to downtown Las Vegas, was typical desert, with scrub and cactus, coyotes and jackrabbits. According to Mother, in the evening when John Gunnerson was hosting, he'd get into his trusty Jeep and go spotlighting, bucking and bouncing across the desert, scaring up all types of strange wildlife to the amazement of his citified guests.

The weekend I spent there was quiet, even the Gunnersons weren't around, and I completely unwound, swimming in the pool or lolling on an air mattress with a tall, cool drink. As the pool was surrounded by cottonwoods, when I wanted to sunbathe, I climbed up on the flat roof of the chuck wagon, and peeled down to my next-to-nothings; it was a perfect private spot for getting a complete tan. At least it was for the first day, but when I climbed up on the roof Sunday morning to complete my tan, a flight of private planes took off from McCarren Field and began showing off like barnstormers, swooping and rolling and dipping their wings—I got the message fast, draped my shape, and took off for the shady seclusion of the cottonwoods.

The evening before, Mother had asked if I wanted to go to town and hit the tables. I nixed it as I really didn't enjoy gambling, and we spent a fun evening reminiscing. I think we must've touched on everything since the day I was born. When we were through—at least I thought we were through—I looked at Mother and could tell she still had something on her mind.

"What's up, Mumsy? Looks like you're wondering if you should tell me something."

She looked at me with a wistful smile and told me an almost unbelievable story of chance, in a city famous for it.

It appears she recently bumped into the Burtons. Beryl and Jim Burton had been very close friends of Mother and Dad in China back "in the good old days," and they'd come to Las Vegas to see if they wanted to retire there.

"Our chance meeting is so unbelievable when you think of the turmoil in the world today, and how all our friends are scattered to the four winds," Mother said, adding, "If I'd been a few minutes earlier … or later; if I'd been in the store, instead of just entering it; if Jim and Beryl hadn't stepped out of their taxi just at that moment, we would never have met! Such exquisite timing has to have a divine hand in it."

It was obvious the Burtons felt the same way, as they'd been trying to find Mother for several years. They had a message for her from Dad—his last words—and they felt honor-bound to deliver them personally.

When Mother learned they'd been sitting by his bedside in Tientsin when he passed away, she was stunned. She wanted to hear what they had to say, but guilt engulfed her; she'd not been with him when he died, as she had promised she would.

Beryl must've seen her agony, because she said, "Gee, believe me, George was at peace when he died. I can't remember his exact words, but I'll do the best I can. He said, 'Please tell Gee I love her, and that I'm not afraid any more. Tell her Mother and Dad and Rose are here to take me home. And please ask Margo to forgive me. I'm terribly sorry for all I did to her—I'd do anything to undo it.' I don't know why it meant so much to him for Margo to forgive him, or who Rose was," Beryl continued, "but, of course, we knew his mother and father, they were such good people. He was actually smiling when his hand slipped out of mine."

As silent tears crept down Mother's cheeks, she said she had told Beryl that Rose was Dad's favorite older sister, and that she'd been killed in the London Blitz. She didn't mention if she'd explained to Beryl about the feud between Dad and Margo. Actually, the feud was all on Dad's part; Margo would have done anything to have him acknowledge she was his stepdaughter by marriage, but he couldn't get over the fact that Mother had loved someone before him, and he took out his jealous wrath on Margo every time he could.

I thought back to the short, harrowing cable from China telling of Dad's death; of Wil Pryor's letter about his funeral; of his ashes scattered on the Gulf of Chihli; of Mother's ongoing nightmare with the London solicitors; and the final, sad, miserly pittance that she received from his carefully saved retirement fund. Everything had been heartbreaking and negative. And now, almost miraculously, she had a beautiful, positive message from Dad through long-lost friends whom we'd almost forgotten in our day-to-day fight for existence.

Dad had always been a tortured soul, steeped in fears that only the truly sensitive can feel. He hated war, and had been deeply scarred by the two World Wars he'd lived through. He loved art, music, and poetry, but most of all, he loved Mother. He openly admitted that it was her strength he drew on when his own seemed to fail him. When Mother died, forty years later, I found a neatly folded slip of paper in her wallet, the words on it faded by time. It was the closing lines of his last letter to her—*my dear sympathetic, understanding lover. Always your own G who adores you.* And I knew then that she had loved him as totally as he had loved her.

"You're right, Mumsy," I said, "there's no way on earth that was a chance meeting with the Burtons, it had to be the hand of God." Then I looked at her and realized that by telling me about it, the last vestiges of guilt she'd been carrying around since Dad's death had been lifted from her shoulders.

Several nights later, when I was back in my dinky little apartment, I had the strangest dream. It was so vivid, I could paint a picture of it to this day. I was in Montmartre in Paris. I'd never been there. I only knew it through Dad's wonderful little sketches, some in black and white, some with color washes, and some in colored pencil. I was walking down the shady side of a narrow street, flowers tumbled from window boxes, and sunlight burst through alleyways warming patches along my way. I looked over to the sunny side of the street, trying to make up my mind whether to cross over, when I saw a man enjoying the warmth, walking slower than I was, but slightly ahead of me, and in the same direction. Although I could only see his back, he looked so familiar, I kept wondering where I'd seen him before.

He was wearing grey slacks, a tweed jacket with leather patches on the elbows, and a dark green porkpie hat with a feather in the band. I couldn't stand the suspense, and hurried to pass him so I could look back and see his face. He stopped to look in a bakery window, and when he started up again, I glanced over my right shoulder and looked him straight in the eye. It was Dad! He saw me, smiled, and waved.

Startled, I woke thinking, *"Of course Dad's in Paris. Paris was always heaven to him."*

∼

The weekend away had done worlds for me. Not that things were much better, but they were definitely in better perspective. I didn't feel overwhelmed anymore, even when I found out that while I was away, Vicki had got in touch with Jay. I learned about it on Monday, when Jay called me and asked if there was any way I could get Vicki a modeling job at Vyola's.

"I thought she was teaching at Veloz and Yolanda," I said tersely.

"She is, but being the latest hire, she's not getting many hours. She's so in debt, she's got to get extra work to pay off her bills."

I wasn't too enthusiastic about it, but said I'd see what I could do, and wrote down her phone number. That evening, working with Vy, I asked if she might need another model.

"Timing's perfect," she said with a smile. "Alyssa Tomlin is pregnant, and it's just beginning to show. What's this Vicki look like?"

"Haven't the foggiest. Didn't know she existed until last week. She's Jay's ex. I believe she's a blonde, that's all I know." Then I told Vy how Jerry had lined her up with a teaching job at Veloz and Yolanda, adding it didn't pay enough to keep her afloat. I didn't mention she was deep in debt.

"I thought you said Veloz and Yolanda didn't have any openings?" Vy said.

"Well, now we know that was a lie," I said, ruefully. "Of course you know the reason … it's these great clothes you've made me. According to Jay, they think I'm filthy rich, that I don't need the job, and that I'm good for many more expensive hours of instruction."

"What are you doing about it?" the ever-practical Vy asked.

"I'll give 'em a bit more time to come through. Meanwhile I'm getting my ducks lined up in the event I have to sue. I hate the idea, but the way I look at it, they're taking me to the cleaners, and I don't like it."

"Atta girl! Go for it!"

Through the weeks that followed, Jerry slowly slipped

out of the picture, and Jay was my steady date most evenings when he wasn't at the studio. Friday and Saturday nights were our special times. That's when Jay donned his beautifully cut Louis Roth suits, and I wore my extravagant wardrobe, and we did the Strip. Our favorite haunts were Ciro's and the Mocambo, mostly because they had dance floors almost large enough to dance on.

Benny, the head waiter at the Mocambo, took a special interest in us. I noticed after the first drink we never paid for another, but there was always a fresh one at our table when we came back from the dance floor. Benny would always smile and say, "Compliments of the house," or he'd point to another table, and we'd bow to them, and hold up our drinks in a silent toast. Quite often, between shows, we'd find we were the only couple dancing, and Jay, having been a professional dancer for years, just took it in stride. I didn't. I was a nervous wreck, hoping I wouldn't let him down. I shouldn't have worried, as he had a way of making a girl look great on the floor regardless of her footwork. I guess the applause we got when we stepped off the floor should have told me all went well, but I still got butterflies every time I found we were doing a solo.

It was during one of these dreamy evenings that this career girl, who wanted nothing but a successful future in the business world, found she'd gotten engaged. Somehow, it just seemed right.

Jay was my complete opposite. He didn't like confrontations of any kind, and I reveled in them. He accepted the world and what it tossed at him. I didn't, I always tried to change it, spin it around on its heels to see what dropped out of its pockets. One thing we did have in common—neither of us was afraid of work. We thrived on it.

There was something about him that always intrigued me:

a "lost little boy" something. His early life was nothing like mine. I never realized how privileged mine had been, except in the broad way all Westerners were considered privileged in the Orient, but compared to what Jay had lived through, I would have been considered a spoiled little rich girl. Although we lost just about everything in the war, I came out of it still believing I could accomplish anything I set my heart on. Jay, ten years my senior, didn't; he was full of doubts. Actually, he was what I needed to bring me down to earth, to make me realize I couldn't pick and choose what I would or wouldn't do. But none of these differences raised its head when we first were engaged. Our love was a deep response to a need for each other, and it was sweet and exhilarating at the same time.

I remember him laughing outright when he realized Jerry would have to be told of our engagement.

"S-o-o-o ... ?" I queried.

"Want to make book?"

"On what?"

"Well, everything I've done, Jerry has followed suit. Dancing, golf, tennis, you name it. Bet you that when he hears we're engaged, he'll go and do likewise!"

"You're nuts, you know," I said with a laugh.

"No, I'm not. Jerry not only has to copy me, he has to outdo me. I just enjoy his company, he enjoys trying to beat me at every turn. If he only knew I couldn't care less, I think he would be devastated."

It hadn't taken me long to realize Jay was a natural-born athlete. He excelled in anything physical. He became a powerful swimmer by training against the flow in the Detroit River, and helped pay his way in college by teaching swimming and becoming a lifeguard. I also learned he played serious ice hockey and football, and only gave the latter up when he had a couple of bad injuries. I thought Jerry was athletic, too, and in a way he was, only where Jay was a natural, Jerry had to work at it.

"Have you noticed that when Jerry and I get together on a weekend and I suggest that we go play some tennis or golf, he always defers it to some time later in the week?"

"Well, he probably doesn't feel like playing just because you do. What's wrong with that?"

"That's not the reason. It's so he can go out on Monday, Tuesday, and Wednesday evening and practice with a pro."

"You're kidding?"

He chuckled. "No, I'm not. For Jerry, winning is everything."

Jay was almost right.

I say that because when Jerry learned of our engagement, he didn't do what Jay thought he'd do; instead, he called me up and asked me for a date.

"Jerry, didn't you hear that Jay and I were engaged?" I said, wondering where the sam hill he was coming from.

"Yes, but that's not the end of the world."

"No, but it's a wonderful beginning, and you're out of line."

"Well!" he exclaimed, his nose obviously out of joint.

"Hey, I know girls find you irresistible, Jerry, but I don't. Let's pretend you never said anything." And I let it die right there.

A couple of weeks later Jay was gloating, "What did I tell you? Jerry's engaged!"

"Who's the lucky girl?" I asked.

"Sarah Lowenthal. Think she's a senior at USC, or something." Then he added, "According to Jerry, she comes from an orthodox Jewish family. Very straightlaced."

"That should be interesting," I said, wondering how this *bon vivant* playboy was going to like settling down.

~

A week or so later, Jay and I decided to enjoy a Sunday on the beach at Malibu. He said he'd come by bright and early, we'd pick up a picnic lunch along the way, and spend the day doing absolutely nothing. It sounded like a day made in heaven.

That morning, I woke around six to a loud pounding on my door. *That doesn't sound like Jay,* I thought sleepily. The pounding got louder and more insistent. When I put on my robe and stumbled to the door, I found it was the police with Jay in tow, looking totally bewildered and frustrated.

"Who is this man?" one of the officers demanded.

"He's my fiancé," I said. "He's picking me up to go to the beach for the day."

"Really? What's his full name and address?"

I gave it to them, and now Jay and I were both bewildered.

Slowly shaking his head from side to side, the officer said, "Don't you know why we're here?"

"Haven't the foggiest," I said, still half asleep.

"This is a *raid,*" he said, emphasizing the last word. "We're rounding up all the gals and their johns! This is one of the most famous bordellos in the Beverly Hills area. Don't you know that?!" He sounded incredulous.

I guess he must've seen the dumb look on both our faces, as a great, big grin spread over his, and he said, *"Get out of here now!* Come on guys, help her pack. You too, fiancé. We'll hold up the raid till you're out of here."

Running back and forth, they pitched all my clothes, books, and paraphernalia into Jay's open Packard convertible, and we took off like a rocket to the moon!

Of course, we didn't spend a lovely day on the beach, we

spent it looking for a new apartment, and I finally lucked out with a new, clean, spartan place out in Fox Hills.

While we'd been driving around, the Murphy bed fiasco came to mind, and I said laughingly, "No wonder Mr. Hollywood Big Shot lit up like a Christmas tree when I gave him my address!"

"What are you talking about?" Jay asked.

"Oh, nothing," I said quickly, remembering I hadn't told him about that wild incident, as I'd wisely decided he might not see the humor in it.

∼

When I wrote Mother about our engagement, she took off running. She was so well-liked at the ranch, the Gunnersons had introduced her to everyone of consequence in Las Vegas, and she had made so many friends on her own, that she immediately planned a gala affair.

Oh, boy, I thought, this I don't need.

I was still mulling over how I could get her to keep it simple when I arrived at Vy's for our Saturday morning sketch session. My mind was a million miles away, and I was completely out of sync when I saw this stunning blonde angel slipping into one of Vy's latest creations. She was a total knockout, and I stopped dead in my tracks, thinking, *Ye gods,* this *is my competition?!*

I guess Vyola saw the weird look on my face because she said quickly, "Pam, this is Vicki. Vicki, this is Pam." Then she added, "We're going to sketch the dresses today while Vicki models them. We'll be able to get a wonderful feel for the drape."

Vicki smiled, and put out her hand. "Pam, I want to thank you for lining me up with Vyola. Isn't she a gem?"

"Yes, she is, and a really great friend, too," I said, not quite knowing how to assess this latest dimension to my life.

When we broke for lunch, Vy let out that Jay and I were engaged, and a change suddenly came over Vicki. She stopped with a forkful of salad to her mouth, and said, "Good *luck!*"

I didn't quite know how to take it. Was it a warning, or sour grapes? Or was she planning some little surprise? But through the rest of the lunch she never lost her sweet expression.

I wish I could believe she's as angelic as she looks ...

That evening I asked Jay when his divorce would be final.

"Vicki says it was final last week, on November 10," he said.

"How could that be?" I asked. "Did you sign any papers?"

"Didn't have to. Vicki said she divorced me by default."

"So, it *is* final?" I persisted.

"According to Vicki."

During lunch on Monday, I walked down to the Hall of Records and asked to see the final decrees for November 10. The clerk was very helpful, and showed me the list for that date. There was no Jay or Vicki Masters listed. I didn't like the feeling I was getting. I asked the clerk if it was not listed, how would I find out its status.

"Do you know when it was filed?" she asked.

"No."

"That's okay, I can go through the alphabetical records. It might take a while." It took more than a "while," and my lunch break was running on overtime when she finally pulled up the information. There it was in black and white: the divorce was still pending!

I thanked her profusely, went back to the office, and stewed for the rest of the afternoon. The last thing I wanted to do was be a bitch, but Vicki had lied, dammit! What was her game? Did she want to let us get married and then throw a bigamy charge on Jay?

Stop being so dramatic, Pamela, it was just an innocent oversight.

But my musings wouldn't stop there, they kept consuming me. *You know damn well there's nothing innocent about that lady! She's as transparent as a martini!*

I was still stewing when Jay came over that evening.

"Your divorce is not final!" I blurted out before he got through the door.

"You're wrong! Vicki says it is."

"Well, I spent my lunch hour at the Hall of Records and it's still open on the books!"

"You don't like her, do you?" he said, changing the subject, and making it sound like it was all my fault.

"I don't like being lied to," I said, sidestepping his query.

"I'll call her tomorrow."

"Call her now!" I said, steering him to the phone.

When he hung up, he said, "She said it wasn't her fault. Her attorney told her it was final. She'll see him tomorrow and take care of it."

And I'll go back down to the Hall of Records in a couple of days to be sure she does ...

Chapter 11

This time, when I went to the Hall of Records, I didn't need the help of the records clerk, I pulled up the final decrees for the previous week, and found the entry with no problem.

Well, at least I'm not engaged to a married man! I said under my breath.

Back at my gypsum job, things were coming to a head, and I knew I must leave or go bonkers. I also knew my freelance accounts couldn't keep me afloat. Nothing had materialized at Veloz and Yolanda, and with the wisdom of hindsight, I realized even if it did, as a new hire, I'd barely make enough hours to get by. So much for the headline in the *L.A. Times* ad, "Enjoy the Fabulous Life of a Dance Instructor." On top of that, the nice new little apartment in Fox Hills wasn't working out as it required several bus transfers to get to work and to my accounts. And Jay was complaining that his commute to Woodland Hills in the San Fernando Valley was a pain in the butt. Something had to be done. But what?

It was Jay who came up with the solution.

"Let's get married!"

"We can't. What about the gala wedding Mother's planning?"

"She doesn't need to know about it. If she insists on the big wedding, we'll go through with it … what the heck!"

He really made sense, so we went to Santa Monica, applied for a marriage license, got our blood tests, and started the ball rolling.

Kitty-corner from the Hollywood Towers, where we'd lived before Ursula's wedding, was a pretty little nondenominational church called the Church Around the Corner. I went there early in the week and asked Pastor Babbit if he could marry us the following Saturday evening.

"I've got a very big wedding scheduled for Saturday at seven o'clock, but if you come at six sharp, I'll be happy to marry you."

Lucille, a Catholic, was my maid of honor, and Jerry, an un-Orthodox Jew, was Jay's best man. Talk about an ecumenical wedding!

When we got to the church it was spectacular. I'd never seen such decorations. It was all done up in white, with giant bows at the end of each of the light oak pews, white gladioli and chrysanthemums on the altar, and tall white tapers everywhere. I had the feeling that the reverend lit the tapers just for us, and their glow was magical. Everything was perfect, especially the service. Pastor Babbit spoke from the heart, never once referring to notes or the Bible, not even when he quoted from Corinthians 1:13.

When it was over, I cried. I wished all my family had been there to witness it. I cried for what they had missed, and I cried for what I had received. I know Jay felt as I did: this marriage would be one for the books.

In our excitement, none of us had remembered to bring a camera, but even without pictures, I knew December 17, 1949, would always be a beautiful memory.

Jerry had made arrangements at an Italian restaurant in West Los Angeles for our wedding supper, and it turned out a wonderful choice. When the little orchestra played *The Anniversary Waltz,* and Jay and I stepped out onto the crowded floor, my cup was brimming over. When the number was over we received a standing ovation, and I never knew if it was because Jay and I were the only couple left on the floor, or because the other patrons had been told it was our wedding night!

As we came back to our table, Jerry offered a toast. "To Pam and Jay, may you have a long and happy life together." Then he winked at us and said, "If you two ever get together—and I don't mean in bed, but in business—*look out world!"*

Now, as I look back, I feel a little tinge of regret, because the only time we ever worked together no one knew we were a team ...

~

Earlier, when Mother had insisted I spend Christmas at the ranch, I told her that would be great. I asked her how many would be there, and she said just the Gunnersons, a Mrs. McCall, who was there for the umpteenth time, and her son Greg, a Pan Am pilot. *And now,* I thought, *you'll get to meet my Jay ...*

I'd told Lucille about it back in November when Mumsy invited me, and said I'd get a little gift for each of the guests to put under the tree.

"That's going to run into money," Lucy said. "These people are loaded, and you can't give them some little trinket from the five-and-dime."

"So, I'll get a Broadway credit card," I said with a shrug. Credit cards were coming into their own that year.

"Can I use it too?" she asked.

"You bet!"

To no one's surprise, the Broadway was happy to extend me credit, and it didn't take long for me to run up a formidable tab. My problem was, I didn't tally up the sales receipts as I made my purchases, and it wasn't until Christmas was over, and I got my first statement, that I was almost blown out of the water. I found the simple, elegant little gifts I bought came to over three hundred dollars; Lucille didn't fare much better. The total we both owed stood at around six hundred—which would be the equivalent of six thousand dollars today. It took me ten months at thirty-plus dollars a month, along with Lucille's contribution, to pay off the balance. Needless to say, I canceled the credit card the minute the debt was cleared.

Christmas Day fell on Sunday that year, and when Jay and I rolled up to the Bar-W on Christmas Eve, the festivities were well underway. Of course Mother, not knowing we were married, had Jay in a guest cottage and me staying with her. Jay and I had a quiet chuckle over it, but I still decided not to tell her, as I didn't know how far the wedding plans had progressed, and if she could cancel them or not, and I felt Christmas was not the time to discuss it.

I could see now why Mother had such a soft spot for the Gunner-sons. They were good people, both tall and lean, with strong features and an air of complete assurance. Karen had an extra bonus; along with her striking good looks, she had flaming red hair that made her stand out in any crowd. Bridie McCall was a little charmer, and her son Greg *thought* he was. Maybe I should have held him in a little more esteem as he was a Pan Am pilot, currently on the San Francisco to Orient run, but he'd already cornered the market on self-importance, so any adulation on my part would have added nothing. Still, he was a lot of fun when the three of us piled into the Packard and did the rounds of the casinos that first night.

Our first stop was at a craps table, and I watched the play but couldn't figure out what the heck was going on. I didn't notice when Jay and Greg moved off to some other table, and when I was handed the dice, I started to roll. I kept watching the excitement build and still couldn't figure out why. Every time I rolled someone would count, *nine ... ten ... eleven,* and then it got to *sixteen ... seventeen ... eighteen,* and they were screaming and placing bets, but I still couldn't figure out what all the excitement was about. I rolled again, and someone sang out, *nineteen ... then twenty ... twenty-one,* and Then I heard a groan and everyone started to leave the table. I looked around to ask Jay what had happened, and noticed he'd left.

When I found them playing blackjack, I told them about the craps table, and Greg said incredulously, "Good Lord, the house record is twenty-three passes!"

I didn't know what he was talking about, and asked wistfully, "Could I have made some money?"

"Oh, *yeah!*" he said, his eyebrows shooting up into his hairline. "Hey, Jay, from here on out we stick to this lady like glue."

It was too late; whatever spell I might have had on the craps table didn't follow me through the rest of the evening.

~

Christmas Day was like no other I'd ever spent. And the dinner, prepared by Mother with help from Karen and me, was special. Mother had asked Karen if it would be okay to serve a traditional English plum pudding with hard sauce in lieu of pumpkin or apple pie. Karen said she'd love it. But I don't think anyone was prepared for the extravaganza Mother brought in on a silver platter, soaked in brandy and rum, and flaming like a baked alaska. John jumped
up to help serve, and the great dollops of hard sauce melted like spring snow when they hit the sizzling pudding.

I know Mother must have made it at least a couple of

months earlier, she always did, then kept bringing it down from the shelf and pouring more booze over it. I don't know why they call it a plum pudding, because it's more like a steamed Christmas cake, with nuts and candied fruits of all kinds—raisins, currants, sultanas, chopped dates, and if there's any room left, maybe a few plums.

After dinner we all sat around the tree and opened gifts. It was as though we'd known each other for years. Just when we felt like calling it a night, John said it was time to go spotlighting, and to wish all the little desert critters a merry Christmas. So that's what we did. I was the only girl in the party, and I found it was loads of fun, the bouncing Jeep becoming a wonderful way to jog down my big dinner!

∼

We drove home on Monday and got a ticket in the desert. The road was in disgraceful condition, with deep fissures running across it from right to left, and left to right, turning it into an hairy obstacle course. As there wasn't any other traffic on the road, Jay swerved back and forth to try to miss most of them. Unknown to us, a California Highway Patrol car was hiding behind one of the numerous billboards luring the drivers to Las Vegas, and before we knew it, lights were flashing, sirens were blaring, and we were pulled over. The CHP officer cited us for erratic and hazardous driving in heavy traffic! It took him over fifteen minutes to write up the ticket, and only one car passed us in all that time, heading to Vegas. He was also rude and insulting, especially after I read the citation and asked him how he could justify what he'd written. When a smirk crossed his face I realized that was a dumb question. If we took it to court, we'd have no witnesses, and it would be his word again Jay's—my word wouldn't count, since I was

Jay's wife. He knew he'd won, and he strutted back to his patrol car and gave us a mocking salute.

I looked at the yellow copy of the ticket he'd handed us, and saw his name and badge number. *Well, officer, you'll be hearing from me ...*

∼

Furious and frustrated at the unjust ticket, and just plain exhausted from the long weekend, it didn't take much for us to fall asleep in my tiny little apartment in Fox Hills.

It must have been around two o'clock when the phone rang shrilly, cutting through my dreamless slumber. Jay, unthinking, reached for it and said a groggy, "Hello?" There was a long pause, and then he said, "Just a minute, you need Pam," and handed me the phone with the weirdest expression on his face.

It was Mother. *Ye gods!* I thought as I heard her voice.

"What's Jay doing there at this ungodly hour?" she hissed.

"It's okay, Mumsy. We're married," I said. "Have been since the seventeenth."

"And you never told me? You never *told* me!" Her voice was rising in her anger.

"Couldn't during Christmas, as I didn't want to spoil the fun," I said lamely.

"When were you going to do it?" she said, obviously trying to get control of herself.

"That's moot now, isn't it?" I replied. Then, trying to end the uncomfortable silence that followed, I asked, "Mumsy, why did you call? Is it Grandma?"

"Yes, Donald called to say she's had a massive stroke, and is in a Burbank hospital. Could you go and see her right away, and let me know how bad it is?" She gave me the name of the hospital and the address.

"Sure. We'll get dressed and go right away. Will get back to you as soon as we can."

Grandma had survived the stroke. She was more twisted and tinier than ever, but her strong little heart was still beating, and I got the feeling she'd recover and be around for many years to come. I called Mother and gave her the news.

"Where are you calling from?" she asked.

"The hospital."

"Is Donald there?"

"No, I haven't seen him."

"Please call him and tell him I'm on my way."

What followed was heartbreaking. It was as though Grandma was not Donald's mother. There was no concern in his demeanor, and I could see he expected Mother, as the only daughter in the family, to handle everything.

Karen and John Gunnerson kept calling to find out how Mother was holding up, and how Grandma was doing. I told them that she was looking for a nursing home for her mother, and could feel their concern was as much for Mother as for the great job she was doing at the Bar-W. They didn't want to lose her, and I couldn't blame them.

I was with Mother when she made the fateful decision to quit the Bar-W and stay and take care of Grandma. It was the result of many little things, not the least of which was Donald's attitude toward his mother and Marian's refusing to have anything to do with her, coupled with the fact that the expense of a full-time nursing home was entirely beyond the scope of Mother's limited finances.

"Donald, when you sold Mother's home in '43, what did you get for it?" she asked.

The figure he told her was ridiculous considering wartime prices and the need for homes.

"For God's sake, why? It was a three-bedroom home, sitting on a fenced half-acre of land! You could've gotten twice that amount and you wouldn't have been out of line."

"I needed the money."

"For what?"

"To pay off our place on Victory," he said angrily, as though it were none of Mother's business.

"What happened to *my* half of that money?" she asked.

"What do you mean, *your* half? Hell, you were in a Japanese prison camp—no one gets out of them alive!" I could see Mother spinning from his callous remark.

"I'm sorry I disappointed you by surviving," she said quietly. Turning to me, she said, "Come on, Pam, let's go."

As we climbed into the car, I couldn't help remembering her remark after Dad's death, when his demented sister had tried to get her hands on his retirement fund. Mother had said "that would never happen with the Henderson side of the family, I guarantee you!" and now I could feel her shock and disbelief.

To handle the situation, Mother ended up wiping out the last of her tiny bank account and buying a lovely little log home up in Idyllwild in the San Jacinto Mountains. It was obvious she wanted to be as far away from Donald as possible.

Somehow, it all came together. She took Grandma up in that lovely clear air, and Mrs. McCall came aboard too, as a paying guest. And, with that money, plus Grandma's tiny pittance from the London school board, and also her allotment as a Spanish-American War widow, Mother was able to run a beautiful home. To this day, I don't know how she did it.

∼

When things settled down a bit, the first thing Jay and I did was find a new, larger apartment. It was back on good old

North Beachwood Drive in the Hollywood Hills. We found a nice furnished place with one bedroom, a kitchen I could actually work in, and a neat little dinette. The only problem with it was the Packard had to sit out on the street, and I know Jay fretted about that, as it's almost impossible to lock up a convertible and make it secure. But nothing could spoil my optimism, as I was going to start my new job the first of the week. Jay was the only one who knew I'd quit US Gypsum. I did it just before we left for Vegas.

When I was in the Architects Building, I'd walk a short block to the huge Los Angeles Public Library on my lunch hour, and do research on design that spanned the ages. It was then that I'd look across at the imposing Southern California Edison building on the corner of Fifth and Grand, and say quietly to myself, *I'm going to work there someday.* So it was no surprise to me when I left the gypsum job that I found myself walking up the street to the Edison Company. The inside of the building was even more impressive than the outside, with marble columns, walls, and floors that echoed with every footstep I made. Striding into the vaulted lobby, I took a sharp turn to my right, walked boldly into the Commercial Sales department, and asked for a job. It was like it was preordained ... that they'd been waiting for me. I was hired on the spot.

I've always loved good omens.

I learned that Southern California Edison supplied power all the way up from the outskirts of San Diego in the south to Visalia and Hanford in the north, in the heart of the San Joaquin Valley. The city of Los Angeles was not in their territory; it came under the umbrella of the Department of Water and Power, a non-taxpaying public utility. I soon learned why the city's rates were so much lower than Edison's; apart from not having to pay the millions of dollars in taxes that private utilities have to pay, if the Department of Water and Power's revenues didn't cover their expenses, they could always dip into city taxes to make up the shortfall. I don't know if that's the situation today, but when I started in Edison's Commercial Sales department, and customers would come in furious about our rates, I'd carefully explain to them that they were paying a just rate approved by the Public Utilities Commission, and point out that if city dwellers added part of their local taxes to their electric bill they'd be coming out much closer to the actual cost of city power. I always enjoyed seeing the look of comprehension dawn in their eyes.

I never forget the dear little old lady who came in to ask what it cost to run an electric clock because her landlord had just jacked up her rent five bucks to cover the expense. Again, five dollars was the equivalent of fifty dollars today. I told her it cost two cents a month to run an electric clock, and she just about flipped out.

"Could you put that in writing?" she asked.

"Sure," I said, giving her my friendliest smile. "I'll do even better than that. Here is our standard breakdown on the monthly cost of running every electric appliance in your home. Tell your landlord he's got to come up with a better excuse for raising your rent."

She snatched the brochure from me and said, "Thank you, honey, thank you!"

I guess I'd been at Edison for about a year when they ran a feature story on me in their employee newsletter. I wish I'd kept a copy of it, as it was really quite good. It had some bad aftershocks, though. Ray Waltham, one of the top managers in Commercial Sales, came in and thanked me for breaking up his marriage.

"I did *what* to your marriage?" I asked, dumbfounded.

"My wife is a very jealous person, and she's absolutely furious. You see, I was in the Marine Corps in Tientsin right after the war—although we never met—and I always told her not to worry about me with other women because there were only gooks in China. When she saw that article and your picture, she said you sure didn't look like a gook to her. I mean she exploded, saying 'Sonofabitch! There you go, lying to me again!'"

I shrugged and started to chuckle. "Sorry," I said, "I don't think there's anything I can say to her now that'll help matters much."

"Oh, God, no! Stay out of it!" he said, vehemently, adding, "I only hope she doesn't meet you at some company function—she's liable to deck you!"

"It sounds like you lead a very interesting home life," I said, smiling, recalling his reputation at work for being a hard-nosed bully and always getting his way. Guess he was making up for being browbeaten at home.

My immediate boss at Edison was John Addison. He had a managerial job, the definition of which I found hard to define. I only knew that, if there was a lousy detail no one else wanted to handle, it was always palmed off on him. I don't know if he realized he was being used; he was such a simple, uncomplicated man, he probably felt flattered that they thought of him. I know he'd been with Edison for years and years and loved working for the company.

Although all the bigwigs in Commercial Sales always went over to the Jonathan Club or some other equally distinguished place for lunch, John Addison either ate in the employee cafeteria, or brown bagged it in his office. Quite often, when he brought his lunch, I'd go in and visit with him. He was like a father to me, and I enjoyed his quiet, thoughtful ways. He had one idiosyncrasy: he was so afraid of germs that every day, before the phones started ringing, I would have to go into his office and wipe them off with alcohol so that any bugs that landed on them the day before, or through the night, would not contaminate him during the day. He had a family he dearly loved, and never got tired of talking about them, where they were, and what they were doing. He was the personification of a family man.

I remember when his twenty-fifth anniversary with Edison came around and the men in Commercial Sales decided to throw him a big bash at the Jonathan Club. It was to be a surprise luncheon, and I was told not to let on to him in any way.

When the great day arrived, I noticed his office door was shut and thought nothing of it. He was so fastidious, he always closed it when he wasn't there. I was sitting at my desk out in the bull-pen, thinking how proud and happy he must be to be finally enjoying the company of all his peers and, more than likely, receiving an elegant gold watch for his years of service to the company, when suddenly Ray Waltham burst into the sales department. I gave him a strange, startled look, but he didn't stop, he rushed right past me to Addison's office, threw open the door and said jocularly, "Ah, there you are! Come with me." Then he rushed out of the building with Addison in tow.

I learned later that the "good old boys" had gotten all the way to dessert and were preparing to say a few well-chosen words in honor of John Addison when someone noticed the honoree was not at the party!

When they finally came back to the office around three-thirty, slapping John Addison on the back and telling him what a great guy he was, I saw the look on his face and almost cried. When he could, he broke away, and slipped into his office. The door was shut once more, and I knew better than to go in. He was never the same after that, although he was always kind to me.

A month or so later, when an opening came up in Kitchen Planning, a promotional arm of Commercial Sales, he put my name forward and I got the job.

I gave him a hug and said, "Mr. Addison, you're a gem!"

His eyes misted over, and he said, "I'm going to miss you, gal."

A year later he died of pancreatic cancer.

∽

Kitchen Planning turned into my dream job.

The girl who'd had it before me did beautiful work—when she wasn't busy elsewhere. Elsewhere turned out to be entertaining the big shots in Commercial Sales. Her little private office off the main sales area was a perfect spot to set up trysts and assignations. I found out about it when one of the gentlemen came into the office, ogling me as I was standing at my drawing board, and asked if I was going to carry on in the "Sheryl tradition." I gave him the strangest look, and he pinched me on the fanny and winked. I turned and slugged him in the gut, and told him to get the hell out of my office.

I guess word got around, because I was never bothered again, but it was enough to tell me what had been going on in Kitchen Planning before I got there.

I really lucked out in that department. The '50s was the time of the great building boom in Edison territory, especially in Orange and Pomona counties. Tract houses were springing up like Johnson weed, and our wiring specialists were all over them to see that they had adequate wiring to handle all the new appliances coming onto the market. I asked them to be sure to let the builders know of our kitchen planning services. I only had to ask once. We were swamped with plans from all over, and I found my days were so busy I didn't have time to worry about my predecessor and her so-called tradition.

The neat thing about tract homes was that I only had to design a kitchen for one of them, and it was repeated hundreds of times in a slew of look-alike models. There was only one stipulation: the kitchens had to be all-electric to get our free service, and to win the coveted Gold Medallion award. The builders loved it. So did the appliance manufacturers, who continually tried to bribe me with appliances so that I would stipulate their brand when I laid out the kitchens. To Edison's credit, we only planned the kitchens after the builders had picked out the brand of appliances they wanted to run with.

Chapter 12

Vicki was turning into a terrific, cooperative model, and I could see Vyola really liked her. She had a great flare with clothes and was available whenever Vy needed her. I hated to think I might've been wrong about her, but it looked as if I'd have to eat a lot of crow.

One Saturday morning early in February, I went into Vy's and found Vicki already there, checking out accessories and pumps to go with the dresses she'd be modeling later in the day for some out-of-town buyers. The mood was light, but I got the feeling I'd interrupted something. It didn't take long to find out what the subject was when they reverted to the interrupted conversation, and I realized they'd been talking about Jay. After a while, Vicki looked at me and said musingly, "I don't know if I should tell you this …"

"Try me," I said sharply. One, because they were discussing Jay behind my back and it made me mad. And two, because I hate it when people preface their remarks with "I don't know if I should tell you," as you know darn well they're going to anyhow.

"Well," she said with a meaningful pause, "I heard from a friend that Jay was seen at the Mocambo the other night with a luscious blonde. He was all over her. It was really something!"

I looked at her, and then at Vy, my world suddenly spinning out of control.

Vy nodded her head.

"Who told you?" I asked Vicki, trying to keep my emotions in check.

"That doesn't matter," she said, adding, "I trust her, she wouldn't make up a thing like that."

"Where does she know Jay from?" I persisted.

"The dance studio," was her prompt reply.

Vy then put in her two cents. "Pam, I've told you. You can never trust a man. Remember how Doc told me he loved me and there was never anyone else? Remember how I found out he was lying, and had been lying all the time."

I didn't say anything, but I remembered it well. Every time Vy found a really nice man she'd have him followed and find out if he was on the up-and-up. She just couldn't trust men. I also remember reminding her it was obvious Doc must have had many girlfriends before he met her, and possibly had some loose ends to tie off. She said it was nothing like that: he'd told her he was visiting his sister, and that she'd invited him over. "He must think I'm a *fool* to believe *that* one," she'd said.

"Did you check to find out if it really was his sister?"

"No. What was the point?"

"The point was he found out you'd been spying on him. How did he take it?" I asked.

"Oh, he was furious. Actually, that's when he came up with the silly sister story."

"Ever think he might be telling the truth?"

"Never!"

Needless to say, that was the last time she ever saw or heard from Doc. And he was such a neat guy. Vyola had more notches on her gun than anyone I knew, but they were all for losing her man, not getting one.

Looking at her now, it was as if she wanted me to suffer like she always did, and I decided I wasn't going to go down that road. Marriages are built on trust, and I was stubborn enough to know I wasn't about to rely on the accusations of an ex-wife with an axe to grind.

A couple of weeks later, Jay and I were at the Mocambo, and Benny asked us where we wanted to sit.

"Benny," I said with a smile, "you know there's only one booth we like."

"Yes, but the last time you were here you threw me a curve and sat over there," he said, pointing to a booth in a dark corner.

"We did? I think you're confused, Benny …"

Suddenly his face flushed a deep red, he glanced nervously at Jay and said, "Yes … yes, of course, I am confused. I mixed you up with another couple."

A little red flag went up for a moment, but then I forgot it and enjoyed the evening.

A while later when I was back at Vy's, Vicki came in, and I could see she was trying to figure out if I'd accused Jay of infidelity. She had that, *Okay, so what happened?* look on her face. The two of them had obviously not forgotten our earlier conversation and were ready to stir things up again.

Damn, I thought, *this has got to end.* I recalled Benny's remark about the booth, and a thought struck me. I looked Vicki straight in the eye and said, "Vicki, if that was *you* at the Mocambo with Jay, and you want him back, you can have him! I don't believe in divorce. Do it now, before I get into this any deeper."

I could see she was startled, as was Vy. I also knew I'd hit the bull's-eye.

"Oh, Pam, how could you?" she said, her angelic eyes moist with tears. "It wasn't me! I don't want him. Dead love is worse than cold potatoes. What I'm telling you is what I was told. You don't have to believe me if you don't want to."

I turned away and started to get out my sketch pad and pencils, and she started up again, talking to my back. "Pam, this is hard for me to say, but maybe you should break it off now. Not because of me, but because of Jay. He's a lying, two-timing sonofabitch. You'll never know where you are with him." When I turned, she still had that angelic look, but there were no tears in eyes now, only a look of deep concern for my welfare.

God, she's good; she should be an actress, not a model ...

"Let's change the subject," I said, and promptly asked, "How are things going at Veloz and Yolanda?"

"They're hiring like mad, and I'm finally getting some good hours in."

"Great," I said, and silently vowed to sue them.

∾

The following Monday, I called Edison's legal office and was put in touch with a new, young counselor named Nigel Connor, and we made an appointment for later in the afternoon.

When I arrived for the meeting, I told him what had happened, and that I wanted to sue for breach of contract.

"That's going to be tough," he said. "Dance studios have batteries of lawyers just to see they don't end up in court."

"You saying you don't want the case?"

"That depends. What have you got to fight them with? It's your word against theirs."

"Not quite," I said. "I have a letter, signed by Frank Veloz, guaranteeing me a job when I finished my instruction."

"Well," he said, his eyes lighting up, "that puts a whole different slant on things. Have you got it on you?"

"Yes, here it is," I said, fishing in my handbag, and handing it to him.

"Good Lord, doesn't he remember writing this?" Nigel asked, after reading it over carefully.

"He probably doesn't, as he was 'feeling no pain,' as my mother puts it."

"I have to be honest with you, I'm not a litigator, I'm a corporate attorney. I've never been in court and fought a case."

"Damn," I said impolitely.

"Hey, I didn't say I didn't want to. I just felt I had to tell you this isn't normally my cup of tea."

"Are you or aren't you going to take the case?" I asked, impatiently.

"I wouldn't miss it for words!"

"Do you want a retainer?" I said, hoping he'd say no, as I really didn't have anything to give him.

"No, I'll take the case on contingency. If we win, I'll take one-third in payment. If we lose, I get nothing."

"Great! Is there anything further you need from me?"

"Not now. I'll have to file. Then we'll get a response from his attorneys and go to court to get a date. It could take several months, depending on the court calendar."

When I left his office I felt good. It reminded me of the complaint I wrote to the California Highway Patrol about the officer who gave us a ticket on our way home from Las Vegas. Jay told me it was a waste of time, but I stubbornly persisted. To my surprise

I got a prompt reply, telling me that the officer had been suspended, and that measures were being taken as mine was the fifth complaint they had received in the last couple of months. They sent me a formal complaint form to fill out, which I dutifully did, giving his name and number off the ticket. I followed through a month or so later and found out that he was no longer on the force. I also learned that we were the lucky ones. Others had been pushed around by him, one of the drivers had been slugged, and two of his accusers stated he was very drunk when he stopped them.

I hope Veloz remembers me when this is over, like the CHP officer must be doing now.

∽

The confidence I felt as a businesswoman didn't follow me into my home life, especially when it came to fixing meals. As a comparatively new bride, I quickly got fed up hearing what a wonderful cook Jay's mother was. If it wasn't her piroshki, it was her pirogi, and if not that, her darn tapioca pudding, made with huge pearl tapioca. Lord, that last haunted me! Every time I made tapioca, Jay's favorite dessert, he'd say it was nice but not like his mom's. One day on my way home from work, I found some pearl tapioca in Safeway, and I bought a packet. I'd show him I could make tapioca as good as, or better than, his mom!

When I got home and read the instructions, I realized it wasn't instant tapioca, and that it took a lot of soaking and cooking before it was ready. Being the impatient type, I decided there was only one way to do it fast so that we could have it for dessert that evening ... I'd do it in the pressure cooker. Bet his mom never thought of *that!*

I got out my pressure cooker cookbook, but couldn't find a recipe for pearl tapioca, so I used the one for rice. In the place of four cups of water and two cups of rice, I put in four cups of milk and two cups of tapioca, added sugar and vanilla, sealed the lid down tight, set the gage, and when it came up to the right pressure, turned on the timer. Then I sat down happily to wait for Jay to come home.

When he came through the door, I said with a grin, "Guess what's for dessert tonight?"

"Can't."

"*Real* tapioca!" I said proudly.

"*NO! Like Mom's?*"

"Better than your mom's!" I said confidently.

And with that, there was a huge hissing explosion in the kitchen. I rushed in, and it looked like Carlsbad Caverns. Stalactites of dripping tapioca hung down from the ceiling, dripping onto counters, tables, chairs, and every item they could find. The glass cabinet doors were festooned with the gummy mess. How two cups of pearl tapioca could cover an entire kitchen was beyond me!

With a perfectly straight face, Jay said, "I don't recall Mom ever making it quite like that."

I won't tell you how long it took us to clean the bloody mess up. After several false starts, with the darn gooey stuff dripping down on us, we finally decided to scrape everything off the ceiling first, then start working downwards, ending on the floor on our hands and knees. The dual shower we took after we were through was as comic as the caper in the kitchen.

And at least Jay had the good grace not to mention his mom again …

∽

I was careful not to let Vyola know that I was suing Veloz and Yolanda, as I was afraid she might tell Vicki, and word would get to the studio. Actually, we were so busy at the salon, there was hardly room for idle chatter. Vyola and her PR girl had come up with an exciting promotion that would do as much for Vicki as it would for Vy.

They'd planned a trip across the States by rail, starting at Los Angeles, with Vicki dressed to kill in one of Vy's fabulous creations, and photographed as she was stepping aboard the train. The heading was to be something like "California Model Heads for New York." It had all been carefully orchestrated so that at each one of the major cities along the route, Vicki would step off the train in another stunning outfit and be photographed, the pictures to be used in the women's section of the different major dailies, along with ongoing copy about her high hopes of making it in New York, where it was to end with a lot of additional hoopla. It was a golden opportunity for Vicki to make the big time, and when Vy saw her off at Union Station she reminded her that both their futures were riding on her success.

When I saw Vy later she said, "God, I hope this works, I've sunk thousands into it, not counting the wardrobe."

"I hope Vicki appreciates what you're doing for her," I said, wondering deep down inside if she could carry it off.

Her first major stop was Salt Lake City, and according to Vy everything went like clockwork. The next stop was to be Denver. Vicki never got there. She just disappeared with the fabulous wardrobe worth thousands, and was never heard from again!

Although I was glad Vicki was now out of my life, I was sick for Vyola. I couldn't help remembering that I was the one who had introduced them, and I felt personally responsible for Vy's horrible loss.

That evening, remembering all Vicki's lies and subterfuge, I asked Jay outright, "Did you and Vicki go to the Mocambo early in February?"

"What brought that up?" he asked in a defensive tone.

"Well, Vicki told me she'd heard you'd been seen there with a luscious blonde. Then Benny, the head waiter, made that cryptic remark about you sitting in some other booth the last time you were there. When I asked Vicki if she was your date, she insisted she was not, and that she'd heard about it from one of the teachers at Veloz and Yolanda."

"Well, that's a lot of rot!" he said, then in a puzzled tone, "Why's it taken you so long to ask?"

I tried to make light of it, and said in a singsong voice, "Old Chinese custom. Velly patient. I wait. You tell."

"I don't know why she lied to you," he said, then added, "Yes, I was there with Vicki. It was after a teaching session one evening. She asked if we could go to the Mocambo as she had to talk to me. When we got there she blurted right out she wanted us to get back together again."

Stay calm, Pam, don't blow it …

"And then?" I asked, still trying to make light of it.

"I told her no way, I loved *you*. That's when she got really mad, cussed me out and told me that the least I could do was give her back her skis, furs, and jewelry. I told her I'd had to sell them to pay her bills. It was *not* a good evening."

"Why didn't you tell me about it?"

"What was the point?"

"The point is she's been needling me about it ever since. Telling me you were a two-timing sonofabitch, and insisting you always had been."

"I'm sorry, I didn't know she'd dragged you into it."

"Well, *are* you a two-timing sonofabitch?" I asked bluntly.

"Let's go to bed and discuss it," he said with a wicked grin.

∼

Good to his word, Nigel Connor called me a month or so later and asked if I was ready to go to court.

"Veloz and Yolanda?" I asked

"Yep. I asked them if they wanted to settle out of court, and they said, No thank you! Said they had a really strong case against you and that they'd see you in court!"

A wave of nausea swept over me, and I felt like a criminal going to the gallows.

"Wha-a-a-t do they mean, a really strong case?" I stammered.

"You tell *me!*"

"Nigel, I *have* told you. I've told you everything just as it happened. And there is nothing to refute Frank's letter promising me a job when I finished the course."

"Good! That's what I wanted to hear. Come on up to my office later today, and we'll go over the questions I'll ask you. They will be simple and to the point."

Basically, when we went over the testimony I would give in court. Nigel asked me my name, address, the type of course I'd signed up for with the dance studio, when I started, how the instructors rated me, and if I'd received any guarantees that I'd get a job when I was through.

"Our only witness will be Frank Veloz. I will ask him to verify the letter and his signature. I told Judge Cole we should be in and out within thirty minutes. That's how I was able to get the case on the expedited calendar."

"When do we go to court?" I asked.

"Next Tuesday, ten sharp. I'll meet you in your office at nine-fifteen, and we'll walk to the court house. It's close, and that's easier than trying to find parking around the civic center."

On the fateful day, after a sleepless night, I found myself walking beside Nigel, who was noticeably nervous. I put it down to courtroom jitters, and the fact he'd never tried a case before, and attempted to make a little small talk. He relaxed a bit, then said, "By the way, you might be interested—I called the *Times, Mirror,* and several of the outlying papers and told them we were suing Frank Veloz for breach of contract and that they might find it a very interesting case."

"Ye gods, you didn't?!"

"Why not? Little girl fights big Goliath. It's always good for a human interest story."

As we started up the courthouse steps, I saw Frank Veloz surrounded by a phalanx of attorneys.

"Oh, Lord! It's really happening, isn't it?"

"Yes, and if I'm not mistaken, those men going up to Frank now are the Fourth Estate, the press," Nigel said smugly.

I watched as one of them held up his camera, and there was a flash. One of Frank's attorneys strong-armed him, and I could see him toeing it out with the hapless man.

"Stay here," Nigel said. "Turn around so they can't recognize you. I'm going to go up and make like a reporter and find out what's going on. Here, take my briefcase."

I took it, tucked it under my arm, and wished I had eyes in the back of my head.

Several minutes later Nigel came back down the steps. "Well, I just saw the free press in action. Frank's attorneys told them if one word, or one picture, appeared in any of their papers they'd pull all their advertising! And, of course, that runs into tens of thousands of dollars of revenue a year!"

I turned my head and looked over my shoulder, and sure enough, all the reporters had left, or were leaving, some still talking among themselves.

Round one to Frank Veloz ...

The courtroom had dark paneling, and a crowded, claustrophobic feeling that did nothing to flush the butterflies out of my stomach. Nigel and I sat at the plaintiff's table waiting for the judge to appear.

At ten on the dot the bailiff announced Judge Cole, and he walked into the courtroom, arranging his robe and looking around at the people present. I felt instantly at ease. He looked just like Dad—only his hair was dark—but he had the same build, and moustache, and kindly eyes.

"Okay, showtime!" Nigel whispered in my ear, and the next thing I remember is being ushered up to the witness stand and being sworn in. I was suddenly calm and collected, knowing my cause was just.

After I sat down, carefully crossing my ankles and arranging my skirt, I glanced over at the defendant's table. Frank, with his swarthy good looks, in a beautifully tailored suit, sat flanked by his five attorneys; he looked up just as I glanced his way, and our eyes locked. I stared right back for a moment or two, then my eyes traveled up into the dim gallery behind the bar and I saw at least ten of the instructors I'd worked with sitting and looking expectant, and my heart stopped and my head started to spin.

What the sam hill are they doing here?

Nigel approached the witness stand about then, and asked the now familiar questions, which I answered as best I could. I say "as best I could" because every time I opened my mouth and said a word, the stenotypist asked me to spell it. After I'd spelled Pamela, then Masters, followed by every broad-A word that came up, I felt I wasn't making any sense whatsoever, and a quiet panic set in. When Nigel was through, and sat down, the judge asked the defense if they had any questions.

The lead counsel stood up and said, "No questions, your honor," and I almost ran back to my seat.

"You may call your next witness," the judge said to Nigel, and he stood up and called Frank Veloz.

Frank got up from the table, straightened his tie, smiled at his attorneys, and then glanced at his instructors with a look that said, "Watch me make mincemeat out of these clowns!"

He really had a presence, and he knew it. He was a star, and he didn't let anyone forget it. He took the oath as if he and God were on the same footing, and sat down gracefully, looking around the courtroom as though waiting for applause. I know he wished there'd been a jury there for him to play to, but he had to settle for just us clowns, and make the best of it.

Nigel asked him the usual identifying questions, and then, without further preamble, brought out the handwritten letter and asked Veloz if he recognized it. The moment was electric. Frank looked as though he'd been hit in the gut, and his counsel caught on immediately, demanding to see the letter. The judge told them to approach, and Nigel handed it over. I couldn't hear what was said, but it was entered as evidence, and the case proceeded.

"Mr. Veloz," Nigel continued, as if there'd been no interruption, "would you please read the letter?"

Veloz rushed through the reading, obviously hoping the full impact would be lost. As he got to the end, Nigel asked, "And is that your signature on the letter, Mr. Veloz?"

Frank gave another panicked look at his lead counsel, who nodded his head up and down slowly, and then he said, almost in a whisper, "Yes."

The stenotypist asked him to please repeat his answer, and I found myself saying softly, *Man, you don't know how I have lived for this moment!*

Nigel was speaking again, "We rest our case, your honor," and came and sat down quietly beside me. I know he felt as good as I did. What a moment! Our full presentation had taken less than twenty minutes.

Judge Cole looked at the defense and asked if they were ready. A minor minion stood up and said, "Yes, your honor, I call Gene Hampton to the stand," and I watched as my favorite instructor took the oath and sat down.

Nigel looked at me questioningly, and I shook my head.

After the usual preliminaries, I think my mouth must've fallen open, as I sat and listened to outright perjury. Hampton's main argument was that one evening, after four hours of dancing, I told him I had a cramp in my foot, and when he massaged it, he felt scar tissue on the sole. He said I told him that I'd had major surgery on the foot after I got out of the prison camp, and it was a wonder I could still walk!

"You didn't tell me about this," Nigel hissed.

"I didn't tell *Hampton* either," I said, disgustedly. "He did massage my foot, he felt the scar tissue, and I told him it was nothing, I'd had some minor surgery after the prison camp because my hand-hewn shoes didn't fit that well. The rest is pure lies!"

Two more witnesses came on, and the story was mostly the same.

"How can they put their hand on a Bible and swear to tell the truth, the whole truth, and nothing but the truth, and perjure themselves like that?" I asked.

"It's the old story of the Big Lie," Nigel said as we sat eating our lunch. "It's your word against theirs, and there are a hell of a lot more of them. Don't worry, Pam, the only thing that counts is Frank Veloz's signature on that letter. You notice they haven't brought it up once."

"Meanwhile, I'm being made to look like a complete klutz," I said in disgust.

After lunch, when court resumed, four more instructors gave varying testimony as to my ability, or inability, to be an instructor. The only thing that kept me on an even keel was I kept remembering that fabulous dance routine I'd done with Frank Veloz before he'd written his damning letter. Damning for him, that is.

Finally around three o'clock Judge Cole exploded.

"Frank Veloz, I don't want to hear one more word from your so-called witnesses. I don't care if Mrs. Masters is boss-eyed, cross-eyed, and has three left feet, what I want to know is, did you or didn't you write that letter?"

At the prompting of his counsel, Frank Veloz stood up and said, "I did."

"Mr. Veloz, I've always admired you and your wife. You have to be a superb dance team, and I've always enjoyed going to your performances. But this has nothing to do with dancing. This has to do with business. I'm only going to tell you this once: don't ever sign a contract you don't mean to keep! Am I clear?"

"Yes, your honor," Frank said meekly.

"This case could have been over in thirty minutes. Instead, you and your counsel have dragged it out all day, wrecked the court's calendar, and never once refuted the plaintiff's cause for action. The case is awarded to the plaintiff. Frank Veloz is to pay the plaintiff the cost of her tuition, plus interest to be stipulated by the court, plus all court costs."

With Vicki out of my life, and Veloz vanquished, I felt like shouting, *Bring on the world, I can handle anything!*

Chapter 13

As it turned out, I never saw a dime of the judgment against Frank Veloz. By the time Nigel Connor had taken out his one-third and I'd paid off my debt to Mother, there wasn't anything left for little ole me. In fact, I got quite angry with Nigel when he insisted that, as we had won, we should be generous and bow to the opposing lawyers' request that they pay me off in several installments so that the award would not go on public record. At that time in California, any judgment under a thousand dollars was not recorded against the company involved.

"Then why the sam hill did I fight this case?" I asked.

"To recover the money you put out," Nigel said patiently.

"That was only part of it. I wanted others to know if they ever got taken as I did, they could sue and win! Now, there is no record. Frank Veloz got out of this scot-free, except for paying back my tuition with interest."

"And court costs," Nigel reminded me.

"So what? He could take that out of petty cash, and not even miss it!"

For the first time in my life, although I'd won, I felt like a failure. I could see he was getting impatient with my attitude, and I said, "I'm sorry, Nigel, I do appreciate your good fight, but somehow, to me, it's turned into a Pyrrhic victory."

∽

Meanwhile, back at the Edison Company, I was building up a kitchen planning department second to none, and enjoying every minute of it. I don't know why I always felt guilty picking up a paycheck for doing something I loved—it must go back to some previous life where I was a drudge or galley slave.

With my dreams of being a dance instructor squelched, I put all my efforts into the dress design classes I was taking at UCLA's night school extension in the RKO Building in downtown Los Angeles. My instructor, Mrs. Henner, was the personification of *haute couture*. She was tall, slim, and striking, in her mid-thirties, with beautiful prematurely white hair swept up in a French twist, who always wore a wide-brimmed hat and carried an elegantly rolled up umbrella, come rain or shine. She said she carried the umbrella as an extension of her *self* and, frankly, she'd have looked undressed without it. When she swept into class all eyes were on her, and she commanded instant admiration and respect.

I know I was nuts over her. And I believe most of the other students felt the same way. I'm not sure if the two Jewish businessmen did. They were short, portly, and very charming, but I just couldn't see what they were doing there, as neither of them seemed to have an ounce of talent when it came to sketching and design. I remember asking Mrs. Henner about them, and her reply was right to the point. "Oh, they're from Mode-O-Day, I believe, or some other such chain. They make no bones to me about the fact that they're here to see what new, fresh, young ideas my students come up with so that they can follow the trend."

All of a sudden the incident with the sassy little boutique and the famous dress designer on the Strip flashed in my mind. "You mean, they're here to swipe our ideas, don't you?"

"Touché!" she said, adding, "Got problems with that, Pam?"

"Lots of them. I'm getting wiser, but it's all uphill. I found my designs on Sunset Strip, but I hadn't been paid for them; and I saw some of my fabric design concepts on La Cienega at those interior decorating houses. The tumbling Oriental spider chrysanthemums; the footsteps and sunglasses in the sand, reflecting California scenes in their dark lenses; Chinese chopsticks and bowls of rice. Abstracts galore. It's been heartbreaking. They just change a leaf here, or a petal there, or alter a scene by adding more palm trees, or taking them out. It's so simple. I knew nothing of copyrights when I came to the States. And, frankly, I don't think they're worth much even when I do use them."

"You're right, it *is* heartrending. That's why most of our top dress designers work in Paris. In France they're protected. The Dior look. The Chanel look. The Fogarty look. No one dares copy them, or they're fined and can't show for several seasons.

"When American buyers go over to Paris they're never shown the top of the line because, although they put up a huge bond, the French know they're going to forfeit it, and steal everything they can. When they get back to the States, they don't use the designs as-is. They break them up, a detail here, a drape there. It's all very subtle, and if they were in France, it would be quite illegal. What can I say, Pam? Unless you can afford to go to Paris, you're going to be copied by all the Mode-O-Days and catalog houses, whose buyers, like the gentlemen here, are looking for fresh, young ideas."

Nothing daunted, I came away from her classes fired up and ready to do battle. I remember her telling me that when she went to college before the war, she was one of the oldest students in her class, and for that reason she wouldn't settle for anything less than straight As. She said when she graduated, the strain had been so great she had a total nervous breakdown and her hair turned pure white. "Now, that I'm over it, I like my hair, it's different and makes me stand out, but at the time I was devastated, and it seemed to take forever for me to get over my breakdown."

"I think your hair is absolutely beautiful," I said admiringly.

"Thank you, but the reason I'm telling you this is that straight As don't mean beans when you're out in the business world. It's the degree that counts. You've got so much on your plate today, Pam, I worry about you. Come to class, do your best, and I'll help you all I can."

At the end of the year, when I got my grades, she gave me a B+ and I told her she'd just made history. She laughed and said, "You would've had an A+, but you missed some classes."

"I couldn't help it," I said. "I had freelance assignments I had to get out. They help pay my bills."

She just smiled and said, "Remember what I told you, it's the degree that counts, not the straights As. Stick with it."

∽

I should have taken Mrs. Henner's advice and stopped piling more things on my plate, but I'm not built that way.

Our apartment had rather thin walls, and a couple of nights a week I could hear meetings going on next door, and actually heard what was being said. The only voice I recognized was that of the hairy tenant I'd met several times on the stairs, a strange-looking individual who kept to himself. Through the months we'd learned to mostly ignore each other as if by mutual consent until, of course, he started to hold those fateful meetings that I unintentionally overheard. Joe McCarthy would have been proud of me: I'd just stumbled onto one of Hollywood's famous Communist cells!

Not surprisingly, when I told Jay I was going to report it to the FBI, he said, "No, you're not! Keep your darn nose out of it."

Believe me, I tried. But after several weeks, with more and more weird people coming and going next door, I couldn't hold back, and called the Los Angeles field office of the FBI. I got an agent named Fox, who pumped me rather extensively, and then of all things asked if I would join the cell. He said it would be simple for me, as I lived next door and could easily spin a story of being intrigued by the meetings.

"I'm sorry, but I can't do it. I just got out of China before the Communist takeover; I'm applying for my American citizenship, and I sure as heck don't want anything to jeopardize that."

"It won't. In fact, it could help, by showing your loyalty to the United States."

"By joining a Communist cell?! I'd have to become a Communist—you must be kidding!"

"We need your help, ma'am," he said softly, giving me the granddaddy of all guilt complexes.

I could feel myself squirming, and said, "I'll ask my husband. If he agrees, then I will do it," knowing full well what Jay's answer would be.

∽

Not long after that, Jay and I came home from work to find an ambulance outside the apartment building, and the whole place in a hubbub. Don Savage, our neighbor from across the hall, met us at the top of the stairs and said that the old lady in 207 had been found dead in her apartment.

"She wasn't that old, was she?" I asked, perplexed. I'd never seen her, only heard about her, as she was a total recluse.

Don's wife Jean came up just then and said, "I guess she'd been ill for a while, but no one knew about it. It seems her immediate neighbors heard cats crying, and knocked on the door. When she didn't answer, they called the manager. The place is a complete mess. You'll never believe how she lived."

Our curiosity piqued, Jay and I decided to go down the hall and see for ourselves.

The door was wide open with yellow tape across it, and the windows were also open. From the stench that came out into the hall, it was obvious the medical crew had had to let in fresh air so that they could work. Although we couldn't enter, we saw the living room, and through the big archway, what had once been a kitchen, similar to ours. It was now a kitty hostel. All the cabinet doors had been taken off, and the different shelves made into tiers of apartments for the lady's feline friends. Surprisingly, none of the cats tried to go out through the open door, and I learned later that they never had been outside the apartment to anyone's knowledge.

The story I learned, in bits and pieces from other tenants, was sweetly tragic. The lady's name was Alice Preston, and she had been the confidante and close friend of one of Hollywood's earlier stars. Alice's immediate neighbor said it was Marilyn Miller, an actress who'd died in '36 at a very young age. I wasn't able to verify this, but according to the neighbor, the actress asked Alice to take care of her two beloved cats if anything happened to her. Right after that, Marilyn Miller—if that's who she truly was—died, and a heartbroken Alice took the cats to her apartment. Soon after, to her surprise, she found she'd been written into the star's will: it wasn't a huge sum, just enough to take care of the two cats, with a little left over to help Alice along the way.

As the story unfolded, I was convinced the actress had meant for Alice to take care of just those two cats—not any progeny. But Alice must've been a simple soul, because before long the original two critters begat a passel of kitties, and through the years second, third, fourth, and umpteen-more generations all did their bit to add to her feline family. Being kind-hearted, it was also obvious Alice did nothing to prevent the litters from multiplying, possibly feeling it was all part of her obligation to the actress, and never giving a second thought to the eventual outcome.

While we were getting the story, Animal Control arrived. I learned that at the final count there were thirty-seven adult cats in that small apartment, with at least five more squirming litters that the humane personnel hadn't been able to count. What really got to me was a comment I heard made that they hadn't found any edible food in the place for Alice, only cases and cases of cat food and kitty litter, and I couldn't help wondering if Alice had died of starvation or malnutrition…

∽

One night, not long after that, Don Savage's big black German shepherd dropped through the roof of our convertible, then panicked and tried to claw his way out of the car. The damage he did was unbelievable.

"Oh, God," Don said when he saw the mess. "Last evening I kept thinking I'd forgotten to do something, but I couldn't think what it was. Now I know. I forgot to put Buster in the cab of the pickup for the night. I guess he didn't like sitting out on the sidewalk, so he tried to get into your car."

"You mean you leave him locked up in the cab of your pickup all night?" Jay asked incredulously.

"Well, the damn landlord won't let me have him in the apartment, so what can I do?"

I couldn't help thinking that was rather unfair of the landlord as he'd let another tenant have thirty-seven plus cats in her apartment, but I bit my tongue and let the men duke it out.

"I hate to tell you," Jay said angrily, "but the top is going to cost you a pretty penny."

"I hate to tell *you* I don't have any insurance," Don said with a smirk. "You'll just have to get it repaired …"

"You mean 'replaced' …" Jay interrupted.

"Whatever. And I'll pay you off at five bucks a month!"

"That's not acceptable. I'll get a couple of estimates, and you'd better find some money to pay for the job."

"See you in hell first!" Don said, and stormed off.

We walked back into our apartment and I said to Jay, "I always thought Don was easy-going, but he's beginning to look like the type who'd do more damage to the car, just for spite. What should we do?"

"Well, there *is* a solution. Beecher told me there's a brand new apartment complex on La Tijera Boulevard in Westchester." Beecher Brown was Jay's immediate boss, and he and his wife Margie were a couple of our closest friends.

"You saying we've got to move again?" I said without enthusiasm. I'd gotten to hate moving.

"Well, we'd be stupid to sit around and wait to see what Don'll do next."

"He can move too, you know, and then we'll never get him to pay up."

"There's a difference, I *know* where he works, and I'll find him," Jay said firmly.

∽

The apartment on La Tijera was so new, the paint on the walls still felt damp. It smelled and looked lovely. There were a couple drawbacks, though, but Jay couldn't see them. The first was that it was not furnished, and we didn't have a stick of furniture. The only thing that came with the place was a range, a refrigerator, and a chrome and Formica breakfast table with four chairs. The second thing was, we had to pay the first and last month's rent—a brand-new concept to protect the landlord from unscrupulous tenants. We were just able to make the rent and security deposit, but it left us without a nickel to spare. The only thing we had to eat for the following week was one can of Campbell's tomato soup and some stale crackers.

"Well, we'll just have to see if it works," I said, being deliberately ambiguous.

"What works?" Jay asked.

"In famine-ridden China and Africa, mothers strap a large stone against their children's bellies to keep the pain of starvation away, and to stop them crying."

Jay looked at me and shook his head, as if I'd already dropped over the edge. I shrugged and said a little prayer.

We had box springs and a mattress on the floor in the bedroom with an orange crate beside it for a bedside table. The mattress Jay had gotten from one of his buddies at work who was looking to throw it out. He'd also given us a nine-by-twelve-foot carpet that he didn't want. When I looked at it, it was so bad I told Jay I'd rather go without; at least the brand-new hardwood floors looked beautiful and were easy to keep clean, so Jay rolled the carpet up and put it on the shelf in the carport, where the Packard was parked, happily protected from the elements.

"Thank God I got a monthly pass for the bus," I said. I got it before I knew we had to pay the first and the last month's rent, and it was one of the reasons we were behind the eight ball now.

The apartment building was one-story, and built in a U-shape, with lawns and newly planted trees in the area between the two arms facing the street. We had the first apartment on the right-hand side, and stepped out of the front door onto a nice wide sidewalk. I'd just finished putting the towels and sheets in the linen closet and hanging up our clothes in the bedroom closet, and was walking out to the kitchen to put the lone can of tomato soup away, when I heard a rap on the back door.

It was Mrs. Helbrick, our landlady, and I invited her in. I saw her look around with a puzzled expression, so I quickly smiled and said, "We've always rented furnished apartments before, but we plan to get some living room furniture next payday." As I finished talking I heard my stomach growl, and wondered where I could find a brick, hoping our landlady hadn't heard it.

Jay came in from the bedroom about then, and Mrs. Helbrick, who insisted we call her Martha, asked him what he planned to do with the carpet he had rolled up in the carport.

"I guess I'm waiting to find time to go to the dump," he said ruefully.

"Don't do that. I need it to put under my living room carpet. Here's ten dollars, will that cover it?"

"Oh, *yes!*" I said, almost snatching the bill from her and shoving it in my pocket.

"Do you want to take the carpet now?" Jay asked. "I could help you install it."

"Oh, would you? That would be wonderful."

When they'd both left, I looked heavenward and said, *She didn't hear my stomach growl, but You obviously did. Thank you!*

Jay and I had budgeted our groceries at five dollars a week, and had lived pretty well on that frugal figure. *Well, we've got money for two weeks' groceries,* I told the empty kitchen.

When Jay came back, he smiled and said, "How the heck do you do it? Every time it looks as though we're on the rocks, broke and desperate, money comes from heaven and falls into your hands."

"It's because I believe in guardian angels," I said.

I have to say, not long after that incident, my guardian angel must have thrown up her hands in disgust.

We got paid every other Friday, and as soon as I received my check, I went up to the Security Pacific Bank branch on Edison's fourth floor, and cashed it. It was a ritual. And when I got home, I divided the money up between groceries, utilities, car payments, and miscellaneous bills, each amount carefully stashed in labeled envelopes against the day the bills had to be paid.

Going home in the evening, I was always the first on the bus, and the driver and I became a good friends. He knew I liked to sit on the right-hand side of the bus, in the front row, and when the sun was low and shining brightly through the windshield, he'd pull the screen down on my side so I wouldn't get blinded. It was a sweet gesture, and it made me feel special. Another little courtesy he showed me, almost from the start, was to stop in front of our building and let me off the bus so I wouldn't have to walk almost a half mile back to our apartment.

One Friday evening, several weeks after we moved, he stopped and let me off, then waited to see I was safely across the street before pulling out, waving as he moved back into the traffic.

Jay, who worked at North American's facility by the Los Angeles Airport, invariably got home ahead of me. That evening, as usual, I dashed into the apartment, gave him a hug and a smooch, and started to throw things together for dinner.

Then, while the meal was in the oven, I went to my handbag to get out my wallet and divvy up the money.

There was no wallet!

"Oh ... my ... God!" I said, and Jay immediately caught up on the tone of my voice.

"What's up?"

"I must've left my wallet on the bus!" I said, trying to keep the desperation out of my voice.

"Who else was on the bus?" he asked.

"Just a group of kids who always sit across the back row, the driver, and me."

"Where do you sit?" he asked.

"The front row, across from the driver." I shuddered when I thought about it. No one getting in or off the bus could miss a wallet lying on that seat.

"Well, I guess you worked for nothing the last two weeks," Jay said dully.

"No! I can't accept that. Let's get the Packard and go over to the bus barns. There's only one stop after I get off, and we'll search all the busses till we find my wallet."

"It's a waste of time," he said, then noticing my stubborn look, added, "Do you remember the number of the bus"?

"No, but it's a Crenshaw bus. We'll find it!"

Fifteen minutes later we were at the bus barns. Lord, I couldn't believe how many busses there were! All the drivers had left, and the maintenance crews were going through them, one by one, when we started down the lines.

"Excuse, me," I said to one of the workers, "would you know where the last Crenshaw bus would be parked?" He waved over to the far northwest corner of the barn and said that would be a good place to start. So we did.

Luckily, when the drivers left their vehicles they also left the doors open for the maintenance crews. I don't believe I've ever climbed in and out of so many busses in my life; the only thing that shortened our search was that if the wallet was in one of them it would have to be either on the front seat, or on the floor under it.

I could see Jay was losing heart, and have to admit, I felt my usual optimism dwindling, too.

"Well, that's all the Crenshaw busses," he said, stepping off the last one.

"You don't know that," I said. "Some of these with blank destinations could be Crenshaws, but the driver rolled back the signage before getting off."

"You're a dreamer!".

"Worth a try," I remarked, as I climbed into the first of the unmarked busses.

And there it was! Lying on the front seat, the wad of bills sticking out of it for all the world to see. I let out a unbelieving scream.

"What's up?"

"It's here!"

"And the money?"

"It's here, too!" I started to cry, and I couldn't stop.

Jay just shook his head, hugged me, and steered me back to where we'd parked the Packard.

It was right after this incredible incident that I learned from Dr. Brobeck, Margie Brown's gynecologist, that I was pregnant, and he told me it looked like we'd be proud parents the first week in September.

Chapter 14

Through all of this, Jay and I became a part of the '50s building boom. We'd bought an acre of land in Woodland Hills in the west end of the San Fernando Valley, and he spent most of his weekends out there working on the property, getting ready to build. I was eight months pregnant, and on a leave of absence from the Edison Company at the time, so it was up to me to get our building permit, and be available whenever the inspectors came out to check the different phases of construction.

I think the day I got the permit from the Los Angeles County Building Department was the highlight of the year, at least it was till then. I'd drawn up all the blueprints myself, followed the building code out the window, and was really proud of my work. The plan checker seemed pretty impressed, too, until he came to the upstairs bathroom, off the master bedroom, that was in a loft overlooking the family room, which had a swinging door into the kitchen.

"You can't do that," he said, pointing out that there was only one door between the bathroom and the kitchen; the swinging saloon doors didn't count, and the building code said there had to be two doors between any bathroom and food preparation area.

"Why?" I asked.

"That's the law," he said, adding, "I'm sorry, but you're

going to have to either enclose the kitchen and put in an acceptable door, or enclose the loft, and put a door at the head of the stairs."

"What about airflow? What about my beautiful, open plan?" I wailed.

"What can I say? I can't approve these plans as they're currently drawn up," he said firmly.

"You mean there are *no* mitigating circumstances?" I said, trying to keep my voice under control.

"No, ma'am."

Then I lost it. "Tough! I'm nine-and-a-half months pregnant," I lied without a blush, "and I'm going to stay here until I have the baby if that's what it takes to have you approve my plans!"

His face turned all shades of red, and he started to flounder, completely out of his depth.

"I wonder if you could find me a more comfortable chair," I said in a more conciliatory tone. "This one's beginning to make my back ache."

"Just a minute! Just a minute!" he said, jumping up out of his chair and moving it around the desk for me to sit on. Then, grabbing the set of plans, he rushed out of the room.

I sat there wondering what was going on, and hoping whatever the plan checker was doing wouldn't jack up the cost of the building permit.

Half an hour later he came back in with a smile on his face, and handed me the plans. "I got them approved. I had them write a variance for you. You can go ahead and start building as soon as you see the cashier, and pay the fee. Here's an additional sheet of instructions telling you what to do as each phase of the building is completed. You do know that each phase has to be checked by an building inspector?"

I told him I did, thanked him profusely, paid the cashier—noticing the permit hadn't gone up in price—and floated home on cloud nine. A month later, Jay had all the footings dug, and I called for an inspection before we poured.

Everything seemed to be on time except the arrival of the newest member of our family. The first week in September came and went. Also the second, third, and fourth, but nothing happened. The first week in October, I asked Jay to take me for a long, bumpy ride, hoping it would start someone thinking seriously about joining our world. Jay took me up Topanga Canyon and Malibu Canyon, on two separate occasions, and we wound off onto rutted, bumpy fire roads; still nothing happened.

Those last six weeks had to be the longest I've ever spent in my life. It was like reliving the last months in the Japanese prison camp when we were surrounded by Chinese Communists and couldn't get out, only now I was horribly uncomfortable, as big as the Hindenburg, and flopping around like a beached whale.

Finally, in the wee hours of October 20, 1952, my little tummy guest decided it was time, and Jay rushed me to the Centinela Community Hospital, where, sixteen hours later, after a hellish labor, Rebel let out her first yell and entered the world! Jay said I'd never looked prouder or happier than when I was being wheeled down the hall to my room with our littlest in my arms.

He was right. I'd already forgotten the painful delivery for the sheer joy of seeing her, all golden and glorious, with flaming red hair!

"Okay, the only person I know with red hair is the milkman," he said, with a grin a mile wide. "Want to tell me about it?" In those days our milk was delivered at dawn by the Arden Dairy.

"Not particularly," I said, as an attendant took her from me, and the nurse helped me up onto the bed. When I was comfortable, she handed Rebel back to me.

I kissed her fuzzy little head and asked Jay, "Want to hold her?"

"*Oh, my God!* Oh, my God ... supposing I drop her!" There was pure panic in his voice.

The nurse, who was cranking up the bed, laughed. "Believe me, you won't drop her. Here, let me show you," she said, taking her from me gently and handing her to Jay, showing him how to support her head.

Then it was my turn to look on the happy face of the proudest father in the world!

A while later when the birthing nurse came in to see how I was doing, I told her Jay was giving me a bad time about Rebel's red hair. "That's normal when one of the parents is blonde and the other very dark-haired like you are. She'll lose it in a couple of weeks and her regular hair will grow out. It's usually a toss-up whether she'll be a blonde or brunette."

I liked the lady, she was so down-to-earth, and I asked her another question. "How can a baby be over six weeks late?"

"Babies can't be late ... but doctors can be wrong. Anyhow, your little girl was waiting for a full moon to light her way."

I looked out the window then, and sure enough, a beautiful full moon was sailing up into the autumn sky.

The nurse was talking again. "Every time there's a full moon we have a slew of babies, but when I tell them to double the crew on the maternity floor, they look at me as though I were nuts!"

"How many babies were born tonight?" I asked.

"So far, five. Four boys and Rebel ... I sure love that name."

I'll never forget when we got home, and I had to change

her for the first time. "Jay!" I called in a panic. "How can she have scrambled eggs in her diapers when she's only had milk to drink?"

"Lord, you're going to make *some* mother!"

"So, I'm new at this, I can learn."

"You'd better do it in a hurry, our littlest Rebel doesn't look like she's going to put up with much incompetence on your part."

"How many babies have *you* had?" I asked, annoyed at his mocking tone.

"When you put it that way—none."

"At least I keep my incompetence in the family," I said, recalling a crazy incident one night in early August, when our apartment shook like a train on a rickety trestle, and Jay leapt out of bed shouting, "Earthquake!" then charged out through the front door onto La Tijera Boulevard, bare-assed naked!

I raced out after him, shouting, "Get your robe on, idiot!"

"I'm not going back in that building!" he shouted back.

When I came back out with his robe, all the neighbors were yelling and whistling at him, but he didn't seem to notice. I threw the robe over his shoulders and started to steer him back toward the apartment just as the complex across the street suddenly shot a tidal wave of pool water over the roof, catching and drenching us both.

Mrs. Helbrick came up to us then, still laughing, and said, "For you neo-Californians, that's called an aftershock."

"What are you talking about ... the earthquake or Jay?" I asked.

I always got a boot out of remembering that incident, it had a lovely way of leveling the playing field after I'd said or done something really stupid or outrageous.

"When was I ever incompetent?" he asked, as I finished

changing Rebel. I could tell his feathers were ruffled.

"Maybe 'incompetent' isn't the right word," I said. "Maybe I should have called you an exhibitionist."

When he still looked dense, I said with a smug grin, "Earthquake!" and his face turned to flame.

"You'll never let me live that down, will you?"

"Not unless you forget scrambled eggs," I said with a smile.

∽

I don't want to even mention what we did after that: We moved again! This time to a dear little caretaker's cottage on Rosie and Larry Bauer's ranch off Fallbrook Avenue, a mile or so from our property in Woodland Hills. Jay was right. It was a lot more convenient for him and his ongoing building program.

The thing that really clinched the move was Rosie. She and Larry had two great boys, ten and eleven respectively, but no girls, and Rosie had always wanted a girl. To say Rebel was spoiled rotten would be an understatement. Rosie had been a nightclub singer, and still had a lovely voice, and the boys, Rusty and Randy, were both very musical, so more often than not we'd come home to find the three of them entertaining Rebel with delightful songs, accompanied by the piano, guitar, and drums!

We also found, to our great surprise, there was a huge colony of commuters who went to downtown Los Angeles, and over Sepulveda to the aircraft industry around the international airport, and we both found excellent car-pools. Actually, Jay car-pooled and I rode with a neat couple who had two other passengers. The driver, Larry Copeland, worked a couple of blocks from Edison, and his wife Amy and the other two passengers worked with me, so Larry would drop us all off at Edison's main rotunda every morning, and pick us up there in the evening. Boy, that was hard to take!

Like everything, though, there was a downside too. I had to stop taking Mrs. Henner's classes at the night school, and any talks I gave on kitchen planning had to be during working hours, at lunch, or some such time. As I watched my degree drift farther and farther away, I knew from here on out all my higher education had to be on-the-job, or hands-on training, as it was called.

The days would start with us dropping Rebel off at the "big house" with Rosie, and Jay and I would then ride to Topanga Canyon Boulevard where I'd pick up my ride, and he'd go on to North American with his car-pool. The days he wasn't driving, he'd leave the Packard in a shady spot along Topanga Canyon Boulevard. I always got back at least twenty minutes ahead of him, so I'd sit in the car and read, or knit.

I'd been doing this for several weeks when I slipped into the car and found a mash note from Jean Barkley, asking Jay what had happened, and why he didn't come around any more. She sounded absolutely heartbroken. Jean was the daughter of Bob and Roz Barkley, and Jay had rented a room in their big ranch when he was batching it in the valley. I guess when he moved out, he neglected to tell them why, and left a lot of loose ends dangling. When he got back from his commute, and slid behind the wheel, I handed him the note.

"Haven't you told Jean and Roz that you're married?" I asked.

"No."

"You must've seen them in the last three years. Why didn't you?"

"I didn't want a scene."

"How long are you going to play this game? Heck, you've got a daughter now!"

"You're right. I'll do it this weekend."

The following week there was another note. He'd obviously not spoken to either of them. The week after, still another, each sounding more and more heartbroken.

I couldn't stand it! Maybe Jay couldn't face a confrontation, but I couldn't face not setting things right. I wrote to them both, telling about our marriage, and our darling daughter, and inviting them over to visit when they had time. I enclosed a snapshot of Rebel at her cutest.

The timing was perfect. The following weekend I was in the J.C. Penney store in Canoga Park, and Jay was outside with Rebel nuzzling against his shoulder, when Jean and Roz came up. I was just leaving the store, but stood back for a minute to see what would happen.

I saw Jay quickly turn his back and try to walk away, but Roz went right up to him and said, "So this is your lovely little Rebel? Lord, she's cute!" Jean didn't look quite as happy about it, but she smiled and said, "Hi."

The look on Jay's face was priceless. "You know about Rebel?"

"Yes, Pam wrote us and told us all about you two and your new daughter. Why didn't you tell us, Jay?"

Rather than watch him squirm, I came out of the store and introduced myself. After they left, Jay turned to me and said quietly, "Thank you."

I wanted to say, *Let that be a lesson,* but I knew it would be useless. Some people just can't handle confrontations.

Well, I thought, *I've got rid of Vicki ... and I've got rid of Jean ... I don't think Roz was ever a threat ... and Doria I deep-sixed way back.*

That's right, I didn't mention Doria, did I? I should have. She was one of Jay's earlier romances, and very wealthy. I guess she took their affair seriously and decided she was going to marry him. He lived in a house trailer at the time, and the refrigerator went out, so she gifted him with a new one. When she learned he was married she sent him a bill for it. I would've probably done the same thing. Jay ignored the bill. I was cleaning out the bedside-table drawer when I found it, along with a couple of follow-ups, each with an angrier note scrawled on it. I was just planning to juggle the budget and pay her off when I got a phone call. "This is Doria Harris. You don't know me …"

"Oh, yes, I do, Doria. I'm glad you called," I said, in a sweet, gushing voice.

There was a slight pause at the other end, then she said tersely, "You won't be when I'm through."

"Really? Why?" Still playing the ingenue.

"I've decided to add a few items to a statement I sent Jay. I gave him a refrigerator because I thought we were going to be married. Now tell him I'm adding the woods, the ski jacket, the cashmere socks …"

"No, you're not!" I said, with a complete change of tone. "We were just getting ready to send you a check for the refrigerator. It's a big item, and it's understandable that you'd like to be reimbursed for it. But the rest were obviously gifts. Just as I know Jay gave you gifts. The check for the refrigerator will be in the mail today if you give me your address."

Actually, I paid the darn thing off with some freelance money, and Jay never knew a thing about it.

Like I told Vyola when she got mad at Doc—I knew Jay had not been living in a vacuum before he met me, but I couldn't stand tripping over all his loose ends. Maybe it went back to Bill, and him not having the guts to tell me personally that he'd gotten married.

∼

Our little studio cottage had one large sunny room, with the bathroom, dressing area, and clothes closets off one side, and the kitchen and dinette off the other. The Thomasville couch, end tables, lamps, and rocker, all in Early American maple that we'd bought for the La Tijera apartment, fit nicely, with the big double bed, now on a strong steel frame, placed under the window and covered with a heavy spread to complement the upholstery. It was cozy, and home to our precious family of three, but by no stretch of the imagination was there space for one more person!

Unknown to me, Jay had written his mother, obviously exaggerating the size of the cottage, and told her how happy we were in our new little home. He probably left out the word "little," because, when January rolled around, his mother, Florence McCullough, who asked to be called Nana after Rebel was born, arrived by train from Windsor, Canada, for an extended visit. The timing couldn't have been worse.

She'd just been through a radical mastectomy, and was depressed and picky as all get out. There was nothing I could do right. She was supposed to be recuperating from major surgery, but she didn't know how to relax. On top of that, Jay and I were gone all day and there were no interesting places close by for her to visit, and nothing she could do to while away the days. She outwore her welcome at the "big house" very quickly when she told Rosie she didn't know how to take care of Rebel. To Rosie's credit, she stayed calm and sweet and told Nana that Jay and I were more than happy with the care she was giving our little daughter, then politely shooed her out of the house.

Back in our little place, with nothing to do, she started cleaning and polishing, always being careful to be on her hands and knees, scrubbing the kitchen floor, when we returned from work, and complaining under her breath about what a rotten housekeeper I was. She must've scoured the floor at least six times in the first two weeks. It was a cheap, patterned linoleum when she arrived, but there was hardly any pattern left on it when I finally blew my stack.

It happened when she said, "Your dear cousin Madeleine is such a wonderful housekeeper, you can eat off her floors!"

That's when I lost it, and spat out, "When it becomes fashionable to eat off the floor, I assure you, my floors will be clean enough!"

Jay told me to shut up!

I told *him* to shut up, and all hell broke loose!

The following day I called Mother and wailed my woes. She was living in Altadena now, as she'd had to sell the pretty log cabin in Idyllwild when Bridie McCall passed away, and she couldn't find a job there to help stretch out Grandma's pensions. She'd done wonders to the home, and got a nice price for it, which she turned around and put on a big fixer-upper on Windsor Avenue in Altadena. The choice of locale was predicated by the job she'd landed at Cal Tech.

"I'll take Florence for a couple of weeks, Pam, and you and Jay must try and patch things up. I'll pick her up on Saturday. Here, she'll be close enough to town and transportation to be able to go places and do things, and she'll have a room all to herself."

"How about Grandma?" I asked.

"She's doing great. Of course she isn't well enough to go places with Florence, but they just might hit it off together, and the company will do her good."

When Nana left with Mumsy early Saturday morning, even Jay had to admit it felt good to have the place to ourselves again.

But it didn't last.

Mother called me at work the following Thursday, and without preamble said, "I'm bringing Florence back. I've had as much as I can take. I've had five solid days of her telling me what a dreadful daughter I have; that she's a lazy good-for-nothing whose house is a pigsty, and that she's not half good enough for her precious son! It was all I could do not to respond in kind! Every darn thing that came out of her mouth was negative. Saturday, after we got home, I took her shopping at some of our best stores, she went through them as though they had a bad smell. Sunday I took her and Mother for a drive, but all she did was gripe about the traffic and say she thought Southern California was horribly overrated, and didn't know how anyone could stand to live here. Not a word of thanks. Nothing!"

"I'm so sorry, Mumsy, I'd no idea it wouldn't work out. Thank you so much for taking her for the days you did. There's peace in our valley once more, and I hope I'll be able to keep it that way."

"You're young; you have the strength … I don't!"

So Nana came back. This time she didn't scrub and clean, she went through all our personal possessions and made herself quite at home. The first evening after she was back, when we got home from work, she was sitting in the rocker repairing little snags on my lingerie, and sewing loose lace back on my panties.

I felt as though my privacy had been invaded. I tried to tell myself that she wasn't well, that she was going through hell from her surgery and needed all kinds of loving. It took all the patience I had not to explode, and patience is not a virtue I have in abundance. Somehow I got through to Sunday evening, and then she let slip that she'd been reading my personal correspondence, and I went ballistic.

"So, what am I supposed to do all day," she whined, "sit here and do nothing?"

"Nana, we have books. Lots of books. You can read *them!*"

"My eyes get too tired to read."

"But not too tired to read someone else's personal letters!" I shouted.

Jay didn't help. "Don't you dare talk to my mother like that! She's older than you, you must show her respect."

"Respect? Was that what she was showing when she went through my lingerie? And when she read my personal letters?"

Jay reamed me out up one side and down the other, backing his mother to the hilt. I'd had it! The following day I went up to see Nigel Connor and came right to the point.

"Do you handle divorces?"

"Whoa! What brought that on? I thought you were now a loving threesome; who's moved into your happy little home?"

"Is it that obvious?" I said, astounded.

"Don't answer a question with a question. Who has moved in with you? In-laws?"

"I'm afraid so." And I told him the whole sorry story.

"Well, to begin with, neither your mother-in-law, father-in-law, aunts, uncles, cousins, or anyone else, has a say in *your* home. Age has nothing to do with it. And you'd better put Jay straight about that, too."

"Let's get back to my first question … about a divorce."

"Let's not. There's a much simpler solution. Send your mother-in-law home! If you don't have the money for her fare, I'll pay for it out of my own pocket, and I don't want to be repaid."

"Oh, we can afford it, but I know Jay won't go for it," I said.

"He will, if you tell him what I just told you. No one can usurp your rights in your own home!"

He got up, and I knew the talk was at an end. I thanked him for his advice, and left his office.

"What's eating you, girl?" Amy asked, as we were driving home.

"Nothing I can't handle," I said, knowing I was lying in my teeth.

When Jay got into the car on Topanga, I was waiting for a frigid look, instead he leaned over and kissed me. It was so unlike him, I flinched.

"What's that for?" I asked. I'd been expecting another tirade, not this.

"I learned something today."

"Really? What?" My voice was still bristling from his treatment of the day before.

"When I got to North American, I saw the employees' attorney. She told me you were perfectly within your rights to put Mother in her place. No one can usurp ..."

"... my rights in my own home!" I said, ending the sentence for him.

"How did you know?"

"I saw Nigel Connor, and he said the same thing. He even went so far as to offer to buy her ticket home."

"You're kidding. So did North American's attorney!"

We both laughed, and I began to feel good about myself again. Mother had no way of knowing that all the beastly things she told me Nana had said about me had really hit home. Many people can fluff off mean remarks; I can't, I take them all too personally, and let them gnaw away at little parts of me like ravenous piranhas.

A couple of days later, on our way to Union Station to see

Nana off on the train, she told us that her doctor had asked her what she did for exercise. She told him she walked a lot, and did housework. According to her, he told her that was great, he wanted to see her scrub her floors at least three times a week to build up the muscle tissue in her arms! And all the way downtown she talked like she'd been wound up with an extra large key. She kept saying how lucky we were to live in such a lovely state, everything was so beautiful, the houses, the trees, even the traffic was well-behaved; in fact, it was all the nice things that Mother would have loved to have heard her say when she took her on the drive the previous weekend ...

What's going on here? I wondered.

It took me several years to find out what made Nana tick. It happened when Jay, Rebel, and I went up to Medicine Hat in Alberta to visit his Uncle Frank, who surprisingly was only two years older than Jay, and his wife, the fabled Madeleine. Both of them preferred to be called "cousins" because of the very slight age difference. Madeleine was also a councilwoman for the district, and I wasn't at all certain I wanted to meet her.

When we got there, Frank and Jay immediately started to horse around. I got out of the car, took Rebel out of her car seat and was trailing her by the hand, when Madeleine came toward me with outstretched arms, saying, "I've always wanted to meet this paragon of virtue whose damn kitchen floors are so clean you can eat off them!"

I guess my mouth fell open.

"What's the matter, Pamela? I didn't offend you, did I?"

"Far from it," I said, and burst out laughing. "Oh, Lord, I don't believe what I'm hearing!" And I told her about Nana's visit, and her complaining about my filthy home, rotten housekeeping, and spendthrift ways. When I was through she said, "Boy, that sounds familiar!"

Needless to say, we were kindred spirits from thereon out.

After the train pulled out of Union Station, I said to Jay, "Let's wait until we have a real guest room before we invite anyone else to stay with us ... okay?"

I got a wide grin in response.

∼

I was glad Nana wasn't with us when an earthquake hit again. It was on a weekend, and the littlest Rebel was taking her afternoon nap on our big bed under the window. There was a long mug rack over it, and as I didn't have any mugs to put on it, I decorated it with sprays of greenery and huge sugar pinecones. When the quake hit, the shelf rattled like crazy, and the huge pinecones came tumbling down. I couldn't move fast enough to grab Rebel, and one cut her scalp open and blood gushed everywhere. My first thought was that it had landed on her head, but it hadn't, it had landed on the bed and bounced up and hit her a glancing blow that cut a long, horrible gash through her now light blonde hair.

Rosie came rushing over to see if we were okay. When she saw my face she said, "What happened?!"

"Rebel's been hurt, and I can't reach my doctor—what am I going to do?"

"Hey, I've got two boys, I'm a born nurse. Let me see her."

I'd wrapped her head in a clean white towel, and when Rosie took it off, it was still bleeding, but not as fiercely.

"Does she need stitches?" I asked apprehensively.

"No, I've been through worse with both Rusty and Randy. They were always banging and busting their heads. And heads always bleed like the devil. Let's clean it off and put on a couple of butterfly clamps."

I brought her the first aid kit, and before long Rebel was nicely patched up and back in the land of Nod.

I couldn't help remembering the first time I learned of butterfly clamps. It was when I was doing an assignment on the dinette table in our La Tijera apartment, and our overhead kitchen light exploded. I found out later that I'd put in the wrong size bulbs and screwed the lampshade on so tight it couldn't expand with the heat. A big chunk of the heavy glass shade came crashing down and cut a gash over my right eye, knocking me out cold. Once more, my guardian angel was standing by, and must have whispered in our landlady's ear, because within minutes Martha Helbrick came over for a visit and found me lying in a pool of blood. She propped me up, and cleaned off the gash, as I slowly came to. She said the cut looked bad, and was hanging open like a third eye, but surprisingly, the bleeding was slowing down. I told her I was lucky that way, and asked for a paper towel to press over it to stanch the flow.

That same angel must've been on overtime, because Jay walked in just then, and I removed the pressure and showed him the gash.

"Think we should take her to the hospital?" Martha asked. "That's going to leave a horrible scar if we don't have it stitched."

"No. I'll butterfly clamp it, and it will be fine," Jay said, and methodically cut little Band-Aids into butterfly wings and, holding the gash together, he placed about three across the cut. It healed beautifully, and all I have today is a little scar tissue in my brow-line that I touch up with an eyebrow pencil.

Chapter 15

That August, I lined up a new account: Eva of Beverly Hills, who made a line of exquisitely beaded and embroidered evening sweaters and stoles. It was the classic story of a little cottage industry that started out in a garage burgeoning into a million-dollar industry. Eva was loud, flamboyant, rather overweight, with ash blonde hair that definitely was not her natural color, and who favored lavender clothes to go with her lilac Cadillac. One thing about her, she never entered a room without all heads turning her way, and it was obvious she loved the attention.

I didn't like Eva's husband, Bernie, though. He was number three or four in a line of husbands, and had been a sporting goods salesman in Brooklyn before they married. According to Eva, he convinced her that her business was getting so big she needed a full-time manager, and proceeded to take over the job. I found out his qualifications were nil, but dear Eva was nuts about him, and he could do no wrong.

Eva's reason for having me design a line for her was that she wanted to get into high-fashion sweaters with a lot less handwork on them as it was killing her bottom line. I loved the challenge. Using some of the ideas I'd worked up for my La Cienega account that were too sophisticated for that salon's older clientele, we came up with a new line, simple but chic.

Before long I noticed a strange glow in Bernie's eyes when

he saw my sketches, so I quickly got in touch with Nigel Connor and had him draw up a contract specifically spelling out that the designs could only be used by Eva of Beverly Hills for her *haute couture* line, and that any other use would violate the contract and be grounds for suit. It also stated that if Eva wanted to use any of the numbers in her Junior Line, or any other line, the contract could be renegotiated to cover additional royalties to be paid to the designer.

"Let me see them wriggle out of this one," Nigel had said smugly as he handed me the contract, adding, "Go get their signatures on that before they know what's hit them!"

Armed with the contract, which I considered as binding as Frank Veloz's letter, I started to spend a large part of my Saturdays down in the Los Angeles garment district working with Eva. I even worked with her knitting mills to see that they understood how to set up their machines to do the work. I insisted all seams had to be woven, and all welts and trim had to be part of the knitted piece, something few American mills liked to do. I even went so far as to buy a huge commercial knitting machine at auction that I set up in our new garage, so that I knew I was not demanding the impossible.

I loved the challenge, and I loved Eva. She was a generous, kindhearted soul, who always saw good in everyone.

∽

And of course, Kitchen Planning at Edison was my five-day-a-week challenge. Although the subdivision work was flowing smoothly, I was getting more and more calls for remodels in the Beverly Hills-Bel Air area. I remember one home had a dining room that jutted out onto a wide sweep of lawn, and was so large that it had booths on all three outer walls under huge picture windows, with a banquet table in the center that easily sat twenty! It was like a picturesque restaurant, and the stainless steel kitchen that went with it fronted on tennis courts, with a fast-food service counter for hungry athletes. The equipment in the kitchen rivaled any hospital or restaurant kitchen I'd ever worked on, only there was no thought given to food flow. It was as though the contractor just moved in all the high-priced equipment he could find without thinking of the poor chef and cooks who would be working there.

The remodel was running in the tens of thousands, and I came up with an excellent plan that would cut down steps, work, and cleanup for the kitchen staff. I was really proud of my layout until the lady of the house saw it, and said it wouldn't work.

I looked at her and asked, astonished, "Why not?"

"You moved the kitchen sink!"

"That's right, it was interrupting the food flow, and actually it had been poorly placed," I said by way of explanation.

"You can't move the sink," she said adamantly. "You'll have to come up with another plan."

I knew budget wasn't the problem, and couldn't fathom why she was so insistent the sink stay where it was. I guess I must've looked confused, because she said, "You don't seem to understand, it's taken me ages to teach my cat to come in and go out through the cat door under the sink. I won't go through that again! Sorry, the sink and the cat door stay!"

I thought of a lot of smart-aleck remarks about what I'd do if that were my cat, but I bit my tongue and came up with another layout. It was good, but not as good as the original one.

~

To our surprise, late in October, just after Rebel's first birthday, Jay's dad reappeared. He'd been popping in and out of our lives recently as he moved around the States in his capacity as a hotel management specialist. He was known in the hotel circle as "The Hatchet Man," and was hired to clean up unprofitable hotels, restasurants and clubs, and put them back in the black. I understand he was a wizard at it, and had a success record second to none.

I didn't like him, though. I guess it was because I knew he had abandoned Jay and his mother, saying he wasn't ready for fatherhood. That was back in 1917 when there was no such thing as aid for dependent children, or any such lifeline. Jay had bumped into him, off and on, as he grew up, but every time it happened his father would disown him and say he was no son of his. It had a terrible effect on Jay and his understanding of what a real family was all about.

His mother'd had a really rough time for several years after Jay's birth until she met James McCullough, a rugged Irish Protestant with no tolerance for Catholics. Florence had been raised a Catholic in Bohemia, and led a tortured life after she came to the States because her church didn't believe in divorce, yet she still needed the security that McCullough offered her and her son. That was the family Jay was raised in, and I'm sure he, like so many children, blamed himself for all his mother's woes.

As for James McCullough—he was a tough but fair man with only one love in his life, Jay's mother Florence. As far as Jay was concerned, he'd give him a roof over his head, and food for his belly, but he had no more love to spare, only approval or disapproval. It was a very empty life for a sensitive boy who needed much more than that.

When we heard from his father in October, we learned he was managing the Mapes Hotel in Reno, and he asked us if we could spend Christmas with him and Edith, his latest wife. If it hadn't been for Edith, I would have suggested we not go, but I'd met her earlier and she had to be one of the nicest people I knew—even if I couldn't figure out what she saw in Jay's dad.

Jay was very surprised at the invitation, and kept wondering what his father was up to.

"He's never done this before ... what's he got up his sleeve? It's just not like him."

"He's been bitten by the Christmas bug," I said, happily. "It's about time he remembered he had a family."

"Somehow that doesn't sound like Dad," Jay insisted.

When we were first married, Jay and I would often spend our weekends in the high country, hiking in the Sierra or fishing its rivers and streams, as that was about all we could afford to do. Since the arrival of Rebel, we'd been spending more and more weekends on the property building our new home, and our love of the outdoors had been put on hold, so we decided to make Christmas a combined holiday this year. We'd stop over and visit with his dad and Edith in Reno, then go up north on State Route 395 to Alturas for pass shooting. Goose Lake was just north of there, and was one of the winter migration grounds for Canadian honkers.

I was really looking forward to the time off, because after the first of the year I would be interviewing for someone to help me in Kitchen Planning, a department that didn't know how to slow down. I was looking forward to the help, and dreading it at the same time. I loved my privacy and neat little office, and knew it would take me a while to get used to someone sharing my space. I decided Christmas was going to be a time of rest for me and, hopefully, a time of healing for Jay and his dad.

When we arrived in Reno, it had just snowed, and the city looked lovely with its whisper of white. The Mapes was rather a dark and dreary hotel, and as we came into the foyer, Jay's dad came out of his office and greeted us warmly. He showed us up to our room, which adjoined their suite, and Edith took one look at Rebel and became putty in her tiny little hands. It felt good. It finally felt like family, and I knew we were going to have a great time.

"When you kids have relaxed a bit and tidied up, we're going to meet friends in the lobby for drinks," Dad said.

I took a shower and changed, then dressed Rebel in a pretty little black velvet dress with a white lace collar, and she looked perfectly edible. When Jay came out of the shower, he donned his favorite light grey suit, and I couldn't help thinking it really looked great on his tall, lean frame. The three of us checked Dad's rooms and found he and Edith had already gone downstairs, so we took the elevator, walked across the lobby, and stepped into the cocktail lounge. Dad was sitting at a table for six, facing the entrance so he could spot us as we came in, and he waved us over.

"There's Grandpa," I said to Rebel, and that was all she needed. She bounded across the lounge to his table.

When we got there, a very good-looking man stood up. Dad introduced him as Jim Johnson, and we shook hands.

"I think you know his wife," Dad said, and as I turned to greet her, I saw it was Vicki! She jumped up from her seat and gave me a hug, then proceeded to give Jay more than a hug! I could see Jim didn't like it, but Dad was enjoying every moment of the little charade, and I couldn't help thinking that Jay knew his old man much better than I did.

He just loved to make people squirm. I guess it came from putting so many employees on the hot seat before he fired them for stealing! He insisted that when he moved into a business that was running in the red, the first thing he did was find out who had slippery fingers, and who was helping himself, or herself, to booze, high-priced steaks and lobster, and dipping into the cash drawer. There were lots of other items involved, but those were the main categories with the biggest impact on the bottom line. Quite often, when the employees learned Dad was being hired to turn the operation around, they'd disappear before he arrived rather than face him and the possibility of prosecution for theft.

Vicki, it seemed, had done well for herself. She had a talk show on a local television station several afternoons a week. Nothing really spectacular, but she gave it a friendly, hometown spin, interviewing locals and tourists, and getting an interesting slant on life in Reno, northern Nevada's gambling Mecca.

Jay's dad wasn't to know, but he'd just done me a favor with his petty little game, because the first thing I decided to do when I could get to a phone was let Vy know where Vicki was. I still felt guilty for introducing them, and my loyalty would always be to Vyola. How she handled Vicki after I called her was entirely up to her, as I felt no qualms as far as that lady was concerned. By the time the evening was coming to a close, I was mad enough to consider disposing of Vicki myself!

Dad and Edith had gone up to bed around ten and taken Rebel with them. Edith insisted she'd love to tuck her up and put her to bed, so we let her, and stayed down to enjoy the smooth little orchestra and some great dance music.

Vicki kept draping herself all over Jay, and treating Jim like a pesky pup. When the music started up, she dragged Jay onto the floor—it didn't take much dragging, I have to admit—and clung to him like honeysuckle. I could see Jim was getting madder by the minute, and so was I. Finally, after several numbers without a break, I looked at Jim and said,

"We don't have to put up with this, you know. We can play her little game just as well as she can!"

His eyes lit up, and he said, "Let's do it!"

The next number was a slow one, and Vicki was already nuzzling Jay for all she was worth, when Jim and I stepped onto the floor. She didn't notice us at first as she was too wrapped up in Jay, but when she saw Jim whispering sweet nothings in my ear, and me nestling up to him and giggling at his remarks, she went ballistic! I'd never seen such rage. She came over to us and I thought she was going to belt either him or me, or both of us.

I quickly stepped back from Jim and burst out laughing.

"Well, Jim, it worked! The lady can dish it, but she can't take it!" Turning to Vicki I said, "You should see your face! You're a nut case! Come on, Jay, let's go up to bed," and I took his hand and we left.

In the elevator I said, "Why the hell did you let her go on like that? You knew it was driving Jim mad. They're married, for heaven's sake, and you know better!"

"Hey, you're jealous!" Jay said happily.

"'Fraid not. Just disappointed. It would take a lot more than anything that blonde two-timer could come up with to make me jealous. I promise you, when I *am,* you'll definitely know it, and it won't be because of any games Vicki dreamed up!"

A couple of days later, when we started getting dressed to head up north, Jay asked, "Would you mind terribly if we left Rebel behind? Edith wants her to stay with them while we're hunting. Her own two girls are grown up now, and she hasn't had a little one around in ages. I guess you can tell, she's crazy about Rebel."

I couldn't tell Jay it wasn't Edith I was worried about, it was Vicki. A weird scenario went through my mind: Vicki taking

Rebel, and holding her in exchange for my silence. She was too late though, as I'd already called Vyola. In my paranoid state, I didn't know if that was a plus or a minus, and I knew if I told Jay how I felt about Vicki he'd think I was off my rocker. He, like everyone who saw Vicki, couldn't believe she was anything but a sweet, loving angel. So, against my better judgment, I ended up agreeing to leave Rebel with her grandparents.

The drive up Route 395 was lovely. The sky was a brittle blue with delicate cirrus clouds swirling across its icy face. Many hours later, as the winter sun started to set, we approached a little town called Likely, and saw a quaint, homemade sign for a bed and breakfast two miles ahead.

"That's what I've been looking for, but I couldn't remember the name of the town," Jay said.

"You've been looking for that bed and breakfast sign?"

"Yes. Some of the guys at the North American Rod and Gun Club told me about it. Seems it's the favorite hangout of hunters and railway workers because they serve fabulous food."

As there were only half a dozen buildings in the whole town, the bed and breakfast was easy to spot. It was a lovely old two-storied farmhouse, sitting back away from the road. It needed a paint job, and so did the fence, but to two tired, hungry travelers, it sure looked inviting.

The inside reflected the history of the building, too. Its large dining room, which was part of the former country kitchen, had a huge old wood stove that was used as a central heating system in every sense of the word. It was in the dead center of the room with a giant flue rising up through the two floors. When we were shown up to our cozy room, the double bed with its light fluffy eiderdown comforter was placed along the central wall, and if you touched it you could feel the warmth from the kitchen below.

If I recall, we paid five dollars a night, which included dinner and a hearty breakfast. We arrived in time for dinner, joining a group of railroad workers. It was served farm-style, with all the platters of food placed piping hot on a refectory table with benches along both sides. There was a baked ham with a spicy honey glaze, gobs of real whipped potatoes slathered in butter, bowls of steaming vegetables, and platters of homemade hot biscuits, all topped off by a fruit pie with pastry to die for.

I believe the current owners must have been the original farmers, as they kept farming hours. We asked them if they would be kind enough to wake us at five-thirty as we wanted to get out early for our shoot. They laughed and told us not to worry, we'd wake by ourselves from the smell of cooking coming up from below, as breakfast was between five-thirty and six-thirty. Definitely farmers' hours.

And they were right about us waking to the aroma from the kitchen: it was so enticing we raced through our dressing to get down in time.

If dinner was big, breakfast was bigger. They had platters of T-bone steaks, eggs, bacon, home hash browns, fresh-baked bread, coffee that was strong enough to wake the dead, and jugs of orange juice. I gorged myself once more, and enjoyed every mouthful.

The pass shooting was terrific, and before long we got our limit. We only kept two of the honkers, though, and gave the rest to the farmer, who thanked us profusely and insisted on cleaning and packing our two in dry ice for the trip south. It had to be one of the most memorable shoots we'd ever been on, and we told him so. I know Jay would have loved staying another day, but I was still antsy about being away from

Rebel, and worrying if she was missing us as much as we were missing her.

When we got back to Reno, Rebel was nowhere to be found, and I panicked. On top of that, we couldn't find Jay's dad. When we finally located him in the hotel kitchen, he told us not to worry, and led us up to the suite where Edith was watching television. Rebel wasn't with her, and I just knew something was wrong. "Where's Rebel?" I almost screamed.

Edith turned, laughing, and said excitedly, "On television! Come quick!"

"Wh-a-a-t!?" I exclaimed, unbelieving.

Sure enough, the program was just starting, and there was our darling daughter sitting in a booster chair beside Vicki, stealing the complete show! Edith said she was back by popular demand. This was her second appearance in as many days!

"And you were worrying about her *missing* us?" Jay said, laughing.

Vicki did a delightful job interviewing Rebel, whom she introduced as her niece, and Rebel, who was just fourteen months old, came back with her precious, limited repartee, giggling and smiling and waving at the cameraman—all things for which adults would be chased off the set.

Chapter 16

It's strange how I never asked Vyola if she'd pressed charges against Vicki. I guess it was because I was chicken; I didn't want to open an old wound. All I hoped was that Vicki would stay out of the picture for the rest of my life. I think Vy realized I felt that way, because she never once brought the subject up, but knowing her as I did, I felt she had weighed all the pros and cons, and decided there was no way she could get blood out of a turnip, as the old saw goes, and cut her losses.

As for my three neat freelance accounts, the yarn boutique, Vyola, and Eva of Beverly Hills, I always let them think that each was the only account I had. It was easier that way: then they couldn't accuse me of spending more time with one than the other, or think I might share, or steal a design. The last seemed rather ridiculous on the face of it, as I had so many designs bouncing around in my head I knew I'd never run out of them, or have to steal from one account to satisfy the other.

I still felt guilty for being paid to do things I loved so much. Kitchen Planning, my full-time job, was such fun it had to be illegal. Apart from domestic kitchen planning, I also laid out hospital and restaurant kitchens, and fast-food installations. And although I didn't have a degree, like Edison's Home Economics director, Polly Eliker, or all the other home economists she had working for her, I was totally enthralled and involved with that part of Edison's sales promotion as well.

I remember thinking when Polly nervously started Edison's soon-to-be-famous television cooking schools, that she shouldn't have been nervous, she was a natural. And I also remember the first MC she got to warm up her audiences: it was Bob Barker, the same Bob Barker who was spotted by Art Linkletter, and who went on to great heights in television game shows. He and his wife and manager, Dorothy Jo, were two of the most down-to-earth, delightful people I'd ever met.

There was only one hitch to all this peripheral promotion—it gave Kitchen Planning such a boost I couldn't put off hiring another planner to keep up with the flood of work coming in. Although, contrary to Mrs. Henner's admonition, I'd never felt handicapped by not having a sheepskin, I decided to interview only college graduates for the position, preferably ones with a degree in interior design. I felt that with such a background it should be a cinch to train them in the time-and-motion/food-flow concept of kitchen planning. It turned out to be a wise choice, but often entailed my insisting on some *House Beautiful* kitchen layout being rearranged to include a more functional approach.

"Hey, if beautiful *functional* kitchens were easy to design, there'd be no need for our kitchen planning department!" I told Maria Pinetta, the outstanding grad from UCLA whom I had picked. "The challenge comes when you can combine the best in interior design with the best step-saving kitchen layout."

As Maria filtered most of the phone calls now, she always took first dibs on any remodel jobs in Bel Air, Beverly Hills, or Palos Verdes Estates. It got to be quite a contest to see who finally went out on an assignment. But one thing that helped immensely was that, with two of us now in the department,

I could give talks or attend appliance conventions and company functions without having to worry that the workload wasn't being handled.

I remember early in '55, Polly and I were to be honored at a luncheon at the Jonathan Club for outstanding achievement in the field of sales promotion.

"Good Lord, are they actually going to allow us gals into that holy of holies?" I asked Ray Waltham when he told us about the awards.

"You're darn right they are! I told them who you were, what you'd done, and that they'd better roll out the red carpet for you both."

When the great day arrived—with Polly and me dressed to kill—we were escorted to the Jonathan Club by all the big brass in Edison's Commercial Sales division. Talk about feeling grand! It was only a short block to the club, and I felt euphoric all the way—that is, until we arrived at its august portals and were told by the doorman we couldn't enter!

Edison's management team looked very uncomfortable, and gave Waltham an accusing look that seemed to say, *How could you do this to us?* But to Ray's credit, he exploded in our defense.

"Dammit, call the manager! This has all been arranged. The ladies are coming in and are going to be treated as honored guests."

"Just a minute," the doorman said in a panic, running into the foyer and buttonholing the obsequious manager, who I could see was gushing over the Los Angeles mayor and his entourage.

"I'm sorry, Mr. Waltham," the manager said as he stepped through the imposing doors. "I agreed to let the ladies have luncheon here, but in no way did I agree they could enter the premises through the front entrance. They will have to go to the rear and take the service elevator up to the banquet room."

Ray started to cuss, remembered we were present, offered us each an arm, and said, "Okay, ladies, you heard the gentleman—and I use that word loosely—we will use the service entrance." He gave the sales managers a questioning look, but they all bolted through the front door and left Ray to do the honors.

Going through the employees' entrance and up in the service elevator along with the Jonathan Club's famous platters of pungent corned beef and cabbage had to be *the* ego-deflater of the year!

~

As the year progressed, so did the saber rattling. Although the Korean conflict—it was never actually called a war—was long over, the Cold War was heating up, and the Russians were catching up with us in the space race. It was then I started to think it really wouldn't matter a hill of beans if Mrs. America had the best-planned kitchen in the world, if she wasn't free to enjoy it.

That's the problem with us Aquarians: we always have to look at the big picture. And Jay had inadvertently fueled my fire by telling me about North American's new rocket facility out in Canoga Park, just a whoop and holler from the lovely home he was building us in Woodland Hills.

On top of that, Maria had started complaining that we needed to hire another girl in Kitchen Planning, as the work was getting more than the two of us could handle.

"You'd better get *two* more girls," I said, stressing the two. "I'm quitting and going to work for Rocketdyne in Canoga Park."

Somehow, I just knew I was going to work there, just as I'd known back in 1950 that I'd get a job with Southern

California Edison. Anyhow, I'd broken all my records by staying six years in the same job.

So, a couple of days before my twenty-ninth birthday, I started to work for what I fondly learned to call the "rocket racket."

What an about-face!

For six years I'd worked for a privately owned utility, where every paperclip and rubber band was accounted for, where every strip of masking tape was used over and over until there was no stickum left. All this, in order that Edison's shareholders could earn the dividends they were entitled to for investing their hard-earned money in a giant operation. I came from a responsible, private enterprise to a cost-plus government-financed entity, where "fun" was taking huge sheets of expensive art paper, at several bucks a sheet, and cutting it up to make happy little *origami* birds, or dumping a full gallon of rubber cement, at thirty-five dollars a gallon, onto an art table, letting it set for a while, then picking it up and molding it into a bouncing ball to be tossed all over the art bay. As much as I liked most of the people I worked with and for, I had a problem adapting to their *laissez-faire* attitude.

On top of that, I couldn't get over the irony of the situation. Here I was, working in a facility that was directly connected to Werner von Braun and the German V-2, the precursor of which had wiped out all but one member of my father's family.

I'd been there just over six months when Bob Nelson, my immediate supervisor, put me in for an upgrade, from the unexciting job of plotting flowcharts to a technical artist's position. He said it was a tonic watching me work. He'd always thought the output of the different art groups could be improved, but never had a yardstick to measure by until I arrived. I didn't like that. It made me feel like I was showing everyone else up, and all I wanted to do was meld into the group and not make waves.

As excited as I was about the new position I'd been offered, there was a catch: it called for a Top Secret classification and I doubted I could get one. How the sam hill could anyone here in the States check my background? I had been born and raised in China and had left the country just before it fell to Communism. Not much there to recommend me for Top Secret clearance.

For once, my feeling of invincibility abandoned me. I filled out the required paperwork, positive it was an act of futility, and turned it in for processing.

"It takes several months to get clearance," Nelson said, "so meanwhile you'll have to keep working for me, if you can stand it."

"Bob, you know you're one of the neatest guys to work for. If it wasn't for you I'd have tossed this dull job long ago." When I said that, I also said a silent prayer that I'd get clearance, as there was nowhere I could go in the space program without it.

Right after that I had an occasion to go into the girls' john. For once it was empty, and pleasantly quiet. After washing my hands, I started to tidy my hair and coil my ponytail up into something a little more sophisticated, when the group of junior chart techs I worked with came in and marched towards me in a body. Crowding me up against the washbasins, Jean Watson, their leader, said, "Who the *hell* do you think you are?"

Another one piped up, "You're a stoolie!" There was a sneer in her voice. "Nelson just told us we had to shape up—he didn't say *like you,* but it was obvious—or we'd be shipped out. We know you're his sweetie pie. Bet you're sleeping with him. Before you came here it was fun coming to work."

I got mad. "Oh, really? You call what you're doing *work?* You treat this place like a country club. You waste supplies and precious time while the Russians are getting ahead of us in the space race." My words were full of contempt.

"Grow up. Where've you been? The Russians are a bunch of dumbheads who'll never catch up with us!"

"Don't bet on it! If your output is the measure of our effort, a turtle could pass us with loads of time to spare. Dammit, you're two-dollaring the rocket program to death!"

"S-o-o-o, Uncle Sam can afford it!" Jean said, hands on her hips.

"Can *you?*" I asked

"No skin off *my* nose," she said with a toss of her head.

"That's what *you* think. In case it hasn't sunk in to your thick skulls yet, we're all self-employed. The taxes, that Uncle Sam enjoys taking out of our paychecks, pay our wages. Haven't you ever figured that out?"

"Bullshit!"

"'Fraid not. The more time you waste on the job, the more the space race is going to cost, and the more taxes will be taken out of our paychecks to cover those costs. It's as simple as that."

"You're full of it. Who the hell put you on earth to light our way?"

"No one. But if you can play games all day, pick up a paycheck for doing nothing, and then sleep nights, be my guest. I can't do it."

"Boy, I wish you could hear yourself! You sound so damn smug, you self-righteous *bitch,* you make me *barf!*"

I knew now why the girls had picked Jean as their leader; she certainly had a great way with words.

I looked each one in the eye, shoved Jean out of the way,

and stalked out of the john without looking back. I knew the lines had been drawn, but I'd faced worse in my life. *To hell with all of you,* I muttered, as I stepped out into the bay.

"You okay?" Bob Nelson asked nervously. He was standing in the aisle, a few feet from the door, with a worried look on his face. "I'm sorry, I saw the girls eyeing you when I gave them my ultimatum, and when I was through, I watched as they stormed off after you to the john. I swear, I didn't mention your name."

"Don't worry." I shrugged. "It's nothing I can't handle. Just hope I don't meet any of them in an alley some dark night."

Three weeks later, to my complete surprise, I was called into Greg Freeman's office—he was the general manager of the whole art department—and he handed me my clearance papers with a broad smile.

"You've just broken some record," he said. "It usually takes anywhere from three to four months to get clearance. Sometimes, even longer than that."

"How the sam hill did Washington check my China background?" I asked, dumbfounded, remembering the runaround we'd had years ago when we tried unsuccessfully to get verification on the Chinese clerks who had witnessed Dad's will.

"They didn't have to do a check. You worked for the Marine Corps after the war, and your CO gave you such a terrific recommendation, you got clearance ahead of all the others. Welcome aboard!"

My new supervisor was Vic Rodman, and before long I was doing complete exploded views of the Jupiter and Thor engines. I thought that rather ludicrous, and told Vic it was a waste of time, all they had to do was send a diver down off the Florida coast with a camera, and he could shoot all the exploded rocket engines we needed right there on the seabed. For some reason, he didn't think my remark humorous.

A few weeks later, I was being nosy and, walking through my section of the art bay, I found six other artists doing exploded drawings of the same engine I'd just completed. I went over to the ever-present Employee Suggestion Box, got out a form, and wrote up my suggestion. I wrote, instead of seven renderings of the same engine, we could do one and file it, and it could be used in all the technical manuals we did, instead of doing a separate illustration for *each* manual. I sent it up the chain of command to Greg Freeman for his signature, thinking I would get a nice bonus for my brainchild.

Later in the week I got called into Freeman's office. I was elated, and asked him what he thought of my suggestion. Without so much as a blush, he looked me straight in the eye and said, "I won't sign it. You must understand, Pam, if I sign it, all I'll need to hire is one low-paid file clerk. If I don't, I'll have to hire ten highly paid artists. It's called empire building," he said with a wry smile, making no bones about it.

I learned later from Bob Nelson that Freeman got paid by the bodies he hired and not by their output, and realized that Bob Nelson, like John Addison at Edison, was too conscientious for his own good. That seemed to be the pattern for all the direct supervision; they struggled to get production up, while the bigwigs at the top were busy looking for ways to pad the contracts.

Along the same lines, they kept playing musical chairs with our desks. At least seven times in the four years I was with Rocketdyne, my desk was moved. At the beginning, that was no big deal, just annoying when I came to work and couldn't find where I'd been moved to. But when I received Top Secret clearance, any unfinished classified art I was working on had to be covered with a heavy canvas sheet at night. With a hundred and twenty-eight artists in the bay, the search could be very time-consuming. And later, when I became an airbrush artist, it wasn't only my desk that was moved, it was all the pipes, hoses, and paraphernalia that went with airbrush graphics. After the first couple of times, I learned that Rocketdyne got paid hundreds of dollars a desk whenever one was moved; with all the art groups involved, that became quite lucrative, especially as it didn't matter how far the desks were moved, or for what reason.

The last time I was moved, my desk was placed alongside a group of cartoonists whose job it was to lighten up the dull subject of job safety with wild cartoons of what could happen if safety were ignored. Their minds were fertile, their imaginations wild, and I loved them all, especially Bob Sullivan. He found fun in everything. I remember the time I came back from the girls' john complaining it was so crowded they were stacked three-deep. Within seconds he handed me a cartoon of a closed stall door, showing three sets of feet under it, indicating each was sitting on the other's lap!

I recall once on lunch break—there weren't any restaurants around, so we usually brown bagged it—when a group of us were discussing one of our favorite topics: space travel.

"Wouldn't it be awesome," I said, "if at some later date, our astronauts were to land on a distant planet only to find the ground rolling, mountains heaving, darkness at noon, and the crucifixion taking place all over again?"

I got some weird looks from several of the artists, and to defend my remark I added, "You know, we're not the *only* planet in the universe that God has visited?"

Bob Sullivan was one of the group, and he said, "You sound so positive."

"I *am* positive!"

He grinned and tweaked my ponytail. "Sorry. If I can't laugh at it, I won't think about it."

Surprisingly, that random thought, thrown out for what it was worth, brought discussions on the religious aspects of space travel that made me realize I hardly knew my friends and fellow artists that I'd had taken so much for granted.

∼

About that time, Jay transferred from North American, Downey, to Rocketdyne, spending most of his time out at Edwards Air Force Base as a field service rep.

It turned out to be the only way we could work together, as both North American and its Rocketdyne subsidiary had a policy that husbands and wives could not work in the same department.

Just to be on the safe side, though, when Jay came in from the field for briefings, or to turn in his reports, we were careful not to be seen together. A few of my closest friends knew who he was, and of course Ross Pettit, my new supervisor in the airbrush section, knew, because he and Jay had originally worked together in the training department at North American's Downey facility.

When Jay was in town, I didn't car-pool. We'd quietly meet out in the parking lot, climb into the Packard, and head for home. Ditto in the morning, always trying to keep a low profile. Guess it didn't work too well, as one morning, while we were getting out of the car, I overheard one of the secretaries say to her girlfriend, "See those two? *They're sleeping together, I just know it!*" She sounded so happy with this juicy tidbit that I burst out laughing, heading for the art bay while Jay veered off to the offices and conference rooms.

His job in the field was instructing military personnel on

rocket telemetry, and he told me he'd never enjoyed a job so much. The students came from all over the world: England, France, Italy, Greece, Turkey—the latter two countries, once mortal enemies, were now our allies against the threat of Communism. He said the group he enjoyed most were the Brits. He couldn't get over the low noncom ratings they held when they were such sharp, well-trained men. The Americans outranked them in every field, and he didn't think that fair. He got in the habit of bringing some of them home for the weekend, and they'd camp out in the family room, enjoying my simple home cooking and a place to flop. It wasn't long before we had a good old dart board up on the wall, and I learned to leave their beer out of the refrigerator, as they preferred it warm! Their accents came from all over England, and quite often Jay would ask me on the q.t. to translate, as he couldn't understand them. I hated to tell him, I had the same problem every once in a while.

One weekend, Jay, Rebel—who was now going on five—and five Brits somehow managed to squeeze into the convertible, and took off for Disneyland. I was unable to join them as I now was on a six-day work schedule. I'd even had to give up all my freelance accounts, which I found really tough.

Actually, I only had to give up Vyola and the knitting boutique, as Eva had fallen by the wayside a year earlier. It all happened innocently enough one Saturday, after I'd been designing her very successful line for several seasons. Things were going along swimmingly; we'd just put in a exceptionally busy morning, and decided it was time to break for lunch. When Eva, Bernie, and I got in the elevator to go down to the deli, we found there was a passenger already on board. When he saw Eva, he grinned widely and asked her when he could come in and sketch his next season's line.

"Any time, Hymie, any time," she said, smiling.

When he got off, and we continued on down to the lobby, I said, my voice bristling with anger, "Did I hear him right? He sketches your exclusive line and runs it the same season you do?"

"Pam, you have to be realistic. This is business. If I don't let him sketch the line now, he'll wait till it's out in the stores and sketch it anyway, and come out one season later. This way he's happy, and we remain friends. Friends are important in this type of a business."

"I'm glad to hear that," I said, barely controlling my rage. "I thought *I* was a friend. I can't believe you have knowingly violated your contract with me!"

"You're being stupid, Pam," Bernie said, not mincing words. "I've already knocked this season's line off under a new label. Even Eva doesn't know about it!"

I looked at Eva. She turned white, then slowly turned purple. Bernie didn't seem to notice, but went on jubilantly, "I've beaten Hymie at his own game—how *about* that?"

Eva, still looking as though she'd been hit by a wrecking ball, started to steer me into the deli on the ground floor. The odor of pungent kosher cooking and the heartbreaking news I'd just received made me nauseous, and I said, "I'm sorry, Eva, I've just lost my appetite," and turning on my heel, I fled the building.

You dumb broad! Don't you remember Mrs. Henner said American designers have no protection in their own country?

∽

When the noisy group got back from Disneyland, the stories they told could have filled a book. I guess the highlight of the day came when they went to see a group of Sioux from the Rosebud Reservation in Nebraska doing a tribal raindance.

Jay recognized some of them, as he'd spent time on the reservation on a construction job back before the war, and when the exhibition was over, one of them saw him and yelled, "Hey, *Whitey!*" They all came around and started slapping him on the back and reminiscing, and Jay asked what had happened to Mendota, the Indian girl he was nuts over. "Ah, Mendota," her cousin said sadly, "you know, she never got over you. She left the reservation right after you did, and never came back. I hear she never married either." Then, with a wide grin he added, "See what you do to our women, Whitey!"

Of course, the Brits didn't miss a word, and Jay got teased unmercifully for the rest of the day. In fact, it was the Yorkshire boy, Wally Chumley, who told the story when they got home in the evening, embellishing it as only the British can, while through it all the other men softly sang snatches from bawdy beer hall songs in the background, and I cracked up laughing.

Chapter 17

When October 4, 1957, came around it had no landmark significance for me. But all that changed dramatically when I poured my first cup of coffee and turned on the news to find that Russia had just launched a satellite into space.

Those dumbheads who could never catch up with us ... ?

A while later at work, when I was talking somberly with Bob Nelson, one of his chart techs came by and said laughingly, "The Russians sure have a *silly* name for their satellite—what's a *Sputnik*, for God's sake?"

"It's a *wake-up call,* if you really want to know," Nelson said, looking disturbed at the girl's lack of understanding. Then turning to me he said, "I can just see the smug look on the faces of our top honchos now as they write up proposals for additional megabucks to cover the space program."

"Well, you have to admit, it would be legit," I said. Then, thinking of Nelson's concern regarding production, I added, "Wouldn't it be ironic if we had to install the Russian program of rewarding workers for their output? I can just see it now: all of us lining up and having Freeman pin stars on our chests with different colored ribbons, designating whether we were Comrade First Class, Second Class, or Third Class. I wonder if top supervision will now back you, Rodman, and the others, and insist on better production figures."

"You're a dreamer!" he said with a weak smile, as we went our separate ways.

But it did seem to make a difference, and I noticed a lot less goofing off and a lot more serious effort in the art bay.

So *Sputnik* was only a one-hundred-and-eighty-four-pound unmanned satellite, it still *was in orbit,* something we had not been able to achieve to date, and circling the earth every ninety-six minutes at an astronomical eighteen thousand miles an hour. Personally, I loved the additional challenge. It's always more exciting when you have to overcome something tangible, or beat someone, and you've got a valid target in view.

But none of that eliminated the seriousness of the situation, and when Rebel's birthday arrived towards the end of October, I looked at her and prayed that she would grow up in a safe world. The space race had become very real to me. The idea that there could be global war from outer space within her lifetime put a damper on my mood. I kept thinking of the old expression, get the lead out, and hoped all the industries involved in our space program would realize the time for fun and games was over. We were in this for keeps, and we'd better give it all we had. I thought of the girls who'd pushed me around in the john, and wondered if they really understood the element of peril hanging over us … literally and figuratively.

I knew it, of course. I'd lived through it, thousands of miles away in another country. In another world. I'd seen the devastation, the horrendous human loss, the ruined lives, the unending trauma. And I also knew I couldn't impart that very real threat to anyone who'd never lived through it. It was one of the reasons why I understood and enjoyed the company of the GIs who'd been lucky enough to return home. We were all kindred spirits.

Of course, I didn't let my fears interfere with Rebel's

happy birthday party that followed a couple of weeks after the launching. It's strange how we take so many events for granted—like Christmas and Easter, Mother's Day and Father's Day, Memorial Day, the Fourth of July, Labor Day, Thanksgiving and, of course, birthdays. Those are all celebrations taken for granted by free people, but the element that makes them possible is anything but "free."

And then to my horror, I started having nightmares about an atomic attack. The last one I'd had was in the prison camp right after our liberation, when the devastation of Hiroshima and Nagasaki was still fresh in our minds. It was the first time I can remember dreaming in full, bloody color, and I woke up sweating in terror. The ones I was having now were just as bad. The city around me was collapsing like a house of cards, dust and debris were everywhere, and I couldn't breathe, as the bomb had sucked all the oxygen out of the air. It would end with me waiting for the blast to come and turn me to blistering dust. Then blessedly, I'd wake up, only to start choking over the horror I'd seen.

I knew most of the nightmares were brought on by exhaustion at the pace I'd set for myself. I'd find I'd have to force myself to relax—and it took a while for me to grab hold once more of the excitement of being part of a program that was designed to prevent these dread dreams from ever becoming reality.

I didn't dwell on them much after I got my Senior Artist rating. In fact, I stopped having them entirely after I was assigned to working with what I considered fantastic rocket engineers and scientists. Their minds were so free and unencumbered that nothing appeared impossible to them. I would literally sit and hold their hands as they came up with ideas that I would sketch for them while they dreamed on. Solid and liquid rocket concepts, space stations, which upon launching, opened up like Swiss army knives, their ragged antennae and dishes hailing limitless space with a spunky, "Hey, I'm here! What are you going to do about it?!" And I could visualize life on the other planets saying, "Good Lord, that little upstart Planet Earth is becoming a major player!"

The thing that amazed me the most was that although the engineers' ideas seemed way-out in terms of what we knew at the time, they made their application so practical and possible I could feel the tide turning. I knew we were on the right track. I knew we would ultimately beat everyone in the field. And once more I was proud to be a part of all that excitement.

There was only one time when I had a terrible letdown; when I had to acknowledge Mrs. Henner was right again. That was when a couple of Rocketdyne's most brilliant men—one had never finished high school, the other barely walked through the halls of higher learning—were going to pitch their concepts in Washington in the hope of gaining lucrative research and development contracts for Rocketdyne.

I just knew their enthusiasm and knowledge would knock the lawmakers' socks off, and I was thrilled for them. I remember one of them saying, "This could only happen in America!" They had so much more on the ball than many of the others whose names were loaded down with academic degrees. It wasn't that the latter didn't have excellent theoretical knowledge, it was that many of them lacked vision. According to my two happy iconoclasts, when you thought "big" you didn't need textbooks to tell you that it couldn't be done ... *you just did it!* And they were living proof of that.

Then came the letdown. Just days before they were to leave for Washington, they were told they would have to explain their concepts to a couple of colleagues who had the right credentials to make the presentation. And being men of integrity, that's what they did.

I believe I was the only one at work who really knew how hard the blow had been, not just to their egos, but to their idea of what being an American really meant. I tried to laugh at it, and said, "If you think that's bad, how about me? I don't have a degree either, but I've enjoyed working with you, and if you're not acceptable, then neither am I. Maybe we shouldn't let them take all the graphics and flip charts we've worked up to illustrate the presentations. Let's face it, they were obviously drawn up by an incompetent!"

That brought on gales of laughter, and they asked me to go out and get drunk with them. It sounded good, but I declined as it was Friday, and I knew Jay was careering home from Edwards AFB.

∽

Jay spent the following week at the Canoga Park facility, and I was assigned by my boss, Ross Pettit, to work with him on a set of training aids he needed for Edwards. It was fun, and we got a lot accomplished. As I mentioned earlier, only a couple of old friends knew we were married, so we kept up the pretense. On our way home, several evenings into the week, Jay said, "You missed something today. After you left my desk, Joe Danforth, who sits right by me, watched you walk away and said, 'How'd you like to take *that* to bed with you?' I didn't know whether to say I did, or deck him."

I couldn't help laughing, remembering my earlier rhumba lessons, and a comment Gene Hampton, my dance instructor, had made: "You're the only gal I know who has a built-in rhumba-roll. You sure as heck don't need any lessons!" And I remember thinking at that time that it was unfair that one seldom got to see their own "walkaway."

As the work got more demanding, so did the need to let off steam. The section of the art group I was in let down its hair with parties. Preferably costume affairs, but anything was considered a reason for a blowout. Dorothy Marsh had just built a new home—the price of an invitation to her housewarming was a framed, signed painting or sketch, to be hung in her new art gallery. She didn't care what the subject matter was: abstract, conventional, comic, cubist, anything and everything was acceptable. Mine was an oil painting of my recollection of the Taoist temple in Peking; it was one of the saner ones. Most were flights of fancy, or rather fantasy, depicting the cosmos, intergalactic travel, and exploding nova, interspersed with some wild nudes, and wilder cartoons, and surprisingly, a few true masterpieces—leaving me wondering how that last great talent had been harnessed to the plough horse called technical illustration.

I remember a party at Sergei Malakoff's home. He was a Russian immigrant, and I couldn't help wondering how he had got his Top Secret clearance. Regardless, he threw a Halloween party and, of course, we had to come in costume. I came as a geisha, with a modified hairdo as I couldn't find an appropriate wig, my hair piled up with tall Oriental combs, flowers, and jiggling butterflies. Jay first said I couldn't get him to dress up if I wanted to, then relented, and came in the formal tails he wore as a professional dancer. He looked great, but I didn't think he was really in costume. The others made up for him, though, as pirates, princes, courtesans, caballeros, and most of history's great heroes and heroines. And typical of Russian bashes, every costume, and every wacky incident, was an occasion for a toast. Before long, the strain of the workplace was forgotten in the "anything goes" atmosphere of the party.

Sergei had a great selection of music, and among his

records was our favorite, *Canadian Sunset*. Jay and I had made it "our song" when it came out, as he had so many ties to Canada he considered himself almost a Canuck. Towards the end of the evening he suggested we should go home, but that he'd put on *Canadian Sunset* one more time, and we would have our last dance together before we left.

We had our dance, and while I looked around for Sergei to thank him and tell him we were leaving, Jay wandered off to the kitchen.

I couldn't find Sergei anywhere. Wandering through the crowd and wondering where he had disappeared to, I decided to ask Bob Nelson's cute wife if she'd seen him.

Laughing, she said, "He's standing right behind you!" Then added, with a mischievous smile, "He's been two steps behind you all through your search."

I turned, just as he was reaching to tap me on the shoulder, and said, "Darn you, Sergei! I was looking for you to thank you for a wonderful evening. It's been a great party, but Jay and I are going to have to leave now."

"I don't think so," he said, and at my perplexed expression, added, "Jay's in the kitchen telling one of his wild stories, there's no way you're leaving now. Let's dance."

He was good, and we danced several light numbers. All the while, I kept glancing toward the kitchen, but the laughter and stories were still bursting out through the door, and I knew Jay was really wound up. Then *Malaguanya* came on, a tango I just loved, and Sergei grabbed me and said, "This is mine—forget Jay!"

We must've looked a riot: A Cossack and a geisha doing a tango! He was only a few inches taller than I was, and we fit together like yin and yang. I had some trouble with my kimono flying open and showing a lot of leg, but hell, that's what a tango's all about. Unknown to me, Jay had spotted us from the kitchen, and came storming out.

"How dare you dance with anyone after we had the *last dance!*"

I looked at him flabbergasted. "That was almost half an hour ago! I'll be darned I'm going to stand around like a wallflower while you regale 'em with your shaggy stories."

I gave Sergei a hug and thanked him again for a great evening, while Jay started dragging me out to the car.

As he slammed the passenger door on me, and stormed around to the driver's side, he yelled, "What the hell got into you?!"

He dropped behind the wheel and turned on me, and for the first time in my life *I was scared.* I'd never seen him like this. He *never* lost his cool or raised his voice.

I took a deep breath and said to myself, *Watch it, this is jealous rage ... take it easy, gal.* I knew I should've been flattered, but this was new territory for me. I thought about quipping that it was okay for him to flirt with every girl he met, but that I had to walk the straight and narrow, then decided to drop it as I watched him struggle to gain control of himself.

As the '50s came to a close, many of the tech service reps were spending more and more time in the office, and less time out in the field, and I knew Jay, who was one of them, loathed being pinned to a desk.

In October of '59, he was approached by a recruiter for Aerojet, Rocketdyne's competition in Northern California, and offered the position of tech rep at Vandenberg AFB. He asked me if he could accept. What could I say? We only go around once, and we'd better enjoy every minute of it.

Several weeks later, after a sad goodbye to his buddies at Rocketdyne, and a sadder goodbye to Rebel and me, he took off for Rancho Cordova, a suburb of Sacramento, and home to the Aerojet facility. Good to the company's word, he was soon assigned to Vandenberg AFB, and although it was a lot further away than Edwards, he drove home every weekend.

It was during this time that I almost killed him. It was late one Thursday and I was trying to sleep, but I was overtired and kept thrashing around in bed, my legs aching, and my lower back reminding me it could just take so much abuse. I guess I must've finally dropped off, because I woke with a start when I heard the outside door to the family room open and someone start furtively up the stairwell. I was terrified. Trying not to make a sound, I reached under the mattress and pulled out the Colt .38 Jay had given me, and silently slid the safety off. My heart was thudding so hard I could hardly breathe. I'd never been so scared in all my life. As I saw the head and shoulders of a figure appear above the loft floor, I sputtered in a shaky voice, "Stop, or I'll shoot!"

"For God's sake put that away! It's ME! JAY!"

I lost it then, and burst into tears. I was shaking so badly I almost dropped the pistol. He took it carefully out of my hand, slid the safety back on, and put it under the mattress.

"I'm sorry, hon, I thought I could slip into bed without waking you."

"When you come in late like that," I said, finding my voice, "you better yell, *'I'm home!'* or you'll be dead."

"Hey, you're not the only one who was scared!"

"Today isn't Friday—how come you're home?" I asked, realizing that, subconsciously, that was what had terrified me.

"Around six this evening they called off the test firing tomorrow, and told us we could go home and have a nice long weekend. Thought you'd be happy to see me." The last was said in a hurt little-boy voice.

"I am! But don't *ever* do that again!"

Luckily, we hadn't woken Rebel in her nursery downstairs, and the lovemaking was extra sweet that night. Probably because we both realized we'd come so close to never making love again.

∽

Life turned into a hectic, chopped-up existence after that, and I got to thinking there had to be a better way to live. I'd given four years of my life to Rocketdyne and loved it there, but the smog and traffic in the San Fernando Valley, where we lived, were becoming unbearable, and for Rebel's health, if for no other reason, I started to consider moving up north with Jay.

When I told him the following weekend, he was thrilled. I suggested it would be best if I came up in June after school was out. That would give him time to find a place for us to live, and me time to sell the house.

After he'd gone back to the base, I got out a pad and pencil and started making a list of little things that needed to be done before we could sell our home. Stuff he wasn't able to keep up with on the weekends when he came home, such as some baseboards, door trim, touch-up painting, and gobs of miscellaneous little odds and ends. There was no way I could do it. I was working six days a week and spent my precious Sundays with Rebel or doing minor housework; I'd had a weekly housekeeper for several years for the heavy work. Luckily, our neighbor across the street was a comfy lady with a brood of kids, and she didn't think anything of adding one more. She had a daughter just Rebel's age, and the two of them were inseparable. Her husband worked for the city, and she enjoyed having the extra cash to spend.

In March I took a few days off, and Rebel and I drove up to Sacramento to get a feel for the area. That's when I fell in love with Northern California! I'd never seen such a landscape: luscious rolling green hills dotted with languid cattle and gnarled oak trees just turning to bud, and the air so clean it just begged to be breathed. In the shimmering distance, billowing white thunderheads climbed up over the snow-capped Sierra. I had just turned thirty-three, and I knew I'd finally found my one-and-only lasting home.

Earlier, when Jay asked me where I wanted to live, I'd said I didn't care just so long as it was east of Aerojet, so that I'd have the sun behind me on my commute to and from work. I'd suffered through heavy traffic with the sun in my eyes coming and going to work all through my years down south, and if I had a choice, it was not going to happen again.

With the help of a garrulous old real estate agent who knew everyone and everything in El Dorado, a county in the Sierra Foothills that adjoined Sacramento County, Rebel and I were shown some delightful little pear and apple orchards. The trouble was, they were in the Georgetown Divide area, between the south and middle forks of the American River, and the drive up to them over twisting, turning mountain roads was often blocked by slow-moving lumber trucks, canceled out any advantage gained by being east of Aerojet, and added the hazard of driving on unfamiliar mountain roads.

"Sorry, darling. I love the ranches, but you've just doubled my commute time by being so far out. Is there anything closer to Highway 50?"

"Oh, sure," the old man said. "The Pardi Ranch is for sale in the heart of Placerville, right up on Big Cut. I'll have to call them first, but I'm sure they'll let me show it to you."

On the way back down the mountain, on tortuous Highway 193, he rambled on about the history of Big Cut. It seems back in the Gold Rush, a city slicker from New York came to town and asked a bunch of sourdoughs, as the miners were called, where the best gold could be found. They figured if he was so dumb he thought they'd tell him, they might as well give him a run for his money. With a perfectly straight face, one of the miners said, "See that hill rising right outta town? Well, at the very top we know there's a lotta gold. Trouble is, we'd work it ourselves, but we can't afford the equipment we'd need to mine it!"

"Son-of-a-gun, if the crazy New Yorker didn't bite, hook, line and sinker," the real estate agent went on. "He moved crews and equipment up to the top of the hill and proceeded to cut a great gash out of it—hence the name Big Cut—while the old sourdoughs sat back and laughed their heads off.

"Surprisingly, the city slicker got the last laugh, because he *did* find gold! Enough to pay off all his expenses and make him a rich man. It soon played out though, and he moved on."

"That's a true story?" I asked.

"Every word of it. Believe you can check it out in the old *Mountain Democrat.*"

Then he rambled on about Fremont, Kit Carson, and the Pony Express, all part of El Dorado's golden history, and like the poor city slicker, I knew I'd succumbed, hook, line, and sinker.

The Pardis were delightful, and I loved their property overlooking the city of Placerville, the county seat for El Dorado. The views went on forever, and were absolutely breathtaking. I had one concern though: the western boundary of their pear orchard hung over the sharp cliff that the New Yorker had cut away in his search for gold, and the drop to the road below was deadly.

"Oh, I wouldn't worry about that," Mr. Pardi said. "We've only lost one cow. It dropped off the ledge and was killed."

"It isn't cows I'm worrying about," I said. "It's my little seven-year-old daughter."

"Oh, you could put a fence up, I guess, if you're really worried about it," he said, "but we never found a need for it, and we raised our whole family here."

"What do you think, hon?" Jay asked, as the real estate agent dropped us off at his office on Main Street, and we got back into our car to head down to Jay's tiny apartment in Rancho Cordova.

"I love it! Did you see the views? My God, it would be like living on top of the world. Wait till I tell the kids at Rocketdyne. They'll just drool!"

Chapter 18

In April, Jay called to tell me the Pardi sale had fallen through.

"Why, for heaven's sake? I loved that place!"

"The orchard's been hit badly with pear decline. They're pulling out all the trees to stop it from spreading. They've decided to keep the place and retire on it." Pear decline, or psylla, was the scourge of the '60s for the pear crops in El Dorado County.

"Oh, *d-a-m-n!*"

"Don't worry, hon, I've already found another, and I know you'll love it."

I was dying to see the new orchard that he said was in Camino, four miles east of Placerville, but I couldn't get away as we had deadlines galore to meet at work. May came upon me before I knew it, and I rushed around looking for a handyman to finish up the odds and ends we needed done on the house. He wound up the work in June, a week before school was out, and in a panic, I started to look for a real estate agent. She came to see me on Saturday morning to look the place over. She said she didn't think we'd have any problem selling it, as it had everything going for it.

"What are you asking for it?" she asked.

I knew that would come up, and had already figured out a price. I took the amount we'd paid for the land, added the price of all the materials we'd used to build the house, doubled that to cover Jay's labor, and decided to triple it to give us a nice profit. I gave her the figure, expecting her to shoot me down, but she said, "That's sounds just about right. Let's try it."

Next day, Sunday, she brought a couple over and they fell in love with the place. They put a down payment on it, and then on Monday came over with a check for the balance! I paid off the real estate agent and told Jay all systems were go!

I didn't even have to worry about my next job. The week after I told Jay I'd move north with him, he took my resumé into Aerojet's employment office and I was hired on the spot, with a nice fat raise! The only problem was, they kept hounding him and asking if I couldn't get up there sooner than June, as they needed me desperately in Technical Manuals ... *"Now!"*

It was nice to know that as far as jobs were concerned I was still invincible!

～

Leaving Rocketdyne was bittersweet. I'd had great jobs all my life, but none as exciting or fulfilling as this one. I'd learned so much, met so many terrific people, made so many friends, it was sad to say goodbye. I still have the huge going-away card that Howard Marson made for me. It's a brightly colored wash cartoon on black paper of me in jeans in an orchard, an old farmhouse in the background with a bright red Chinese pagoda roof on it, and smoke curling out of a huge, incongruous brick chimney. I'm climbing a ladder with a bucket of paint in one hand and a brush in the other, painting the pears on the trees all different colors! The caption reads, "Now, isn't that more artistic?" I placed the signature page, with close to a hundred names and kind wishes, behind the picture when I had it framed. Who knows, someday I may take it apart and reminisce over each and every one of them ...

I'd no sooner said my goodbyes than North American Van Lines came to haul all our belongings up north. The crew told me to go visit a neighbor while they packed and that I was not to worry as they wouldn't miss a thing. I have to admit Aerojet really took care of its employees in grand style.

I'd already packed all our clothing and loaded it into the ranch wagon, and was rounding up Thor and Jupiter, our two cats, and Cali, our liver-and-white English Springer, when Jay came roaring up to the house in his new VW bug.

"We've got a problem," I said. "We've got three cars and only two drivers. What are we going to do?"

"Oh, I forgot to tell you. Last weekend I sold the Packard to Ronny, the kid next door, for $500. It's not a car that's good in a northern climate. I'd left the keys to it in my apartment in Rancho, that's why he hasn't already taken it. I'm going to leave the keys with his folks now."

"Are you sure you want to *sell* it?" I asked, remembering how he'd loved that car through the years.

"Yup! We don't need it!"

We might not have *needed* it, but he kicked himself around the block the rest of his life for letting that car go, especially after Packard folded and it became a classic.

∼

When Jay took Rebel and me out to the ranch in Camino for the first time and introduced us, I saw the Olsens' stunned expressions and watched as their daughter, Catherine, turned deep red, spun on her heel, and rushed out of the room, fighting back tears.

What the hell's going on? I thought.

I couldn't dwell on it, as the Olsens started to show us the old homestead. They insisted it was only a few years old, but I interpreted that to mean they'd only finished working on it a few years ago, as it was definitely at least thirty years old. It was a typical two-story farmhouse, with a high pitched gable roof to handle the snow load, two pretty porches, and a patio. Downstairs there was a lovely big farm kitchen with a mudroom off it, a living room with an adjoining full dining room, two bedrooms, and a bathroom. Upstairs were two more very large bedrooms, but no bathroom, and a huge landing that I mentally turned into my studio. From its window I looked down on a sweep of lawn and a huge swimming pool.

Rebel jumped up and down and screamed excitedly, "O-o-h, a pool! A *swimming* pool!"

About fifty yards beyond it and slightly downhill were the pickers' quarters, and below them, two large barns. One was open to the elements, where they stacked tree props, picking and pruning ladders, and odd items. The second, with sliding wooden doors, housed the tractors. The spray rig was on a concrete landing just below it.

After we'd viewed everything around the main house, Henrik Olsen showed us the foreman's house facing the head of the steep driveway, then took us down into the orchard where the original little homestead-cum-worker's cabin nestled in among the Bartlett pears. The more I saw of the ranch, the more I loved it. It was even prettier than the Pardi place, if that were possible, and much larger. And for Jay, it had another plus: it wasn't in the city. He was not a city dweller; he loved the great outdoors, wildlife, and the wonderful feeling of freedom that came with it.

As we drove away, I said, "I *love* the place!" Then I added, "What have you been telling the Olsens?"

"What do you mean?"

"Come *on!* You must've seen the stunned looks on their

faces when you introduced Rebel and me. Didn't they know you were married?"

"I told them we were separated."

"*Why?*"

"Because technically we were ... until you moved up."

He said it so nonchalantly, I could've slugged him.

"Dammit, Jay. Didn't you see the look on Catherine's face? You hurt the gal badly. How could you?"

"I wanted the ranch."

"And you thought if you appeared eligible you'd have a better chance of getting it? *I don't believe it!*"

Although we'd had a double-ring ceremony, Jay never wore his wedding band, saying it could be hazardous in the work he was doing. *Yeah, and it would sure spoil all your fun, too ...*

As we couldn't take possession of the ranch until that year's crop was in, we moved into a little house-trailer that the Olsens had let Jay place between the pool and the pickers' quarters. We found the reason they needed to sell was that Henrik Olsen, in his late sixties, had had several strokes and couldn't do the work anymore. It was obvious he liked having Jay working for free on the ranch when he got back from Aerojet in the evenings and on the weekends. Actually, Jay could only work on Sundays, as the Olsens were Seventh Day Adventists and didn't work from sundown Friday to sundown Saturday. They were so strict about it, they wouldn't let Jay work either, although there was a lot that needed to be done. We weren't allowed to do anything, not even swim in the pool, and I had a hard time explaining that to Rebel.

Sundays I started going to St. Patrick's Church in Placerville, and Jay and I planned to join the church. That got tossed out of the window fast when Henrik came down to the trailer around five-thirty Sunday morning and told Jay to rise and shine as it was the first day of the week. It wasn't on *our* calendar, but that didn't seem to matter to the Olsens. Jay wanted desperately to learn all he could about farming, and it really rankled when he had to sit around and do nothing on Saturdays. I tried to get him to go sightseeing, come on a picnic, or take Rebel to a park—anything to get him away from the place, but, manlike, he insisted on staying in the trailer and stewing.

∼

I'll never forget the euphoria of our first harvest, and of making the first installment on the ranch. After all our expenses had been paid, I asked Jay if we had enough to cover the mortgage, and he said grinning, "You bet we do!"

The following day was Saturday, so I knew we would have to wait till the first of the week—*our* week, that is—before Jay could pay Henrik. Jay had a different idea.

Saturday lunch, while I was making sandwiches, he roared up the driveway, slammed on the brakes, and came in doubled over with laughter.

Rebel looked up at him with an excited, "Hi-ee Daddy!"

Smiling to match his happy face, I said in a bewildered voice, "What's up?"

"I just made the mortgage payment to the Olsens!" he said with a grin as wide as a sickle moon.

I couldn't believe it, and said, "Oh, Jay, how could you! It's Saturday. It's their *Sabbath!*"

"Hell, it made up for all those Saturdays I had to sit around twiddling my thumbs, and all those Sundays I couldn't join you and Rebel in church."

I didn't point out that he still didn't come to church with us, and now he had no excuse.

"Did they accept the check?" I asked, surprised. "They are not allowed to conduct business of any kind on Saturday."

"You *bet* they accepted the check!"

"You sonofabitch ..." I said softly, wondering where he got the gall. And for the next seven years, after each harvest he'd wait until Saturday came around to make the mortgage payment.

That first year had not been without its disasters, though. Early in the picking season, the short, hardworking Filipino pickers had nothing but trouble with the tall twelve- and fourteen-foot ladders. The first casualty was a badly sprained back that required hospitalization; the second was when one of the men fell off a ladder and broke his arm in several places. More hospitalization. And that was followed by an accident in our own immediate family.

Darling seven-year-old Rebel was out of school for the summer, and she totally enjoyed "helping" her dad with the harvest. She always rode with him in the Chevy truck to the Placerville Fruit Growers, where the fruit was processed, packed, and distributed. Heading back to the ranch one evening, she was sitting beside him on a coil of rope that he'd used to tie down the bins of fruit earlier. It made her sit taller in the seat, and she felt very important. Going around one of the sharp inside curves on North Canyon, the passenger door flew open, and she was flung out into the road. It was all Jay could do to control the truck, crimping the wheels so he wouldn't run her over with the wide rear bed. Pulling over as close as he could to the inside bank, he parked and rushed back to where she lay. She was a bloody mess from head to toe, but was being a little stoic, more worried about her dad than herself. She kept saying, "I'm all right, Daddy. I'm all right," all the while trying her darnedest not to cry.

The only thing Jay could do was lift her gently into the truck and lay her across the front seat, then he closed the door and locked it once more. Slipping in the driver's side, he put her bloody head on his lap and drove the quarter mile to the ranch, transferred her to our new Ford Falcon pickup, and rushed her to the hospital.

She was already in the emergency room when I got a call at Aerojet notifying me of the accident. Howard Hillman, who was our car-pool driver that day, dropped everything and rushed me to Marshal Hospital. When we arrived, I could hear Rebel's screams all the way out to the parking lot, and I leapt out of the car, bent on clobbering anyone hurting her.

The first person I saw was Jay, and he was a total wreck. I asked him what happened and what they were doing to Rebel to cause such agonizing screams. He put his arms around me, tears cutting through the dust and grime on his face, and said, *"Oh, God, Pam!* She fell out of the fruit truck as we were rounding the sharp bend just past the dump. She's covered in gravel burns from head to foot and looks like raw hamburger. They have to scrub all the gravel out with hard brushes to stop any infection, but they can't give her an anesthetic because they don't know how bad her injuries are."

I thought of stories I'd heard of interrogators torturing children to make their parents talk, and now I knew the horror of their anguish. All I wanted to do was kill all of them for hurting my Rebel.

Finally, they wheeled her into X-ray and found she had a broken back. I looked at Jay, and could see that his guilt was killing him. He kept saying, "It shouldn't have happened. I know I locked her in. I swear I did! That door should never have flown open."

As bad as her back was, they couldn't put a cast on until the gravel burns had completely healed, so they covered her from head to foot in a new ointment with special healing properties and then wrapped her like a mummy. She never cried again. Our littlest Rebel had to be the toughest little girl I'd ever known.

A week later, when they removed the bandages, there was hardly any scar tissue to be seen, and they were able to put her in a total body cast. I have never seen anyone adapt like she did. The cast covered her entire torso from her neck to her thighs, yet somehow she got around almost like a normal kid. Of course, she couldn't sit, so she'd plop down on her knees when she was tired of standing, and from there she would flop onto her back, side, or tummy if she wanted to lie down. All this in the heat of late summer, with that damn swimming pool beckoning to her...

One thing did get cleared up almost immediately. The weigh-master at the packing shed told Jay he'd seen him lock Rebel into the truck cab that fateful evening.

"You're positive?" Jay said.

"Positive," he replied.

"Then how the hell did it happen? I had that handle changed so that instead of pressing down to release it, you had to pull up on it. I did it just so that Rebel couldn't lean on it and unlock it."

They both went over, opened the passenger door, and looked in the cab.

"Was she sitting on that coil of rope?" the weigh-master asked.

"Yes, she liked the extra height."

"Well, that's the culprit. When you went around that curve the rope slid across the seat and caught under the handle and released it. The only suggestion I've got now is that you strap her to the back of the seat so she *can't* slide out." That was well before the harness seat belt law.

Needless to say, Rebel didn't make any more trips with her dad that harvest season. And although Jay still blamed himself, he knew at least that he hadn't been careless about locking her in, only about not realizing a hazard still existed.

I remember when I was at the hospital for hours on end, Aerojet having given me all the time off I needed. I'd go from Rebel's room, when she was sleeping, to visit our hospitalized Filipino pickers. On one of these trips, a young orderly came up to me and said with a perfectly straight face, "With all the people you've got in the hospital, Mrs. Masters, don't you think you should consider dedicating a wing?"

∽

If Rocketdyne's art department was a country club, Aerojet's had to be the Mickey Mouse Club!

It was not that Technical Manuals didn't have some very excellent fine-artists heading up the department, it was that I couldn't find one who was a technical illustrator, trained in reading and working from blueprints. If there was one thing my work at Edison and Rocketdyne had taught me over the years, it was how to read blueprints, both architectural and engineering. I loved it. And I loved how I could take a stack of flat, one-dimensional drawings, and turn them into a fully visual home, kitchen, or rocket engine! I also loved how I could take a rocket engine illustration and, by rendering it in full-color airbrush, make it look like a photo of the actual thing. Not surprisingly, with this background I was assigned to the airbrush section of Tech Manuals—and my immediate supervisor, Brian Tibbets, turned out to be an ex-window dresser.

His knowledge of airbrush art extended to freehanding autumn leaves on store windows with a wide sweep of vibrant color and a lot of panache. I often found him sweating bullets, trying to cut itty-bitty friskets, or stencils, around odd engine parts, and then using a hairline airbrush to capture the photographic appearance of the item. When I tried to explain parts that tiny were best rendered with a paint brush and their edges later softened with the airbrush, he told me to go to hell. Realizing he was already there, I decided to go elsewhere.

My first assignment was to illustrate an exploded view of a gimbal, the device on a rocket engine that allows it to alter course and keep the rocket on track. If Tech Manuals was a joke, Aerojet's engineering department more than made up for it by being superb. I fell in love with their design ability, it was so clean and logical. Where Rocketdyne installed umpteen additional controls and valves to take over in the event of an engine failure, Aerojet built safeguards into each component so that it would automatically shut down if it sensed a malfunction.

A-a-a-h, the beauty of it!

To my surprise I found I'd been allowed two hundred hours to complete my gimbal assignment. I must've looked weird, because Dom Ragazza, who handed me the job, said, "What's the matter?" And before I could answer, added brusquely, "Okay, so how much time *do* you want?"

"That's a forty-hour job, Dom," I said softly.

"Oh, yeah? Show me!" he said.

"I will, if I can get all the blueprints." That turned out to be a hassle, but I finally ended up with a stack of prints a foot high and started to really enjoy myself. It took me twenty-two hours to draw up the gimbal, and another eighteen to render it in full-color. I turned it in on Friday afternoon, at the end of the workweek, and had the pleasure of seeing Dom almost choke on it.

I'd been in Tech Manuals about three months when all hell broke loose. It was during the lunch hour and Brian, the ex-window dresser, was standing back admiring his rocket engine rendering. He'd put over two hundred painstaking hours in it, and all the guys in the department were raving over it. Just then someone moved awkwardly, tripped, and dropped a tuna fish sandwich right in the middle of it. Brian went ballistic.

"Two hundred hours! You just ruined *two hundred hours* of artwork! You bloody fool, I could kill you!" I looked at his purple face and bulging eyes, and didn't doubt it for a minute.

I walked over and studied the mess. "I can clean that up for you with no problem," I said, trying to defuse the moment. To my surprise, it only made things worse.

"You keep your damn hands off it! Don't you dare touch it!" Dom grabbed Brian just as he started to swing at me.

I got mad. "You want to put another two hundred hours into this damn piece of art, or are you willing to learn something for a change?" I stormed. Then I stared them all down and asked them to stub out their cigarettes.

"What are you going to do? You can't touch that, it's *my* art!" Brian yelled.

"I'll clue you in, it's not *art* anymore," I said, still fuming. "What have you got to lose by letting me clean it up?"

For once Dom seemed to see the logic in what I was saying and told Brian to shut up and let me go ahead.

I did.

First I gently wiped off all the greasy tuna and mayonnaise I could, then, checking to see that all cigarettes had been stubbed out, I picked up a squirt bottle of Bestine, a highly flammable rubber cement thinner that we used to make friskets, and squirted it over the damaged area. After letting it sit for a spell to soak up the grease, I took a Kimwipe and carefully cleaned up the art. When I was through, I felt a wave of smug satisfaction when I saw that the colors, if possible, were brighter and sharper than ever.

Dom was the only one who had the decency to say, "Nice work, Pamela."

The following week I was called into Darren's Bullard's office—he was the department manager—and told I was being loaned out on a GWR, or General Work Release, to the Titan Training Division.

Ah, there is a God, I said silently. And life was fun and challenging once more, with only one little snag: Jay and I were both working together again in the same department!

Chapter 19

It turned out I didn't have to worry about working with Jay in the same department, as Aerojet didn't appear to have the same restrictions as Rocketdyne. Either that, or they needed the positions filled so badly they were willing to overlook any infractions.

As usual, Jay and I got along great, causing one of his buddies to remark, "How come you two get along so well together? How come you don't fight?"

With a sweeping gesture, I pointed to all the people working around us and said with a smile, "Too many referees!"

Although I enjoyed working with Jay and the other tech reps in the training division, I could see Jay was getting restless again. He couldn't stand being a desk jockey. If he wasn't outdoors under a limitless sky, he felt like a caged animal. Before long, when word came down that the Vandenberg operation was closing down and the reps would be assigned new jobs at the Rancho facility, I wasn't surprised when Jay asked me if he could quit. As we'd met all our goals to date, I said, "Why not? The ranch has turned into a full-time job, but Frank doesn't seem to realize it." Frank was our foreman, who, unknown to us at the time, spent his days fishing at Slab Creek, getting back to the orchard just before we got home from work. Jay couldn't understand how jobs that should've taken a day at the most never seemed to get done in under a week.

"You're right. I can let Frank go and handle the whole thing myself. It'll be interesting to find out if I'm really as far off on my calculations as I appear to be when I give Frank a job to do." But before Jay turned in his resignation, he said he wanted to buy a plane.

"Bob Anderson has a 1949 Navion for sale. I've seen it. It's one of the originals built by North American, and it's a beaut. He wants five thousand for it, and he needs the cash badly."

"Can we swing it?" I asked.

"Yes."

"Then do it! You've always wanted a plane."

"Are you sure? Do you think we can make it on just your salary?" He always got nervous if we weren't both working. It had to be a throwback to his early years when he was on his own, living from hand to mouth, never knowing what tomorrow would bring.

Seeing his hesitation, I smiled and said, "But it's *not* just my salary. You're making one too. Only you get paid once a year, while I get paid once a week. Go for it!"

So the next thing I knew, Jay had met one of his life's goals: he was the proud owner of a sleek, low-winged plane, modeled after North American's famous P-51 fighter of WWII. He had another lady in his life now, and he loved her as fiercely as he loved Rebel and me.

∼

When Jay started working full-time on the ranch, he tossed all his nice business clothes and began looking like the world's worst bum. He loved it. He said no one expected anything from a bum, so he could get away with murder. And an incident that followed right after our first harvest proved his point.

The only industry in Camino, apart from agriculture, was a large lumber mill. Michigan-California Lumber Company owned just about all the houses in the little town of Camino and employed most of the workers, except for a few who worked in the orchards. The lumber company was nonunion, and nobody seemed to care except a union organizer named Sheldon James who lived over the fence from us in a house-trailer. He wasn't land-locked so wasn't supposed to use our driveway, but he did; also, the fence was on our property, so he wasn't supposed to cut through it to get to his property, but he did. And quite understandably, Jay got to hate his guts. The feeling appeared to be mutual, although Sheldon had never met Jay. Possibly he needed someone to vent on as he was getting nowhere trying to organize the men at the mill. Whatever the reason, one day when Jay came up out of the orchard looking like some dirty old field hand, Sheldon hailed him. Trooper, a big golden lab we had somehow acquired, went loping over to him, so Jay decided to follow.

Sheldon started to tell Jay what he thought of the s-o-b in the big white house, pointing to our home. He went on and on about what an ornery cuss he was, how he thought he owned the world, how he kept closing up the hole in the fence that Sheldon had cut. It became obvious that if anyone thought he owned the world, it was Sheldon, but he didn't see it that way. Finally he said to Jay, "I don't know how you can work for that s-o-b." Then he added, reaching out to shake Jay's grubby hand, "By the way, I'm Sheldon James, and you … ?"

"I'm the s-o-b who lives in the big white house," Jay said without batting an eye, then he turned and called Trooper and walked back into the orchard.

When Jay told me about the incident that evening, I could see he had enjoyed every minute of it.

"How can you do that?" I asked. It was contrary to all I knew of him. Here was a man who couldn't stand confrontations of any kind deliberately causing one. It was years before I learned it was "a control thing," as Rebel put it when she was in her teens. "Daddy hates confrontations unless he starts them and is in control. When that happens, he *loves* them!"

Another character, whom *I* unintentionally rubbed the wrong way, was Jeff Weaver. He was one of our car-poolers, and a rabid socialist. Between him and Howard Hillman, a staunch Seventh Day Adventist, the conversations on the commute could get really dicey. I was the only one who liked to mix it up. The other two in the car-pool, Jerry Smith and Arlene Nicols, whom we picked up in Placerville, just sat and let us go at it.

One thing I noticed, Jeff always patched things up at the end of the day so that he and his wife could come over for a swim. Not just once or twice a week, but *every* evening. I felt sorry for them, their little house was so hot and uncomfortable, and I thought it was the least we could do, but I could see it irked Jay, as we never seemed to have the pool to ourselves. For Rebel, it was just a case of the more the merrier, and she bounced in and out of the water like a happy beach ball.

There was a downside to all the pool play for me, though. At that time, there was no such thing as pool service, so I had to spend at least three hours every Saturday morning vacuuming and adjusting the chemicals. One time Jay came up out of the orchard for lunch as I was winding up the job, and said, "I want you to get Jeff and his wife to come in on alternate Saturdays to help you. They monopolize the pool every evening but never offer to help keep it clean."

"I don't think they realize we have to," I said.

"So tell them! Tell them they're welcome to use the pool as long as they help us keep it up."

I got to thinking about it and decided it was a great idea.

The following Friday evening I asked Jeff if he and Jenny would help me vacuum the pool the next morning. You'd have thought I'd asked them to clean out the septic tank with their bare hands.

Ron looked at me and exploded, "How dare you! We're not your servants!"

"I'm sorry, but I'm not *your* servant either! I have to clean that pool every Saturday, and I'm just asking for a little help."

"You know, Pamela, that's the trouble with you rich landowners, you think you can make everybody do your work for you!"

"Hold it! One, we're not rich! Five years ago Jay and I were scrabbling just like you two kids. Two, we work hellish long hours every day and only have crews in to help at harvest and pruning. You've got some wild notions, Jeff. I'm fed up with you calling me an elitist snob in the car-pool, and saying we should feel privileged to pay extra taxes to help the poor. I'll bet when you and Jenny get ahead, you won't be singing that same tune."

"Come on, Jenny, let's get out of here," he said, grabbing their towels with one hand and her arm with the other.

"See you tomorrow?" I asked sweetly.

"Go to hell!"

Well, we didn't have to worry about them monopolizing the pool anymore, but it sure didn't help me with the cleaning job.

~

My new supervisor in the Titan training division was Nathan Cramer, who preferred to be called Nate. He was such a pro I couldn't help putting him up on a pedestal. Like most of the top men at Aerojet, he'd been recruited from a competitor in San Diego. He headed up the handbook section of propulsion training, and the first thing he did was make me his art director. When I pointed out that I was only on loan to training, he said, "That's okay, I'll take care of it!" And he did.

I would've loved to have been a bug on the wall when Darren and his compatriots learned that the witch they'd sent over to training "to put her in her place" had landed right-side-up ... *again.*

It was a while before I met Nate's boss, Gerald Hayes. Somehow, during the birth of Aerojet's Sacramento facility, he'd moved up from some lower position and slipped into line with the big boys. He appeared to be totally out of his element, but he knew how to play all the angles. I commented quietly to Nate one day, while we were waiting for Gerald to make his appearance at one of our production meetings, that Aerojet should pay him to stay home for all the good he did. That got a twitter out of the senior editor, Jan Gardner, and the top tech writer, Carl Kendall.

"No such luck," Carl said quietly as Gerald came into the room, apologizing grandiosely about having just got out of a meeting with "The Board." He made a bunch of inane remarks, dropping the given names and nicknames of members of one of Aerojet's top management teams. I looked around the table to see if anyone was impressed, and caught a few feigned yawns.

Nate interrupted him with a "'Morning, Gerald. We're running quite a tight schedule today and need to get back on the job. Here's a lineup on the project so that you'll be up to speed with management." And referring to his notes, he proceeded to fill Gerald in. One thing about Gerald, he appeared to have total recall, and could reel off all he was told as though his was the mastermind behind all the projects in the technical training group. It was his only plus as far as I was concerned, as among his shortcomings was his desperate need to have everything yesterday, without consideration of the requirements for research and implementation. The only thing that mattered in Gerald's book was that he be made to look good up at the top, where the big boys played.

One of the projects Nate and I worked on was devising inking standards so that the giant illustrated flip charts of rocket components, viewed across a room in military briefings, could be reduced in size, and hold up line for line, to be used in the pocket-size propulsion handbooks that were our ultimate product. It was a challenge, taking a lot of testing and retesting, using camera reductions down to infinitesimal percentages, but the final illustrations were so sharp and clear, it was worth every minute spent on it.

As my job turned out to be that of an art director with no artists to direct, we had to send an overview of our project and a request for bid to Technical Manuals to bid on. I moaned when Nate told me, as I felt positive they would be out of their depth. I also knew that they would not deign to follow any illustration and inking standards that I'd had a hand in. The sample art we had requested, along with the bid request, proved me right on both counts. The bid figure they came up with cinched it, as they used their favorite two hundred hours per illustration rule of thumb, and priced themselves out of the picture.

"So, what do we do now?" I asked Nate in a quandary.

"Get a list of job shops here in Sacramento and the Bay Area, and we'll go out for bids."

We did, and the competitive figures were so good, the samples of artwork so sharp, we had a hard time picking a contractor. It finally boiled down to a company in the Bay Area that would guarantee turnaround, offering to eat any overtime that might be necessary to meet our deadlines.

"Now what?" I asked. "Do I have to move to the Bay Area?"

"You don't have to go anywhere, Pam. They have to move up here, and the figure they bid covers housing all their personnel as well."

"Ye gods, how can they do that and still come out ahead?"

"They guaranteed it—let's see them do it!" was all Nate said.

∽

The team of technical illustrators from Webley Graphics turned up a week or so later, after the company had made a frantic search for housing in Rancho Cordova. The city was already bursting at the seams with the influx of Aerojet personnel and, as expected, the housing finally arranged was minimal and the crowding abysmal.

I felt sorry for one of the girls, a terrific technical artist by the name of Frances Shaffer who had more hidden talents than anyone I'd ever met. I mentioned her to Jay, and in his easygoing way he said, "Why can't she live here with us and commute with you to Aerojet?"

"She's a *hippy*, Jay," I said, knowing how he felt about the new subculture that had its roots in San Francisco. "I think you'd have a hard time with her after a while," not mentioning that *I* might have a hard time with her, especially as I had to work with her all day as well. But Jay insisted, and Frances happily moved into the big upstairs guest room.

Rebel was thrilled. Frances had a way with kids that had them following her around like she was the Pied Piper. As she clumped upstairs with her umpteen suitcases and her guitar, I could see how she would never have fit into the confines of the limited housing provided by Webley.

She couldn't read a note of music but had perfect ear and

pitch. She only had to hear a piece of music and she could play it unerringly in any key. The first evening, while I was putting dinner together, she sat down at the upright piano in the dining room and started to play *The Blue Danube*. Rebel was mesmerized, and when Jay came in out of the orchard, all mucky from changing water lines, he just stood in the kitchen doorway, messing up the floor, with a rapt look on his face.

I nodded my head in the direction of the dining room and said, "That's Frances. I told you she was talented."

He shook his head, went back into the mudroom, dropped his clothes, and started down the hall.

"Yo, man!" I said quickly. "You can't do that anymore, we've got a houseguest now!"

"Oops! Go up and get me some clean clothes, will you. I'll go into the bathroom."

We soon learned we were more worried about offending Frances than she was at taking offense. She just loved being in a home, as she hadn't had one for years. She said she'd started life in Hollywood as a child bit-actress. Her father was one of the top cameramen of the '30s and '40s, and she just loved the bohemian life they'd led. But when she was in her early teens, her father succumbed to the pressures of the job and started to drink, ending up as a skid row bum in Los Angeles. Frances and her mother managed to get along somehow, and when she was old enough to strike out on her own, she did. At the time she was staying with us, she hadn't seen either of her parents in years.

I recall a day in the fall of '62 when the easygoing Webley crew was just bristling with antagonism. It wasn't anything I could put my finger on, but where they'd taken suggestions and art direction eagerly before, they now snapped and growled when I said anything. My terse "You gotta *problem* with that?"

only brought on more snide remarks under their breath. I wanted to think the fact that they were crowded together day and night was beginning to take its toll.

That evening I asked Frances what the hell was the matter with the crew at work.

"*You!*" she said briefly.

"Meaning?"

"They think you're a miserable *bitch!*"

"Oh, come *on* now. What did I do?"

"You're too damn demanding. They hate your guts."

"They told you that, when they know you're living with me?" I asked, dumbfounded.

"Sure."

"And you said … ?" I asked, hoping to hear she defended me.

"*I agreed with them!*"

I was at the sink, rinsing salad greens for dinner at the time, and I turned and looked at her. She was lolling against the hall door, seemingly unaware of how deeply her remark had hurt me.

"Thanks a heap, Frances. With friends like you, I sure as hell don't need any enemies!" Somehow I got the rest of the dinner put together, and slammed it down on the table.

"What's eating you?" Jay asked, as I almost flung the bottle of salad dressing at him.

"Nothing! A-b-s-o-*lutely nothing!*" I said, giving Frances a withering look.

After dinner, I cleared the table and went out to wash the dishes. I was still seething, and when I'm mad I can work twice as fact as when I'm not. I was pitching dishes into the sink, scrubbing saucepans, and flouncing around like an ostrich with a bug up its butt when I heard a guitar softly playing.

It was Frances. She was leaning against the hall door again, softly singing *My Buddy*. When she was through, she said, "I don't know how to apologize."

"You already have," I said, touched beyond words.

Things went a lot smoother at work after that, and I hated to admit that Frances's blunt comment probably had a lot to do with it.

~

In January of '63, after eighteen months of hellish work, the contract was finally winding down. It looked as though we'd meet all our deadlines, and the feeling in Titan training was euphoric.

"Nice work, crew," Nate said to all of us, including the Webley gang, and I suddenly realized that Frances would be gone within a couple of weeks. I knew I'd miss her. And so would Rebel, who loved to monopolize her while I did household chores. That's one thing Frances never did; I don't believe she worried whether the house was clean, or dinner was on time, or about any of the mundane things that hold a family together. But then, she was Frances, and somehow I never expected her to pitch in; I just expected her to entertain. And that she did with a flourish.

That night she got a phone call. I was surprised, as she'd never received one all the time she was staying with us.

When she put the phone down, she looked ghastly, and I said, "What's the matter? What was the call about?"

"My dad. They think he's dead. They've picked up a bum on skid row that might be him, and the L.A. police want me to come down and identify the body."

"How did they know you were here?" I asked, surprised.

"I always left my name and address with Paramount in case he touched base with them. I guess some old buddy of his from the studio was contacted, and they got in touch with Webley, who then called me here. I hope you don't mind, but I gave Webley your phone number when I moved in with you."

"Sure, that's okay," I said, then added, "Frances, I'm *so sorry* ..."

"I've dreamed of this happening for so many years," she said quietly. "It's always been that I'm called to identify him, and he's lying out, frozen, with a tag on his toe. But I never dreamed it would really happen."

I could feel her anguish and asked, "You got money for the trip?"

"Yeah, I got paid yesterday. I'm fine."

"You be sure and call now? Promise."

"I will."

"Frances, *call me!* Call me collect, but call me ... either way. Take care, gal, we love you."

But weeks passed, and Frances didn't call. She'd left with all her baggage and her old beat-up guitar, and she left us with a great hole in our lives. It was like the summer of '40 all over again, when I was thirteen and happily living in a little treaty port in North China, where the war seemed so far away. That was the year that tall, gangling Anne Newmarch waltzed into our lives. I don't know if she was a musician like Frances, but she had to be the greatest thirteen-year-old artist and playwright I'd ever known. And as we were both the same age, I could speak with authority. That summer had been a blast, and when it was over she left, and we never heard from her again. The darn war did things like that to friendships: people got scattered all over the world never to meet up again.

I found myself thinking back to the prison camp. To Guy, who in an indelible way had marked my life forever. I would always remember him as my worst nightmare and my sweetest dream. If anyone could love and loathe someone at the same time, we had perfected the process. And Dan, my sweet buddy, who'd survived the camp only to become a paraplegic from spinal meningitis he contracted during the last few months. I did hear from him: he was so darn upbeat, so full of living, even though only half of him was still alive. And I thought of zany Gladys, and hoped she'd found a man big enough to handle her and her overwhelming love. And Jock Allen, with his dry wit and unflappable calm in the face of utter terror. Pete Fox stepped in and out of my musings, always with a giggle and a crazy anecdote.

Where were they all? What were they doing? Most of them left the camp with barely a pot to piss in. We left as we'd arrived, all leveled by the same circumstances. I wondered how they all made out, even the Japanese commandant, a repatriated diplomat who epitomized all I'd learned of the graciousness of Japanese civilians. He'd helped make our camp a haven of hope in a world racked by brutality. Then I thought of Frances again, and couldn't help thinking, *Oh, God, I hope that's not Frances's final goodbye.*

Chapter 20

I'll never forget November 22, 1963. We were all working on the latest propulsion handbook, scrambling to get it done, hoping to meet one horrendous time frame. It didn't seem anything could drag us away from those last hectic days before we went to press, but that only goes to show how wrong one can be. When the silence was so total all you could hear was the slow tick, tick, tick of the electric wall clock, someone rushed into the office and shouted, "The President's been shot!"

My concentration had been so complete, it took a few moments for me to comprehend what he'd said. The first to find his voice was Carl Kendall. *"Oh, God, no!"*

Someone said, "Where, how, when ..."

"Dallas, motorcade—he was shot in the head, they're rushing him to the hospital."

The rest of the day was a blur. We were glued to a radio that had been brought in from somewhere, and we listened mesmerized as the news grew grimmer.

The days that followed weren't much better. Lyndon Johnson had been sworn in on the presidential plane at the Dallas airport immediately following the assassination. Two days later Jack Ruby, a nightclub owner, shot suspected assassin Lee Harvey Oswald to death. And the country was still reeling from shock when the slow drumroll that accompanied Kennedy's funeral procession through Washington to Arlington Cemetery beat mercilessly into everyone's brain.

I knew the assassination went way beyond any political affiliation, and I kept thinking ... *Presidents don't get shot in America. Maybe in Yugoslavia or Peru, or anywhere else in the world, but not here, not America! We might not agree with a President or his party, but we never shoot him, we just work to see he isn't elected for another term. That's what democracy is all about ...*

Finally, we were able to put the tragedy behind us and get on with the task at hand.

Once more we'd had to turn to Webley Graphics for tech illustrators, but this time we only needed two. Although there were sizeable differences both in text and artwork from the original handbooks, most of the illustrations could be adapted without having to draw up complete new illustrations.

To my happy surprise, Frances Shaffer was one of the artists assigned to us. She came into the office with a close friend, Jeanne Robins, and told me they'd found a neat little apartment in Folsom for their stay.

"God, it's good to see you!" I said, giving her a hug. "I didn't know you were still with Webley."

"Where else would I go?" she asked. "I asked them to send me—wouldn't have missed this for words."

Recalling the last time I'd seen her, I said, "You never called. Was that your dad the L.A. police called about?" I dreaded to hear her reply.

"Oh, no, it was some poor old wino. Didn't even look like Dad," she said offhandedly, putting her supplies down on the art table she'd been assigned.

Remembering the horror of her last leaving, I'm afraid I lost it. "I could throttle you! Do you realize how Jay and

I have worried about you? Dammit, gal, you could be a bit more considerate!"

"I'm sorry. Except for Jeanne here, you're the only people who care about me. Should've called, I know, but it was such a relief I forgot all about it."

It didn't take long for Gerald Hayes to start riding herd on us, demanding we meet all deadlines, totally ignoring the fact that they were now almost unreachable.

I remember our last meeting: Nate asked us all how we felt about the handbook. Jan Gardner said she felt it was as good as it was going to get. I seconded her as far as the illustrations were concerned.

"Okay, it's a go!" Nate said. "Jan, first thing next week, you and I'll go down to Cal Central Press and get this baby on the road."

∽

The weekend that followed, I totally relaxed. I even found time to put up the badminton net on the lawn and play some fun games with Rebel.

That swath of lawn between the house and the pool had been the site of many great times. In fact, I can still remember the first time I lay on it and looked up at that glorious clear night sky with all the constellations beckoning me, and I yelled to Jay and Rebel that I could see a shooting star.

"Where?" Rebel asked excitedly. "There!" I said, pointing to a star racing across the sky, only to have Jay laugh and say, "Hell, that's no shooting star, that's a satellite!" And as I watched it travel from west to east, a feeling of pride crept over me: *our* satellites were up there now. Maybe they didn't have the payload of the Russian *Sputniks,* but technologically they were far superior. *Natch!*

The following Monday at our early morning staff meeting,

my little art group was assigned the job of preparing the training transparencies for the Apollo engine. When we adjourned, Nate and Jan left for Cal Central with the manuscript and art for the newest handbook.

It took a while for me to round up all the Apollo prints, as much of the work was still in the research stage, and we were advised by the engineers that drawings might have to be modified before they were finalized.

It was while we were working on the Apollo project that the galleys for the propulsion handbook came back from Cal Central for proofing. I checked all the art and call-outs and signed them off, while Jan, Carl, and the writing crew did a comprehensive final edit on all the copy.

"*Dammit,* when am I going to be able to take a finished copy of that book up to the big boys?" Hayes said as he wandered through the department, hounding each person while they worked on their sections. I could sense their frustration; it never dawned on Hayes that every interruption interfered with concentration, something needed desperately when proofing technical material.

God, I would've loved to have slugged him!

I have to say though, the Apollo project intrigued me. We were finally going to the moon, and I was going along for the ride whether I wanted to or not! Of course, it was an earthbound ride and I'd never go into orbit, but quite often as I worked on the job I felt as though I were. My part of the project, the Apollo engine training graphics, wasn't a big job, measured by all the other effort put into the moonshot, but it was just as vital, and I loved every minute of it. When we completed the job, on time and under budget, Nate's "Great work, Pam!" made me glow. I felt he'd just awarded me the Croix de Guerre with an oak leaf cluster, and

I thanked Frances and Jeanne for their outstanding work.

Once more I said goodbye to Frances, but this time it had no tragic undertones.

And then it was time for the propulsion handbooks to be delivered. They looked fabulous—worth all our blood, sweat, and tears. Nate, Jan, and Carl each took a copy home to go over minutely in the quiet of their respective homes. Gerald Hayes did, also.

The following day, Nate came in with a look of utter frustration on his usually happy face. Jan and Carl followed him, tight-lipped and unsmiling. It turned out they'd found quite a few typos and glitches that had not been caught in the final hurried—and continually interrupted—edit. Before I could commiserate with them, Gerald Hayes came in, and he was sizzling.

"*Nate, get into my office!*" he bellowed, and then I heard him shout, "*Goddam sonofabitch, how could you do this to me? You know my future is riding on this book. What am I going to tell the guys upstairs. You're fired! The whole damn writing crew is fired! Clean out your desks—you're outta here!*"

I saw Jan and Carl. They were so furious, they just upended their desk drawers on the floor, grabbed a few personal items, and stormed out. The other writers mumbled among themselves; they could get transferred to other departments, so their positions were not as dire as those of Nate, Jan, and Carl.

Nate quietly went to his desk, took his wife's picture off it, reached into the front drawer and took a few personal items out of it, and turned to leave.

I jumped up and ran to him. "No, you don't! You can't go without saying goodbye, Nate." I gave him a heartfelt hug. "I'm going to miss you. *Dammit,* I'm going to miss you! We all are. You're the best thing that ever happened to Aerojet; we all know who should be going out the door."

He hugged me back, tried to say something, choked, spun on his heel, and was gone so fast I felt the swoosh of his leaving.

I turned slowly, and looked in Hayes's office.

He was standing behind his desk, literally foaming at the mouth, and I lost it. I marched into his office and gave him a look that could shrivel a slug.

"Yes, Pamela?" he asked in a soft voice, belying the anger in his eyes.

"I just came to tell you, *I'm OUTTA HERE!*"

"Why? I didn't fire *you*. Your work was excellent."

"My work was excellent," I said slowly, "because I got input from the best writers I know." My voice was shaking with rage.

All the sweetness was out of his voice now, and he said brusquely, "Pamela, there's one thing you have to learn: it's always smart to get rid of your problems before the big boys get rid of you!"

I couldn't hide my disgust. "I could *never* work for a man who lines up his troops and shoots them down to save his own bloody neck!"

"Please, Pam, reconsider." His voice was back to a gentler tone, almost a whine. "You're one of the top women at Aerojet. You know your work, and it shows."

"You can go to *hell!*" I spat. I spun on my heel and slammed out of his office—straight over to Chuck Winslow, the head of another tech writing group on the far side of the bay.

"Could you do with another writer?" I asked.

It was obvious Chuck had heard the blowout in our department—everyone in the bay had—because he smiled and said, "Only if you promise to write *and* do the artwork."

"Why *not?*" I asked facetiously.

"You're hired!"

As we shook on it, I asked if there was anything I had to do to arrange the transfer. "Nothing. I'll take care of it. Welcome aboard!"

Shades of darling Nate! He'd used almost the same exact words when I originally came over from Technical Manuals.

After moving my tools and paraphernalia over to my new desk, I sat down and thought about what I'd done. I knew I had to be one of the luckiest people in the world. Most people would give their eyeteeth to tell their bosses to take a hike sometimes, even point them in the right direction as I had just done, but they'd have to stop and think about their commitments, their families, their mortgages—and I knew when I got home and told Jay what I'd done, he'd smile and possibly say something like, "Good for you, gal, I never did care for that bastard anyway!"

∽

I'd no sooner transferred to Tech Writing than the whole department was moved to an old cannery building at Thirty-third and C Street in downtown Sacramento. That meant no more car-pooling and, as the freeway system had not been built yet, added almost another full hour both ways to my commute.

Except for the commute, I enjoyed the job. I hardly did any writing though, because each one of the writers continually asked me to illustrate some part, or problem, they had to explain. The work was not precise; a simple line sketch using a visual from some valve or component would usually do, rather than drawing from blueprints. It was a nice change, and I liked it.

As I say, the only thing that got me down was the commute. I never had any time with Jay and Rebel anymore. The weekends were spent on doing so much catch-up they seemed almost like a extension of my workdays at Aerojet. Although

Jay had surprised me in late 1960 by replacing the little '49 VW with a gorgeous gold '61 Thunderbird with a white landau top—he'd seen a few accidents involving VWs, and wanted me in a safer car—I hated all the miles and wear and tear I was putting on the T-bird.

Then, just to add to my woes, that summer we were all put on a six-day workweek, and when August came around, I think I got pregnant out of desperation! It definitely was not planned, but I got the feeling the Good Lord didn't want me to wear myself out behind the wheel.

I took maternity leave in February of '65, just in time to help Jay plant four thousand pear trees on Frank Ringer's property in Ione. Frank had seen what a great job Jay had done planting acreage on Windmill Hill, the name we gave the Olsen ranch, and on Twin Hills, the second ranch he'd bought in '64. Jay's argument for buying the second ranch was very sound: he said thirty acres wasn't enough land to make a living off of, and bought almost thirty more to make his efforts worthwhile.

The story behind the second ranch is priceless. Jay went to a meeting put on by the California Farm Advisor's Office about what happens to untended orchards that are then abandoned. As Jay watched the slide presentation, he recognized the property as the twenty-seven-plus acres at the bottom of our long driveway. The following day he found the owner and gave him ten thousand dollars cash for the land. They shook hands on it, took the paperwork to Inter County Title, and the whole transaction was signed, sealed, and delivered within the week.

He told me that while I was doing my thing at Aerojet he went into the orchard, introduced himself to the trees, and told them what he expected of them. Then he had a dump-bed put on one of our orchard trucks, went over to Schubin's Chicken Farm in Gold Hill and hauled out all the free chicken fertilizer old Mr. Schubin had, and spread it under the trees. The property smelled pretty ripe for a while, but the trees were so happy and did so well that we saw a complete turnaround within one season.

As usual, Jay was having a running battle with the state over taxation without grower representation. He took great pleasure in putting huge signs on the side of the stinking truck bed that read "One More Load of —— from Pat Brown," our erstwhile governor. It was obvious to me that Rebel was right—Jay didn't mind confrontations as long as he instigated them!

I still remember the figure Jay gave Frank Ringer to plant his trees: sixty-five cents a tree. Frank thought the figure sounded great but was positive Jay would lose his shirt.

Frank didn't know my guy.

The first thing Jay did was go out and check the land. It was nice and flat and Frank had had it disked, so Jay and I surveyed it, lined up all the stakes on a diamond, and when everything looked true, we hauled his old Ford-N tractor, with a posthole digger attached, over to Ione. The following day, with three Mexican field hands, we started the planting. Frank had bought the rootstock, which Jay kept soaked in wet burlap, and we loaded the trees into bins on a low trailer behind a farm tractor. With one of the Mexicans driving that tractor and Jay on the Ford-N, the work began. Jay would drop a posthole, I'd get down on my hands and knees—that was fun, as I was just beginning to get really ungainly—and I'd drop in a small scoop of chemical fertilizer and a large scoop of soil on top of it, then stand back while the remaining two Mexican workers placed a tree in the hole, lined it up, shoveled the earth back down around it, and tamped it down firmly.

Of course, while we were doing this, Jay was digging the next hole. The job got to be unending, and I felt like the sorcerer's apprentice on an ceaseless treadmill, not to mention that by the evening my back was aching like the devil.

In less than a week, Jay handed Frank an invoice for twenty-six hundred dollars, and Frank just about flipped out.

"Does a guarantee go with this?" he asked facetiously.

"It sure does," Jay said. "Any trees that don't make it, I'll replace gratis."

We never had to replace a single tree, and within a few years the established orchard looked terrific, and Frank started getting a nice crop off it.

Right after that happy planting project, Jay went to work for a contractor who was putting in a huge dam on Slab Creek about a mile from our Twin Hills orchard. He loved the outdoor job, especially the pay, and we rented the orchard cottage to the senior engineer on the project. He turned out to be a militiaman, with weapons and ammo caches hidden all over California and the western states. I'd never met anyone so "right" he was almost wrong. If he honestly believed all the horror stories he told us, our country was in dire straits.

All that took a backseat when, in the wee hours of June 16, Jay rushed me to Marshall Hospital. Dr. Fitzpatrick had told us earlier that by the baby's heartbeat he was positive Jay would get the son he wanted, and I had one really happy man waiting for the miraculous event.

It was a very rugged delivery that took hours, and when the baby finally arrived late in the evening, it wasn't a boy, but another adorable girl. Jay had been called back to the ranch in the meantime, and I was waiting in bed, with Gillian in my arms, when they rolled in a woman to the second bed in my room. She was crying softly, and I asked her what was the matter. She said, "Thank God it's a boy. Michael would never have forgiven me if I'd had a girl!"

I couldn't believe what I was hearing. "Is this your first child?" I asked.

"No, but he's a high school coach and he only wants sons."

He came in just then and was so strutting proud I wanted to bop him. I could tell by his wife's tone that she'd been praying for a girl, and that her tears were really from disappointment more than happiness at pleasing her husband.

Jay came in soon after that, and I smiled and said, "Doc Fitz was wrong, honey. We've got another precious daughter."

The smile he gave me and Gillian melted my heart. Knowing he might've been a little disappointed, I said quickly, and just loud enough for Michael to hear, "Hon, it's a known fact of history that all the world's greatest lovers always had daughters, *never* sons."

The kiss he gave both of us said it all …

By the time my maternity leave was up, I found Aerojet had cost-plussed itself out of some big contracts and was back down to a workable size, with the writing group once more at the main plant in Rancho Cordova.

Before I started back to work, I found a sweet family in Placerville, who loved children and needed the extra cash, to take care of Gillian. It was tough having to leave her every morning on my way to work, but I took her in her little bassinet, and she barely woke on the trip over and was asleep in the arms of her "other mother" before I climbed back into the car.

Ah, yes … I forgot: Jay traded my lovely golden T-bird in for a huge dark-red paneled Mercury ranch wagon without saying a word to me. He said that now there were four in the family we definitely had to have a ranch wagon. Lord, that was a big car. It was loaded with power-everything! I remember the car salesman saying when he drove it up to the ranch, "Here's your five-thousand-dollar playpen!"

In 1966 that was a lot of money to pay for a car!

∽

I'd love to say all was sweetness and light on the home front, but that was not the case. Rebel didn't turn out to be a happy thirteen-year-old babysitter for her new little sister as all my gushing girlfriends had predicted. Instead, she turned into a green-eyed monster. No one was going to steal her daddy from her.

It was so darn understandable. She had been Jay's little princess from the day she entered the world. It was no good my telling her that her daddy had enough love for both his darling daughters. She was his, and he was hers, and *nobody* was going to get in between! In the past, as I was gone so much of the time, she'd never really had to share him with anyone, and the new situation was almost unbearable for her. I wanted to hug her and make it all right again, but she wouldn't have any of it. It's tough when you're entering your teens to find your wonderful world had just been flipped on its tail.

And the toughest part was that as Gillian grew, she completely adored her big sister. She wanted to be around her all the time; for her, Rebel could do no wrong. But sadly, for Rebel, Gillian could do no right.

That was the year that Rebel started attending El Dorado High. She was a leader, not a follower, and dressed to prove the point, always in skirts and dresses, wearing a cute felt hat and a look that said, "I own the world!" The heartbreak was, when she came home she didn't "own the world"—she had to share it with a baby sister. And that was intolerable.

As 1966 wound down, she spent most of her hours at home

shut in her room, playing loud music to block out any "family" sounds.

That was also the year that it snowed unmercifully. I'll never forget the week before Christmas. Right after buying a fabulous, fat, twenty-four-pound turkey, the power went off. I kept the bird in the refrigerator in the garage for a while, but when it started to thaw out, I buried the bird in a huge snowdrift outside the kitchen window, along with all the other perishables I'd bought earlier for Christmas dinner. The other items weren't in trouble, but when Christmas day arrived, still with no power, I knew I had to cook the turkey or lose it, especially since I'd seen coyote tracks around the house that morning and knew it would be just a matter of time before those starving animals smelled the bird.

"What am I going to do?" I asked Jay. "Is there any way I can cook this darn bird on the Coleman stove in the cellar?"

"You could try. I've got a lot of fuel for it," he said.

So I seasoned the un-stuffed turkey, wrapped it in heavy aluminum foil, leaving the top open, placed it on the Coleman stove on a sturdy rack in a large roasting pan full of water, and sealed the whole thing with a huge tent of more foil. While it was cooking—at least, I *hoped* it was cooking—I decorated the dining room table with candles, pinecones, pyracantha berries, and sprays of cedar. It looked so colorful, it outshone the unlit Christmas tree. I debated putting candles on the tree but felt that would be a bit too hazardous. As I had no potatoes, gravy, or cooked vegetables to serve, I decided to make sandwiches and serve a salad with them. If that darn bird ever cooked, we'd at least have some lovely hot turkey sandwiches!

After almost eight hours, I carefully opened the tent and looked at the bird. It looked moist and thoroughly cooked, with lots of good pan juices, but it had to be the ugliest bird

I'd ever seen: white as the snow outside, and covered in huge water blisters! *Oh, God, how am I going to serve that?* I said silently, as I trudged up the stairs, holding the heavy, steaming pan with thick hot-mitts.

"How's it look?" Jay asked, clearing a counter off for me to place it on.

"You don't want to know! If we all shut our eyes, we might be able to eat it, but it looks ghastly. *God, I wish the power would come on!*"

I hadn't realized it was a prayer, but just as I said it, the power came back on!

I turned the oven up to four hundred degrees, uncovered the turkey, ladled out all the pan juices, then threw the bird in the oven. While it was browning, I fixed instant mashed potatoes, green peas with parsley, and a delicious thick brown gravy. Thirty minutes later, we all sat down to a scrumptious turkey dinner with everything except Jay's favorite oyster dressing.

And then the power went off for another three days!

∽

By the following year, the situation between Rebel and Gillian hadn't improved one whit, and Jay suggested Rebel might be happier attending a school away from home. Recalling how I'd enjoyed the years I'd spent as a boarder in a convent in China, I agreed. At least Rebel wouldn't have to put up with a doting little sister who was always underfoot. That summer we visited several girls' schools around the Bay Area and Napa Valley, and Rebel picked a Catholic girls' school in the wine country run by a teaching order.

It appeared to be an excellent school. I say "appeared" as I really had no yardstick. I found myself comparing it with the Catholic convent in North China where I'd been raised, where rules were so strict that, if I got caught talking in line or was tardy to class, my one-Sunday-a-month outing would be forfeited. Here was Rebel, coming home *every* weekend; most of the time her dad would pick her up in the plane at a little air strip near the school. If he couldn't do it, I'd drive over and bring her home, driving her back Sunday evening. I don't believe that depriving the girls of home visitation was ever contemplated as punishment for infractions.

The school nestled up against rolling hills, and Rebel told me that quite often the girls would go out in the evening and sit quietly up in the hills and smoke pot. It shocked the blazes out of me, and I asked her if the Sisters knew about it.

"I doubt it," she said. "They're too busy demonstrating and getting involved with Cesar Chavez and the farm movement."

"How can they find time for that?" I asked, flabbergasted.

"Oh, they *make* time."

"Meanwhile, what happens at school with you girls?"

"We're on our honor," she said. "Mom, they don't *all* go! A lot of them stay to take care of us, get our meals, do the laundry and such."

"That's big of them! What if there's an emergency, or something?"

"Oh, Mom, it's no *big thing!*" she said with a dismissive shrug.

Well, it might not have been for Rebel, but I couldn't help thinking of all the other girls and wondering if their parents knew what was going on.

Betsy Stoddard, another girl from Placerville who attended the school, didn't go home weekends but spent them with her aunt who lived nearby.

"How do you get along with Betsy?" I asked.

"Why?"

"I'd feel a lot better knowing you could get in touch with her aunt if you needed to."

"Oh, I know her aunt well. She comes every weekend to pick Betsy up, and we chat quite often. She's a neat person."

"Good," I said, somewhat relieved at the situation. "I'll call her and enlist her aid if it's needed."

∽

Back at Aerojet, I was going nuts. I'd done all the artwork necessary to illustrate any problems that needed troubleshooting, and had set up a filing and cross-filing system so that the writers could pull up whatever art they needed, and I began to feel antsy like Jay did when he was called back from the air bases. He loved the outdoors; I loved graphic art. When we weren't doing what we loved, we were pretty hard to get along with. *Anyhow,* I rationalized, *I've spent more time at Aerojet than on any job in my life. Hell, it's been over seven years, I've got to get moving on …*

I told Chuck Winslow I'd set up all the files his crew needed; all he needed now was a file clerk, not a high-priced art director.

"I think that's my decision, Pam," he said with a smile.

"I'm afraid not," I said gently. "I can't do make-work; I have to be challenged. I'm sorry, but I'm moving on. Thank you for all you've done for me," and I handed him my letter of resignation.

I'd no sooner got back to my desk to clean it out than I got a call from Aerojet's personnel office. *That didn't take Chuck long,* I thought.

As I walked into the office, a striking woman stood up and said, "I hope I didn't hear right."

"About my leaving?" I asked, shaking her hand.

"Yes."

"I'm afraid you did. I'm leaving. Aerojet's been good to me, but I have to be challenged."

"Think carefully before you do this. You'll never find another job as good as this one, or that pays as well. You've proved women can go a long way in the space industry. Please think about it."

"I have. I thank you. But I'm leaving."

I went back to my office, collected my things, said a few heartfelt goodbyes, and left.

It was eleven o'clock in the morning. Too early for lunch yet. *What to do?*

Instead of heading east toward home, I turned south, and headed for the Douglas Sacramento Test Center out on Douglas Road, just for the fun of it … and was hired on the spot as the base artist, with a hundred-dollar-a-week raise.

When I got home late in the evening, after being thoroughly processed, Jay said, "Aren't you rather late today?"

"Yeah, I quit Aerojet," I said. Seeing the look on his face, I quickly added, "But I was hired out at the Douglas test facility with a nice fat raise. I'm starting there Monday."

"Good Lord, woman, how the hell do you luck out like that every *single* time?"

Chapter 21

The job at the Douglas Sacramento Test Center, which started at seven in the morning and was over by four in the afternoon, turned out to be a little of everything. I did some technical illustration, put out a monthly newsletter, silk-screened signs for all over the base, made posters for different occasions, learned how to do phototypesetting, and was responsible for the daily upkeep of a huge lighted bulletin board in the lobby that held each day's schedule of events, especially testing and firing. It was strictly public relations for all the visiting dignitaries to see, as Douglas was one of the main contractors on the Saturn booster that was to put the Apollo into orbit.

God, that rocket was a big bruiser! You just knew by looking at it that it could put an American on the moon!

One of the first things I was told was that after every test firing I was to go out and silkscreen the date and test results in six-inch block letters on the concrete base of the test stand. One day, several months after I'd been there, I was out setting up for just such a silk-screening when a test supervisor in a hard hat stopped and asked me what I thought I was doing.

"Putting the results of yesterday's test on the stand," I replied.

"Hell, we almost blew the *damn* stand up! What are you doing?"

"Recording the test," I said stubbornly.

"Oh, no, you're *not!* We don't record failures. Only successes," he said firmly.

"Then it's not a record: it's just another *attaboy!*"

"Call it what you like, we don't record flubs."

"Yes, sir," I said aloud, and under my breath I added, *Score one more for PR!*

I found that Douglas believed utterly and completely in public relations, and under that guise, I was loaned out all over the place. At that time, Ronald Reagan was governor of California, and the Douglas management team had me doing a huge display for the capitol rotunda promoting Reagan's Creative Citizenship award, along with a scaled-down version for the display window outside his office. I liked the idea behind the program: it was to reward people and organizations that helped those in need without seeking state or federal handouts. It was surprising how many remarkable people and causes there were, and the Douglas team that ran with the ball for the governor went meticulously through all the resumés and records, winnowing them down to around ten from which Reagan would pick out the three winners.

In all the work and preparation that had gone into the project, one item was overlooked. When I arrived at work on the great day, I asked where the awards were. I knew the trophies had been designed and donated by a well-known California sculptor down south, and although I'd worked from photos of the awards to make the two displays, I'd never actually seen them.

"Go ask Shep," one of the men said.

Willis Shephard headed up the Douglas management team in Sacramento, and he'd been fairly gloating over the success of the project, but now it looked as though, after all the careful work that had been done, they were about to drop the ball with a resounding thud.

I knocked on his office cubicle. "Hate to disturb you, Shep, but where are the awards for this afternoon's ceremony?"

The look on his face said it all. "Oh, my God, they're still down south!"

"If you can find out where they are," I said, "I'll call home and see if Jay can fly down and get them, and be back here by two."

"Do it, gal, do it! I'll locate them."

So Jay took off in his trusty Navion for the little Ontario Airport, only to find to his horror, when he dropped over the San Gabriel Mountains, that he couldn't see Los Angeles, let alone Ontario! They were both socked in with L.A.'s famous brown smog. Jay had never found time to go for his instrument rating, so there was nothing he could do but call March AFB in Riverside, tell them he was on an errand for the governor, and ask to be vectored in. I learned later that was one heck of a maneuver: they not only vectored him in, they put him down right in front of the freight terminal where the crates were waiting!

Yes, he made it back in time and, yes, the award ceremony was a total success. I don't believe Governor Reagan ever knew of those hectic last hours, but according to the news media, the recipients were overwhelmed by their justly deserved awards.

~

Back at Rebel's school, my worst fears were realized when Rebel got a severe allergic reaction to something she ate. While the Sisters were gone stirring up the troops for Cesar Chavez, her throat swelled up and she couldn't breathe! She called me in a panic, and I could barely understand what she was saying, so I phoned Betsy's aunt, who, bless her heart, dropped everything and got her to the hospital in time.

That summer when Rebel came home and started to pal around with her old gang from El Dorado High, I wasn't disappointed when she said she didn't want to go back to that school. I won't go into what she put us through while she finished high school at El Dorado, but I will say I wished I'd named her Faith, Hope, or Charity instead of Rebel, because she sure lived up to her name!

∼

At the test facility the following winter, the countdown to the Apollo moonshot was foremost on all our minds. Everything was going smoothly. A big hurdle had been overcome: transportation of the huge Saturn rocket from the West Coast to Cape Canaveral had been licked. I'd learned earlier that, after the contract had been let, it was found that there was no workable overland route to the East Coast due to low overpasses, bridges, and tunnels, so a special plane had to be built, and it was dubbed the Pregnant Guppy.

As base artist for the Douglas test facility, I had to go to Mather AFB in Rancho Cordova, home base for a squadron of B-52s, and sketch a simulated loading of the Saturn rocket into the Pregnant Guppy. The big bird was there, and they were opening up the tail section and getting it ready for me. I'd already done a line drawing of the Saturn rocket in position, with the idea of sketching the huge plane in relation to the rocket, along with blocking in crew members overseeing the loading. All this was for a VIP briefing that was coming up.

As usual, I got bored waiting for everything to be in place, and I wandered off to get a better look at those sleek B-52s. I was sauntering down the ramp towards them in my hard hat and overalls when I felt myself being jacked up at the elbows by two of the tallest, toughest MPs I'd ever seen.

Squirming and kicking like hell, I hissed, "What are you *doing?*"

I think the MPs were as surprised as I was, but still holding on to me and doing a smart about-face, they said, "This is a restricted area, *ma-a-a-am!*" They let me know just how they felt about me by their emphasis on that last word.

"Put me down, dammit!" I snapped, still kicking.

"No, *ma-a-a-am!*"

Marching me back up to the loading area, they dumped me unceremoniously down in front of all the Air Force personnel, who were roaring with laughter.

"Dammit, you'd think I was going to blow up those bloody planes!" I said, determined to get in the last word.

"One never knows …" the base commander said in an ominous voice, spoiling it with a delightful smile.

∽

The summer of '69 was full of exciting anticipation, and after a very successful Apollo liftoff in mid-July, the weekend of the nineteenth and twentieth had me glued to the television set. There was no doubt about it, I was under the spell of space—if I couldn't be an astronaut, at least I was an ardent follower.

Only one incident took me away from the moonshot: it was on Saturday morning, a news flash from Kowloon, across the bay from Hong Kong. A feisty little Franciscan Sister, Mother Thomas à Becket, my eighth grade teacher in the convent, was being interviewed regarding her trek out of Communist China. I'd lost touch with all of the Sisters when I came to the States, and was learning for the first time that they'd been held captive in Peking and allowed to teach the children of the foreign embassies until Mother Superior got so ill she became a burden on the state, then they were told they could leave. No one helped them, or found them transportation; that little group of Franciscans had trudged all the way from Peking to Kowloon, pushing a dying Mother Superior in a wheelbarrow!

My mind flashed back to my years in North China. To Tientsin, where I'd attended boarding school, and where the White Sisters, as they were called, tried so hard to make me a lady. Mother Superior never gave up. She, who preferred to be called Mother Montana, was a jovial, loving person, who, unlike my father, believed completely in the humanity of man. Mother Thomas had been the only firebrand in that group of dedicated women, her flaming hair continually breaking loose from her wimple, her nostrils and brows flaring, and her eyes flashing at the slightest provocation. She must've lived through hell as she trudged the length of China, being spat on and reviled all the way! She'd never learned acceptance as the other Sisters had, and always spoke her mind—just as she was doing now to the consternation of her interviewer. The bitterness in her voice made me wince, and I cried with her when she told the interviewer that Mother Superior had died when she saw her little flock had made it safely over the border into Kowloon, leaving the horror of Communist China behind them.

The following day, Sunday, July 20, 1969, I completely forgot that tragic news story as Neil Armstrong and Buzz Aldrin stepped on the moon—and I went into orbit!

∼

By the following spring, the Douglas Sacramento Test Center was almost closed down. It was as though Washington didn't need us anymore. We'd proved we could put a man on the moon, and although I kept hoping for an encore—bigger and better things, like a manned flight to Mars—it didn't happen. The closest I could get to a flight of any kind was a fly-in down to Ojai.

Funny, I can still remember it, probably because it was the first time I can remember wearing jeans. In fact, I had to go out and buy them just for the occasion. We'd joined the Fun Flyers and I found that flying was very awkward in a skirt, especially climbing in and out of Jay's low-winged Navion with its sliding canopy top. For a girl who'd worn skirts and heels all her life because her work demanded it, I found the freedom of jeans and flats almost intoxicating.

We'd picked the perfect weekend for a fly-in, and the easygoing members of the club made it even more enjoyable. Sunday evening, tired but happy, we climbed into the plane for our flight home. On the way, Jay told me he was concerned about our bachelor tenant, a gifted pianist, who was renting the big foreman's house.

"I haven't seen Jim Frazier since Tuesday," he said. "I noticed his dog whining when we left the ranch yesterday. We were on a tight schedule, so I didn't say anything, but I thought the critter looked hungry."

"Think Jim's ill?" I asked.

"Could be. When I saw him Tuesday, he said he was feeling pretty rotten. But I can't help thinking he must've been really ill if he didn't feed his dog—he sure loves that mutt."

"Let's check on him when we get home," I suggested.

After tying down the plane at the Cameron Park airport, we drove home. As I crested our driveway, Jay looked across at the foreman's house, only to hear the dog howling piteously.

"Stop! I'm getting out! Something's very wrong!" Before I came to a full stop, Jay leapt out of the car and raced to the front door.

I drove up to our house and took our gear out of the car. While I was sorting it out on the kitchen counter, the phone rang. It was Jay. "Call the sheriff! Jim's dead!"

"Oh, my God. How did he die?"

"Suicide. Call them, please!" Jay sounded frantic.

Two sheriff's cars came wailing up the driveway within ten minutes. Jay was waiting for them outside Jim's place, and after greeting them, he picked up the scared dog and brought it up to the house.

He put it down, and it was shaking so badly I was afraid it would bolt if I made a sudden move. I slipped quietly into the house, got it a big bowl of water, and another of dried food, and carefully put them down near him, trying to coax him to eat. He lapped the water thirstily but ignored the food.

As I went back up the steps and into the kitchen, I found Jay standing over the sink putting a match to a piece of paper.

"What are you *doing?*" I asked, surprised.

"Nothing."

"Come on, you're burning a note. What is it?"

"Jim's suicide note," he said tersely.

"My God, you're destroying evidence! You can't *do* that!"

"You didn't see me."

"For God's sake, Jay, why?"

"Jim's always been in love with Laurie Galloway. He told me that one day when he came down into the orchard while I was working. In his note, he left her his undying love and all his worldly possessions, including his two pianos."

"So?"

"Those *are* his sole worldly possessions. I didn't tell you, he hasn't been able to pay the rent for several months, and if this note became public, it would ruin Les's career, not to mention Laurie's reputation ... for *what?* A couple of pianos and a pledge of love?"

I could see his point. Laurie's husband, Les, had just been elected to public office; he was highly regarded in the community and definitely on his way up the political ladder.

"Where did you find the note?"

"On his desk in the living room, weighted down with an ashtray."

"How did he die?"

"OD'd on sleeping pills. The empty bottle is still on his bed stand."

I looked out to see the deputy approaching, and stepped outside in case he frightened the dog.

"You find the body?" he asked. I crouched down and held the dog, and heard water running in the sink; I knew Jay was flushing the evidence away and cleaning up, and said, "No, my husband did. He'll be right out."

A few moments later Jay stood at the top of the steps and nodded a greeting to the sheriff.

"Sorry you had to find him like that," the deputy said. "The coroner says by the decomposition of the body, he's been dead at least since Thursday. Hard to pinpoint the exact time, as he was under an electric blanket."

"In July?" I asked in amazement.

"Guess after he OD'd he got the chills and put it on without thinking." Then he added, "We'll send in a crew to clean up the place, fumigate it, and get rid of the smell as best we can. That's a nice house, and that's a horrible thing to have happen in it."

"Jim was our friend. It's a terrible blow," Jay said.

The deputy nodded. "Do you want to make a statement now, or would you rather come down to the sheriff's office tomorrow?"

"I'll come down tomorrow. We've just got back from a trip and we're both pretty bushed. We still have to go over to the neighbors and pick up our girls. Nine in the morning okay?"

"Sure, fine. Ask for Deputy Watson; I'll be waiting for you."

We waited till the entourage of cars had left and the rental house was sealed before picking up Rebel at her girlfriend Terry's home, and Gillian at the Garretts'. Her best friend was Sylvia, the Garretts' youngest daughter, and now that Gillian was of school age, she went home with Sylvia on the bus every day and stayed at the Garretts' till I picked her up on my way home from work.

When Jay got back from the sheriff's office the next morning, he said, "Now they're not sure it's suicide, as they found a couple of bullet holes in the screen on the bedroom window."

"What about the sleeping pills?"

"Hard to tell how many pills he took, as his body was too decomposed to do a thorough autopsy. So now the case is listed as a possible homicide."

I let out a sigh of exasperation. "All because you destroyed his suicide note …"

"Listen, Pam, you're *never* to speak about that again. Especially don't say a word to Laurie. I know she's a good friend of yours, but don't do it! Think how you would feel if you knew someone who loved you had committed suicide. If you told her, she'd probably think she was to blame."

"Oh, Jay, it's so sad …" I was still having a problem coming to terms with Jim's death.

"It is. But there's a hell of a lot more to it than just unrequited love for Laurie. Jim told me he was a bomber pilot in World War II. It got to him. On their last run—they'd bombed some huge dam and were returning home—he realized they might not make it as they were running low on fuel. He said he asked the crew if they wanted to try to make it, or ditch the plane and walk out. They were flying over the Balkans at the time, and they could put it down safely and walk away. He knew the crew was as fed up as he was over the devastating bombing they'd been doing, and was not surprised when they said for him to land the plane and they'd take their chances. That's what he did. But Jim said his desertion had haunted him ever since. I think that's the real reason he couldn't go on. Promise me you'll never say a word about this or the note to anyone … at least not while I'm alive."

"I promise."

After the county crew had come out and cleaned up the place as best they could, we found they'd told the welfare department that there was a vacant home out on our ranch, and before we knew it, a case worker came out and said they needed to rent the house for a single mother with two children, and that welfare would be responsible for the rent being paid on time.

Jay, who hated to have rentals without tenants, jumped at the offer, and Hannalee, Tessica, and Adam moved in.

As I was gone from five-thirty in the morning to five-thirty at night, I knew nothing about them, or what Hannalee had done to the house. It was Jay who filled me in at dinner one evening.

"Well, I told Hannalee that the house could do with a painting, and that I would supply the paint if she wanted to do it. She jumped at it. I let her pick out the paint, and I'm afraid every room's a different color. Not quite what I thought she'd do. And she also took all the inside doors down and put them in the cellar. In their place she's hung curtains of beads, and she burns incense all through the house. Actually it helps kill the odor the cleanup crew wasn't able to get rid of, so I can't complain. She's put decals on all the kitchen cabinets and scattered psychedelic throw rugs all over the floors. I guess that's her idea of hippy heaven."

"Is it clean?" I asked anxiously.

"Oh, yes, she's a good housekeeper. But she sure has weird friends. A big bearded black man has moved in. She told me he's her guru, whatever that is, and she treats him like God."

One Sunday, a month or so later, while I was working in the kitchen and Gillian was playing outside, I saw Tessica come running up. She whispered something in Gillian's ear, then I heard her say, "Quick! Quick!" Gillian said she'd have to ask me first, and came into the kitchen on the run, saying, "Mommy, Mommy, Tessy wants me to come down and watch her mommy make babies. Can I go?"

Ye gods, is that considered child entertainment today?

I tried not to look too flustered and hurriedly said, "I was just going to make your lunch, honey. Why don't you ask Tessy if she'd like to join you? Tell her to go call her brother, and we'll have a picnic out by the pool."

The picnic turned out to be another eye-opener. To make conversation as we all sat around on the lawn, I asked them what they usually had for lunch. "Peanuts!" Adam and Tessica said in unison.

"Oh, peanut butter sandwiches?" I asked with a smile.

"No. Peanuts and milk."

"And for dinner?" I asked, getting really nosy.

"Peanuts and milk."

I didn't dare ask what they had for breakfast.

∽

Late in the summer of '70, the Douglas Sacramento Test Center closed down permanently, and I was once more out of work. I knew I could've gone back to Aerojet, but the challenge was gone. Anyhow, I was getting awfully tired of long commutes and decided to look for a job closer to home. Although I figured the pay would be less, it would more than likely offset the wear and tear on my car, not to mention the expense of gas and tires.

My new boss turned out to be George Fisher, owner of Pioneer Press in Placerville, five miles from our home ranch. I got the job by accident. I'd started freelancing, and I walked into his shop to see if he needed any graphic design or brochures. He was sitting at his desk, holding his head, and looked as though he had the granddaddy of all headaches. When I asked him if he needed any artwork, he said, "No, not now ... what I need *now* is a camera/stripper. Ever done that?"

"No, but I've seen it done, and I sure can learn."

And that's how I went from being one of the highest paid women in the space industry to a camera operator/film stripper on minimum wage! As usual, I learned how to do nearly everything—up to, but not including, running the presses. I still had a fearful respect for them, going back to the days when I lost the tip of my index finger in the mimeograph machine.

I soon discovered that George was gone most of the time. He was a super salesman, and was also involved with both the city and county chambers, and umpteen service clubs, so I more or less took over the front office as well as all the camera work and plate-making. That I threw in my graphics for good measure goes without saying. If a job needed artwork, it got artwork. I became philosophical about it, telling myself I was being paid to go to school.

The job lasted for three years or, I should say, I lasted for three years. When George bought a travel agency, I thought, *Hey, we must be doing okay,* although I'd never seen his bottom line. When he and his wife took off on trips all over the world, my philosophical bent got bent a little further, and when they came back from a two-week trip to Tahiti and George gave us each a bonus for racking up the best month in the history of Pioneer Press, I said, *"Enough!"*

I was working anywhere from ten to fourteen hours a day; I might have gotten rid of the commute but sure as hell not the long hours. George had inadvertently taught me how to run a printing business, how to get along with customers, how to do everything required to get a print job ready for the presses. Bless his heart, he'd even shown me there was enough work in the town to support *two* commercial printers!

When I went into his office and told him I was leaving to start my own business, he responded like the personnel manager at Aerojet: he didn't say I'd be sorry, but he implied it. I said the only way I could find out was by doing it. Realizing he couldn't dissuade me, he said I could go with one stipulation: I had to be available to do artwork for him whenever he needed it. I agreed, and we shook on it.

Now, looking back, I realize I never thought of failure. I was programmed for success, just as in the prison camp I'd been programmed for survival.

The future would always be my greatest challenge …

Chapter 22

Meanwhile, back at the ranch ... Hannalee was long gone, and Jay had found a delightful, slow, but oh-so-thorough foreman by the name of Henry Boone. What Henry didn't know about farming wasn't worth knowing. Likewise, what he didn't know about the work ethic wasn't worth knowing, either. He'd been raised on a farm, and because he'd been put to work at the age of six, he'd never gone to school; when he was ten he learned to drive a tractor and to handle all the chores thrown at him. And in his tough, rough world, he'd learned that animals could be trusted better than humans. People had often been unkind to him, laughed at him because of his slowness and because he couldn't read or write, but animals never hurt him; they knew he loved them, and they loved him in return.

He came with a mother, a dear lady whose sun rose and set on Henry. I never learned her first name; she was always Mrs. Boone. The two were both homely and beautiful at the same time. When Jay asked Henry if he would like to work for him and be his foreman, Henry just about dropped down on his knees and kissed Jay's feet. From there on out, whenever he was on an errand for Jay he'd introduce himself by saying, "I'm Mr. Masters's *foreman*, Henry Boone ..." and it was easy to see he was so proud of that title.

One thing Jay soon learned, though, was that Henry didn't have a driver's license. He hadn't needed one on the big spread he'd grown up on; like everything else to do with farming, he just *knew* how to drive. Trouble was, in California a person had to have a driver's license, which meant he had to know how to read to pass the written test. Jay went down to the Department of Motor Vehicles and asked if they would give Henry an oral test. They were very helpful and said they would, then gave Jay the latest state motor vehicle code booklet. The two of them sat down, and Jay coached Henry on every single rule of the road till he had it memorized. It took a long time, but not as long as it would have taken to teach him how to read well. When Henry felt confident he could pass the oral test, Jay took him down to the DMV and he aced it. There'd never been any doubt that he would pass the actual driving test. Now Henry was the proud owner of a Class B driver's license and could go into town, run errands for his mother—instead of the other way around—and he'd just grown ten feet tall in his own estimation. Jay explained to Henry that before harvest season, he would have to get a Class A license to legally drive a truck, and as the months rolled by, Jay coached him further, and once more he took a driving test and got his Class A with flying colors.

One incident I remember so clearly: one Saturday morning I came racing up the driveway and told Henry the little foal that had been born the previous day was dead. It wasn't moving, just lying on its side in the grass in the lower meadow. I started to cry, and Henry said, "It's not dead. It's getting its vitamin C. Animals do that."

"Oh, no, Henry, it's *dead*," I insisted. "We better let the owners know."

Henry, in his quiet way, knew there was only one way to put my heart at ease, so he stopped what he was doing and started down the driveway, and I followed him. When we got to the meadow, Henry leaned on the fence, and looking at the "dead" foal, he made some gentle Dr. Doolittle sounds. I watched amazed as the still wobbly-legged critter rose like Lazarus and came slowly over to the fence, its neck arched and ears flicking.

Well, now Jay had his much-needed ranch help ... but there was still Gillian, especially in the summer months when school was out. Rebel had moved out right after her eighteenth birthday and had her own apartment, so she wasn't available to keep her eye on her little sister, although they were getting along much better now. I was still on a treadmill; instead of long commutes first thing in the morning, it was chamber breakfasts and council meetings that took a big slice out of my early hours. I knew I had to find someone to be with Gillian, and then it struck me—*How about Mother?* She'd lost dear Walter, her third husband, several years earlier and was living alone up in White Rock in British Columbia. I wrote and told her I needed her, and asked if she would consider living in a mobile home on the ranch. Her response was overwhelming: "I never dreamed anyone would ever *need* me again. Of course I'll come!"

So we leveled out an area between our home and the foreman's house, put in a pad, a septic tank, and a propane tank for heating and cooking, then moved a one-bedroom mobile home in, laying a red brick patio under its metal awning. And when Mother arrived, looking a good ten years younger than her eighty-four years, the first things she did were plant a small rose garden, hang tubs of petunias from the filigreed awning brackets, and paint a couple of Adirondack chairs she'd brought with her a stunning bright yellow. Once again she lit up her corner of the world. That was a wonderful knack she had; she could turn any place into a home. She'd done it in our lovely rambling homes in China, she'd even done it in the prison camp, and she did it again and again wherever she'd landed in the States and Canada.

I remember the following year, when she decided to pay a visit to some dear friends in Canada, how I'd had to remind her eighty-five was her age, not the speed limit! She loved to drive up to British Columbia, her little cairn terrier in the seat beside her, breaking the long trip with a stay-over at Margo and Jack's home in Albany, Oregon. I said a silent prayer that I would be as active as she was at her age.

When Mother arrived, Sierra Gold Graphics had been in existence just over a year. At the time I'd opened my doors, George Fisher's Pioneer Press was the only other commercial printing business in Placerville, as Doc Phipps's Line and Letter was more or less a captive shop to American Title Company and El Dorado Savings. But before my presses had time to really warm up, Ace Copy and Placerville Press opened their doors. They were tiny family operations, with limited equipment and equally limited know-how. I told them there was enough work to go around for all of us, so there'd be no need for undercutting or poor-mouthing competition. I offered to help whenever they might need me and, surprisingly, got quite a lot of work from them when they bid a job then found they didn't have the equipment or, sometimes, the ability to do it. Part of my operation became what's known in the printing business as a "trade shop"; unknown to their customers, I would do the work for the copy shops at a reduced figure so they could make a profit. Not as big a profit as they could make if they'd done the job themselves. That was deliberate, so they wouldn't take advantage of me. It soon developed that when they got a really complicated job, they wouldn't even bid on it but would recommend the customer come to Sierra Gold. And that's how I liked it, especially as I was not a copy shop and was quite happy to send them a lot of copy work in return. It always surprised me how the public seldom knew the difference between a commercial printing business and a simple copy shop.

I opened my doors on August 8, 1974, figuring that, as eight was my lucky number, a double-eight would double my luck. It didn't take me long to find out success had very little to do with luck, and a heck of a lot more to do with hard work. I also found out that I couldn't get away with blowing my stack, telling customers to take a hike, or any of the little stunts I'd pulled in my earlier career. Regardless of how I felt or how crazy a customer's printing request might be, the adage "the customer's always right" kept coming into play, and I would have to bite my tongue, smile sweetly, and agree their idea was terrific.

For me, it was a whole new exercise in self-restraint, but I quickly got a handle on it, especially when I saw how thrilled they were when some brochure, catalog, poster, or flyer they'd dreamed up became a reality. Quite often they'd come into the shop with no concept of what they wanted, and I'd design a whole package, starting with a logo for business cards, then going to brochures, letterheads, invoices, and the whole shooting match. Usually they'd be starting out on a shoestring, as I had done, and I'd suggest they forget everything but a really sharp business card and possibly a simple brochure. I'd suggest that to get word out, they should join either one, or both, of our chambers of commerce. I'd recommend after they'd got their foot in the door and business was coming in, they use the money they'd made to get the balance of their printing done. That way the business would be generating its own income, and they wouldn't have to dig too deep into their start-up funds. I think they really liked the idea that I understood what starting a new business cost, because they came back again and again, and I never had to do any other advertising myself. It intrigued me that several years after I'd been in business I heard a story going the rounds, "If you want to stay in business, have Sierra Gold design your logo, and you've got it made!" That sure didn't hurt business any!

Of course, as far as the chambers were concerned, I got really involved. Before I could blink, I found I was chairing the county chamber's membership committee, an excellent place to find out about all the new businesses starting up and to learn the names of the established ones that weren't as well-known as our few big industries. I also joined a couple of service clubs and became involved in many community projects. I had to smile whenever I thought about it, because it was George—my only *real* competition—who'd taught me how to build a business.

Then, out of the blue, George sold Pioneer Press to a couple who hadn't the foggiest idea what they were buying. They must have thought they were getting a little mom and pop print shop, and they were out of their depth within months. And within the year they went belly-up, and George got it back.

After trying to find a new buyer, he came to me and asked if I wanted to buy Pioneer Press. He was such a nice person, and I hated telling him he had nothing I wanted. His equipment was old, his client base had vanished, and the figure he was asking would buy me a heck of a lot of new equipment that I would soon be needing.

George was nothing if not gracious, and said, "I know, if I

were in your shoes I'd have given the same answer. You can't blame me for trying." Then he auctioned off all his equipment, closed his doors, and started another venture.

I was soon to find there was a wonderful plus to owning a printing business in Placerville: I went from not knowing a soul in the county to knowing just about everyone. Of course, as always, there were upsides and downsides, like the afternoon I was tooling down Highway 50 after making deliveries to Michigan-Cal Lumber in Camino. Just as I was making the bend by Merryman's Corner, I noticed a Highway Patrol car behind me with its damn lights flashing.

Now, what the sam hill did I do? I said under my breath as I found a spot to pull over.

A CHP officer stepped out of the car and came up to my window, and looking up, I saw it was Mac McPherson.

"Okay, what did I do?" I asked with a frown.

"That depends."

"On … ?"

"Whether you got the Pony Express Re-Run flyers out yet!"

"Good God, Mac, you just ruined my reputation to ask if the *Pony Express flyers* were done?"

"Yeah," he said with a wicked smile, "and I enjoyed doing it!"

"You know what?" I asked acidly. "I think I should have you walk the straight and narrow with your finger on your nose! *I'd* enjoy doing that!"

"Bet you would! Can I pick up the flyers this afternoon when I get off duty?"

"Sure … what the heck. It's a good thing they didn't give out citations when the Pony Express was running," I said, laughing.

"You know, David Young is still trying to live down the time he pulled you over on North Canyon."

When I looked perplexed, he said, "You remember. He tried to ticket you for cutting all the corners, and asked if you hadn't seen him following you. Your reply was that yes, you'd seen him, you'd also seen there was no traffic approaching so you decided to straighten out North Canyon and save your tires!"

"If I recall, I didn't get a ticket," I said smugly.

"That's right. According to Dave, he was laughing so hard he couldn't have written a ticket if he'd wanted to."

"You just made my day!" I said with a grin.

As I pulled back out onto the highway, my mind flashed back to the real estate agent who'd first told us about the Pony Express. I'd learned through the years, and through the annual Pony Express Re-Runs, that the young, unarmed riders had run flat out from St. Joseph, Missouri, to Sacramento, California, protected by a hard-won treaty with the many Indian tribes along the route. After the Paiute Indian War of May 1860, the Indians honored the treaty and learned to admire and respect the young riders, who almost to a man were in their early teens, and were also orphans. William H. Russell, of the freight hauling firm of Russell, Majors, and Waddell, and the mastermind behind the enterprise, insisted on this last stipulation in order to keep expenses down by not having to pay compensation to bereaved families in the event a rider was killed. It wasn't entirely callous, as in addition to the riders, there were around four hundred other employees, and the expense of running all the way stations along the route, keeping the remounts in top shape for their short all-out dashes, and the myriad challenges they had to meet on a daily basis was excessive.

The Pony Express ran for just over eighteen months, from May 1860 to the end of 1861, when it was replaced by the Transcontinental Telegraph, but the riders' record of sheer gut-slugging bravery and honor to duty became a legend. Only one rider was killed, and the Indians who found his body gave him a warrior's funeral.

∽

In case I've left the impression I never lost my temper or had a problem remembering "the customer is always right," I have to admit I did lose it a couple of times.

Once a corporation ordered stationery for its new office in Pollock Pines, but neglected to tell us that between the time they'd ordered the printing and came to pick it up, they'd moved to a better location. When they came for their stationery, they refused it because the address was wrong. I said it was right when they first ordered it, but they still refused to take it.

"That's okay by me," I said, "I'll round-file it. But you *will* pay for it … and *now!*"

I guess I can be quite intimidating, because they wrote out a check for the full amount, picked up all the printing, and stormed out of the shop.

I don't know what made me, but I glanced through the window as they walked out the door to their Mercedes, threw the boxes into the backseat, and climbed into the car. They conferred for a moment, then a cat-in-the-cream look came over their faces, and they nodded and drove off.

I looked at the check, saw it was drawn on a local bank, and asked Rebel, who was now my new bookkeeper/manager, to call the bank and have them call us if a stop-payment was put on the check. Rebel called, giving the account and check number, and within ten minutes the bank called with the not-unexpected news.

"What do we do now?" I asked Rebel, who'd worked for a bank before coming aboard.

"Call the sheriff and have them picked up for theft. It's almost grand theft."

Needless to say, when we called the bank back several hours later, the check had been made good, and Rebel rushed over and deposited it. It was great having her in the office because she knew every in-and-out a person could take to manipulate the banking system.

There were a couple of other accounts I'd eased out the door. To be honest, I *shoved* them out the door. One never came back, and I was happy about that, but the second, to my dismay, returned, all contrite. He said he'd never been squeezed like a lemon before, or pitched out of a door like a bum, but he'd tried all the other shops in town and still liked us best.

What could I do but accept his roundabout apology and take him back?

∽

One day in the spring of '76, two very clean-cut young men came to the shop. They needed packaging for an item they had designed and asked if I could help them with it. They introduced themselves as elders of the Mormon Church, and the project they were working on was a fund-raiser for the Boy Scouts. It was a simple safety-lock that could be produced for under fifty cents that the Scouts should easily be able to sell for around two dollars. I told Jay about it, and he said, "Give it all you've got, hon, what could be safer than the Mormon Church and the Boy Scouts of America!"

Looked at in that light, I had to agree.

During the course of designing the packaging, Joe Austin, whom I thought was a surprisingly smooth number for a church elder, and Mike Hammond, who personified that office, said they were having trouble getting the item manufactured and wondered if we knew of any outfit that could do it for them. Jay studied the idea carefully and, following the recommendation he'd given me, found them a manufacturer in Sacramento. They were very grateful, but it appeared they didn't even have enough money to get the dies made, so Jay said he'd fund that part of the operation if they set up a corporation and made everything legitimate. The agreement finally boiled down to their being in charge of marketing and selling the items to all the different Scout troops in California, while we took care of production and packaging. They were only too happy with the arrangement, and a corporation was formed. Jay put up the money to get the ball rolling, and all systems were go.

We not only handled all their manufacturing and printed all their packaging, we spent night after night assembling the items that went into each packet, sealing them, crating them, and readying them for shipment, and then warehousing them while we waited for orders to come in.

They only trickled in. And soon we learned that Mike had had to get back to his full-time job down south, and we were left dealing with Joe, a self-styled entrepreneur with lots of ideas but no work ethic. Every time I went out to the warehouse behind our pressroom, I'd shudder when I saw all those neatly stacked cartons collecting dust. We'd given their project everything, spent money we really didn't have, and for *what?*

There was no point in brooding; I had too much other work in the shop for that. We had a wonderful account base by then, which included the county offices, the hospital, a couple of lumber mills, and most, if not all, the professional offices in Placerville and round about. We also had some lovely winery accounts, as wine-making was now becoming one of El Dorado County's newest agricultural enterprises.

And then the bottom fell out of our world!

Officer Watson, the same deputy who had handled Jim Frazier's suicide, came up to the ranch one evening to deliver a subpoena and said with a broad grin, "Guess you're going to have to dig into the petty cash. I see here you're being sued by the Boy Scouts of America for two million dollars!"

I said, "*Come on,* you're kidding, right? What the sam hill did we do to the Boy Scouts?"

"Dunno, but it looks serious," he said as he got back into his squad car.

As he drove off, Jay came out of the house and asked, "What was all that about?" I handed him the summons. I should have prepared him first, because his face went dead white and I thought he was going to collapse.

"Good God, we couldn't raise two million if we sold everything we've got! What the hell has happened?"

The following day I called down to the director of the Golden Empire Council in the Los Angeles area and asked what the suit was all about. I was told that Joe Austin had been taking money from the different Scout troops all over California but not shipping the product and, as we were the organization behind the project, the BSA was suing us for unfilled orders and miscellaneous damages.

What we needed now was a good corporate attorney. The only one I could think of was Nigel Connor, who'd won my case against Veloz and Yolanda, and I said a little prayer that he was still working for Southern California Edison.

I called Edison and found Nigel was up at Carson City, just over the Sierra from us, working on some big private power tax problem. I was given his phone number in Carson City, and he seemed genuinely happy to hear from me and said he'd see what he could do for us. We set up an appointment for early the following Tuesday, and Jay and I flew up on Monday, dropped our overnight bags at a motel, and went to meet Nigel for dinner. When we found him in the bar, he was already three sheets to the wind and insisted we had to drive to Incline Village on the east shore of Lake Tahoe because it had the only good restaurant for miles. I gave him one look and asked for the keys to his car, as there was no way I was going to trust him behind the wheel.

The night was beautiful with a full moon, and the rental turned out to be a sleek, white Firebird, loaded with everything, so I really enjoyed myself. That's the first time I'd ever seen a man lap Manhattans like they were Shirley Temples; he put five away in the course of the dinner, which was really excellent—the dinner I mean, not his drinking. When we dropped him off at his apartment, which was adjacent to his office, I hoped he had great curative powers because we didn't need him with a hangover on the following day.

Back at the motel, I found Jay was terribly uptight about the same thing and, being a woman, I knew instinctively how to get his mind off his problems.

We woke the next morning refreshed, had a shower and a good breakfast, then went to see what condition Nigel was in.

I couldn't believe it! There was no hangover: he was sharp and dapper, and got right to the point.

"Where are your corporate papers?"

Jay handed them to him, and after he'd studied them for several minutes he said, "Who wrote these up?"

His tone had me worried, and I looked nervously over at Jay.

"I did," Jay said. "Anything wrong with them?"

"Not a damn thing. The Boy Scouts haven't got a case."

We both drew a long sigh of relief.

"You should be a lawyer, Jay," he said. "That clause stating the corporation is not responsible for any transactions carried out before its formation gets you both off the hook."

"How come?" I asked baffled. "We made the items, and Joe sold them but didn't ship them."

"That's right, but look at the dates on the orders cited: they were all *before* you ever formed the corporation, hence Mr. Austin is the only person the Boy Scouts can sue."

"But he hasn't got a nickel to bless his name," I said.

"That's going to be tough on the Boy Scouts of America, but not on you. I'll send a letter to the Golden Empire Council stating the case, and I'll send you a copy and a token bill for my services."

The whole thing reminded me of the addendum Jay had put on our purchase contract for the home ranch back in '60. It was the first such agreement to have a "seven year interest only" clause in it in the event the orchard was hit with pear decline, as it took seven years to get pear trees into full production. There was no doubt Jay had a cool head when it came to business.

I gave Nigel a big hug. "Thank you. I knew you'd know how to handle it."

"Do you have to leave now?" he asked, and he sounded really disappointed.

"Yes, we really do. Orchard work is backing up on me," Jay said, shaking Nigel's hand and thanking him for all he'd done.

"Well, if you must go, I'll drive you to the airport." And this time I had no qualms being in a car with Nigel behind the wheel.

The relief on the flight home was so great, I felt I could've flown without a plane!

~

On Friday, July the first, several weeks after our trip to Carson City, I was out on the patio watering my geraniums when Jay came staggering up out of the orchard. He was clutching his chest, and I could see he was in the throes of a heart attack. Aghast, I bundled him into the car and raced him to Marshall Hospital. After they'd stabilized him, he was put in intensive care. Sitting by his bed, with him connected to every type of machine imaginable, I got to thinking about his age, sixty, and of his dad who'd died of a massive heart attack at the age of sixty-three, and I said a silent prayer that Jay didn't have his father's genes.

Chapter 23

Saturday morning when I went to the hospital to see Jay, he'd been moved from intensive care. His color was back, and so was his sassy upbeat outlook. "The doctor says I can go home. I'm to take this attack as a stern warning, but I can go home," he said with one of his lovely wide smiles.

"What did you do? Tell the doctor you'd have another heart attack if they kept you here?" I asked, knowing his devious ways.

"Not quite. Would you check at the desk and see if my paperwork's ready? I really want to get out of here." To my surprise, it was. Small hospitals are wonderful that way.

Home again, he was his happy old self. The girls were all over him, waiting on him hand and foot, and Mother came over to add her welcome-home wishes.

Sunday after church, I found him resting quietly in the living room, watching a sports program on television. "I'm supposed to go to an art exhibit at Friday House this afternoon," I said. "Will you be okay if I leave you?"

"Sure."

"Positive?"

"Yep."

"I'll fix your lunch and then take off."

The showing at Friday House was delightful. George, Jean, and Carol Mathis, a very talented father, mother, and daughter team, were the leading artists of the history of the Mother Lode. I'd met George at Aerojet, where he was their signature artist. Like Ross Pettit, my last supervisor at Rocketdyne, George painted fabulous pictures of rocket launchings and interplanetary travel, along with great portraits of all Aerojet's top management. When he bought the charming old rambling house in the little town of Coloma, the site of Sutter's Mill and the original gold strike, they named it Friday House, as that was the happiest day of the week, when they could all get together and George could look forward to a weekend of painting the historic Gold Rush scenes for which he was so famous.

I bought a lovely water color of a snow scene Carol had painted, and was looking forward to hanging it in a special spot where I knew it would look great.

Driving home that evening on twisting, turning Highway 49—called the Golden Chain because it had originally linked up all the mining towns in the Mother Lode—was pleasant, and for once, probably because it was a Sunday afternoon, there were no logging trucks to slow me down. When I got home, I parked under the huge tulip tree that shaded the top of our circular driveway and got out of the car. As I went around the passenger side and reached into the backseat for the painting, I heard my name called in a panic-struck voice. I glanced up over the top of the car and saw Mother standing by her mobile home with a neighbor.

"Jay's had another heart attack," the neighbor said. "I took him to the hospital. I would've stayed with him, but I wanted to be sure you got the message as soon as you got home."

"How is he?" I asked, dread in my voice.

"I'm sorry, darling, he's very bad," Mother said gently. And recalling all the years she'd spent with Dad, who'd also had a bad heart, I knew it was dire.

"How did it happen? When?" I asked.

"Right after you left, he got dressed and went down into the orchard. I watched him," Mother said, "but what could I do but wave to let him know I'd seen him?"

I handed her Carol's water color and jumped back into the car, my mind in a whirl. I couldn't understand why I hadn't received a message of some kind. I'd enjoyed the afternoon, thinking everything was great at home. That was so unlike the two of us: Jay always felt pain when I did, and vice versa. We were so finely attuned, he told me once he swore he felt every labor pain I went through when I delivered our two girls. Why hadn't I had some premonition all was not well … ?

When I got to the hospital, they were stabilizing him, getting him ready to transport to Mercy General in Sacramento. Dr. Riley, our family doctor, told me Mercy was setting up for an immediate angiogram, and that a Dr. Davis would be taking over. Riley was gentle but blunt, and told me I should prepare myself for the worst.

As so often happens when I'm totally stressed out, I don't remember the drive down behind the ambulance, or anything that happened prior to Jay being rolled into the operating room. It was as though I were in a trance that only ended when Dr. Davis came out after the angiogram, which had turned into an angioplasty, to tell me that the left half of Jay's heart had been very badly damaged and that he would never be able to live the way he had or do the things he'd done before.

I knew then, without anyone telling me, that the stress of our possibly losing the ranch had been the cause of the heart attack. It was as though all the old insecurity that I'd thought Jay had overcome had come back to slug him. How could I let him know that there was nothing on earth worth his losing his health over?

A week or so later, after he'd been taken off the critical list, I came into his room and saw a pretty little Sister climbing up on the low, wide window sill. I asked what she was doing. She smiled sweetly and said, "Mr. Masters told me the sun was in his eyes and asked if I could lower the blind, but it got stuck, so I'm having to loosen it."

"Let me do that, Sister," I said, ready to clobber Jay, who was smiling in a wicked way.

"Oh, that's all right, Mrs. Masters, I've done it now!" And with that, the blind dropped with a plop, and she stepped down from the sill, smiled again, and glided out of the room.

"You *sonofabitch!* You were getting your jollies, weren't you?"

"Honestly, hon, I didn't know her habit was transparent until she stood in the sunlight!"

I gave him a kiss and couldn't help laughing. Some people are just born incorrigible.

A week later, back home once more, he defied all the odds, worked like nothing had ever stopped him, and got stronger by the day. A year later, when I took him in for a physical and stress EKG, Dr. Davis couldn't believe the results.

"I don't know what you've been doing, but what I'm seeing is almost miraculous. Your secondary blood vessels have taken over and repaired most of the damage your heart sustained last year. I wouldn't have believed it if I hadn't seen it with my own eyes."

To say Jay was one happy man would be the understatement of the year!

∼

As the '70s came to a close, I found I was getting more and more bored with my work. I needed a change. Any change. Heck, I'd been doing the same thing for almost six years, and it was getting me down. That was one thing I hadn't thought of when I started Sierra Gold Graphics. You can't just walk away and leave a business you own like you can any other boring job. You have to stick it out, or find someone to buy you out. I really didn't want to sell it so much as to have more time on my hands to do other things. A partner would be good. Someone to bounce things off and run the show while I went picking daisies in greener pastures.

I was mulling over different alternatives one afternoon when I got a call from Marshall Hospital. This time it wasn't Jay, it was Mother. They said she had just been admitted, and would I please come over.

When I got there, I found she'd had a massive stroke while driving her car. One of our tenants, whose brother was an EMT, had seen her slumped over the wheel, off to the side of Pony Express Trail, and had immediately called the fire department. The ambulance ride from Pollock Pines to Marshall Hospital had been long and grueling. Her heart had stopped several times, and when I saw her, she was badly bruised from all the measures they'd had to take, but she was alive. Daisy Mason, the counseling nurse and one of my favorite people, asked if Mother had left any instructions. I told her she had: there were to be no heroic measures taken. Daisy asked if it would be okay to leave a tube in her throat to keep her airways open, and I told her that would be all right, but that was all they could do, as I knew my Mother's wishes. Daisy said to be prepared; there was very little chance Mom would make it through the night.

I went home, totally shaken. Jay was there to help me, and Rebel and Gillian, but Mom had never been as close, brave, or wonderful to them as she was to me. I consoled myself by remembering all the things Mother had told me, especially how she'd asked God to let her leave this world doing the one thing she loved—driving her car. Her worst nightmare had been that she would grow so old she would lose her driver's license; she'd had one for so many years. In fact, that's how she met Dad: she was an ambulance driver on the Western Front in the First World War, and he was a captain in charge of a contingent of Chinese coolies that he'd brought over from the Orient to dig trenches and graves for the Allies. They met one day when one of Mother's wounded soldiers died on the way to the field hospital, and Dad had taken over. That had been the beginning of a long, tempestuous love affair that had lasted well after Dad's death. And, as shaken as I was, I thanked God for answering Mom's last prayer. She'd been on her way home after having her hair done; she was beautifully coifed and was driving along with her precious dog beside her when God reached down …

~

I went to the hospital early the following morning, bolstering myself for the inevitable. Although I'd been quietly surprised that I hadn't had a call in the night, I got to thinking, *Why would they call me and disturb my sleep to tell me Mom had slipped into her eternal rest … ?*

The cold, moist touch of another dawn reached out to me as I walked through the almost empty visitors' parking lot, then through the unattended lobby, and down the hall to her room. A nurse joined me when I passed the nurses' station, and said, "You're in for a wonderful surprise! It's almost unbelievable, but your mother rallied in the night. Isn't that great?"

I couldn't help thinking, *Was it?* That depended on so many things.

"Will there be any permanent damage?" I asked, voicing my main fear.

"More than likely. You'll have to ask Dr. Riley."

I looked at Mom's precious face, all slipped out of shape. Her vacant eyes and labored breathing. The tube was still down her throat, and I could see it was paining her; I didn't know if she couldn't speak because of the tube or because of the stroke. I sat beside her and took her cold, transparent hand in mine, and tried to will my own strength into her.

Mother was eighty-seven. She'd led a fascinating life, hardly any of it easy, but she'd given me her strength, her bounce-back, and her in-your-face attitude, and it only seemed right for me to try to give some of it back now.

The following day when I went to see her, the tube had been removed and Dr. Riley was standing by her bed. When I joined him, he said softly, "Pam, your mother will never recover completely; she'll always be an invalid. Her days of being active are over. How much damage was done to her brain remains to be seen."

"Will she ever be able to talk again?" I asked, fearing his reply.

"To be honest, it's doubtful."

"Can she *hear* us now?" I asked, as I didn't want her to hear these dire predictions.

"Again, it's doubtful, she's still very much unaware of what's going on." Then he added, "She'll always need round-the-clock care, and that means a full-care convalescent home. Placerville Pines next door would be my choice. They're great with their patients."

But later, when we checked it out, we found the Pines didn't have an opening. It sounded callous, but I would have to wait for one of their patients to die before Mother could be admitted. It was a sobering thought.

I asked Daisy if there was another convalescent home Mother could go to, and was told not for someone who needed twenty-four hour care. There were several very good homes for ambulatory "guests," but they didn't take anyone who was bedridden. So Mother stayed at Marshall for a full month before I was able to get her into the Pines.

I visited her every day at Marshall, and started the ritual of coming at lunchtime to help feed her, as the hospital was full to capacity. Sometimes a Pink Lady would come in and talk to me; they were the volunteers who fed Mother in the morning and evening, and their gentle solicitude was lovely to see.

When she was finally moved to the Pines, I learned firsthand what Doc Riley meant about loving care. I dropped in and fed her at lunch time, and a couple of times a week I'd take her for a drive on our winding country roads. Although she was still very frail, the nurses helped me settle her in the car, and she was able to sit up and see everything around her. She seemed to like the drives, but sadly they didn't last long. While she was at Marshall, she'd chafed her heel on the bedsheet, and as her skin was very fragile, it had broken. With no circulation in her legs, the tiny sore had turned into a gangrenous mess, which before long threatened her leg. The surgeon, a very caring person, asked me for permission to amputate it.

"Don't ask me," I said. "Ask Mother."

He looked perplexed.

"She understands," I said. "Ask her."

Even I was surprised when she said, haltingly, "Do it!"

He look at me in total shock, and said quietly, "What do you think, should I amputate above or below the knee?"

I said again, "Ask *her*." And he did.

Her halting reply was classic Mother: "I made *my* decision, doctor, that one is *yours*."

He bent over to hear her, then kissed her forehead and said, "Yes, *ma'am!*" and amputated her leg just above the knee.

I didn't know it at the time, but those were to be the last intelligible words she would speak except for a whispered "thank you" now and then.

Several months later, the second leg had to be amputated as well, and although both were taken just above the knee, sitting for any length of time was very tiring and painful for her.

Through the years—yes, she was there for seven years—I learned to communicate with her on a different level. It was sort of a mind-to-mind communication. In China, and when I was first in the States, while I was still more British than American, I'd always called her Mumsy, not Mom; when I started to call her that again, I saw her eyes light up. So it stuck, and even the nurses and aides started calling her Mumsy. "Mumsy's doing great today." "Mumsy ate all her breakfast." "Mumsy's been getting impatient waiting for you."

My lunch hour became a ritual. When I first came to feed her the food was too hot, and I'd have to sit and wait almost fifteen minutes for it to cool off. I told the aides I'd prefer it if they would leave her tray on the cart with its cover on, and when I arrived it would be ready for me to feed her. It was a simple thing, but it helped immensely. I left the shop at noon, walked the uphill mile to the Pines, and by the time I got there, the food was just right for her to eat. While I fed her, I'd tell her all that was going on at home, how her little dog was getting along—her little cairn terrier had died right after she'd returned from her last trip to Canada, and she'd bought a cute, wiggling little dachshund she named Pretzel—and somehow the time just flew.

Then one day I came to the Pines, and everything was in an uproar. The state inspector was going through the home throwing her weight around and being obnoxious. I went to get Mother's tray from the cart, but it wasn't there.

"Where's Mumsy's tray?" I asked one of my favorite aides.

"The inspector made us put it back and keep it hot," she said. "I'm so sorry, Pam."

"You're not as sorry as she's going to be," I said, furious. "Where *is* she?"

"In the office with the administrator."

"Thank you!" I said brusquely, and started to march off.

"Don't, don't ... you can't go into the office!" she pleaded.

I pretended not to hear and barged right in.

"I came to see the state inspector," I said in my most officious voice.

"Ye-e-es? And, what can I do for you?" Ah, what a *sweet* voice she had ... I felt like wringing her neck!

"You can stop changing the instructions I gave for the care of my mother!" I said angrily.

"Excuse me?" The sugary tone had been replaced with one of clipped authority.

"You heard! I have a one-hour lunch break. It takes me fifteen minutes to walk here, thirty minutes to feed my mother, and another fifteen minutes to walk back to my work." I didn't tell her I owned my own business and could take as long as I damn well pleased, but I laid it out in language she could understand. "When you come and tell the girls to take my mother's lunch off the cart and to keep it hot, you've just added another fifteen minutes I don't have to my lunch hour, because that's how long it takes for the darn food to cool off before I can feed Mother. *Capisce?*"

"They have to keep it at a certain temperature—it's the law!" she said, letting me know who was boss in no uncertain terms.

"No, it's not, it's *bullshit!*" I said rudely. "Are you telling me that it's safer for Mother's food to sit *uncovered* in a dining room while I wait for it to cool off than it is to sit *covered* on a cart?"

She started to burble and make weird noises, but I cut her off. "Don't *ever* interfere with me, or my mother, or any orders I give the personnel here. Go throw your weight around somewhere else. I'm not impressed."

Darn my voice ... it always carries! When I came storming out of the office, every one of the nurses and aides was trying to hide their smiles and outright laughter. Even Mother's eyes were sparkling. On the plus side—*I* might have gotten heated over the whole situation, but Mother's lunch had cooled off just enough for me to feed her ...

∼

In the early '80s Jay drove up to Redding and bought an old steel building that was being torn down to be replaced by a much larger and more modern one. Lord knows how big the new one must have been, because the one he bought was fifty by one hundred feet! He had it taken apart, piece by piece, all the parts stacked and numbered for easy reassembly, and then had it shipped to Camino.

In California, farm buildings without electricity or plumbing—like barns, stables, and such—don't require a building permit. So Jay engineered the whole job, photographing every step along the way and recording every measurement he made, and except for having some steelworkers come in and help him with the roof, he reassembled the whole thing himself. Sadly, Henry had left, having been offered a higher-paying job in a lumber mill up north. It was bittersweet for Jay, as Henry only got the job because Jay had spent all the time he could helping him learn how to read and write.

The building turned out so well that Jay decided to make it more than a storage building. He'd already started to fill it up with farm equipment, lumber, and irrigation pipe when he decided to build an office in the front overlooking North Canyon. At the time he'd poured the original foundation for the building, he'd added a twelve-foot gallery along the front, and a huge octagonal rotunda off the southwest corner. When I'd seen the foundation I instantly drew up an elevation, showing a beautiful red-and-white tent top over the rotunda and a covered gallery with hanging baskets of flowers across the front of the building. When Jay saw the sketch, which I'd livened up with color, he said, "How did you know that's what I wanted to do? That's it—we're going to build it just like that, only we're going to add a pie kitchen too! You can't sell apples in Apple Hill without a pie kitchen."

The trouble was, all the additions had taken it way beyond the definition of a farm building. It now had to be permitted and required electricity, plumbing and, of course, a complete set of plans drawn up by a bona fide civil engineer, all of which would then require step-by-step building inspections. That's when Jay realized he'd have to have the help of Clifford Logan, a civil engineer who knew his way around the county building department.

Cliff checked all the work Jay had already done and all the photos of the work in progress, approved it, drew it up, and then laid out plans for the pie kitchen, a detached employees' toilet and washroom, and a ramp up to the gallery for handicapped visitors, and then he and Jay went down to the building department to get the necessary permits.

Not surprisingly, all hell broke loose. Why hadn't the building been permitted in the first place? The explanation that it started out as a farm building and, like Topsy, it just grew didn't seem to make a dent on some thick skulls. Cliff, if nothing else, knew his business inside out, and had the patience needed to deal with public servants. Jay didn't!

One morning at Sierra Gold, in the midst of all these goings-on, I got a frantic call from Cliff to get down to the building department—Jay had just threatened them and the situation was dicey!

I rushed down to the county offices, one of my best printing accounts, and found Clifford Logan trying to soothe some very put-out planning personnel.

"Where's Jay?" I asked without preamble.

Cliff gave a sigh of relief, took me by the arm and, leading me out of earshot, said, "I took him down to the cafeteria to cool off. Whatever you do, don't let him come back up here again or he'll be arrested. He threatened to go home and get his gun and blow them all away! He's absolutely furious at all their crazy nit-picking and doesn't understand that's what makes bureaucratic wheels go round."

I thanked Cliff for saving the day, then went down to the cafeteria to collect my man. As it was midmorning, there was no one else around except the girls who ran the place, and they were sitting with Jay, commiserating with him and trying to get him out of his black mood. They'd done a pretty good job by the time I arrived, and I thanked them in turn. Luckily, Jay had arrived in Cliff's pickup, so we had no extra wheels to worry about, and I drove him home.

Somehow the necessary permits were issued, three-phase power activated, inspections made, and after the kitchen, toilet, and handicapped ramp were built, everything met with county requirements and the building was signed off. *Lord, what a relief!*

Chapter 24

In '82 I had the dubious distinction of becoming the president of the County Chamber of Commerce. It was a year very much like all the ones that had preceded it, only I put in more hours, if that were possible. The management of Sierra Gold Graphics fell more and more on Rebel's shoulders and, as one day ran into the other, I found myself coming in after hours and working late into the night doing all the catch-up needed in the shop. I still handled all the art direction, camera work, and stripping. In the former I left copious notes and sketches for the graphic artist, always secretly wishing Sierra Gold was smaller so I could still do all the fun work myself, and in the latter I'd stack the stripped-up jobs by priority and leave them for the pressmen to plate the following morning. There was no doubt about it, I was definitely on a treadmill.

Other print shops had opened, and some had folded, but we still led the pack. It was a good feeling, but I seldom had time to relish it or think about it.

It was while I was chamber president that a group of our old friends from the Orient decided to make a pilgrimage back to China. Nixon had opened the door in '79 with his historic visit to Peking, and travel and trade with China were slowly expanding. My sister Ursula was going with the group and asked me to join her. I'd have loved to have gone, but there was no way I could leave that year. Surprisingly, when she got back and I saw all the photos she'd taken, I was glad I hadn't made the trip.

The convent we attended as students in the city of Tientsin had been severely damaged by the humongous earthquake in July of 1976. That quake, with its official toll of 242,000 lives and an estimated death toll as high as 655,000, had centered on the Tangshan mines, with over 100,000 of the dead being coal miners who were buried alive. These were the mines the Kailan had run from the turn of the century until the Communist takeover in 1949.

The Kailan Mining Administration, or KMA, was a Chinese-British consortium that Dad had worked for until his death, and had been one of the prime targets of the Japanese invasion of China in the 1930s. I thought of all the history wrapped in that company, where every managerial job was headed by both a British and a Chinese executive, and of my dad's counterpart and fellow accountant in the little treaty port, the gracious Mr. George Wang. But most of all I thought of my happy youth in that great country, and I felt the quake had not only destroyed hundreds of thousands of lives and caused property damage in the millions of dollars, it had also permanently severed my last ties with China.

Ursula, with her journalist's eye, had taken many great pictures: The convent, clearly unsafe with its crumbling walls and cracked windows shored up with wood and cement, served as a school. The chapel, its glorious stained glass windows and pink marble columns shattered beyond repair, was being used as a huge storeroom. Then there were pictures of our lovely rambling home in the little treaty port of Chinwangtao, now housing five Chinese families, with laundry festooned from the rafters of the picturesque outdoor veranda. The beautiful semi-formal front garden commanding a glorious view of the Bay of

Chihli now housed a three-story red brick tenement that completely blocked the view of the bluffs and the sea. The wooded hills surrounding our home were studded with smelting pits, a relic from the Great Leap Forward of the '50s and '60s. The bungalows on Long Beach, once filled with life and laughter in the summer months, were all gone. The big but unpretentious summer home of Teddy Nathan, the British CEO of the Kailan, had been replaced by an ugly People's Hostel to reward productive comrades who exceeded their yearly work quotas.

No, I don't need to see that. I'll remember my Camelot in all its natural beauty, abounding in a love for life …

~

Several years later, the huge barn that Jay had built on Twin Hills became his prized apple stand, where apple and cider sales vied with charming, original handcrafted items made by a small group of local artisans. On the weekends when I stopped by, I got a yen to throw in the towel at Sierra Gold and help Jay at the stand, especially as I saw how all the work was beginning to take a toll on his health once more. Before long, that made me start looking around seriously for someone to buy my printing business.

There was also a personal reason why I needed to sell. I hadn't realized it until the morning I came into the shop after a chamber breakfast and found Missy, one of our top pressmen—I refused to call her a pressperson—spotting negatives I had readied for platemaking the night before. I got quite angry with her, and said, "And *what's the matter* with my negs?"

Missy hadn't heard me come in and got very flustered. "I'm sorry, Pam, when I started to plate them I found a lot of pinholes."

"I don't believe it!"

She started to squirm in embarrassment, and I grabbed

the loupe, a high resolution magnifying glass, and skimmed over the surface of the culprit negs.

"Good Lord!" I said, equally embarrassed. "I'm sorry, I must've had my eyes closed when I spotted these last night. Has it happened before?"

"Yes, I'm afraid so. I always have to check them before I plate them."

I smiled and apologized again for being short with her, then thought, *I guess there's only one solution—I've got to get glasses, dammit!*

It was obvious, all the tight graphics I'd done for years had finally taken a toll on my sight. And I thought back to when I'd gone down south to visit Margo when we first arrived in the States, and I saw a specialist in New Orleans. He'd checked my sight because I was having trouble, and I learned I'd really abused my eyes in the prison camp trying to read at night by the wavering light of a wick burning in my precious ration of peanut oil. After he handed me a prescription, I asked him how long I'd have to wear glasses, and he said bluntly, "How long to you expect to live?"

For a person who hated crutches of any kind, that was a blow I didn't need. It wasn't until I'd gone to work for Edison several years later that I learned about the Bates Method of eye training, found a wonderful instructor, and within a year had my sight back to normal. I think the happiest day was when I went for my driver's license and got it without any restrictions.

Oh, well, I guess I should expect glasses by now, I am going on sixty ...

When I put out the word I was looking to sell Sierra Gold, my chamber contacts helped. The news spread, and a sales executive from a big media company became interested in the shop. I met him, liked him, and suggested that until he got the feel of the business and met a lot of its established customers, he couldn't do better than have Rebel run the office and handle the accounts she knew so well.

He was all for it until I had lunch with both him and his wife, and the lady said that no one outside the family would be allowed to handle the books or the office. I thought of all Rebel's loyalty and hard work, and decided to chuck the whole thing, only to go home and find Jay exhausted after another grueling day of work. I had to make a lousy decision: who did I help, Rebel or Jay?

Quite understandably, Jay won, and although Rebel got an excellent position managing a big trade shop in West Sacramento, she had a worse commute than I ever had at Aerojet or Douglas, and I felt about two inches tall.

Once more I changed careers, and once more Jay and I were working together ... yet really apart. He handled the orchards, the pear and apple picking, and cider making, while I handled the apple stand. Now, instead of buying apple pies from a neighboring grower, I made the pies, hundreds of them each week. It took all the fun and romance out of whipping up an apple pie, because I had to install a production line and hire neighboring housewives to help out. When you're making pastry for twelve pies at a clip, likewise peeling and tossing apples with lots of sugar and spices, all meticulously measured out so that each pie tastes just like the one before, there is no such thing as romance left.

Jay's cider was famous on the Hill, and he also made it for several other orchards. They'd supply the apples and he, with a couple of hard-working cider makers, would crush, bottle, and deliver it through the week. Many times he and Gillian would work till one and two in the morning to get the cider ready for early delivery the following day.

As always, he was an utter character, and he, along with the huge red-and-white tent top over the rotunda, became a landmark in Apple Hill, especially when he tooled around county roads on his big Massey Ferguson, forklifts fore and aft loaded with hefty bins of bottled cider. He didn't drive fast, but he somehow got around all the heavy weekend traffic and personally delivered the cider to his accounts. I learned later how much his fellow farmers appreciated his conscientiousness, especially when they started to run low and saw him coming down North Canyon with another load of cider for their thirsty customers.

I'd originally got involved with Apple Hill in the late '60s when I was working for Douglas and one of the top men of the fledgling growers' association asked me if I'd do a promotional piece for the State Fair. I knew the easiest way to do it would be at work, because the test facility had all the phototypesetting equipment I needed. Rather than try to do it on my lunch hour, I went directly to my big boss and asked him if it would be okay for me to do the work on company time.

"If you can work it in and not shortchange your official job here, go for it," he said. "But be sure and let the growers know that the Douglas Test Center is picking up the tab." Once more, public relations came to the fore.

Apple Hill, the new name for the agricultural area around Camino, grew into a marketing phenomena. Except for a map and a sales brochure that were updated each year, all the advertising was done for free … or almost for free. Once a year, just before apple harvest, the association would throw a huge press picnic and invite all the top players in the different media to it. All the news people and their families were paired off with growers, who would take them around Apple Hill to the different ranches, giving a spiel on the background of each one, including any special features, and then plying them with gifts of produce, cider, and baked goods to take home to enjoy. It paid off in hundreds of column-inches of copy, and stories that couldn't be bought at any price.

And it was during this time that one of California's largest supermarket chains came up with a new advertising campaign based on fear. They smugly pitched their produce by stating they were the only chain that cared for the safety of the public. They left no doubt that California farmers were irresponsible and sold inferior produce contaminated by unchecked spray programs. They also inferred that because of this, they'd had to put in their own inspectors and labs to check the produce they sold, and it was only because of their diligence that they could guarantee everything they sold was fresh and contaminant-free.

Boy, did that make my blood boil!

It was easy to understand the fears of the public, who knew nothing of California's agricultural industry or of all the state safety programs and inspections that followed each item of produce on its way to market. But the ad campaign was a degrading insult to the farming community. The state spray programs were so well-regulated that no grower could spray until told to do so, and any produce sprayed could not be sold until the spray residue had completely dissipated; each step was checked and rechecked by state inspectors. As most of the farms were family operations—like our orchards where our girls helped haul the fruit to the weigh stations, working side by side with the hired help—the idea that we would allow our family or our workers to be harmed in any way by working in contaminated orchards or fields was so unthinkable as to be ludicrous.

That campaign spread till it reached the northwest and

brought on the famous Alar scare in Washington State. Even our sales in Apple Hill fell off, and I had to letter a big sign saying we did not use Alar. It was interesting that, after all the loss and damage sustained by the apple industry in Washington, it was found that Alar, except for making the fruit more attractive, had absolutely no ill effect on the consumer. Not surprisingly, when the front page Alar scare was refuted some time later, and the television network and celebrity who had promoted it were made to pay out millions in damages to the apple growers in Washington State, the latter coverage only received a couple of column-inches hidden away on some back page where no one read it.

∼

It was seven years almost to the day after her tragic stroke that I lost precious Mumsy. I got a call from the Pines in the wee hours of an icy March morning, telling me her cold had turned into pneumonia and asking what they should do.

"Nothing," I said quietly. "It's time for her to go."

I sat with her for almost twelve hours, holding her hand, talking to her, and telling her how much I loved her. I watched my gallant ninety-four-year-old mother slowly slip away, knowing at last, God willing, she would get the relief and release she should have received so many years earlier.

Around two in the afternoon, a couple of the aides who'd taken turns sitting with me suggested I take a break and get some lunch, and said they'd stay with her till I got back. I did just that, and when I returned less than an hour later, she had gone. They told me it was as though she was waiting for me to leave … she didn't want me to see her die. Darn her sweet heart, she was strong and stubborn right to the end!

I still miss you, Mumsy …

∼

It wasn't until I worked at the apple stand full-time that I found out how vast Jay's "empire of women" really was. He was just like my dad, he had to have women around him all the time and, by gum, every one of them loved him!

One of the men, a crafter at our apple stand who carved fabulous woodland critters out of tree stumps, said to me one day while we were watching one of the women crafters making a big play for Jay, "Have you ever thought Jay flirts with women to get a rise out of you, to make you jealous?"

I looked at him in surprise. "That's such a wasted emotion," I said, not realizing I was voicing my reluctance to let anyone know how easily they could push my buttons, a reluctance that had been compounded by Bill when he dumped me so many years ago. Of course, in the depths of my heart, I *was* jealous. It hurt to see how Jay thrived on the adulation of all his women, but I kept quietly saying to myself, *Eat your hearts out, gals ... he's mine!*

And it didn't help when well-meaning friends tried to hint that maybe my looking the other way gave Jay ample opportunity to be unfaithful. I found myself wondering if the old saying about a loose rein checking a horse better than a tight one was really true. Was I wrong? Had Jay ever been really unfaithful? I thought of the trips to Paradise to drop off cider to be pasteurized, followed by a visit with Connie on the way home. Connie, with her house full of wildlife, who'd never been able to hide her feelings for Jay. Had that been too much temptation for him, and too stupid of me?

Oh, this is ridiculous ... doesn't he always tell you about her, about the little animals she's found with broken wings and battle scars that need care and healing?

And I thought back to the dumb evening I'd spent, so many years ago, sitting with Vyola in her car outside Doria Harris's apartment. Vy, who'd lost more men than I could count by being jealous, had convinced me that Jay was not teaching night classes but stepping out on me, and I'd sat there, feeling guilty and foolish, only to finally get home and find him pacing the floor, worried sick at my being so late.

And the mother who told me in strictest confidence that Jay had called her daughter at two in the morning and propositioned her? That had happened a couple of days after Jay had told me he'd talked to the romantic, oversexed girl in the parking lot outside Sierra Gold. She'd bragged to him about teaching high school boys how to get the most out of sex, and he'd brushed her off without a comment.

And the Saturday I'd worked on catch-up at Sierra Gold, planning to go from there to work in the wine garden at the county fair. The day grew hot and airless, and I decided to go home first and change into something cooler. As I drove up to the ranch, I noticed a beat-up old blue car in the driveway, and thought it was probably one of the orchard workers trying to find some shade for his car. As I bounded into the house and started up the stairs to our bedroom, I heard voices and laughter. I stopped dead and called, "Jay?" After some scuffling, he stepped into the doorway of the guest room, naked as a jaybird except for a towel around his hips. I spun on my heel and dashed out, too numb and hurt to say a word, tears so close to the surface I knew I'd make a spectacle of myself if I stayed.

That evening when I got home, he was waiting for me.

"Why did you dash off like that?"

"You know damn well why!" I said, anger having replaced my tears.

"No, I don't. Bob Ritter was giving me a massage. My back's been murder for several weeks, and I thought it would help."

"Yeah, and I just fell off a turnip truck …"

He took forever trying to convince me, but as Bob Ritter never came back to give him another massage, at least not while I was there, I still had a problem believing him.

Funny, but it was at the same county fair a year later, while I was working at the Right to Life booth, that I started to chat with a man in the Animal Rescue booth next to mine. He was a neat soul, and we talked for quite a while on just about everything. Finally, curiosity got the better of me, and I asked, "What do you do when you're not looking out for stray animals?"

"I'm a massage therapist."

"And your name … ?"

"Oh, I'm sorry, I forgot to introduce myself—I'm Bob Ritter."

"I'm Pam Masters," I said, reaching out to shake his hand.

"Oh, Jay's wife," he said with a smile.

I shut my eyes for a moment, and it all came rushing back. It finally dawned on me that every coin has two sides. I found myself stepping into Jay's shoes, recalling how, without so much as saying a word, he'd always shown he trusted me. I thought of all the times I'd been the only woman on a project; of business trips I'd taken, one to San Antonio that had lasted well over a week; and of all the different men who in their clumsy ways had tried to proposition me, and how I'd kid them and tell them to forget it. And, as much as I hated to admit it, like Jay I was flattered and enjoyed all their attention.

Okay, Jay, you and I are cut out of the same cloth. There's only one thing I ask—you'd better always be there for me to come home to.

Chapter 25

It was in the spring of '89 that it happened. I was in the living room reading on the couch when I looked up and saw Jay staggering through the hall door, clutching the handle for support. He tried to speak but words wouldn't form, and as I looked at his twisted face, I knew he was having a stroke.

The weeks that followed were a mixture of relief and confusion: relief because the damage was not as severe or permanent as Mother's, and confusion regarding what to do with the ranches, as it was obvious that Jay couldn't keep on farming.

The hours he put in, the heavy work he insisted on doing himself, and the stress of a dwindling market for the Bartlett pears that were our main source of farm income were too much for him. When we started in 1960 there were something like thirty-four packing plants and canneries in California for our fruit; in the late '80s there were only three, and they dictated the price they'd pay for our pears. On top of that, because the Delta fruit came in almost six weeks ahead of our mountain-grown pears, the processors already had their quota before we were ready for market. Although both Rebel and Gillian had married great men, neither was interested in farming as they already had good jobs. That left us with only one option: we had to sell.

That got me to thinking of our girls again, and of their growing-up years on the home ranch, when I'd somehow found time to be a den mother to Rebel's Brownie troop and a cooking instructor for Gillian's 4-H club. Those were wonderful years, even the ones through their "terrible teens," and I'd love to write about them, but the girls made me promise not to mention them except in passing. I don't believe they're shy, but as they're my daughters, I can't change their names and attribute some of the cute but dumb things they did to someone else. Anyhow, in passing—they're the greatest, and I'll never take lightly all the help and love they've given me through the years.

I first decided to tackle the sale of the ranches myself by putting out a colorful brochure targeting Napa Valley wineries. Our soil had been tested as perfect for varietal grapes, and our land prices were much lower than the premium land of the Napa Valley. But it didn't take me long to figure out that making the brochure was the easy part; handling prospects, knowing real estate law, and closing sales took an expertise I didn't have, and frankly didn't want to learn.

Through the years I'd got to know just about every realty house in the county, and decided to call one with a good track record on selling ranches like ours. Bonnie and Carol, partners in the firm I chose, wrote us up a six-month sales agreement, and we started the ball rolling.

By the time the agreement was up, we'd had a disappointing total of three interested parties. Jay and I were home to greet the first couple with their children, but while Bonnie and Carol were out in the orchard showing them the property, Jay said he hoped they weren't being given too strong a sales pitch. "Buyers have to understand that the crops *might* cover the mortgage payments, and possibly the taxes, but they won't cover anything else. It's not like the old days, when we had solid contracts for our fruit. We have to impress on them that they still have to have outside jobs to handle the household expenses, like food, utilities, insurance and so forth." I agreed with him.

When they all came back into the house, I'd just taken a pie out of the oven, and the spicy aroma floated all through the downstairs. I could see they were all starry-eyed and ready to sign, and looked at Jay; he gave me a now-or-never look, then quietly proceeded to give them the hard, cold facts. They left in a much more sober mood.

That evening I got a call from Bonnie telling me the sale had fallen through, and she asked that in the future Jay not be present when they brought prospective buyers to see the property.

The second family that came knew absolutely nothing about orchards or growing fruit. After being taken out and shown around the property, they asked me how many crops of pears and apples we got a year, as though we ran a truck garden!

I looked over at Bonnie and nodded for her to follow me into the kitchen. When we were out of earshot, I said, "These are *screened* prospects? Why are you wasting your time and mine?"

After the children had polished off the last of another pie, this time a la mode, they all left, and while they were piling into their respective cars, Bonnie came back and apologized to me again.

The third party was no more qualified than the other two. When I called the real estate office the day after the showing, I told Bonnie that as winter was now upon us, Jay's workload would lessen, and we'd not renew the contract but might reconsider in the spring.

∼

We did renew the sales agreement in the spring. Bonnie found us a man who was more interested in the land than in the crops, and it sounded like a win-win situation for all concerned.

Several days after we learned of the great new prospect, we had a surprise, and not a pleasant one. We received a notice in our mailbox that we had a registered letter, and after going up to the post office to sign for it, I noticed it was from the DA's office. When I started to read it I almost flipped out: the Department of Fish and Game had brought a criminal indictment against Jay!

I sat down, my stomach in knots, and read the full indictment.

Our home ranch was one parcel of a three-way split of land that had once belonged to three brothers, and the three pieces of land were served by a miner's grant, or water right, dating back to the 1800s. Jed and Maidie Johnson, our neighbors to the east, had the other two parcels of land, and two-thirds of the water to our one-third. Until Jay's heart attack in '77, he'd done most of the work on the ditch, assisted by Manuel, the Johnsons' foreman. Through the years they'd replaced the ditch with a pipeline to cut down on evaporation, and to stop siphoning by people along its route. That didn't endear Jay with the culprits, but it never caused any trouble. After his heart attack, Jay stopped climbing like a mountain goat up and down the canyon walls to service the pipeline. He left that work up to Manuel, and paid the Johnsons for our share of the cost while supplying men whenever Manuel needed them.

The previous year, when Fish and Game notified Jay that there was a hole in the pipeline that had to be repaired, he called Manuel. The foreman found the hole, which was about the size of his little finger and on top of the pipeline, where it would be no problem to repair. Luckily, it was also near the end of the pipeline and easily accessible, so Jay was able to check the repair work, and he congratulated Manuel on an outstanding job.

Now here was this criminal indictment stating that Jay had "willfully, and with criminal intent" allowed water to flow from a break in the pipeline down the canyon wall and cause the formation of sand bars in the American River to the detriment of fish habitat. Attached to the indictment was a hundred-page finding made up by Fish and Game biologists illustrating the horrendous impact of his careless "willful conduct."

After I'd cooled down, I called the DA's office and I got right through. Trying to make light of it, I said, "Wendell, what the sam hill's going on? Jay's just received a criminal indictment from Fish and Game—hasn't your office got anything better to do?"

I could feel the awkward pause on the other end, then Wendell Carr said, "Sorry, Pam, I don't know how to say this, but somehow the paperwork fell through the cracks. Almost a year passed before we found it. In the interest of time, and to comply with Fish and Game's demands, we *had* to file a criminal rather than civil complaint against Jay."

"That's all you've got to say?"

"I'm sorry …"

"You're *sorry?* My husband, *with felonious and criminal intent, deliberately and willfully* destroyed fish habitat?" I knew I was almost shouting, but I didn't care. "You know Jay … he couldn't *deliberately or willfully* hurt or destroy *anything,* especially wildlife! He was an environmentalist before anyone knew what the word meant. This is rot!"

"I'm sorry, Pam, but Fish and Game insisted. We tried to talk sense into them. It was useless."

"You mean you're going to *prosecute?*"

"We have to."

"His heart can't take the stress of a trial," I said in total frustration.

"Then have him plead guilty."

"But he *isn't* guilty, dammit! In fact, if … and that's a very *big* if … either the fish or the river sustained any damage from the pipeline before it was repaired, Jay wasn't responsible because he hasn't been able to work on the pipeline for over thirteen years. The Johnsons have that responsibility now; we just split the costs and supply workers when needed. Why weren't *they* named on the indictment as well? They have two-thirds of the water rights to our one-third."

"Better get an attorney, Pam," Wendell said tiredly, "and try and see if you can get Jay to plea-bargain."

As I put down the phone the absurdity of the indictment struck me. *How could a hole the size of a man's little finger allow enough water to wash down a canyon to destroy fish habitat and form sand bars in the American River? Also, Fish and Game's figures on the fish population were totally out of line …*

I stopped mulling over the mess when I heard Jay drive up.

"You look tired," I said as he came in.

"I am." He sat down and started to take off his grubby boots, picking foxtails out of the laces as he loosened them. Then he looked across at me and asked if I'd picked up the registered letter. Reluctantly I told him I had.

"What's it about?"

"You don't want to know."

"Bad as all that?" He started to look anxious.

"No, not really," I said quickly, trying to lighten the moment. "Actually, it's rather ridiculous. You've been indicted by Fish and Game for damaging fish habitat and causing sandbars in the American River."

He looked up in disbelief. *"What?* Read it to me!"

I read it without relish, then told him as gently as I could about my phone conversation with the DA.

"*Never!* I'll *never* plead guilty! And I'm *damned* if I'll hire an attorney. I'll represent myself." Jay's face turned a ghastly shade of gray, and I thought he was going to have another heart attack or, at the very least, a stroke.

I decided to call the Johnsons, but they weren't in so I left a message on their answering machine. Jay and I sat down to a light supper, to be followed, hopefully, by a long night's sleep.

When the phone rang early the following morning Jay was already out in the orchard. He'd had a terrible night, and I'd heard the television going at all hours. I picked up the phone on the second ring, and knew who the call was from before I heard Maidie's voice.

"Good morning," she said. "What's up?"

When I told her, and read her the indictment, I could sense her anger.

"You know that's baloney," she said. "I'm going to talk to Manuel, then I'm going to check with all the people who live along Brush Creek. I *know* there have never been the fish counts Fish and Game speak of."

During the night I'd had a brainstorm, and I told Maidie I was going to PG&E, the utility that served our area, to look up rainfall figures for the previous spring. I was convinced nothing could wash out the side of a canyon and cause the kind of damage Jay had been cited for, short of a heavy downpour with no letup.

"It did rain a lot last spring, if I recall," Maidie mused.

"You do your thing with the fish, I'll do mine with PG&E. Thanks for helping."

When I got back from the power company, I was jubilant.

The rainfall figures they'd given me for the previous year showed that there'd been record-making rain during the month of March. *That should knock the indictment into a cocked hat!* I thought happily. *It'll be interesting to see if Fish and Game will file criminal charges against the Almighty now!*

Maidie had been no less successful. The people who lived along the creek that paralleled the pipeline insisted they'd never seen more than two or three fish in the stream in any season. "So much for impacting hundreds of native trout," Maidie said happily.

Not aware how criminal charges were handled, I blithely got into my car and drove down to the DA's office. With what Maidie and I had learned, I was positive I could get the charges dropped.

Thirty minutes later, I drove silently home, the unfairness of the whole thing overwhelming me.

Wendell had turned the case over to Assistant DA Phil Amherst, who obviously didn't relish the situation. "They won't drop the charges, Pam. Fish and Game insist on prosecuting. It's almost like a vendetta. What's Jay done to them?"

"Nothing that I know of. Like the tiny hole in the pipeline, this whole damn thing's been blown completely out of proportion."

To my surprise, after I got home Maidie called to say that Fish and Game wanted to have a conference to see if we could come to some kind of a settlement. I said, "Go for it!" and she set up a meeting for the following week in their home.

When I came over on the appointed morning, I was a little early, and we discussed whether we should tape the proceedings. I thought it was a good idea, as Jay couldn't be there. A while later the Fish and Game crew came in—if I recall correctly, there were four of them—and the first thing they did was look around for Jay. I told them he wasn't well and would not be attending, and that I would be acting in his interest. I added that because of that, we would like to tape the proceedings so he could have a complete record of the meeting. One of them asked if Jay planned to plea-bargain, and I shook my head. As Jed started to put the tape recorder on the table, the four men looked at each other, nodded, and without a word turned and walked out. The next thing we heard was their two cars driving off. I still don't know why they left so abruptly. Was it Jay's absence? Our request to record the meeting? Or the fact that Jay refused to plea-bargain?

∽

While we were waiting for the second boot to drop on the Fish and Game matter, our new prospective buyer was impatient to close the sale on the two ranches. Yes, he wanted Twin Hills as well! All I could think of was that it would be great to get everything cleared up once and for all, and for Jay and me to be able to get on with our lives. But it turned out life wasn't handing us a bowl of cherries, at least, not for a while …

It started with the Fish and Game fiasco. Jay tried to represent himself and, just as I feared, the pressures of the courtroom deprived him of speech, his words coming out garbled and unintelligible; the judge got angry and told him to get an attorney, and he was forced to plea-bargain for a crime he hadn't committed.

"Oh, Pam, Pam, I knew what I wanted to say but the words kept changing before they came out of my mouth … what's happening to me?" I saw the fear in his eyes, and it crushed my heart.

"Don't worry about yourself," I said, giving him a hug. "You were fine. You were the only one in court who really knew right from wrong … but no one was listening."

We paid the fine. We paid for our defense, such as it was. And of course, as always, when you're sued by your own government, we paid for our prosecution!

With that heartrending mess behind us, we turned back to the ranch sale once again.

Jay had insisted from the onset that the sale had to be on an as-is basis, as we knew there was residual contamination brought on by years of the once-legal use of DDT. There could also have been mercury residue in the lower orchard from gold mining back in the Gold Rush days. The amounts were probably undetectable, but in all conscience we had to disclose the possibility.

The buyer would not accept Jay's as-is contract, so we spelled out what we would be willing to do: we would be responsible for any cleanup in the area immediately around the diesel and gas tanks up by the garage; the rest of the property would be sold as is. When we received the final amended contract to sign, I queried the additional wording inserted after our disclaimer on the cleanup area involved, which read, "… and leave the property free of contamination."

"That sounds like we're guaranteeing the whole ranch to be contamination-free," I said.

I was assured that the property referred to meant the area immediately around the tanks.

I wanted to add a marginal clarifying that, but was told it was obvious and not necessary. And we were further advised that this final contract had been reviewed by our own attorney and had his approval. So, unhesitatingly, Jay and I both signed.

When I called our attorney to tell him the sale was going through, and to thank him for taking the time to review the final paperwork, he just about choked. "I never saw any contract. I haven't been in touch with your broker!"

I shuddered as I hung up the phone.

The signatures on the contract were hardly dry before the buyer insisted that all the acreage had to be contaminant-free.

So much for it "being obvious" that the property referred to in the disclosure statement was limited to the area immediately around the fuel tanks, I thought with disgust.

Then an additional ingredient was added to the mix: It appeared that the buyer must have co-authored the book on how to buy land with "nothing down," because that became his real game plan. Needless to say, when I now hear glib pitchmen on television telling how easy it is to become a millionaire overnight by buying land for nothing down, I realize there is one little item they conveniently forget to mention: every purchase has a victim. In this case, we were the victims.

The buyer well knew that the type of cleanup he was demanding would financially ruin us. On top of that, he treated us like old fossils, saying he had nothing but time, something we "silly old people" didn't have, and that he could wait us out. He even went so far as to offer to take the contaminated land off our hands.

Such magnanimity!

When it became plain that he was using recent environmental concerns to bolster his case, I cringed. I thought of Jay, and of the winter of '61—the beginning of our first year of operation—when I went into the orchard and watched him burn huge stacks of trimmings that had been cut out of the trees. I was standing with him on a hill, looking down into a low, flat area with a creek running through it, and I saw a humongous pile of brush.

"Hon, that stack down there's much too big, it will get out of control if you burn it," I said.

"Who says I'm going to burn it?" he replied.
"Well, aren't you?"
"No."
"Why not?" It didn't make sense.
"Ask me again in the spring," he said cryptically.

In the spring, he took me down through the budding trees and showed me the pile of trimmings in the flat. Little families of California quail were running in and out of the brush, the proud males with their bobbing topknots, the little females like Japanese mama-sans a couple of bird-paces behind, followed by their obedient little bouncing broods. By not burning that pile of brush he'd made them a safe habitat, and it was so precious I couldn't help giving him a hug.

And then I saw some weird paw prints on the ground, and asked him what animal made them.

"Oh, that's old Cinnamon. He's a big lumbering bear that lives in a cave down where that creek runs out of the property. He came out of hibernation a while back, and his coat is absolutely gorgeous."

"You've seen him?" I asked in awe.

"Oh, sure. He's not a bit afraid of me. Rebel's seen him too."

Now I knew why he loved the land as much as he did: it held his extended wildlife family.

Then I recalled how, to protect the wildlife, he'd gotten rid of the old spray rigs that came with the orchard, and that saturated both the trees and the ground under them, and had driven up to Canada and bought a sprayer that shot a gentle mist onto the fruit trees without letting it fall to the ground to hurt the soil and ground cover.

He was a man who loved the outdoors and did everything he could to protect it. And now his genuine concerns were being used against him by a man who couldn't care less for the environment.

~

As if we didn't have enough on our hands with the ranch sale mess, in early '92 Sierra Gold Graphics got into the act by going belly-up.

I don't know when the mismanagement started, or how, but by January of that year, I got my first inkling that all was not well when my December note payment was missed. It had always been "slow pay," but now it had just turned into "no pay," and by February the business went into Chapter 11. The court-appointed trustee tried every which way to save it for the current owners, but when I studied the debt load, which included state and federal taxes, sales tax, lease payments, disability insurance, paper and ink supplies, and utilities, I realized I was lucky that I'd been paid as long as I had.

The upshot was, after umpteen trips down to the Federal Bankruptcy Court in Sacramento, I ended up convincing the judge that the best deal would be for me to buy back Sierra Gold Graphics for the debt load. Although I didn't want the business, and I sure as hell didn't *need* it, I couldn't see all those well-paying jobs going down the tubes because of mismanagement.

When I got the business back in August of '92, I asked Rebel if she would come in with me as a partner and run the show. She jumped at the opportunity, as the commute to West Sacramento was taking its toll. I couldn't help feeling sorry for the businessman who'd lost Sierra Gold, especially after he came up to me in court and said sadly, "If only I'd done what you suggested and kept Rebel on, this would never have happened."

Of course, the next step was to sit down with the court appointed trustee and all the creditors and establish a payment schedule. I still don't know how Rebel did it, but by the end of '95 she'd paid off the humongous debt load, and I bowed out. It was clearly evident she didn't need me anymore—she was going great guns!

∼

In September of '93, the ranch sale broke out of stagnation. We finally won our first round in court when a settlement agreement was reached in judge's chambers, limiting the area of contamination to the soil around the gas tanks as we'd originally stipulated, and a date in late January of '94 was assigned for the down payment on the ranch.

Excited by the outcome, Jay and I promptly made a ten-thousand-dollar deposit—all we could lay our hands on—on a lovely large home approximately half a mile up the road from our second ranch, Twin Hills. We knew that with the lifting of the *lis pendens*—which had to be cleared before escrow could close—and the court-ordered down payment in January, we'd have no problem paying it off.

Christmas that year was very nostalgic. I knew it was going to be our last in the old homestead, so I spent extra time and care on all the decorations, hoping to make one long-lasting memory of all the wonderful years we'd spent there.

When the January '94 drop-dead date for the down payment was four days away, the buyer came up with a new demand, and we were told that he would never pay the down as long as we were still living on the ranch. Nothing daunted, we moved in the pouring rain to the new home we'd started to purchase. It was a herculean effort, requiring the unstinting aid of our two girls, their families, and umpteen friends.

When the buyer found we'd met this last, almost impossible demand, he came up with more—all of which were granted by the commissioner.

As February moved into history, and March roared in like a lion, we watched our down payment going out the window because it was now being applied at sixteen hundred dollars a month towards rent.

On top of that, it didn't take long for me to figure out we'd made a horrible mistake on the purchase. Apart from not being able to afford it now, the house had two stories, with a steep, straight flight of stairs up to the bedrooms—stairs that scared the heck out of me every time Jay said good night and started up them. If he lost his footing near the top, he'd fall all the way down to the bottom, as there was no landing to break his fall.

I knew we had to move … and soon.

I was pretty low the day I drove around looking for houses for sale that were one story and small enough for us to afford. I don't know what made me, but I found myself turning up Camino Heights Drive, heading for Halmar and Joe Flynn's home. They were really good friends, and maybe they'd know of a place we could buy. I was almost to their street when it suddenly struck me they were in Europe attending the celebration of the fiftieth anniversary of the Normandy invasion. Joe had been a pilot in World War II, and had ferried troops over from Britain to France during that heroic battle. They'd left three months early to visit Israel and travel all over Europe before participating in the nostalgic reunion.

Oh, damn, now what … ? I thought dejectedly.

It was then that I slowed down to get my bearings and saw a For Sale by Owner sign off to my right. I swear it popped up as if by magic. The house was one level, and had a charming sunken front garden with a pocket lawn, lots of tall, beautifully shaped fir trees, and a look that said "Welcome!" I didn't hesitate. I pulled into the apron, got out of the car, and headed straight for the front door. Before I could ring the bell, it was opened. The woman standing there looked vaguely familiar, and I said so.

"You do, too," she said, cocking her head to one side and eyeing me. "I'm Doreen Plotkin."

"Good Lord, I know your husband Bob. We used to work together at the chamber. I saw you several times with him at evening functions. I'm Pam Masters."

"Oh, that's right. I remember you now."

We reminisced for a while. Then she told me she'd just lost Bob, and the house was too full of memories; she needed to move. When she showed me the place, I fell for it. It might be small, but it had been beautifully laid out, with glass sliders leading onto a lovely deck off the large living room and dining area. And best of all, there were no stairs anywhere. Jay could move from room to room, and out on the deck, without a problem. It was perfect, and so was the price. As she was selling the house herself, she knocked the agent's commission off the price instead of pocketing it. What a lady!

When I brought Jay back in the evening to see it, he wasn't as excited about it as I was, as he still loved "big," with lots of land, and this was just the opposite. We were going from almost sixty acres and a rambling, two-story farmhouse to barely one-sixth of an acre and a fifteen-hundred-square-foot home, and I knew it was going to take a lot of adjusting for him. But on the plus side, I found our furniture fit as though it were designed for the place, upkeep would be minimal, and we'd be able to spend lots of time doing the things we loved.

The sale moved through escrow at warp speed, and we moved in within two weeks. I soon found out there was an extra plus for Jay: we were two houses down from the first tee of a nine-hole golf course that wound its way around and through the little community. Jay soon found out that Wednesday was

Ladies' Day at the golf club, and he'd walk up to the first tee and visit with them when they got ready to tee off. He loved it, and so did they. If he missed Ladies' Day they'd come by to see if he was okay. I can't say I was surprised; it was obvious if he hadn't found them, they'd have found him.

∼

Going back to the previous September, and the court-mandated settlement agreement: it became clear to Jay and me that we were now solely responsible for the cleanup of the designated spill area. And it was while we were figuring how to handle the mess that I recalled an account I'd once had when I owned Sierra Gold Graphics. I'd done a brochure for the firm, reducing all the technical data on their intriguing product down to simple layman's English, and I now realized it was just the product we needed!

The CEO, a one-time crop-duster and a true environmentalist, had worried years earlier about the spill from pesticides that so often accompanied the loading of crop-dusting planes. Using his chemistry background, he'd developed a bacterial enzyme that could be activated and sprayed on hazardous waste, cleaning up a spill in thirty to sixty days instead of fifty to a hundred years. I remembered asking him what happened to his happy little bugs after they gobbled up the spill, and being told that when they were through devouring the hazardous material they died, as they were specially formulated to eradicate a specific hazardous waste, such as petroleum products, pesticides, or whatever, the detritus then reverting back to harmless water and carbon dioxide.

We promptly hired his firm, along with a heavy equipment operator. And then, to verify the work, we hired an ex-state inspector who was a contamination specialist to oversee the job, monitoring each step along the way.

The first area we had cleaned up was a diesel spill that had occurred decades earlier when a careless fuel vendor had allowed our tank to overflow while filling it. I was euphoric a couple of months later when the final contamination count on the spill area, measured in parts per billion, was so insignificant, and the instruments used to read it so new, that if it had been done a year earlier no contamination would have been detected. Nothing like being on the cutting edge!

Simultaneously, we double-checked the soil around a steel gas tank used to fuel our pickup trucks. The tank, removed a year earlier, had come out clean and with no corrosion, but we had the area dug up again and rechecked. The non-detect lab report of that test, indicated by a big "N/D," was just icing on the cake!

Back in court later that month, when the would-be buyer learned of the non-detect readings, I thought he would self-destruct. After a hurried consultation with his attorney, the latter said, "Neither my client nor his personnel were present to supervise the work. He insists that the tests be done over, and that his people be present to check all readings."

So we did them over. And this went on and on …

First the fuel spills. Then supposed pesticide contamination in the garage area. It did no good for Jay to tell the buyer that the white powder found by the huge commercial washing machine was washing soda, used to clean cider cloths in the adjoining cider mill. Or that the residue around the cider press was from rice hulls used to aid in crushing overripe apples. He demanded lab tests on everything just to run up our tab and hopefully force us to throw in the towel.

After the fuel and supposed pesticides, it was our household well that had to be checked for contamination. Never mind that it hadn't been used since '64. He insisted that it be drawn down several times, and meticulous lab reports made on each sample taken.

By now, I was immune to his demands. We kept meeting them, and beating them, and he kept getting angrier and angrier as each N/D lab report came in. If I could've been on the sidelines watching the game, it might have been fun, but Jay took everything to heart and his health began to worsen. He had worked over thirty years on the property, loved every inch of it, and had to watch in horror as the delineated area of contamination turned into a war zone. Even the heavy equipment operator was appalled at the demands made on us, and loathed the resulting devastation.

But ultimately, the horror came to an end.

~

I'll never forget the day we went to court for the final disposition on the ranch sale. The hearing was brief. The judge glanced at the buyer, and started to tell him he now had to make the stipulated down payment as all his demands had been met, when the man's attorney interrupted with, "Excuse me, your honor, but all this is moot: my client rescinded the contract yesterday!"

I saw a flash of anger in the judge's eyes, and I turned to our attorney and asked, "Now what?"

"Well, by rescinding the contract, he doesn't have to pay any court costs or your costs. He can walk away scot-free."

"And the property?" I asked anxiously.

"It's all yours!" He couldn't keep the elation out of his voice. "The *lis pendens* is automatically lifted. Go make whoopee!"

"I'd like to, but I feel kinda wiped out right now," I said, then I thanked him for all his hard work, and turned to Rebel and Gillian, who'd taken time off from their respective jobs to be with me. I saw they were both crying softly, so I went over and threw my arms around both of them. Our relief was so great, I found myself crying along with them. It was the first time I'd allowed myself any tears.

As we stepped back from our three-way hug, I said, "You know what, gals? I do believe the old bugger finally met his match!" And we all started to giggle and laugh hysterically.

I'd wanted to call Jay from our attorney's office, down the street from the courthouse, but thinking of how the girls had reacted to what had just happened in court, I decided to wait until I got home.

I've never driven up the hill so fast in all my life ... thank God there were no black-and-whites on patrol!

When I barged in through the garage, Jay was lying on the couch, watching the noon news.

"Forget *that* news," I said excitedly, "*ours* is better!" And when I'd done telling him what had happened in court that morning, he, like the girls, began to sob. It was so understandable.

Kneeling down beside the couch, I hugged him and said, "It's all over, darling. It's ours again!" And I felt his shudder of relief.

～

When harvest season opened a couple of weeks later, it seemed extra special. There was no sword hanging over our heads anymore. No more whens and what-ifs. And the crafters could feel our elation, and responded with caring and love.

Our little "harvest family" was just that. We didn't charge them for their booths; the space was theirs to enjoy with only one stipulation: when we needed help, all we asked was that they pitch in and help us. It worked beautifully. When Jay drove up with more fresh cider, I'd yell, "Cider call!" and they'd come running. The same thing for apples, or any other heavy chore. It was unique on the Hill, as all the other ranches made their concessionaires pay fees for their booth space. But then, most of the other growers were younger than we were, or had large families to pitch in and help.

Like any other family, there were romances, jealous tiffs, and backstabbings, and all the friendly little things real families get into. Every weekend I could expect something new to happen, and every weekend I was never disappointed.

I even found fun in baking pies once more, and I added homemade apple turnovers with puff pastry for the breakfast crowd. We got a great crew of high school girls to help serve in the kitchen, and I only had one problem with them: they were all members of El Dorado High's basketball team, so whenever I asked one of them to do a job, they'd all rush up to do it like they were going after a basket! It was hard not to enjoy their esprit de corps.

Thanksgiving and Christmas that year were real celebrations with no ominous undertones. And the New Year came all smiling and bright, followed by a delightful blossom time, and the promise of another good harvest.

And with spring I found, for the first time in decades, I had leisure time on my hands. When my sisters, Margo and Ursula, asked if I'd like to join them on a Princess cruise of the Mediterranean, I couldn't turn them down.

∾

The languid cruise started in Barcelona and visited Nice, Florence, Rome, Athens, the Greek Isles, and Ephesus in Turkey.

It was in Rome that I lived up to my well-deserved reputation of having absolutely no "bump of direction," indoors or out. We were touring the Vatican, and after being totally overwhelmed by all the glorious paintings, tapestries, mosaics, and statues, our happy little group moved into the Sistine

Chapel. As beautiful as it was, I could hardly see a thing for the dense crowds. It appeared that all the other tour guides had converged on the chapel at the same time we did, and the old Pentecostal story of "speaking in tongues" became a living reality. It was then that I got an extreme attack of agoraphobia, and told Margo and Ursula I had to get out of the chapel, *now!* I headed for the first door I could find, with both of them quietly following. Every stairway, every corridor, and every salon we went through looked familiar and gave me a good feeling. The lovely little gold cross and chain, blessed by the pope, that I'd bought in the Vatican gift shop to commemorate my becoming a full-fledged Catholic the previous Easter, became my talisman, and I just knew we'd meet up with the rest of our tour group at the main entrance without a problem.

Almost two hours later, we staggered out of the Vatican, not through the main entrance, but through what turned out to be a side door into an alley. To make matters worse, it was pouring with rain! Margo and Ursula both deserved medals; not once did they bawl me out for getting us into this hellacious mess.

The Vatican is *big!* And once again I must've led them in the wrong direction, as we walked for what seemed like miles around the walled city's perimeter before we came to the main entrance. Of course, our tour bus had left. In fact, all the buses had left. It wasn't until almost an hour later that a searching Princess Cruises bus spotted us, and we climbed aboard looking like three drowned ducks.

That evening, at dinner, everyone hailed us as we came into the dining saloon, and I didn't know whether to bow or quietly slide under our table!

Back on board the following day, basking in the sun on the

Lido deck, I thought back to when we'd moved up to Camino so many years ago, and Jay and I had taken religious instruction, planning to become Catholics and get married again, this time in St. Patrick's Church.

Instead of being a wonderful, uplifting experience, it turned into a hairy mess. The first problem came to light when Jay wrote his mother, who'd been a devout Catholic earlier in her life, and asked for his baptismal papers, only to learn she'd never had him baptized. And with that eye-opener, I began to find out about his horrible early childhood. His father had taken off when he learned Jay's mother was pregnant, and she was too busy trying to make ends meet after he was born to worry about anything else. Then one day when Jay was three or four, she learned where his father was and got the bright idea that if he could actually see his little son, he'd come running back to her. So she shipped Jay off to his father in Seattle, like some kind of offering, in the care of a sweet old train conductor. Trouble was, his dad had married again, and his new wife wouldn't have anything to do with Jay, so he was placed in an orphanage. When the orphanage became overcrowded some time later, he was sent to a juvenile home for boys. The trauma of that last experience was to mark all the days of his life. When his mother finally found out what had happened, she sent for him. But by that time, she had married again: a tall, flaming-haired Irishman from Northern Ireland, and a devout Protestant.

We told all this to Father O'Connor, who forwarded the information on to the appropriate parties in Sacramento. Then somehow Rome stepped into the picture and insisted on written proof.

We spent days, weeks, months, and years trying to get records from the orphanage, which had changed hands several times since then, and also from the juvenile home, whose records were spotty at best. Almost three years later, when the latter ultimately responded, they said there was no way they would have a baptismal record in their files, as they definitely would not have worried whether a child was baptized or not. So Rome finally accepted Jay's word, saying, as there was no record to the contrary, he could now be baptized and married in the Catholic church. Along with this generous communication came a bill for several hundred dollars.

"I'm supposed to *pay Rome* for telling me I'm not a liar? *Forget it!*" And with that he stopped attending church completely.

It was kind of heartbreaking, because I always felt it could have helped him over some of the setbacks we encountered through the years. If I ever mentioned it to him, though, he'd say he felt closer to God in the orchard and the great outdoors than he ever felt in a man-made building. I couldn't fault him, but I still wanted him with me in church, especially as I was now enjoying all the sacraments.

The return cruise up the Adriatic ended in Venice. Just as we were about to leave for the airport and were thanking the crew for making the trip so memorable, we learned that the Italian air traffic controllers had gone on strike!

Of course, the cruise line took it all in stride, but as we'd vacated our staterooms, all we could do was sit in the various lounges and watch the new passengers coming aboard. Three hours later, while we were wondering what the heck was coming next, the crazy Italians changed their minds, and the strike was called off! Of course, that three-hour delay caused us to miss all our connecting flights at JFK—Ursula to Atlanta, Margo to Portland, and me to Sacramento. Still, nothing could take away from the fun of that fabulous trip, and the lovely, pampered rest I'd had.

A couple of months later, I was at home making myself some loungewear when I heard the horn on Jay's pickup blast without letup. I rushed out to see what was up, and found him trying to get out of the car while holding his left hand. It was swathed in a filthy piece of cloth with blood gushing out of it. I led him over to the passenger side, helped him get back into the cab, then jumped in and drove like hell to Marshall Hospital while he filled me in, as best he could, on what had happened.

I'm still amazed at how he drove home from the ranch. He'd been out at the apple barn using the table saw, he said, and must've blacked out for a moment, because somehow he caught his hand in the saw, slashing all the fingers on his left hand to the bone. When he was wheeled into surgery several hours later—they'd had to wait for a hand specialist—he was pale and, for once, was not giving the nurses a bad time. Two things made the surgery really difficult: as a cardiac patient, he could react at any moment to the anesthetic; and as a stroke victim on blood thinners, he risked extreme blood loss. The surgeon, one of the best in Northern California, came out after a grueling six hours and told me they had not been able to save his index finger, as it was severed all the way through the bone, but he felt that possibly they had been able to save the other three. Only time would tell if the tendons would heal properly.

I thought of Jay, a southpaw, and wondered if he would be able to overcome one more setback. During the five years of litigation, he'd had two more heart attacks and three strokes, each one brought on by the stress of negative court rulings; the last stroke came while he was having his third angioplasty. How he bounced back every time, I'll never know. But I couldn't help noticing that each bounce-back had a little less bounce. After a health check he'd had in 1989, before our ranch sale had put him through the wringer, I had read on the hospital's admitting sheet that he was "a very young seventy-two." They couldn't say that now, because he had turned into a *very old* seventy-nine.

All through apple season that year, he was hampered and frustrated by the things he couldn't do because his left hand was stiff and unresponsive. Simple things, like trying to shave or brush his teeth with his right hand. Trying to soap a face cloth, or wring it out, with only one hand. Dressing became a real chore, and I spent more and more time helping him, and getting bawled out by his therapists for doing so. I agreed with the therapists, but they didn't live in our house; they didn't try to get him to use his bad hand to the point of nagging; they didn't know how darn tough it was see the big, rugged man you loved, who had always been able to do anything and everything, trying to cope with little, inconsequential things, and finally giving up. I found myself alternating between helping him every which way, then getting mad at him for not trying to help himself.

One day I came home from running an errand, and he was missing. I went up to the first tee, but he wasn't there. I went all over the neighborhood looking for him, ending up at the gas station at the top of the street. To my surprise, I found he'd been there, waiting for someone. The attendant said Jay had driven off with a woman, and he described the car and the lady, but I didn't recognize either of them. When they came home several hours later, I asked him why he hadn't left a note to let me know where he was. He said, "You know I can't write anymore!" Then I looked at his girlfriend and said rudely, "You got the same problem?"

She looked like she was going to burst into tears, so I hurriedly said, "I'm sorry, but you don't know what hell I've been through." I promptly went out and bought him an electric typewriter so he could hunt-and-peck messages on it with his right hand. He never did.

As the following summer rolled around and the limitations on the things Jay could do became more evident, we realized we had to try to sell the ranches again, especially as we knew how fast agricultural land goes downhill when it's not tended. The market was a lot softer, and I knew we wouldn't get what we could have back in 1990, but this time I picked the right real estate agent, and he sold both the ranches within three months. In fact, we had to stall the second sale so that it wouldn't appear on the same year's taxes.

And with both the sales, we got a sizeable down and carried the paper. I thought that would give Jay's morale a boost, and it did to an extent, but he was still so frustrated by his limitations. It wasn't just his hand; six months prior to that surgery, he'd had major back surgery, and that was followed by a rotator-cuff repair on his shoulder, both being complicated by his thinned blood and heart condition, and exacerbated by a very slow recovery. For some reason, Jay refused to follow through at home with his therapy, and one hour three days a week just wasn't enough to make the difference.

When he stopped trying to walk up to the first tee to visit with his ladies, I finally knew his get-up-and-go had got up and left him.

Chapter 26

I couldn't help thinking of Mumsy the day I had to call the Sierra Boys' Home and ask them to pick up Jay's wheels. He'd outlived his driving days, and every time he went into the garage and saw his Dodge Rampage pickup it wrenched his heart.

He knew he had to quit driving after he left for town one morning. He drove onto the freeway, then lost his nerve and inched along the outside emergency lane while traffic roared by. Two highway patrol cars pulled up in front and back of him, thinking they had a DUI on their hands. They asked him what his problem was, and in his straightforward, blunt way, he told them. One of them kindly escorted him home, and he never got behind the wheel again.

I'd like to say, as I quietly watched Jay go downhill, that we grew closer together. But it wasn't so. He acted like a wounded animal looking for somewhere to hide. There were no orchards to walk in, no trees to talk to; the house was so small, there was barely room for us two to move around without bumping into each other. More and more, he'd close himself off in the front bedroom known as "Dad's room" for hours on end. If I knocked and looked in, he'd be on the bed, boxes of photos, clippings, and memorabilia scattered all over, with a smile of remembrance on his face.

I knew I couldn't go there. It was as though he was trying to go back to a place that I would never know, and it suddenly dawned on me that that was how he must've felt when I talked about my youth in China. We had grown up so far apart, and although we had become so very close, there were still places we couldn't visit together.

"Hon, why are you dwelling on the past like this? It's a lovely day, let's take a drive." I didn't realize at the time how dumb that question was. Of course he was dwelling on the past, that's all he felt he had left.

One time I came in and he was looking at a picture of his grade school sweetheart, Dorothy Matlock. They'd got in contact again, seventy years later, after the death of his mother in the fall of '95. That was when he learned his mother had never told his stepfather about her first marriage or Jay, instead passing him off as her nephew, the son of a sister who had died. It came about in a strange way: one of his mother's friends called to offer her condolences while we were making the funeral arrangements back in Windsor, Ontario. When Jay answered the phone, she said, "Oh, Jay, you poor boy, I'm so sorry about your dear aunt's death. You were always such a good nephew to her." After he hung up, he looked at me, and it was as though someone had just kicked the world out from under him. Too late he'd learned why his stepfather never looked on him as a son.

Dorothy Matlock starting sending him letters after that, cards at Christmas and on his birthday, and I could see it meant a lot to him. It was a tie to his childhood, when bad things were easily forgotten, and the truth lay hidden. Because he couldn't write any longer and refused to hunt-and-peck on the electric typewriter, he would call her from time to time, and their talks would go on for hours. Then sadly, after several years, there came the day when Dorothy's niece wrote to say her aunt had died, and I saw a little piece of Jay die with her.

And Vicki. She'd died years earlier, and he took her death hard. I couldn't go there. I've always been so positive that life doesn't end in death: that we're only travelers in this world, our life one earthbound trip, and when it's over, we get to go home.

When the century came to a close, I got an invitation to attend an Old China Hands Reunion in Scottsdale. As a director of the Center for Internee Rights, I was to make a pitch to all the ex-POWs of World War II who would be attending, bringing them up-to-date on our ongoing fight to receive reparations from Japan for all our years of imprisonment. I would remind them that the United States had apologized and paid reparations to the Japanese interned here, and Germany had apologized and was making full restitution, but Japan still refused to admit any guilt.

I'd tell them about CFIR's long, uphill battle. How we were not only seeking justice from Japan, but also from our own State and Justice Departments, both of whom were doing everything possible to prevent ex-POWs of the Pacific Theater from receiving reparations. I would remind them that sixty years ago many ex-POWs were asked by a then-grateful nation to stay on in the Orient and the Philippines to protect American interests. And for their sacrifice, they'd been ignored for over half a century, many still suffering from the trauma and tragedy of those years.

The talk would cover our court appearance in Tokyo in the summer of 1998, where Japan, backed by our own government and the spurious San Francisco Peace Treaty of 1951, told us they didn't owe us a dime. And, as if that were not enough, that injustice would be compounded when the Code of Bushido raised its ugly head, and we were told that Japan did not believe in prisoners of war, and as such, we should have all committed mass hara-kiri and not embarrassed our countries!

I was really looking forward to giving that talk. I was hoping I'd sign on many more ex-POWs to add to the clout we were gaining in both the House and the Senate. But it wasn't to be.

That morning, while I was attending a colorful slide presentation of our early days in China, a horrible foreboding grabbed hold of me. I knew the girls were taking turns looking in on Jay, and I'd called him the evening before and he was fine, but I couldn't quell my doubts, so I stepped outside and used my cell phone to call home and see how he was doing. A stranger answered the phone, and he told me he was an EMT and that they were prepping Jay for transportation to the hospital.

I spent the rest of the day on standby at the Phoenix airport, and finally got to Marshall Hospital at around ten-thirty that night. Gillian was there with her son Dakota, and as she gave me a welcoming hug, she whispered in my ear, "Daddy had a panic attack when he woke up and you weren't there. He's stabilized now."

"Should I wake him?" I asked.

"Yes. He's been calling for you all day."

I kissed his brow and said softly, "I'm home."

His drowsy, welcoming smile made every minute of the long, anxious day worthwhile.

Almost a year later, I got an e-mail from John Pritchard, a dear friend in England. He moved in pretty august circles, and was attending a function at the Court of St. James, where he was introduced to the Japanese ambassador. In the course of their conversation he learned the gentleman was the son of the commandant of our prison camp in China! I couldn't help thinking it was so fitting that the repatriated pro-Western diplomat who'd run our camp and shown us such compassion should have a son follow in his footsteps. John told the ambassador about my sisters and me, and about *The Mushroom Years*, the book I'd written of our years in the camp, and the ambassador invited us to London to visit with him before he retired in early October.

I thought about it for a while, and a few days later, I called Margo and Ursula to see if they would join me on the trip. It was still early in the morning, and when I was through talking to them, I went into the living room to see if Jay was ready for breakfast.

"What are you watching? Doesn't look like the news," I said, as a horror scene from some ghastly movie played on the screen.

"It is the news!" Jay said.

And as I stared dumbfounded, all I could say was, *"Oh, my God!"*

The date was September 11, 2001.

Needless to say, any thoughts of flying to London died with all the victims on that tragic day.

Thanksgiving was always a special time. Even the sobering thought of terrorism couldn't dampen our fun. Apart from it being Turkey Day, we celebrated two more of my favorite "turkeys": Rebel's husband, Bob, and Jay had their birthdays on November 23 and 24 respectively, and it was always a triple treat.

Christmas was as lovely as always, but I noticed that Jay was getting weaker and quieter as the days went by. And with the new year, it was all I could do to get him to eat a thing.

One morning in mid-January, while I was pulling up my e-mail—I always did it first thing while Jay watched his news—I realized he hadn't turned on the television, so I went into the bedroom to wake him. He looked so peaceful as I bent over to give him a wake-up kiss, but as my lips brushed his icy brow I knew he'd left me, and I let out an anguished cry.

There was no going back to soothe crumpled feelings. No chance to tell him how much I loved him. My only hope was that where he was now, he knew without my saying a word.

∽

The girls hadn't seen the slow erosion of his health as I had, and although I'd mentioned several times that he was failing, the shock hit them so much harder than it did me. Luckily they each had their men to fall back on. Gillian also had to console Dakota, who'd lost his favorite grandfather, and in doing so she helped heal herself.

We had a beautiful private service for Jay, and my favorite little Filipino Father gave him his last rites. I'd learned back in the convent so many years ago that if a person died before receiving baptism, there was a comforting Baptism of Desire that could be invoked. I knew Jay, who through the years had only gone to St. Patrick's for his girls' first communions or to attend a friend's wedding or funeral, would have liked the simple service Father held. That was balm to our souls. But when I got to thinking about all his friends, I knew they needed to say goodbye, too. In the fifty-three years we'd been married we'd made so many friends, and I told the girls I thought we should have a celebration of his life.

"You mean a wake, don't you?" Rebel said bluntly.

"No, not a wake ... a *celebration*. I don't want tears, because Dad's not hurting any more; he's free from all his pain, and we must celebrate all the wonderful years we had with him."

We decided to have the party at our home, as the living room with its adjoining dining area was nice and large, and could be opened out onto the deck if we needed more room.

"To cater, or not to cater?" I asked.

"Let's do it ourselves," Rebel and Gillian said in unison, and Rebel added, "Anyway, at times like these, friends always like to bring something, so I don't think food will be a problem."

We set a date, Sunday, ten days ahead, and while a close family friend called all our friends to give the time and date of the occasion, I started to make a storyboard of Jay's life. Even that turned out to be a balm, because as I found the photos and remembered the occasions, I recalled the fun that went with them. Like the time Jay was bragging to son-in-law Bob how far his Navion could fly with its new tip-tanks.

"How far?" Bob asked.

"Almost to Hawaii," Jay said proudly.

"*Almost* is not good enough!" Bob had said dryly.

There were pictures of Jay in the orchard at blossom time talking to his trees, to each one of which he'd given a name— a *girl's* name, of course. Then there were shots of him swimming, skiing, golfing, all of which he excelled at, and umpteen pictures of him in the orchard, driving the tractor, hauling fruit, living the life he loved.

I thought the storyboard turned out well, setting a light tone for the afternoon's celebration. When it was time for the festivities to begin I felt I was prepared for anything ... that is, until Jay's girlfriends started to arrive.

Lord, they kept coming!

Some gushing, some teary-eyed, and a surprising number I'd never met before, but it didn't take them long to get into the upbeat mood of the celebration and join in all the priceless reminiscing. At one point I saw Gillian chatting with one of his ladies, and I heard the woman say in a low confidential voice, "You know, Jay always told me *I* was his favorite," and I watched as Gillian gave her a hug and whispered in her ear,

"You'd better get in line. Daddy told that to *all* his girlfriends!" I could've kissed her!

The celebration that was to be from two to five ran well past seven-thirty. When it was over, my little family and I kicked off our shoes and flopped down on the couchesand I could feel that for most of them, closure was gently settling in.

"Was it just me," I asked, "or did anyone else get the feeling that Daddy was here this afternoon?"

"He was here, okay," Gillian said with a grin. "He was enjoying every minute of it. I think even *he* was surprised at all the friends he'd made through the years."

Rebel was still having a rough time, and I knew it had hit her the hardest. She said tearfully, "Daddy was here ... he was *really* here," and she let out a sniffling little laugh that touched me to the core.

Through the days that followed, I found I was still turning to Jay with questions, then catching myself up short. It would happen at the darnedest times. I even called to him once and asked if he'd heard an item of gossip going the rounds, then when I realized what I'd done, I said to him, as if he were standing there, "Okay, so you knew that story before I did, how come you waited for me to tell you first?"

And then it happened!

It was the third Sunday after Easter. I'd slipped into church early and was quietly offering up my mass when I opened my eyes, and there was Jay! He was so young and so *alive!* So happy and healthy, just as he'd been when we'd first met and the magic had started—I caught myself smiling and involuntarily saying, *Sonofabitch, I finally got you to church!* And I knew I couldn't have asked for a sweeter message of life after life.

Afterword

If anyone is disappointed at the lack of detail covering the five years of litigation that followed our first attempt to sell the orchards, I apologize. I have to admit, no one could be more disappointed than I am. It was like living through the old Veloz and Yolanda case, multiplied a thousand times, and after winning, not being able to tell the world to take heart …

No one can bring you down unless you let them.

The original manuscript that I sent to my attorney for an overview covered all the heartbreaking details, and I remember waiting in hopeful anticipation to hear from him. I kept telling myself, "Hell, there isn't anything in that Chapter that isn't truthful and to the point." I even covered all the reversals we had during the first three years, which ultimately broke Jay's health and spirit.

Earlier in our marriage, Jay told me that although he was ten years older than I, I was not to worry if he went before me, as he had planned for our futures—the girls' and mine. He had never believed in insurance; I was the one who insisted on carrying it and paying all the premiums, while he made me promise never to take out life insurance on him. When I asked him why, he told me his economics professor in college told him never to be worth more dead than alive.

I didn't delve too deeply into that, as I didn't quite know how to take it. Be that as it may, Jay said the same professor told his class it was always good to have ample savings: that way you carried your own insurance. And that's just what Jay had done through the years. As the litigation proceeded, taking huge chunks out of those savings, I was sure he felt his old professor had been wrong ...

Then my attorney got back to me. He was blunt and to the point.

"You may think the five-plus years you spent in litigation over the land sale was a killer, but if you publish the chapter on that sale as you've written it, I assure you those five years will seem like a Sunday school picnic. People like the man who put the screws to you wouldn't have a single qualm about doing it all over again."

"How could he sue?" I asked incredulously. "Everything I've written is the truth. I kept a day-to-day journal through that whole nightmare. I've got three cases of legal files to back up everything I wrote."

"You asked for my advice. Here it is: *Don't do it!*"

"How can I be sued for writing the truth?" I repeated.

"It comes down to whether you wrote with malicious intent."

"Oh, for God's sake, I wrote *what happened!* I wrote so that anyone who felt they were being crushed by horrible events would know that they could fight back and win, no matter what the odds. I believe in old Winnie Churchill's slogan: *Never give up!*"

"I'm not saying you wouldn't eventually win, but at what cost? *Don't do it!*"

After I hung up, I thought about Jay. What would he have said? And I knew he would have used much the same words as my attorney.

Don't do it ... life's too short.